MULTIPLICATION TABLE

Something touched Gral's lower hemisphere, a contact flooding him with energy. He recognized the curved surface of the life-support table, the device that would strengthen and nourish him during the coming ordeal. Extending pseudopods, Gral searched for the network of veins that spanned the table, permeable membranes rich with oxygenated blood. Finding one, his essence surrounded it and he fed greedily.

Gral relaxed, letting the rich fluids fill him. Soon, when he was strong enough, he would begin to divide. One would become three.

Then three would be one again.

And the Filitaar would rise to lead the people into the universe.

By Joel Henry Sherman
Published by Ballantine Books:

CORPSEMAN
RANDOM FACTOR

RANDOM FACTOR

Joel Henry Sherman

A Del Rey Book
BALLANTINE BOOKS • NEW YORK

Dedicated
to the memory of Alphonsine M. Sherman,
to Carolyn and Courtney for unconditional support,
and especially,
to Shelly Shapiro, who gave me time to grieve.

A Del Rey Book
Published by Ballantine Books

Library of Congress Catalog Card Number: 90-93574

ISBN 0-345-36226-8

Manufactured in the United States of America

First Edition: April 1991

Cover Art by Paul Chadwick

Plots, true or false, are necessary things,
To raise up commonwealths and ruin kings.

—John Dryden

BOOK ONE

THE SOUTHERN ARM

The first blow is half the battle.
—Oliver Goldsmith

ONE

The star system had died at birth, a single partially accreted planet spinning slowly through the gas clouds and stellar debris that shrouded the stillborn primary.

Eclipsed by the frozen mass of the dead world, the warships of the Ssoorii Unity hung in stationary orbits, the silent battle group invisible within the twisted whorls of the nebula. The Unity had waited for countless standards, systems idle, biological rhythms lowered to barest survival minimums. Its independent elements had long before been absorbed by the central mass, Phura crew and troopers stacked in the suspension lockers like so many slabs of stone.

If so ordered, the Unity would have maintained its position for eternity, holding orbit until long after all energy had been expended and its last living cells had collapsed into dust. A dead fleet for a dead world.

But the Designers had not forgotten the Unity.

A jumpspace transmission penetrated the communication node of the mothership. Several millionths of a microspan elapsed while the small intellect compared protocol and matched sequences with its biological programming, then it dispatched a burst of pulses that activated the main reasoning center and forwarded the informational packet for its scrutiny.

The main reasoning center awakened as the data entered its receptors, the sudden burst of information triggering synapses deep within its logic core. It was aware of the long span of idleness only in the context of the immediate moment, a mark of time that separated past from present. It had no questions. It felt no regrets.

Feeding the data into its processing loop, the reasoning center experienced a sensory expansion; its orders for the immediate future were projected on a thin screen of cells modified for optical imagery. Sequential and spatial coordinates were overlaid on a map of a small star system. The graphic was etched with intersecting vectors, each delineating alien actions and re-actions, probabilities and possibilities. And through the center of the chaos, like a multifractured stroke of wild energy, ran the blood-red track of the Ssoorii Unity's decision template.

The Designers' instructions were incredibly detailed, presenting the Unity with a multitude of options concerning the disposition of the planetary cluster. Its choices ranged from diplomatic negotiation to armed invasion. All possible outcomes were also mapped and ranked by descending order of acceptability. Most were subtle variations on the traditional Oolaanian of domination.

Ordered sequentially, the Unity's options were divided into subsets based on alien response and other external variables. Complexity increased logarithmically along an axis of elapsed time, but the first few hundred commands were without alternative considerations, quickly and easily obeyed.

Impulses flickered out from the reasoning center, and the Unity came suddenly to life, activity spreading from the mothership to the rest of the fleet. Specialized elements were calved from the central mass and shuttled to duty stations on the outlying vessels. Phura crews were extruded from the suspension units and reanimated. Engineering lobes booted long queues of preflight instructions, firing thruster cores and testing maneuvering systems for malfunction.

For the first time in recent memory the Unity was fully operational.

Within three deca-intervals, the fleet was in motion. Cloaked and shielded, the battle group cruised toward the nearest nexus, preparing for the first of three jumps that would carry it halfway across the southern arm to its primary objective: a minor planetary group deep in nonallied space known by its alien inhabitants as the Mael system.

TWO

Hurrying down the deserted passageway, Galagazar again succumbed to the nagging urge to scan for pursuit. He had already checked twice and found the long gray service corridor empty. A third glance still revealed no threat but failed to ease the prickling along his spine.

Galagazar had known going in that the deal involved serious risk. Not that his usual clandestine transactions were not hazardous, but there was a vast difference between leaking cargo manifests or shipping routes to a boosting crew and peddling Oolaanian secrets to the Bureau of Human Affairs. After all, the Oolaan generally plugged leaks with bodies.

His informant, Bezhjenzarthra, was intimate with the Oolaanian sense of justice; Blind Jump Benny had been on Denbair when the Oolaan had stormed the citadel. So the crazy Lling had sold his information for a ridiculously low price and was probably already back aboard his single-ship, his shipping contract with the United Trading Authority forgotten, running for the deep, dark safety of the Gulf. Perhaps there was a lesson in his caution, but heavy credit always involved high risk.

And though the waters were well beyond his usual depth, Galagazar was not planning on a long swim. This was his going-out-of-business sale, one last major score to ensure his financial future before he retired from his position as Authority factor on Mael Station and vanished into the decadent arcologies of Malacar.

The way Galagazar figured it, the rest of the complex would soon be following suit. According to his information, the station was about to become a smoldering ruin along a spreading battlefront. He intended to be on the other side of the galaxy long before the first shots were fired.

As anticipated, the communication booth at the end of the corridor was empty. Few ventured into the maintenance sector during the graveyard shift. Galagazar slipped inside and closed the door, grimacing at the stench left by the last user—a Vost in egg phase, judging by the gummy residue of dried secretions coating the floor. Scanning his body, the booth matched species type, and a fluorescent panel flickered to life above the Engi transmission gear.

His privacy hardware was still clinging to the back of the comm, artfully concealed in a discarded gobbet of narcotic gum. A quick pass with a field detector confirmed that the jamming device was functional.

The machine accepted his card, checked his credit balance, and flashed a ready signal. By memory, he punched in the number for a brokerage firm on an orbital half a galaxy away. Several minutes passed before the unit completed a link to the nearest nexus and the INPUT command appeared on the small screen.

Fingering the keys, he entered a brief message in Patois: "Recent reversals preclude investment in Amalgamated Foods at present. Sell all Intel stock immediately and forward credit. Need funds soonest. Galagazar, E. 117-177-7771."

The brokerage firm on Peklo was a front for the Bureau of Human Affairs. Once Galagazar had used it extensively, but since his arrival at Mael Station his free-lance bulletins had dwindled to a few spare reports of ship movements gleaned from drunken traders, and the credit that subsequently appeared in his drop account had slowed to a trickle. But the drought was almost over.

His identity sequence would trigger a bureau code scanner and reveal the primary message hidden within the multilayered transmission: "Have evidence of Oolaanian activity in Col Restricted Zone. Regular payment inadequate, increase factor by ten. Reply soonest."

Satisfied with the phrasing, he pulsed his dispatch out to the nexus. His credit chit reappeared, minus a healthy chunk of its balance—a business expense that he expected would soon be repaid a hundredfold.

Allowing for travel lag and bureaucratic channels, it would be a full cycle before the Bureau responded to his demands. If his luck held, he would have at least that much time before the Oolaan realized that their secrecy had been compromised.

But Galagazar never counted on luck. Assuming that the Oolaan were already trying to plug the leak, he had commenced his vanishing act several hours earlier, abandoning his office and the comforts of his private lodgings. The small fortune in personal items left behind was a regrettable but necessary waste, giving any visitors the impression that he had stepped out only for a moment—buying additional time while they waited for his return. Another sizable business expense had ensured him a safe haven from which to complete the deal and had secured him an anonymous passage to Malacar.

Galagazar headed for the stimrunner, certain that once he was safely inside, it would seem as if he had been swallowed by the alloy decks of Mael Station.

Located at the edge of the galaxy's southern arm, half its economic sphere sacrificed to the boundaries of the Col Restricted Zone, Mael offered few of the amenities common on wealthier stations. Its Fantasyland boasted a handful of bars, some slanted gambling houses, and a scattering of tired prostitutes.

And then there was the stimrunner.

Ho'oont's shop specialized in artificial stimulation, his stock a dazzling array of chemical and technological wonders. No matter one's species, he had a scratch for any itch, and sooner or later everyone sampled his wares.

His profits were legendary, and that was only the surface trade. Ho'oont also offered a variety of other services—loans, muscle, protection, and, for a stiff fee, a place to disappear from the heat. It was generally believed that even a deity could not get inside one of Ho'oont's playrooms without permission.

The stimrunner was quiet when Galagazar arrived. Ho'oont, the Quorg proprietor, relished silence, and since he could crumple alloy with any of his five extremities, his wishes were usually respected. Holographic posters announcing the latest releases writhed across the curved walls and down the narrow hallway leading to the users' booths. A rack of halogens above the low counter flooded the lobby with an intense white glare, leaving the space beyond in total eclipse.

Galagazar heard the soft whine of an approaching lev-chair and sensed a blocky shape moving in the darkness, halting beyond the edge of the light.

"Ahhhh, Galagazarrrr," Ho'oont said, his sibilant whisper ending in a low, bubbling cough.

The Quorg knew his customers and anticipated their needs. A meter of ropy pink tongue emerged from the dark, a dermal patch and a stim clutched in the slender manipulators sprouting from its tip. Galagazar recognized the patch, a high-powered pharmaceutical designed to amplify the stim's sensual reality. But the cube was a mystery, not his usual software fantasy of the steaming swamps of home and a million newly laid eggs awaiting his milt.

"Isss ssspessshull," the Quorg lisped, his tongue struggling with the awkward syllables of Galactic Patois.

"Special?" Galagazar fingered the anonymous cube. No manufacturer's logo. No trademarks. Nothing. It was smaller than most and impossibly thin; the eight pins gave it the look of a black spider.

Rumors alleged that the Quorg was addicted to everything in his inventory. Galagazar did not believe it, but he figured

Ho'oont had probably sampled every item. A recommendation from a being with such jaded tastes was hard to ignore.

"How much more?" He had paid in advance.

"Sssame." There was a glimmer in the darkness as light reflected from a pair of faceted compound eyes.

"Deal," Galagazar said. He picked up his supplies and made his way into the back of the shop to find an empty stall.

The playrooms were generic boxes, padded and sound-proofed, capable of accommodating the needs of most species. Galagazar chose one at random, a single dim fluoro illuminating the drab interior. Stained green fabric covered every surface. Long gashes etched the ceiling and floor, and tufts of white batting protruded from the ragged tears—evidence of past occupation by something with claws.

Some users liked a little anticipation before booting a program, but Galagazar was paying for a fantasy, not for the grim ambience of a playroom. He palmed the door shut and tore the plastic wrapper from the derm, slapping it against the pebbled skin of his thick neck as he squatted on the floor. Peeling away the Velcro patch from his skull jack, he snapped the cube into place.

And knew he was in serious trouble before his head hit the floor.

For a few dizzy seconds he thought Ho'oont had mistakenly given him a program intended for an alien intellect. But as the palsy began vibrating through his limbs, Galagazar realized with cold certainty that it was no accident. His scream was little more than a low whine that tapered off into silence.

The stim was a brain wipe, a lethal version of the standard shanghai system commonly used to staff mining camps or fill organ banks. The paralysis was instantaneous and selective. All extremities and voluntary muscles were dead. He was still breathing and, from the smell, figured his sphincters were very relaxed. Though his sight was functional, he could not move his eyes. But he could still hear: the door sliding open, the muffled tread of something large crossing the padded floor.

A Phura duo entered his field of vision. Bad sign. Phura rarely lowered themselves to mundane tasks such as a simple shanghai. Their presence implied a contract with personal motives. Oolaan, he guessed. But Galagazar could not be certain; he had numerous enemies.

Mind-bonded, the pair worked in silence, stooping to avoid striking their nerve-rich crests against the ceiling. Highlights gleamed on chitinous, hammer-shaped skulls, illuminating razor edges on ten-centimeter claws. Whether he was headed for the banks or the camps, the Phura did not want his seizures to damage the goods. They glued the stim cube to his skull with a glob of extruded pap, then bound his legs and arms with a skein of fibrous secretions.

His last visual image—before the mind wipe reached his optic lobes—was the maw of one Phura hovering above him, moisture glistening in the sensory pits on both sides of its tripartite jaws.

Four hours later a Vost maintenance tech on duty was jarred out of her nap by a howling siren. She looked up in surprise at a flickering telltale on her monitor screen.

. . . WARNING . . . METHANE LEAK . . . LEVEL FIVE . . . MAIN RECYCLING LINE . . . WARNING . . .

The Vost had no time to react before a pair of sharp explosions rocked the station.

Security and emergency response teams were dispatched to Sector Two on Levels Four and Five. On Five, the recycling plant was a burning tangle of twisted metal and severed piping. Teams arriving on Four found the factor office engulfed in flame, windows shattered, corridor filling with smoke and fire retardant.

One body was found in the rubble of the factor offices: Zer Galagazar, the station factor. His identity was confirmed by genetic analysis of the cremated remains.

Subsequent investigation revealed that a malfunctioning robotic welder had inexplicably struck an arc on the methane line. Pieces of the robot were found embedded in the walls of the recycler.

All similar welders were ordered to maintenance for immediate safety inspections and repairs.

THREE

"Attention. It is 1800 hours. This is your first call."

The computer-generated voice that yanked Casey Rourke from a dead sleep was a product of his own memories—part drill sergeant, part father confessor, and part ex-wife—impossible to ignore. Opening his eyes, Rourke lingered on the suspension field and stared up into the starlit darkness of a summer evening, exhaustion paralyzing him.

Final night, he thought wearily. Another double shift and Ambassador Vetch would be aboard his return flight to Peklo, the trade conference would be history, and Rourke would be crawling back into bed for thirty-six consecutive hours of blissful slumber.

Sleep was always scarce during the Authority's annual madness known as the Pangalactic Trade Conference.

Officially, company historians traced the origins of the United Trading Authority back to the chaos left in the southern arm at the end of the Expansionist Wars, sixty standards before the ratification of the Quadriate Treaty. The original investors were a select group of Vosts and Trelarians—business types who had made their fortunes smuggling arms and food across the battle zones and politicians who valued financial gain over blind patriotism.

The first few stockholder meetings probably had been held in the back rooms of some Trelarian dive, with the board members hanging around after the business session to ram some clusters and hoot at the sky. But two hundred standards of unchecked expansion had transformed the Vost-Trelarian joint venture into one of the largest corporate entities in Quadriate space, and it was still growing, pushing into the unclaimed systems scattered between the borders of the Quadriate and the Human Alliance.

Besides the original Vost and Trelar involvement, the Authority had operational charters with seven of the ten spacefaring races and trading agreements with hundreds of independent colonies. Heavily diversified, its interests included agriculture, manufacturing, port operations, imports, exports, exploration—any venture offering a profit. The printed roster of affiliated businesses was as thick as a respectable set of encyclopedias.

The Pangalactic Trade Conference was the current incarnation of an annual meeting, a valiant but vain attempt to keep Authority stockholders and interested observers apprised of new business developments. It was also by design a gala celebration. Financial statements and profit projections were infinitely more palatable when accompanied by the delicacies of known space, especially when those delicacies were served to beings whose faculties had been dulled by copious amounts of their favorite mind-altering substances. Everyone agreed it was the highlight of the fiscal standard.

Everyone, of course, except for the Authority staff. To those on the payroll, the conference was an eternity of double shifts wedged between brief intervals of sleep. And for security personnel such as Casey Rourke, it was ten cycles in hell.

"Attention. It is now 1805 hours. This is your second call." The voice was slightly more shrill, more reminiscent of his first ex-wife. But still he did not move.

Rourke considered a dependable alarm as much a tool of his trade as a security net or a defense kit, especially during the conference—most of the guests were depending on security to get them to the meetings on schedule. Ten standards of military service had trained Rourke to sleep in any position at any time and had given him the corresponding ability to dream right through the assaults of most conventional alarm clocks.

Knowing his limitations, Rourke had designed his own system. The computer voice grew more strident and irritating with each announcement. After the third call, the thermostat began alternating the room temperature between frigid and inferno. An orthophonic vibration infiltrated the suspension field after the fifth summons, initially just intense enough to make his bones hum but increasing with each passing second. Gradient electric shocks accompanied the tenth reminder, but he seldom reached that point.

And there was no reprieve, no password to shut it down from the warm confines of the field. Disengaging the alarm took time and the manual dexterity required of brain surgeons and bomb squad personnel.

Besides, he could not afford to be late. If Vetch filed one more complaint, Queeblint would have his ass.

"Attention. It is now 1810. This is your third call."

No mistaking the threatening tone. Sensing the inevitable, Rourke rolled from the field.

"Terminate nightfall," he commanded. "Medium lights and clear the windows."

At his words, night became early morning, soft yellow illumination spilling down from panels cunningly recessed into the arched ceiling. He yawned and stretched, his middle-aged joints protesting, and then made his way downstairs.

The split-level apartment was decorated in prewar primitive, its thick foam walls textured to resemble mud wattle. Strategic niches displayed native artifacts from a dozen alien cultures—crude statues, stone tools, lacquered masks. The effect was completed by rattan furniture piled with overstuffed cushions, their coarse-woven fabric the color of dried blood.

Beyond the living area, the small balcony boasted a microcosmic jungle with variegated creepers and vines pressing against the glass doors. The interior curve of Central was visible through the shadowy vegetation, a hazy mist drifting down from the weather station at the core and daylight painting a glittering swath across the structures on the opposite side of the massive cylinder.

Officially listed as a Human-class VIP suite, the apartment was well beyond the salary of an Authority security operative. Rourke had acquired the place during a friendly poker game. One of the Engs from the Real Property Division had foolishly decided that a full house was unbeatable and had made a bet exceeding the balance on his credit chit. Rourke's four queens had caused the wheezing alien considerable embarrassment.

But working in housing provided the Eng with some very creative methods for paying off debts. Two cycles and several computer entries later, the VIP suite was permanently "closed for repairs," and Rourke was sleeping in a first-class suspensor field. After four standards he had grown used to his creature comforts.

Glancing at the digital to confirm his schedule, Rourke headed into the kitchen for a cup of coffee. The coffee was real, bartered from a friend in supplies for a pair of tickets to the klaav playoffs. The art of trading was another skill he had acquired to ease the rigors of military life. Twenty standards later, it was still helping to make life bearable.

Carrying the cup of steaming liquid, he made his way into the hygiene unit.

"Ser Rourke." The computer had reverted to its original voice, soft and flat. "There is a visitor at your door."

Rourke lathered more depilatory cream across the gray stubble on his jaw and rinsed his hands. "Display."

Accessing his remote interface, the computer beamed the visual feed from the suite's security net directly into his optic implants. His vision flickered, then suddenly he was staring at a Col female standing rigidly at attention before his front door. Rourke froze, studying the image. Fragments of memory flickered through his skull: red telltales burning on a single-ship's bridge; stale, hot air reeking of his own sweat and fear; his voice droning out the final words of a last will and testament. Shaking off the flashback, he returned his attention to his visitor.

The Col was formally dressed in a silver tunic and vest. Jangling trinkets festooned the spikes extending from the bony fan behind her skull, and the razor edge of her hawksbill mouth was edged with black lacquer. Dark eyes glittered below the bony occipital ridge. According to the net's remote sensors, she was unarmed, carrying nothing more than a harmless cube of inactive circuitry inside her vest.

Familiar, yes, but there was no damn way it could be Jin Il Leera. Fifteen standards had passed since he had last seen Jin, and even the Col were not immune to age.

"Damn," Rourke muttered, blinking hard to clear his optics. His schedule was tight. He could not afford an interruption, but a visit from one of the reclusive Col was a rare event and had to be important. "Let her in and make her comfortable. I'll be down in a minute."

Activating the wash unit, he stepped into the stinging spray, his thoughts drifting back along the twisted channels of his past.

Rourke's brief stint as a prospector had begun after he had left the ranks of the Humanity's Peacekeepers and had ended abruptly when his single-ship had blown a thruster at the edge of the galactic arm. He had managed to scramble into the life pod before the ship flashed, but the ejection trajectory had sent him spinning into the vast emptiness of the gulf, away from shipping routes and rescue.

Through judicious rationing he had stretched ten cycles worth of emergency supplies into fifteen, occupying the long hours by revising and recording his will or playing with the gaming unit he had been clutching in one hand when the ship had decided to nova. But by the sixteenth cycle Rourke had come to two inevitable conclusions: the game could not be beaten, and the life pod was going to be his coffin.

And then the Col ship had appeared.

It was a double stroke of luck. Not only was he spotted and hauled aboard, but his Col rescuer was a carbon-based life-form with environmental and nutritional parameters similar to his own.

Most pilots would have looked the other way, especially if their craft was designed for one. But not Jin Il Leera. For twenty cycles she shared her food and water, draining her ship's emergency reserves almost dry before they finally reached port.

It should have been a crash course in species interaction, but by the end of the ordeal Rourke found he had learned very little from his taciturn savior. He knew that her pompous attitude was a cultural trait, that a gaping yawn was the Col equivalent of a smile, and that Jin had a weakness for drawing to an inside straight.

What Rourke did not know—at least until he was safely back inside Human Space—was that she had violated a direct order by not blowing his ass to eternity.

Before leaving the loft, Rourke strapped on his defense kit. The belt pack was fully stocked with optic grenades and gas capsules. He checked the charge on his sidearm, slipping the small pistol into its shoulder holster, and took a moment to tune his implant to the suite's output frequency. The Col had done nothing threatening, but such precautions had saved his skin in the past. And certain lessons, once learned, were never forgotten.

At the top of the stairs Rourke paused to scan his guest. The alien was perched on a rattan chair, four limbs drawn up against her slender body, extremities clasped as if in prayer. The holo had blurred the beaded detail of the Col's silver garments and muted the wedge of viridescent feathers spanning her chest. The ebony scales on her limbs and face gleamed as if freshly oiled. No doubt many curious stares had noted her approach to his apartment, even in the jaded corridors of Central, with its throngs of Vost and Eng, Trelar and Quorg.

"Welcome, Leera," Rourke said, dredging the formal greeting from deep in his memory. "My wisdom is enhanced by your presence."

"As is my own." The Col bowed her head, touching beak to entwined digits. Her Patois was flawless. "My apologies for this disturbance."

"Accepted." Rourke bowed in return, his fingers steepled before his face.

"I am Rem Il Leera. Are you Kenneth Christian Rourke?"

"That's right."

Inclining her head, the Col stared at Rourke. The metal bangles wired into her horns jangled softly. "The Rourke I'm seeking had slight misfortune in the gulf, a shipwreck. Same Rourke?"

"That was a long damn time ago."

"By universal reckoning, fifteen point three standards to be exact." Rem opened one pocket on her silver vest and withdrew a small square object. She handed it to him, the device balanced on the tips of her four digits. "Do you recognize this?"

"Yeah." The old gaming unit was a familiar weight in his hand, and Rourke smiled as he ran a finger along the studs. "Jin Il Leera send you?"

"Jin Il Leera no longer exists."

"Dead?"

"The flesh is gone. Her mind has merged."

Rourke glanced down at the worn contacts on the game keyboard, surprised by the sudden pang of grief that stabbed him. He remembered the long hours spent trying to explain the subtleties of poker to the stubborn Col and hoped the end had been quick and painless. Jin had earned that much. "And you came all this way just to return my game?"

"I was asked to do so by Dar Il Chedo."

A relative of Jin's, perhaps? Son or daughter? Whatever the Col called their young. Rourke shrugged. "And?"

"And to remind you that there is a debt owed." Her dark eyes glittered.

"A little late, isn't it?"

The Col did not answer.

"Did this Dar Il Chedo say anything about how I'm supposed to repay the debt?"

"You will be contacted when needed. I was sent only to aid your memory. I know nothing more."

He nodded slowly. "Then I guess you've done your job."

"I know the way out," Rem said as she rose, trinkets jingling. Her bow was formal and precise. "Good-bye, Ser Rourke. May your mind remain sharp and your body strong."

"Yours, too."

For a long time after he heard the door slide shut Rourke stood motionless in the living room. It was doubtful that Dar Il Chedo had any legal claim on him, at least in a Central court. No telling what laws existed inside the Col Restricted Zone.

Rourke had never been burdened by too many hard and fast rules, but he had always considered the repayment of a rightful obligation a point of honor. The truth was simple—he owed Jin Il Leera a debt. His past efforts to contact Jin had all failed, but that did not ease his conscience or cancel the marker. If there was a way to repay her kindness, Rourke would try his best to do it. All somebody had to do was tell him how.

The digital on the wall chimed softly, snapping Rourke back to the present—the last night of the Pangalactic Trade Conference. And, he realized with growing horror, he was seriously late.

Vetch was probably having a frigging coronary.

FOUR

The Green was thick and tangled and alive.

Gral Il Chedo, prefect of the Mael system and guardian of the gateway to Col Space, stood motionless beneath the arching boughs of the habitat and stared up into the verdant snarl. Above him, organic chaos rose in a semisolid mass of intertwining creepers and branches. There was no sign of movement except for the occasional white flicker of girga wings as the flying rodents sought safety deeper within the waxy vegetation. But the faint scent of prey and blood was draped like a thin veil across the jungle. His symbiote sucked a deep breath and whined softly with anticipation; the herd was in the upper canopy, wild chedo feeding on a fresh carcass somewhere near the apex of the temple's curved sky.

With a conscious effort, Gral controlled the rising blood lust and forced his chedo to face the phalanx of hetta bodyguards arrayed on the steps leading up from the tunnels. They stood ready to follow, symbs alert, claws extended, weapons slung for climbing. But Gral believed that certain prayers were best said in solitude.

"Hold here," he commanded. "I will go alone."

"As you wish, my Chedo." Kars, the captain of the guard, somehow managed to urge his jujun symbiote to stiffen beyond its already rigid stance of formal attention. Concern tainted the beast's throaty growl.

The big jujun always worried whenever Gral went hunting alone, but lately his distress had become even more obvious, intensified by Vaz Il Tran's insistence that Gral be kept in sight at all times. Everyone seemed infected by the tran's infernal caution. Even Gral had felt a slight stirring of guilt upon entering the habitat, as if the echoes of the priest's litany of restraint were following him through the corridors of Jurrume.

Still, Gral mused mirthlessly, he was the prefect, and there was no question whose orders took precedence.

"No need to worry, Kars," Gral said, bending to strip off his weapons harness. "If the old bull kills me, you can always give him to the tran in my place. After all, do they not seek the best warrior?"

"They have already found him," Kars replied solemnly. "There is none better than you, my Chedo."

It was a proper answer, the correct display of respect, one that he expected from his subordinates. Yet even such common courtesies had been somehow transformed since the priest had come to Jurrume with his tales of prayers answered and prophecies fulfilled. Gral heard the whispers behind his back, petitions mouthed by the troops in passing, awe in their voices: "All blessings to the Filitaar. Keep and protect him."

At first he had tried to stop such foolishness, meting out punishments when he caught his subordinates in the act of blessing or overheard their prayers. But the ground swell of belief fueled by the tran was beyond his control, and his reprimands soon came to be seen as tests of faith. In defense, he had developed a certain specialized blindness, choosing to ignore their transgressions, for their fervor did nothing to quell his doubts.

"If I am such a formidable warrior," Gral grunted, allowing the chedo to toss its harness to the ground, "then you have nothing to fear." His chedo stretched gratefully, glad to be shed of the weight, and paused to scratch at fur snarled and matted by an excessively tight strap. "I would dismiss you—the troop could use some free time. But I doubt you would leave until I have returned. Do I guess correctly, Kars?"

The jujun did not reply.

"Very well. You may remain on duty. But be warned, I will have the testicles of anyone I see following me." It was not an idle threat—he had several such trophies from other unfortunate hetta who had dared to violate his orders. Yet in truth, they were as old and dried as withered fruit.

"I have been ten standards in your service, my Chedo," Kars replied. He tried vainly to keep his jujun features emotionless, but the optical clusters drooped momentarily, a flash of sly humor. "My beast still ruts like a breeder."

"Then for the sake of jujun females everywhere, I hope you've sense enough to keep your stones in their bag for another ten."

The massive beast dipped its skull in submission. "Good hunting, my Chedo."

"There is no other kind." Gral let his symbiote walk across the thick humus toward a downswept bough from an immature foundation tree, reining hard to keep the beast from breaking into a trot. Directly beneath the branch he stopped and glanced back at the captain and his troop. "I'll bring you an ear for your symb."

A slight relaxation of his iron hold on the lowbrain, and the chedo reached up to grip the twisted branch. Swinging up to crouch on a massive bole, the creature paused for a heartbeat before springing across a narrow gap of emptiness toward the next swaying loop of vine. Twenty spans, and the jungle closed around him, all sign of the doorway back into the complex lost in the dense grip of the tangled foliage.

Despite thirty cycles of inactivity, his symb quickly settled into an easy rhythm, the thrill of the hunt rising within Gral as the creature climbed. Moisture from dripping leaves soon flecked the beast's mottled hide; a pleasant exertion burned in its aching muscles.

Gral allowed the lowbrain to release a flood of endorphins and adrenaline, reveling in the sharp chemical edge and the first tentative flickers of animal satisfaction that seeped past the barriers into his system. He felt good, better than he had for many cycles. The responsibilities of his office and his troops were like a fiction drawn from someone else's life, the pressure of his divinity shed along with the weapons clipped to his harness—even the weight of his sin of complicity with the Oolaan had vanished temporarily.

Jungle running was always a glorious pleasure, the instinctive dance of lunge and grab a fitting prelude to the bloody climax of a kill. Yet as his time in chedo form neared an end, each excursion into the Green grew more acute, even basic survival responses gaining an almost sexual intensity.

There were few who truly understood the depth of his need for the Green. Kars, several of his closest hetta, two or three of his fellow chedo—Gral could mark the number with a single manipulator. Vaz Il Tran was incapable of understanding; too many standards under the oppressive weight of the Coda and the influence of omnivore flesh had killed the priest's spirit. Even the Prime, who had authorized the funds for constructing the massive habitat on Jurrume and pushed it through despite the angry protests of the council, did not really grasp the strength of Gral's addiction, treating the Green like a gift to a pampered youngling instead of a basic requirement for his existence.

His aberrant taste for the primitive was a symptom of a failure to become completely civilized. Yet if he was still wild beneath the surface, there was no one to blame but the tran themselves, for they had plotted the course of his life, his path marked by liberal applications of Coda philosophy. Like all chedo-level Col, he was the result of a hundred generations of careful mergings. Yet while his fellow chedo represented a skillful blending of the castes, Gral's ancestors had all been warriors, a chain forged from three hundred minds chosen for their skills in battle.

Frontline experience in the heretic purges had taught him about the art of war. There was no civilized way to kill, and in combat an excess of civility could be as disabling as a severed limb.

Whether or not the tran had finally achieved that which they sought remained to be seen. But one thing was certain—he was different. The winding path of reproduction had come full circle, creating an entity that was a perfect union of Col intellect and chedo flesh. The beast's needs and his own were inseparable, physically and emotionally.

So it was that Gral preferred to leave the petty exercises of decorum and protocol to those who hunted in the hallowed halls of the council: Dar Il Chedo and his kind. He did not understand the subtle nuances of their speeches and posturings, shifting alliances and veiled barbs. There was no honor in their victories, no permanence in their defeats.

In the solitude of the Green, cause and effect were much simpler, strength and agility decided the issue, and the name of the victor was always written in blood.

The sudden realization that this hunt might be his last caused Gral a moment of sadness. Change was coming. The time of hardening was fast upon the Prime Triad, its death looming larger with each passing day. The three heirs whose intellect would be merged to form the new triad had already been chosen: Dar Il Chedo, Harn Il Chedo, and Gral himself, each waiting for the Prime to draw its final breath.

But Dar and Harn would never rule the Col. If Gral succeeded in his plans, they would not survive elevation, nor would their flawed minds be allowed to dilute his sanctified intellect.

In truth, it was not the belief in his own divinity but rather the threat of merging that had driven Gral to conspire against the Prime. The awful realization that the perfect engine of his mind would cease to exist—continuity destroyed by the comingling of the thoughts and experiences of the two other candidates—had made him vulnerable to any offer that promised escape from the mental suicide of elevation.

So when the tran and the Oolaan had come to him with their whispered suggestions, Gral had made his decision and placed his mark on the alien treaty. He alone would survive the elevation to Prime; and then, with the help of Oolaanian jump-space technology, the expansion of the Col race would be assured. His agreement with the Oolaan had been a moment of rebirth. Now there were two Col races: those who had chosen to follow him and those facing extinction along with the tradition-bound Prime.

Soon he would be the new Prime—or he would be dead. Either way, whether martyr or god, his mind would remain unsullied to the end.

Responding to his mood, the chedo's reproductive organs stirred, swelling with blood. In its simple mind, the alien concepts of nostalgia and melancholy did not fit; only Gral's anticipation survived, though it, too, was altered, translated by the beast's proto-intellect into the primal stimulus of rut. Gral fought the beast's sudden urge to howl and moved higher through the net of limbs and creepers, following the spoor of its quarry up toward the faint blue arc of the dome.

* * *

Shifting his attention from the chedo's motor neuron system to its sensory net, Gral let the beast run, submerging into the flood of sensations that washed over him as his symbiote leapt through the brush.

Vaz would have been horrified to learn that he occasionally gave the chedo its head. Letting the beast assume command of the flesh was a grave transgression of the Coda; Gral doubted that even his suspected divinity would absolve him from such a sin. Civilized intellects never allowed the primitive entity to raise its consciousness to a dominant state. From first creation, all Col were taught to fear the loss of control. Young and old alike constantly practiced the giivva: the ritual exercises and elaborate dances and routines devised to demonstrate mental dominance over unruly flesh.

Control at all times; decorum in all things. The mantra of social survival had been drilled into all of them by hovering priests.

That it was a lie, he had learned only by accident.

The memory had survived from his incarnation as a hetta, one of a few fragments of early identity that had somehow remained intact through his subsequent mergings to become part of the coalescing mental juggernaut that currently defined his being. The image was so clear and sharp that when it was conjured up, it seemed time had somehow been sheared away; he felt the clumsy weight of hetta flesh, the raw brute power of bunched muscle and bone. The hell that was the power generation chamber for the fortress of Dhalgri blossomed around him.

Newly elevated hetta were sent to Dhalgri for basic training. One of the tasks deemed fitting for new flesh was firing the garbage in the incinerators and burning the trash to create steam to power the fortress. There were few tasks more hated than a cycle spent shoveling debris in the sweltering heat of the ovens.

The place was the domain of a crippled leera named Raab. No one knew what accident had scored her Col intellect, but the puckered wound in one deformed lobe had inspired among the troops many tales of crimes and punishments.

Though Gral never understood why, Raab had hated him from the moment she had first spotted him among the young grunts. He had recognized the enmity in her leera's wild eyes as they had locked onto his own, her symb rumbling with satisfaction as it raised one trembling limb to point at him.

"You there. Follow me. I've a special job for big bucks like you." One leg dragged oddly as she led him into a dark alcove. The smell of decay swelled around him, making his hetta's guts churn.

"They bring 'em down," she said as her beast staggered ahead of him. "But I like to keep 'em waiting. Save them for special ones like you." The crippled creature bent down to a dark tarp-shrouded mass. Something foul and slick leaked from beneath the woven fabric.

A quick tug, and the tarp peeled away like old skin, revealing a tangled mound of long-dead herd beasts. Worms, their placid feeding disturbed, twitched and writhed in the orange twilight of the ovens.

"Good job for a stupid buck. Cut 'em up and shove 'em in the fire." She pushed him toward the reeking mound.

His hetta gagged reflexively, an act too quick to stifle.

"What?" the crazed leera shrieked upon spotting his weakness. "Weak, Cadet? No decorum? No control?" The other hetta stopped and stared at the commotion.

"My apologies," he mumbled, embarrassment flooding him, coursing into his beast's system.

"What good are apologies?" Raab moved closer. "You came to Dhalgri to learn. So you must be taught a lesson. Punished, no? Maybe a bite of this flesh would teach you not be so squeamish again, eh?" One claw snaked out and sliced a fragment from a rotting haunch, thrusting it before him. Worms writhed in the dripping clot.

His hetta jerked away, recoiling in terror.

"Eat!" Raab shrieked, lunging again to press the gob against his symb's mouth.

Another reflexive step back. The side of the glowing incinerator was a flash of pain across his hetta's side. Anger exploded within its small brain, rage and fear and sickness all twisted and whirling. Its roar of challenge echoed in the chamber, one limb lashing out and sending Raab tumbling back into the mound of corpses.

The lapse in domination lasted only a second. He drove his mental fingers deep and tightened control over the lowbrain, dissipating the rage.

"Beast!" Raab hissed as her leera staggered to its feet. Blood flowed from a gash in its throat, a claw's width from being a fatal wound. "You saw him!" She turned to the others, her voice quavering. "He let the beast be free!" The gibbering creature backed away cautiously. "It will be reported. You will pay!"

Raab was true to her word. A report went out, and punishments were handed down. He spent many long cycles in the practice Green, moving through the giivva rites until they became unconscious actions.

But nothing they did to him diminished his memory of the moment, the exhilaration of surrendering his will to the rages of the beast.

And though the rest of his life followed the path prescribed by the tran and the Coda, the lesson was ingrained into the tablet of his intellect, never to be forgotten even through the rigors of elevation to raas, leera, and finally chedo levels.

Decorum and control were the province of the weak. Mental withdrawal was a viable tactic. Control could be released and still regained if one was strong enough.

Civilization had no place on the battlefield or in the Green.

Lost in his musings, Gral was surprised when his chedo halted, the stiff fur along its thick neck bristling with alarm and anger. The stench of fresh urine burned around them, yellowed droplets darkening the gnarled bark of the small foundation tree that served as a ladder into the higher reaches of the habitat. The old male must be near; the piss was still warm.

Gral had great hopes for the coming engagement. The wild chedo bull was a prime specimen, shipped in from Verrin thirty cycles earlier. A hetta handler had been killed in transport, overpowered despite tranquilizers and stunners. It had been a supreme test of Gral's patience to wait while the beast acclimated itself to the enclosed environment of the habitat, learning the paths and grottoes of the temple's fifteen thousand tri-spans that sweltered under the huge central dome on Jurrume.

But Gral knew from experience that shortening the time only served to lessen his pleasure. Though waiting had been difficult, thirty cycles had allowed the beast to claim its domain and assume control of the leaderless harem that wandered free on the temple grounds. In its small mind, the presence of Gral's chedo could be perceived only as a threat to survival. When the fight came, it would be to the death.

There was no need for Gral to urge his symbiote forward; the scent of ripe females overpowered the old bull's steaming challenge and instinct directed the beast, narrowing its focus to the basic natural programming of hunt and kill, feed and mate.

The chedo was a perfectly designed arboreal predator: eight appendages shaped for grasping and climbing, powerful limbs to swing and pull. Gral had only to relax his iron hold on the lowbrain and the beast was off, sailing silently up through the branches, senses tuned, ranging out to detect the heat and movement of the herd of wild chedo.

Near the curve of the dome the heady musk of chedo females in high estrus was a distinct perfume amid the competing scents of rot and humus. A few more spans along a network of moss-covered branches and he spotted the troop, feeding on a fresh carcass that was sprawled several layers below upon a thick mat of interlocking vines.

Most chedo would already have challenged his approach, but there was no sign of the old bull. Gral let his symb's senses range but detected nothing. Had the beast fled in terror before him? Or was this some new tactic born of age and experience? Gral was uncertain, but the females beckoned with their aroma and the glowing crimson of their inflamed genitalia. Hesitantly, he let his beast move toward them.

As Gral descended, vegetation exploded on his left, the blurred movement accompanied by the numbing shriek of an enraged chedo male. A hunting adaptation, the scream was a biological mechanism designed to stun prey for an instant of sheer terror. It worked, freezing Gral in place until a crushing blow from a taloned paw sent him reeling. He whirled, spotting the torn vase of a huge jug plant where the male had hidden himself, letting the swollen sac of fluid mask his heat and throw Gral's infrared sense into blindness.

Roaring, the big male sprang again, the impact slamming Gral into a gnarled bole. And then Gral was falling through the net of foliage, bouncing from limb to vine and trunk, coming to rest finally on the spongy surface of a tepia lateral.

Warm fluids pulsed from a gaping wound on one shoulder, the raw flesh exposed beneath a crescent of torn hide. He tried to kill his symbiote's pain, muting it with an increased flow of endorphins. Dimly, he heard the blood-maddened predator crashing after him. No stealth now—brush crackling, death howl ululating endlessly.

His chedo struggled to rise, its flight response dominating all impulses in the lowbrain. But with its wounds, running was impossible. Nor could he face the old bull in straight combat. His only hope lay in surprise, in finding a ploy the aged chedo had never experienced.

Driving his control probes deep, Gral paralyzed his chedo.

He forced the beast to lie back, limbs spread, exposing belly, throat, and genitals to a killing stroke. Its lowbrain surged with panic, hearts pounding.

Crouching on the bough above him, the raging chedo halted, its brutish features puzzled and confused. Spread-eagle submission was a female act. A true male would fight or flee. The actions did not fit any known pattern.

The wild one studied Gral uncertainly for a time before cautiously descending. Bewildered, the animal moved closer, muzzle down, leaning over Gral, nostril pits flaring, sniffing first at the unguarded genitals and then up the motionless chest.

Gral waited until the beast was directly above his chedo's talons. Neck arched, throat vulnerable, the savage let out a dismayed howl. And Gral let his chedo strike, claws ripping up and out, flesh tearing open, blood spewing out in a warm gouty river.

The beast fell back, thrashing in the underbrush, its screams reduced to a hideous fluid rasp. Gral's symbiote was on the old chedo before its spasms subsided, tearing into the flesh of the breast, seeking strength from its still beating hearts.

It was dawn before he resumed control of his chedo and headed back toward the entrance to the compound. Servicing the willing females had left the beast stiff and sore. The gash on its haunch was a brand of fire.

Kars and the troop were still waiting on the steps. They were not alone. Vaz Il Tran squatted beside them on the stone, his doughty beast settled into a stance of meditation. As the chedo swung down from the trees, a single spark of anger flared in its eyes and was quenched. Control resumed.

"I hope you didn't have to wait too long," Gral said, turning so his hetta aide could lace up his weapon harness.

"We all need to review the Coda on occasion," the priest said stiffly. "You are kind to provide me with so many opportunities." There was a hint of sarcasm in the voice but nothing direct, nothing Gral could attack.

"Save your reprimands. I am not in the mood."

"It is my duty to remind you of the dangers of such hunts." The priest pointed toward the slash arcing across the haunch of Gral's symb. "The weight of the Col people rests on your back. Your death would be disastrous to our race."

"Regardless of who you believe I am, I still must have my

time in meditation," Gral snapped, his symb's pain bleeding across his mental barriers.

"There are other forms of devotion."

"Not for a chedo! We were given dominion over the beasts so that each could do service in its chosen way—forage, build, or fight. Chedos are supposed to hunt, else we would all be docile omnivores like you tran."

"I do not wish to anger you, my Chedo." The priest's symbiote's flaccid throat sac fluttered with humility. "But other chedos have learned to be satisfied with safer forms of hunting."

"I am not like other chedos," Gral roared. "If I was, you would not be here."

The priest did not answer, its eyes staring placidly.

Muttering angrily, Gral stalked off to find a medic to treat his symbiote's wounds, afraid that if he remained too long, his beast might rise again. He wanted nothing more than to let his chedo slash the priest's sagging throat. But he could not afford to kill the priest now, not before the impertinent tran had served his purpose.

But once Gral was in place as the new Prime, the purges would begin. Only a fool left a nest of conspirators intact, so the tran themselves would be destroyed.

And Vaz would be among the first to die.

FIVE

As he stood in the darkened alcove of the communication booth, Rourke wished that his life had a rewind function; he wanted nothing more than to return to bed and start his shift again, unraveling the skein of linked events that had conspired to turn a basically lousy day into a disaster.

First, the visit from the Col had put him behind schedule. A massive traffic snarl on the cross-Central tubeway had ensured that he was an hour late when he reached the ambassador's hotel. And, of course, the suite's security net was still scrambled.

He would have preferred to ignore the fried net, which had

been down for three cycles, but company regulations required a systems check on entry to any occupied VIP suite. And being an hour late, Rourke figured that a little external reconnaissance of the ambassador's mood was in order.

Unfortunately, the surveillance hardware was still broadcasting only a blurred infrared image, filling his head with static and confirming that his previous calls had been ignored. Regs demanded another immediate report, just the type of operating procedure his supervisor would check and note on his upcoming performance review. Rourke could not afford any more notations in his file, so he headed for a public comm and contacted maintenance. Besides, the call gave him a few more minutes of relative peace before facing Vetch.

"Sssorry," the Quorg on the comm repeated. "We ssshow no fffailure at that addresssss."

Casey Rourke swallowed a particularly nasty oath and struggled to keep the smile painted on his face. He had learned from painful experience—an entire cycle spent pinned to the ceiling by a sabotaged suspensor field—that it never paid to hassle maintenance or anyone else who had unlimited access to his lodgings.

"Trust me, regardless of what your screen says, the security net is scrambled. And this is my third report."

"Will sssend crew to invessstigate," the Quorg said, consulting its screen again. Its lumpy, misshapen skull looked like a small planetoid hanging in the darkness of its office. "Nothing available now. Three ssscyclesss sssoonessst."

"That's what I was told three cycles ago."

"Want to file a complaint?"

"No." Rourke shook his head. After all, it was the middle of the trade conference, and repair crews were in high demand. "Just get somebody on it as soon as you can."

Breaking the connection, he headed for the ambassador's suite, certain that the system would not be fixed until long after Vetch had returned to Peklo.

Vetch was sprawled on the couch, but despite his corpselike pose, there was no evidence of foul play. An empty crystal decanter was balanced on the edge of the accent table; barely a swallow of bourbon remained in the glass Vetch was clutching in his bloated fist. Any physical damage seemed to have been self-inflicted.

At one time the ambassador must have been a prime example of the Human form, tall and broad-shouldered. But age and excess had softened his muscles and layered his massive frame with fat. To make matters worse, Vetch had somehow managed to stuff his girth into the latest fashion rage—a postmodern tuxedo—and the taut fabric only accentuated his obesity.

Noting Rourke's arrival, the ambassador grunted and levered himself to a sitting position, a thin smile failing to conceal his anger and disgust. At their first meeting Vetch had measured Rourke against some internal scale and had found him lacking. Nine cycles of escort duty had not changed that initial assessment.

"Do you always have problems with schedules, or is mine a special case?" The man's vague accent was as fashionable as his clothing.

"Traffic," Rourke replied.

"But of course." Vetch finished his drink and placed the glass beside the decanter. He rose slowly, his movements effeminate and surprisingly delicate. Pausing, he flicked imaginary lint from the front of his slacks and then brought his hard gray eyes up to meet Rourke's gaze. "Let us hope traffic will not further delay our arrival. It would be most upsetting—for both of us."

Rourke nodded and silently wished he were running security for one of the alien visitors. A Wormat or a Vost, even a bloated Quorg, would have been preferable to this huge parody of a man. But the Authority segregated security by species to ensure understanding and comfort.

He had been hired to take care of Humans, no matter how marginal their pedigree.

On the conference roster, Ambassador Konstantin Vetch of the Commonwealth of Peklo was officially listed as a stockholder representative. Most of the staff thought the Vetch name synonomous with leech, but those who considered him a sycophant kept their opinions to themselves; Vetch was rumored to be extremely well connected.

Peklo was an independent system, one of a growing number located on the frontier between Quadriate space and the Human Alliance. The Quadriate might not have wanted any part of the constant warfare engaged in by the Human Alliance and the Oolaanian Unity, but its companies sought profit anywhere it could be found.

Originally famous as a staging area for privateers and for the exorbitant rates charged to vessels forced to seek repairs at its only port, Peklo had languished in obscurity for half a century.

And then someone in the UTA's Acquisition & Development Department had stumbled across an assay report for the hellish system. Major mineral concentrations: nickel, cadmium, cobalt, iron—the list seemed endless. An immediate courtship had ensued, with offers of serious venture capital in return for a membership charter and stock percentage. Upon the signing of an agreement, the floodgates opened and company credit swept over Peklo's unsuspecting inhabitants. Forty standards later the United Trading Authority owned ninety percent of another independent republic.

Though the fate of his government and constituents was inexorably linked to the Authority's continued existence within the framework of the Quadriate Commercial Compact, Vetch harbored no delusions about his role at the conference. There was nothing he could personally do to affect the financial stability of a corporation as massive as the UTA, so he chose instead to ignore all matters of commerce. By skillful scheduling, he managed to avoid every one of the numerous business sessions and concentrated his efforts on attending as many dinners and parties as humanly possible.

In nine cycles Rourke had seen more of Central's restaurants and clubs than he had in six standards of residence.

The ambassador's mood continued to deteriorate during the commute. The limousine proved too small for a man of his social stature, and traffic delayed their arrival until after the entrance of the Management Committee. Consequently, he missed the open bar before dinner.

"No doubt you're well paid for your incompetence," Vetch hissed as they hurried up the stairs into the Grand Salon. "Rest assured your efforts will not go unmentioned to your superiors." Snagging a drink from a passing tray, the man stalked into the hall.

Rourke headed for the security wardroom. Half his job was over for the night. All that remained was to wait until Vetch ate and drank himself into a coma, then escort him home. If there was one thing Rourke liked about the ambassador, it was his predictability.

The wardroom was actually an elevated passage encircling the Grand Salon. Choked with electronic hardware and surveillance equipment, the windowless corridor was the nerve center of security for the assembly complex. From inside its dimly lit confines, any operative had instant visual and audio access to the salon, all the peripheral meeting rooms, or any part of the associated structure. The gear was sensitive enough to monitor the vital signs of any of the guests. No secrets escaped its scrutiny.

Most of the trade conferences had been relatively free of major security problems, but there had been a few bloody incidents in the past. On the surface, the Authority was a pacifistic organization that preferred to leave politics to the experts employed by the Quadriate. But sometimes visitors brought their local disagreements with them to Central—which explained the Authority's heavy investment in security technology. It was bad business to let members or their guests get killed.

Ninety percent of the technology in the wardroom was of Human origin. Rourke thought it a sad commentary that some of Humanity's major exports were detection devices. But it was the best gear in the galaxy and mated perfectly with his own implants. His remote interface and optical upgrades were the only retirement benefits he had earned after five standards with the Bureau of Human Affairs.

Rourke made his way through the twilight to an empty station between a Trelar in a bulbous environmental suit and a dark-furred Wormat. He took a moment to adjust the gear before logging on to the system. Then his optics picked up the general feed from the net, and he was staring down at the Grand Salon from high overhead.

The salon looked more like a stadium than a conference center. A series of broad, flat tiers, each furnished with tables and appropriate seating, descended to an oval floor. Temporary environmental fields had been erected for the comfort of anaerobic species, and the random scattering of translucent blisters marred the structure's perfect geometry. An enormous holographic projection hung above the central level and provided a clear view of the steering committee to those in the upper strata.

The center was reserved for the members of the Management Committee and their personal acquaintances. All others occupied tables on the elevated tiers. The seating principle was simple: the lower the level, the higher the status.

For a few moments Rourke studied the assemblage. Finding a particular individual in the milling crowd required the aid of the security net. Names entered into the system were matched with the seating roster, and the visuals jump-cut to a close-up of the specified sector.

On impulse, he punched in a name: Rem Il Leera.

A message flashed across his optics: ABSENT . . . ABSENT . . . ABSENT. The Col had not checked in. Maybe she would show up later. Or perhaps, by delivering her message, she had completed her task and was already bound for her homeworld.

He entered a second name: Dar Il Chedo. The jump cut was abrupt and disorienting.

The being that appeared on visual was vastly different from the Col he had spoken with earlier in the evening. His visitor had been reptilian, but Rourke found himself staring at an arboreal predator. Its thick frame had eight sinuous legs tipped with razor claws and a prehensile tale knobbed with a welt of bone. The thick fur was mottled silver and black. As he watched, the alien unhinged a lower jaw fenced with ten-centimeter fangs and popped a wriggling morsel into its mouth.

Suspecting that the computer had made an error, Rourke called up the security file on Dar Il Chedo. His optics flickered, and he was suddenly looking at a holograph. No mistake, it was the same being. So the Col had radically differing physical forms. Another quirk to add to the Col mystique.

He studied the being for a moment longer, wondering what the Col might want as repayment for his old debt. Credit? Service? Legal or illegal? It could be anything.

A damned depressing thought.

The computer found Vetch at the director's table. No doubt anymore—the ambassador had very powerful friends.

Vetch was obviously enjoying his last free meal. He attacked each course like a frenzied shark and paused between bites only to guzzle more wine. His mood became more expansive with each glass, his gestures more dramatic.

By Management Committee directive, all the major events of the trade conference were aired by the holonets. Since most of Central's population was on the Authority payroll, the Personnel Relations Division thought the illusion of employee participation would help boost morale. In reality, everyone knew the major deals were cut in back rooms, not in the Grand Salon, but the shows were still popular because they preempted all other broadcasts.

And, of course, the directors' table was a prime minicam location.

Rourke could only imagine the electronic gymnastics being performed by frantic holotechs trying to edit Vetch's antics from the network feed.

During a dramatic pause in the director's state-of-the-company address, the ambassador's guttural belch assumed mythical proportions. An obscene suggestion whispered to the president of a Wormat conglomerate required the skillful insertion of a commercial to allow a protocol officer time to defuse the ensuing brawl. And then, after dessert, Vetch leaned over and noisily deposited the churned mass of his entire meal into the lap of a Vostian senior legal adviser.

Rourke was disconnected from the net and heading for the lobby before he had even been paged.

The assistant undersecretary of protocol (Human Relations Division) was waiting for Rourke outside the rest rooms. A thin, pale woman, she was one of the few other Humans employed by the Authority whom he had ever encountered. Dark circles beneath her eyes betrayed the strain of the past week. The rest room door failed to muffle Vetch's retching, and every echo made her wince as if in pain. After a moment the ambassador appeared, hanging limply between two liveried Wormat servants.

"The ambassador has taken ill," the woman said stiffly.

"Shall I take him to a hospital or home where he can sleep off his . . . illness?"

"I don' wanna go home," Vetch whined, a strand of spittle oozing between his lips and down his chin. He lurched away from his escorts and wrapped the undersecretary in an amorous embrace. "Unless you take me. We could . . ." His reddened eyes narrowed thoughtfully as he bent and whispered in her ear.

It took both servants to pry the woman from Vetch's grasp.

"Take him to a hospital. Take him home. Or take him to a zoo." She shuddered violently, rubbing at her ear as if to wipe away something foul that still clung to her skin. "Just get him out of here!"

"As you wish."

It was nearly midnight when they reached the hotel. The lobby was empty, no doorbeing in sight. Rourke managed to steer the ambassador across the broad foyer, then leaned the man against the wall, called a lift, and shoved him inside as the energy field opened. Holding Vetch upright, Rourke stabbed at the contacts for the thirtieth level.

"Say . . ." Vetch swung his face slowly toward Rourke. His

breath was sour with wine and stomach acid. "You know any women—real friendly women?"

"Not tonight, Ambassador." Rourke was familiar with any number of working girls, but none who deserved Vetch's company.

"Pay top credit."

"You're sick, Ambassador."

"Never that sick."

"Sure you are." Rourke helped the man stagger into the corridor as the lift stopped. "Now, let's get you to bed."

"Bed, okay. But not alone."

He was still demanding female entertainment when Rourke finally rolled him onto the suspensor unit and killed the lights.

Rourke collapsed into a chair in the living room. His skull was throbbing, and his throat was dry. He reeked of Vetch's regurgitated dinner.

What he needed was a beer. Drinking on the job was strictly against Authority policy, but Rourke figured he had earned at least one. Anyone who had spent more than ten minutes with Vetch would certainly understand.

He glanced in at the sleeping man, set the suite's security unit to send him a pulse if it was tripped, and headed down to the Good Sport for a brew.

Five beers, maybe six. He had lost count, but for the first time all evening Rourke was completely relaxed.

"Six," Mygrazee confirmed as she slid another mug toward Rourke. "This number six. Off early, eh?"

"Late lunch." Rourke grinned and flipped his credit chit onto the bar.

"Liquid lunch." The Eng scooped up the plastic square with one huge webbed fist. "Gonna miss you, Rourke. When you finally get ass caught in crack. Gonna miss you when you gone." Thrumming softly, Myg waded back across the tank and dropped the card into the transfer unit. Dark ripples danced across the surface of the oily sludge in the makeshift pond behind the bar.

Conveniently located across the alley from the rear of the hotel, the Good Sport was his usual stop before heading home, a quiet spot to unwind and catch the last few minutes of a game. Mygrazee, the Engi owner-bartender, had built her fortune on providing home-style entertainment to expatriates from a dozen worlds, serving up their favorite beverages along with a side order of the athletic competition of their choice. Klaav, zero-grav thoat, baseball—there was always a different event playing on each of the six holo screens and a semilegitimate sports book waiting to take any and all bets.

Leaning back on the stool, Rourke stretched and yawned, marveling at how warm and benevolent he had suddenly become.

And then a Code One security pulse started hammering in his skull.

"Frapping hell," Rourke swore, lurching to his feet. A Code One meant serious trouble—life-threatening trouble. He tried to access sensory output from the ambassador's suite, but the system would not respond.

Cursing maintenance, he sprinted for the door.

"Hey!" Myg bellowed after him. "Your chit!"

"Be back for it later."

Rourke sprinted across the alley and through the deserted lobby. Waiting for the lift, he tried to imagine an innocent way in which Vetch could have triggered a Code One. Most likely it was part of the system malfunction. But it might have been something simple like trying to deactivate the unit or opening a window. Or maybe the Wormat Vetch had insulted at dinner had stopped by to finish their discussion.

Rourke checked his arsenal as the elevator shot skyward.

The door to the suite was ajar.

Rourke was suddenly sober. Ignoring the static from the net, he switched his implants to infrared. There were no heat sources in the salon, but he detected a blurred signature in the back bedroom. Muffled voices reached him: shouts and curses.

Sliding one hand into his coat, Rourke eased his pistol from its holster. The Spencer Pinpoint felt heavy and warm in his grip, comfortable. Pinpoint was not really an appropriate name anymore, not since he had modified the optics. Anything he hit would be holed to the diameter of his fist. Pushing open the door, Rourke darted inside, staying low and keeping his silhouette brief and compact.

He switched back to standard visuals, his eyes adjusting slowly to the dim illumination spilling in from the picture windows, the Central night glimmering with neons and holograms. No signs of a struggle, black lacquered furnishings in place. No movement. A frigid draft from the air-conditioning vents chilled the sweat on his face.

He was edging toward the hallway when the first scream ripped through the silence. A bloody, brutal sound, like something being skinned alive.

He stopped thinking, reacting to the layers of preprogrammed conditioning hammered into his skull during his standards as a soldier. The drilled procedures kicked in hard, jacked into his mind with the first sickening rush of adrenaline. Rourke keyed the emergency distress tab on his belt unit; somewhere to the south a tactical team was scrambling for a chopper, sirens blaring through their skulls. Clawing at his belt pack, he snagged a blinder. The small optical grenade was a hard lump in his palm.

The bedroom was locked. Blinking back to infrared, he squinted through the static and spotted three hot forms in the room, one prone and two standing. Another wail of agony echoed through the narrow hall, ending in a fluid gurgle that sounded as if it had been forced through a throat choked with blood.

No time to wait for backup, not if Vetch was going to survive. Rourke blinked hard and opaqued his lenses, screening his eyes against the flash of the blinder. Arming the grenade, he counted to three and drove his fist through the thinnest part of the carved panel. Wood splintered, followed a heartbeat later by the satisfying crump of the blinder's detonation as he flipped it toward the center of the room. Driving his weight against the barrier, Rourke felt the door shatter. Then he was falling into the bedroom, bringing up the pistol instinctively, blind for a heartbeat as his implants countered the incandescent flash of the light bomb.

When his optics cleared, his eyes tuned in on a stunned tableau.

Clots of phosphorus ash hung in the air, and smoke coiled up from smoldering sheets. Two women flanked the bed, bodies oiled, black leather teddies pebbled with chromium studs, bleached hair set in rigid spikes. Working girls. Frozen in position, one held a velvet cat-o'-nine-tails while her partner was caught unbuckling the clasp on one spiked heel, a rictus of glee stretched across her face.

Vetch was spread-eagled, bound hand and foot to the bedposts. His skin was pasty white against the satin sheets, his erection wilting and the rapture on his features fading to shock and rage.

The momentary lull disintegrated into chaos, the women clawing at their eyes and Vetch writhing and straining against his bonds.

"What in the hell?" "Stone cold blind." "Pleasure Guild be suin' somebody's ass!"

Rourke did not know whether to laugh or cry.

By the time backup units reached the suite, he had smothered the fire on the bedspread and assured the victims that the blindness was only temporary. He would let the medics tell them about the UV burns, the red welts of which were already spreading across their backs and buttocks. Rourke gave no explanations to the officer in command of the tac team.

"You'll read it in my report," he said, watching the ambulance staff cart the ambassador off to a hospital for observation.

And there would be a report, in quadruplicate. Probably a review board, too. Beyond that, Rourke was uncertain. Despite his experience, he hadn't a clue as to the penalty for inflicting coitus interruptus on an ambassador.

But it had to be severe.

SIX

There was a man silhouetted on the top of the cliff, leaning slightly into the wind as he stood at ease. His gray uniform seemed cut from the same fabric as the overcast sky.

Ignoring the soldier perched on the rocky outcropping, Alexis Weiss waded out of the icy water and jogged up the beach. His sudden appearance was no surprise; she had been expecting a visitor ever since being awakened in the predawn gloom by the howl of the comm-link. Without bothering to answer the call, she had headed down to the sea for a final morning swim, certain that someone would come for her before the day ended.

As she walked across the pale sand toward the base of the cliff, Alexis scanned the beach a final time. The place had served its purpose. Long days spent watching the rolling breakers crash among fingers of black stone, cool nights listening to the hiss of the wind and the throb of the surf—these had erased the doubts left after Yanda. She was Human again. It was time to return to reality.

The path was steep, a narrow track traversing the cliff in a dozen sharp switchbacks. Focusing her gaze on the spot where the trail split the edge of the bluff, she began to run, concentrating on the rhythm of her stride. She did not look back.

The soldier was standing at attention as Alexis topped the rise, his face expressionless, eyes fixed on a point somewhere on the bleak horizon. She acknowledged his salute with a quick snap of her hand and trotted into the dome.

Thirty minutes later she was dressed and packed, her few belongings stuffed into a nylon bag, all evidence of her three-month stay erased. The hovercraft's engine whined softly as it raised from the ground and slid forward along the narrow dirt road.

The chain of nameless escorts and cramped fliers blurred into a single gestalt of travel. Short jaunts separated a half dozen interstellar jumps. She came down on Headquarters in the waning light of a star half a galaxy distant from the one that had illuminated the morning sky.

Konstantin was waiting at the terminal, a familiar landmark in his ever-present khakis and slouch cap. His shirt was open at the neck, revealing his scars and the snarl of silvery thatch that rose to an arbitrary line at the base of his throat, separating shorn beard from tangled body hair. He measured her approach with a predatory gaze, searching for weakness. Evidently what he saw satisfied him; his smile was genuine.

"You ready?" he asked as he fell into step beside her, his movements surprisingly graceful and fluid.

She nodded slowly.

"Good." His own nod was almost imperceptible. "Ducor's waiting for us."

The big man led her through the sterile corridors of the terminal, past knots of grunts and officers, their salutes as precise as the creases on their spotless uniforms. Another car, another faceless escort waiting for them by the open door.

They rode to the Bureau offices in silence.

Rollie Ducor was bent over a data terminal when they entered the room. He glanced up once, registered their presences, and then returned to the block of text gleaming on the small display. Weiss slid into one of the chairs and waited. No use trying to rush him; Bureau analysts operated on different tracks than did the mainstream. They had different imperatives.

The briefing room was a typical Bureau construct, a generic unit equipped with the omnipresent data terminal and wall-mounted viewscreen. The single table was square and utilitarian, its sickly green hue common to all government installations. The chairs were designed for stacking and were so thinly padded that her tailbone pressed painfully against the abrupt curve of the plastic shell.

Like the room, Weiss herself was equally generic. Her average features were mute testimony to the skill of a Bureau surgeon adept at transforming beauty into something easily forgettable. She could not remember the original curves of her face.

Her augmentations were discreetly camouflaged. The RAM unit lodged in her skull was masked to evade even the most sophisticated detection devices. Her security net was organically wired, state-of-the-art splicing techniques incorporating her neural pathways as circuitry. An image enhancer was concealed in her first cervical vertebra, with projection plates overlaying the bone above her temples. Her optical implants were of broad frequency, capable of a bandwidth triple that of normal vision.

She knew at least ten killing strokes for every sentient species in known space.

"Shall we begin?" Ducor asked as he selected an infocube from the stack inside his metal briefcase. It was a rhetorical question, and he did not wait for an answer. In the bright shaft of light that spilled from the display unit, his pale eyes gleamed. His narrow face was pinched and drawn.

The viewscreen faded from neutral gray to the black of deep space. A few specks of glimmering light appeared, scattered stars gleaming against the velvet backdrop of the gulf. As Alexis watched, a blip of red flashed in the center of the darkness and quickly faded, small against the scale of the sector. The image freeze-framed and recycled into an endless loop.

"What you are looking at is a standard energy scan taken six weeks ago by a remote monitor. The unit is part of the Jumpnet system, used to monitor ship movements through known jump nexuses. This particular scan is of the alpha quadrant of the Durban sector."

Weiss accessed her RAM, a nanosecond of detachment as she performed a file scan. "Durban is fringe space," she said as the data cycled up into her mind. "Edge of the galactic arm. Non-allied. Mainly unclaimed property."

"Correct. The area hasn't been fully explored, but there are no known jump nexuses in Durban Alpha." The man touched a contact, and the image on the screen zoomed into a close-up, the speed increasing so that the red pulse became a steady beacon. "However, six weeks ago this flash triggered our remote and initiated its constant surveillance mode. Despite being a fairly weak signature, analysis confirms that it is a standard jump zone energy release. It's been spotted three more times since the initial sighting. Might be a reflection from a nearby nexus, but if it is a real image, then there's an unclaimed hole in Durban."

"Have they got a fix on the location?"

Ducor shook his head, his wispy hair a halo in the half-light. "No. It's been partially vectored, but we were unable to fix a distance. The signature is very weak. It might be way out in the gulf. But it could also be much closer and being masked by some interference like a gas cloud. Or maybe it's being intentionally shielded."

"Since when have the Oolaan had that capability?"

"No one is certain they don't. And this would be the wrong damn time to find out."

Alexis shook her head slowly. "An unconfirmed sighting by a remote monitor. That's not much to go on."

"There's more," Konstantin said, nodding to Ducor.

The analyst produced another cube from the recesses of his case and traded it with the first. The processor whined softly, the viewscreen sparkling with static.

A grainy image appeared, a long-range shot in alien frequencies, magnified to visual limits: granite cliffs, low scrub, and towering trees, blue sky reflected on the wrinkled surface of a churning sea, and the humped shape of an Oolaanian corporal structure squatting on a crescent of black sand beach. Columns of numbers lined one side of the picture: a ship identity sequence, temperature, time, speed, fuel, a long litany of meaningless information.

"We received this three days ago. It's a ship sensory scan. We haven't been able to trace the identity sequence of the ship. Numbers must be from a local registry. The shot was probably taken using Vost hardware, but from the visual settings it's doubtful a Vost took these pictures. Came through our Hardcore drop by way of a free-lancer who promptly died in an accidental explosion. A very convenient accident. Our source was the chief factor on a Quadriate trading station in the Mael system. Mael is on the perimeter of Durban Alpha.''

A slight chill traced her spine. Alexis swallowed hard. "That's at least fifteen hundred parsecs from the Oolaanian border.''

"Closer to nineteen hundred," Konstantin said. "Hell and gone beyond our southern line.''

"What's the confidence level on this information?''

"So far the sighting is unconfirmed. Our source was terminated before providing any additional substantiation. But Analysis is reasonably sure this picture comes from somewhere along the gulf, probably within the Mael system itself. Surveys establish one planet with similar environmental conditions. Place called Jurrume.

"That's a fully functional corporal unit, which means there must be a full battle group somewhere in the area for support. We've checked all normal routes of entry into the quadrant and found no evidence of Oolaanian movement. So it has to be a new nexus—magnitude ten or better to cross that kind of distance.''

"Which means the Oolaan have the key to our back door," she said softly.

"Exactly. And if they are able to shield it before we fix the exact location, it might be years before we can neutralize the threat. That's an unacceptable scenario.''

"What are our options?''

Ducor raked a nervous hand through his scalp. "Well, if we had a location, we could go in with our own units and force a fight. Tactical is fairly certain that at this early stage we could seize and hold the position if we hit hard and fast.''

"But since it isn't our system, command would like to keep the bloodshed to a minimum." Konstantin smiled tightly. "Most of Durban Alpha has been claimed by the Quadriate. Mael system itself is controlled by a local power known as the Col Empire, but the area has been heavily penetrated by Quadriate colonists and trading groups. We go in without being invited and we're going to look like the initial aggressors. Especially if the Oolaan are there by invitation.''

"That a possibility?''

"Well, since an Oolaanian takeover would probably destroy the local economy, it's doubtful the Quadriate would welcome their presence. In fact, there are some who believe this threat might be the lever necessary to finally force the Quadriate to join with us in a mutual defense pact. That is, if we can demonstrate a clear and present danger. The diplomatic corps is anxiously awaiting our confirmation.''

''What about the Col?''

The Bureau chief shrugged. ''They're pretty much an unknown variable in this equation. With the exception of a trading agreement with the Quadriate, the Col have maintained a strict isolationist policy. But that might be subject to change if the price is right, and God knows what the Oolaan may be offering.''

It was Alexis's turn to smile. ''Only God knows, but you'd sure like to find out.''

''You know me,'' Konstantin said, his teeth showing through his tight grin. ''I don't like secrets.''

''Steps are being taken to confirm and, if necessary, neutralize the threat.'' Ducor sat on the edge of the table, absently ticking off the points on his slender fingers. ''Four chameleon-class spy ships have been secreted into the sector to scan for telltales. A full battle group has been 'disbanded' and reassigned. It will regroup inside Durban Beta in fifteen days. With or without confirmation—or Quadriate authorization—the force will initiate an armed sweep of the Mael system on day seventeen.''

''What's my part?''

''Well, the free-lancer who sent us the picture claimed to have definitive proof of an Oolaanian presence somewhere near Mael. You know the routine. Additional scans and exact coordinates were available for a price. We were still negotiating the fee when he disappeared. Chances are that the Oolaan took him out, but he might have left something behind, ''Some hard evidence which could be used to convince the Quadriate of a threat to its security.'' Command thinks it's worth sending someone in to take a look around. Given the travel interval, you'll have approximately six-point-two local days to try and pinpoint the exact nature of the Oolaanian interest in the Mael system and beam it back to us.'' Ducor retrieved a data pack from his case and slid the pouch across the table. ''This is a full dossier. Cover and background included.''

''Correct me if I'm wrong,'' Alexis said slowly, turning to face Konstantin, ''but I'll bet there can't be more than ten Humans in all of the Durban sector.''

The Bureau chief nodded. ''Human population in the sector is nil—you're going to be highly visible.''

''I'm going to be a frigging target.''

"Command thinks your visibility will be an asset. The Oolaan are probably expecting us to make an appearance. They're going to be scrutinizing every new arrival very closely. So we'll give them something to look at, a distraction. If they're busy watching you, maybe they won't spot your partner."

"Partner?"

"Khurrukkatey the Scrounger." Konstantin grinned. "She's the best inside operative we've got. And damn good in a fight. Besides, paranoia can be a real asset in this business."

"Terrific," Alexis muttered. "Nothing I enjoy more than working with a psychotic Rath. And as an additional bonus, I get to be a decoy in a shooting gallery."

"You don't have to accept the job." Konstantin's face was suddenly sober.

"No, but I will." Alexis stared down at her hands. "And don't bother to act surprised. You knew I wouldn't turn it down even before you asked."

Ducor stood and walked back to his briefcase. "Khurrukkatey is already en route. Since she'll be going in the back door, she'll contact you as soon as she's inside." The analyst stared at her, studying her face with his washed-out gaze. "Any more questions?"

"Hundreds," she answered, standing and gathering up the packet. "But what are dossiers for, right? Keep me busy on the long flight out."

Konstantin met her gaze, his eyes displaying a hint of compassion. "You're authorized to use the battle group if you need it. But consider that a last-resort option. Am I understood?"

"Yeah." She snapped him a loose salute. "Some day, Konstantin, I'm gonna get you for this."

"I hope you get the chance, Weiss." His returning salute was little more than a wave. "I really do."

Alexis turned and walked from the room. The first twinges of fear did not hit until the door was firmly closed behind her.

Forty minutes later Alexis Weiss was aboard a shuttle and headed for a berth on an interstellar transport, the first leg of her long journey to Mael Station.

According to her passport, she was a corporate advance executive scouting the Mael system for a new manufacturing location. She had traded her uniform for a severe business suit. Her hair was blond. Her eyes were hazel.

Her external weaponry had been dismantled, the components

hidden inside a dozen packing crates. They would arrive on Mael in four separate deliveries.

SEVEN

The private transport slid smoothly along the causeway, the cushion of magnetic force erasing the seams and imperfections in the road. Rem Il Leera squatted on the front bench and faced the rear, keeping her symbiote's gaze fixed on the external view. She saw no need to voice her disapproval of Dar Il Chedo's presence in the vehicle; avoiding eye contact was statement enough.

Outside, the shop fronts and businesses of Central sped by in a montage of images: alien patrons lounging outside a small café, glittering shop windows arrayed with trinkets from a hundred worlds, neon mist banners proclaiming sales and bargains in stilted Patois. The crowded buildings towered high above, glass and metal fingers reaching toward the core.

The sterile view of the enormous habitat made her long for the jungles of home. A pang of homesickness seeped from her intellect clusters into her leera's lowbrain. Her mind was tired, her symb exhausted.

Too many changes, Rem thought. Too many affronts to propriety. Several of her recent meetings had left her cold: the visit to the Human called Rourke, an after-hours appointment with a member of the Authority Personnel Office to secure a copy of the Human's employment records. Minor details, yet not explained and perhaps even in violation of the Prime Triad's isolationist policies.

So far from civilization, on this strange habitat filled with alien thought and ideas, the rules of etiquette had lost definition. Rem had been too long away from her own kind. She wanted—not for the first time—nothing more than to go home to Verrin, but the Col homeworld seemed part of another life that she feared would never be regained.

"You are too silent, little one." Dar's sleek chedo was

sprawled on the rear bench, long limbs curled beneath its sinuous body. The creature swiveled both turreted eyes to stare at Rem, its hinged mouth yawning and its yellowed fangs framing a thick slab of pale tongue. "Where are the constant details, the timely confirmations of schedule and procedure on which I greatly depend?" He kept his symb's voice gentle, softly chiding.

"What would you have me say?" Her leera was uncomfortable in the formal vest, fabric stiff and coarse, front pouch weighed down with a Sept offering as heavy as a stone. Wedged in beside the gift, the information packet jabbed into the beast's skin like a thorn caught in its breast feathers. Shifting the packet only made the irritation worse. "Should I ask why you suddenly doubt my abilities? Or thank you for doing my job? Maybe you would rather hear me say I think only a fool would call such a meeting? And only an even greater fool would attend it?"

"There, that is my old Rem. Feel better now?" His chedo purred contentedly.

"I would feel better back at our rooms. Better still at home. Here I only feel foolish and embarrassed."

"It is pleasant to have rituals for support. Very comforting. I know, little Rem. Though many seasons have passed since I wore leera skin, I still remember." The sloping face bared its fangs again—that maddening habit called smiling was a holdover from his leera phase, acquired through too close an association with the Human named Rourke—but there was no mistaking his concern. "I am sorry, Rem. But there are times when propriety must be forfeit to expedience."

"Bah." Rem chuffed loudly and returned her attention to the world outside the darkened windows. Dar's amused rumbling made her symbiote tense with anger.

They finished the ride to the Authority offices in silence.

A vanguard of hetta preceded them into the building, six stooped neuters garbed in the silver and black of the Dar holding, their ceremonial weapons gleaming brightly. Perhaps sensing Rem's foul mood, the lumbering warriors performed their function with sublime precision, marching lockstepped with their sensory organs trained rigidly forward.

The interior of the office complex was enormous, a broad incline rising to an equally broad foyer. Hetta footsteps hammered on a floor fashioned of smooth, white stone veined with flecks of gold and rust. The arched ceiling vaulting high above was a statement about the importance of the facility; here was an installation prominent enough to warrant wasted space.

Holographic scenes lined the walls, each individual panel shifting and changing, displaying a multitude of panoramas drawn from member worlds: ruddy stars viewed through a haze of red dust, mesas and mountains thrusting from yellow sands, the harsh white glare of starlight over a stark, airless landscape. They all spoke of the diversity of the Authority and the broad spectrum of its holdings.

The reception desk was at the center of the foyer; a Lling female was on duty. Her body was hidden behind the planes and angles of the encircling work station, her slender neck arching gracefully above the countertop. She watched in silence as the hetta approached and parted rank, pivoting to face inward and form a corridor of protective flesh between Dar and the desk.

Her precious protocol already damaged by Dar's presence, Rem paused a moment to gather her dignity before advancing, forcing her leera into a slow, exaggerated gait, its trinkets jangling against its horns. Meeting the Lling's yellow-eyed stare, she announced their arrival.

"Dar Il Chedo to see Khiser Ouerrabbi." The phrase was repeated three times, first in Colese out of respect for Dar, then in Galactic Patois, and finally in flawless Lling to show respect for the receptionist. Respect in all things, decorum at all times.

"All blessings and honor," the Lling replied with equal efficiency, carefully following the pattern of Colese, Patois, and Lling. "You are expected."

The long neck bent, bringing the four small limbs protruding from behind the skull down to touch a control panel on the desk. Across the great pavilion, a square opened and a doorway beckoned.

"Through the open corridor to the chamber at its end. The Khiser will be with you shortly." The Lling bowed. "May your mind remain sharp and your body strong."

"And yours also."

Though Dar understood both Engi and Patois, chedo-caste Col never conversed directly with aliens. Rem retraced her steps to the waiting chedo and repeated the conversation. He nodded his approval, and Rem grunted orders to the hetta. Re-forming their ceremonial wedge, the unit marched toward the distant entrance.

The hall beyond the doorway was narrow and featureless. There was no room for the escort, so the hetta assumed positions on either side of the portal, their blades held at guard position. Rem and Dar proceeded alone, following the corridor to an oval chamber at its terminus.

Despite many visits to the interface, Rem was still uncertain about the mechanics of its design. Half the compartment was specifically engineered to accommodate Col dignitaries. The other portion—beyond what appeared to be a clear partition—was a Trelarian habitat. But the divider might have been nothing more than a large viewscreen capable of displaying a live image from anywhere within the complex.

Dar had never before entered the chamber. His chedo bared its fangs in pleasure at the rich scent of humus and rot that filled the interior. Native plants spilled from pots strategically placed along walls covered with tepia bark, imported, no doubt, at great expense from Verrin. The floor was softly padded, including a low pedestal where a leera could sit with its legs drawn up comfortably. There was even a sloping depression provided for chedo comfort, a feature added out of respect since the designers must have known it would never be used. No chedo had ever stooped to such base tasks as diplomacy—until now.

With all the dignity of a cub frolicking in the safety of his home arbor, Dar allowed his symbiote a moment to sniff the plants and touch the fibrous walls before sinking into the waiting hollow. Rem ignored him. Her own symb was trained and disciplined, not pampered like his chedo. It mounted the pedestal and assumed a neutral posture while Rem concentrated on the frozen scene beyond the glass, hoping the icy vista would help cool her fevered mind.

A study in white, the Trelar habitat gleamed with the diamond brilliance of ice and frost. The features were hidden by ashlike clouds of drifting gases, which thinned occasionally to reveal vague humped shapes of ivory and alabaster. No walls. No accents or decorations. Nothing to define or destroy the sense of boundlessness.

Movement in the mists. A single dark obelisk materialized, thrusting up from the floor. More motion, hints of colored lights flashing as if through an open doorway, fading as the portal closed. The tall, slender form of Khiser Ouerrabbi approached.

The Trelar were consummate diplomats, as skilled in the art of negotiations as the Wormats were in single combat. An ancient race. Rumors hinted of a violent past, marauding armies that had once fashioned a huge empire and then turned inward to attack each other and collapse the juggernaut, plunging the

Trelar into ages of civil war. Whatever the truth, they were now generally pacifistic, and their endeavors to maintain peace had earned them positions of trust throughout free space. They had once even spearheaded a failed but valiant effort to negotiate a treaty between Human and Oolaan. It seemed every corporation and political organization had a contingent of the six-limbed beings, the Trelar people themselves having become their own best export.

But despite their positions of trust, Rem had never considered the Trelar particularly trustworthy. Like all aliens, they had their own priorities. The Trelar simply concealed their intentions better than most, hiding all behind a smoke screen of words as thick as the mists of their homeworld.

Khiser Ouerrabbi was a perfectionist. In all their dealings, Rem had never seen the Trelar make the slightest error in Col decorum. And despite the unsettling presence of Dar, Ouerrabbi maintained a perfect facade.

"Blessings, Rem Il Leera. And blessings, too, to the magnificent Dar Il Chedo, who so honors us with his presence." The precise, atonal voice issued directly from the surface of the partition, with no evidence of a speaker or transmitter.

"And blessings to you, Khiser Ouerrabbi. I trust the body is sound and the mind sharp."

"It is so." The Trelar squatted beside the obelisk. Its eye stalks were erect, the auditory organs fully extended to form two crennellated bulges along its cylindrical skull. Treble legs, boneless and infinitely flexible, arched gracefully. Treble arms linked and formed an intricate twining with the legs. The tips moved rhythmically, sensuously, constantly. "We would make a Sept offering for your indulgence."

"And I, too, in the name of Dar Il Chedo, have Sept to give." The Sept offering—a book of quotations from the Coda inscribed on metal-leaf pages—reappeared unbidden in her leera's grasping digits, and the beast placed it into the transfer slot. There were times when Rem marveled at the sensitivity of her symb, moments when she almost believed the creature would have been sentient without her Col intellect.

A flash of light, and the book vanished, replaced by a cleverly fashioned trinket of white stone. It resembled a small animal. A frivolous gift, but no doubt Dar would say the object was pleasing if only to be polite. After turning and displaying the curio to the reclining chedo, Rem placed it inside her vest. Leera fingers brushed against the information packet. The touch flooded Rem's mind with sick panic, strong emotions leaking into her symbiote's lowbrain and making its stomachs churn.

"And now, how can we be of service?" The Trelar waited, the tips of its limbs twining and untwining.

"You are kind to ask—kind to see this humble one." Rem paused, gathering her thoughts. "We have come to express our extreme sorrow and condolences in the matter of the factor on Mael Station. It has recently been brought to our attention that the Eng, Galagazar Vys, died in a tragic accident. His loss will be a great hardship for everyone."

"It is so." One eye stalk swiveled, gleaming in the white haze. "Your concern is appreciated."

"One expects it will be difficult to locate a being of equal stature to fill such a valued position." The lie stabbed her conscience. Rem had visited Mael Station several times and had met Galagazar. Neither had struck her as impressive.

"It is always difficult to replace a valued employee."

Since all interaction between lower-ranking Col and aliens was beneath the notice of a Chedo, Dar was supposed to be ignoring the conversation. He should have been lost deep in the meditation of some soothing passage of the Coda or drilling the lowbrain to sharpen his control, waiting for Rem to provide a complete translation. And though Dar kept his symbiote's eyes politely averted, she could sense the tension in its body, its head held so its aural pits could catch the subtle nuances within the exchange.

Surely if she noticed, so did Ouerrabbi.

"Dar Il Chedo is very concerned with the affairs of the United Trading Authority," Rem continued. "Especially where such affairs affect the stability of the Col. Mael Station is vitally important to our people."

The Trelar sketched an elaborate design in the mist with one tentacle, as if wondering where the discussion was leading or perhaps suspecting and anticipating its conclusion. "The wise being is always concerned with those matters of personal import. Dar Il Chedo again demonstrates his noted wisdom." A perfectly diplomatic response: noncommittal, seemingly impromptu and genuine. The Trelar was very good at its job.

"Dar has given considerable thought to potential replacements."

"And has he some requirements for the new factor?"

"Some suggestions only. He would not presume to do the job

of others, others eminently more qualified. Yet there is one being which seems to embody these qualifications.''

More patterns, then stillness. "The Authority is always willing to consider the needs of its clients. If Dar has a being in mind for the job, it would be an honor to relay such to the proper department.''

"The being, Kenneth Christian Rourke, is already employed by the United Trading Authority. Perhaps this will aid in his selection. Dar has taken the liberty of securing copies of his personnel records. I offer them to you now.''

Despite her earlier praise of its anticipation, her leera froze. She had to force it to withdraw the information packet and place it in the transfer slot. Light flashed. The packet disappeared, reappearing instantly across the divider. Khiser Ouerrabbi made no move toward the parcel.

"Your wishes will be directed to the Department of Factors. Is there anything else you require?'' Ouerrabbi waited expectantly.

There was a whisper of motion behind her; her leera turned to stare at Dar. The chedo had moved! He had allowed his beast to raise its eyes to the Khiser, blatantly displaying his interest in the proceedings. Rem fought with her shock and anger. The offer she was about to make was difficult enough without his insane flouting of tradition. Dar ignored her displeasure, his chedo features rigid, eyes locked on the Trelar.

Rem found her voice. "The Dar wishes me to extend his gratitude for your indulgence.'' A chedo offering personal gratitude! She could hardly force her leera to form the words. "And further indulgences would be favorably received, creating an additional obligation.''

There—she had said it plainly—the offer had been made.

"Gratitude takes many forms, some more pleasing than others.''

"It—it,'' she stammered, unnerved by the chedo at her back and the Khiser at her front, her mind churning with emotions as sharp as thorns. "The appointment of Ser Rourke to the position of factor would be greatly pleasing to Dar Il Chedo. A pleasure he would wish to return in kind.''

"We have no need of material items and would decline gratitude of such a personal nature,'' the Khiser said gently, without rancor.

"The Dar would not be so callous as to assume. But perhaps you would find an ally among the Col leadership to be a valuable asset?'' She fought to maintain control. The offer was patently in violation of Triad decree. To assume the duties of the Triad, usurping powers beyond his stature—it was madness.

"Allies are always valuable. Especially when discussions regarding future contracts arise. It is always good to have a spokesman."

"Favorable treatment now could lead to advocacy in the future."

"And a renewal of the existing contract?"

"Advocacy. Renewal supported certainly. Approved if possible."

Another movement at her shoulder; her leera whirled in horror. The chedo was rising, standing upright to face the Trelar in violation of all orthodox tenets.

"Hear me, Ouerrabbi." His chedo's voice was a harsh whisper, its tongue struggling with the painful linguistics of high Trelarian. "Do this and you will have your advocate. My indebtedness would be eternal. You have my bond."

Despite years of professional training and experience, the Khiser could not hide its surprise. Its tendrils quivered intensely; color suffused the mottled yellow hide.

"I will consider Rourke's appointment a sign of your faith." Turning to Rem, the chedo exposed its fangs, in a parody of a Human smile. That unnerving alien habit! "Let us go."

As quickly as it had begun, Dar's madness passed. Reassuming the aloof, arrogant stance of a chedo-level Col, his beast turned away and headed for the doorway. The meeting had ended.

"Blessings—be to yours," Rem blurted, stumbling through the ritual of parting, her speech pattern shattered, her accent appalling. "May your mind be sharp, body strong."

"And yours, as well." The Trelar was equally distracted, its stalked eyes fixed on Dar's retreating form. "Go in peace and wisdom, Rem Il Leera."

Somehow she managed to compel her skittish symb to bow low and back from the room.

Back in the transport Rem huddled on the front bench. Her leera was distressed to the point of illness, its unsteady limbs drawn tightly against its trembling body. It was poisoned by equal doses of Rem's shame and revulsion; nausea boiled in its guts. She let it stare blindly at the city that flickered by outside the window, hoping the glittering lights and colors would soothe it as she could not.

"And so, little one, I have offended again?" Dar lounged on the rear seat, his chedo absently hooking and releasing the dark fabric with its claws. A satisfied rumble emanated from his beast's broad chest.

"Perhaps I should ask how I have offended you." She did not look at him.

"You are without offense."

"Have I failed in my duties? Would you have me resign?"

"Never. Who else would I trust to give voice to my thoughts?" Rem chuffed loudly. "You seemed not to need my skills with the Khiser."

"Silence, little one." An edge of anger crept into his tone. She had crossed a line of tolerance and challenged his actions. Such a thing was not done.

Gods, she thought. Perhaps the insanity was infectious, the disease spread by too close an association. Another wave of sickness surged through her leera, and Rem fought back the urge to retch.

"I've no desire to cause you distress, little Rem." The chedo rolled to an upright position, resting on its back haunches. "It pains me greatly to tilt your precious traditions. But in times of change, traditions are often the first victims.

"I spoke without you. But not without reason. Do you think the significance was lost on Ouerrabbi? Hardly. He will see that Rourke is transferred."

"Perhaps he will see only that Rem Il Leera is incapable of performing her job," Rem said petulantly.

"In that respect, it is only my opinion that matters. Change, Rem. You must accept it. So, too, must all Col, or be trampled by the rest of the universe." His chedo exhaled sharply. "This will not be the last time I offend you. It will not be the last time I ask indulgence and sacrifice of you, little one. Despite all, I will need your support. I cannot survive without it. Will you stand with me?" The beast reached out one forelimb, its long claws scratching soothingly through the ruff of feathers on her symbiote's breast.

Rem looked at him closely: sleek and strong, her master for more standards than she cared to remember. Loyalty welled inside her mind, dispelling the nausea. She felt his strength, his power. Dar was, despite his temporary lapse, a magnificent chedo, one of the heirs of the dying Prime Triad. Her support would always be unquestioned, no matter his sins.

The ritual of obedience was instinctive. Rem found herself in the middle of the rite before she was conscious of moving.

And there was comfort in the traditional gestures.

EIGHT

Rourke finished the form on the computer, printed the ident, and punched NEXT. Another monolithic block of text and blank spaces waiting to be filled appeared on the screen. He mouthed a tired oath and scrolled ahead, the lines flickering past endlessly.

Big damn mistake, Rourke thought, putting the Vost in charge of UTA paperwork. But it was a logical mistake. Vost were fanatics about documentation; their hives were stuffed with dockets and ledgers. Clan workers burrowed through ever-expanding libraries of hard copy, thousands of standards worth of contracts and memorandums layering their dark nests like sedimentary strata.

In his five standards with the Authority Rourke had been involved in the occasional "incident" and had completed his share of reports. Even small matters required reams of text. He had come to think of the paperwork as a potential avalanche hanging over his head, waiting for a single noise to send it crashing down to bury him.

On the corporate Richter scale, the Vetch incident had been the equivalent of a small nuclear strike.

He had been at the terminal all shift—REPORT OF INCIDENT, REPORT OF ASSAULT, REPORT OF WEAPON DISCHARGE, REPORT OF DAMAGE—dealing with a continuous procession of official company forms. His back was stiff and aching, and his eyes felt as if they had been sprayed with sand.

The wail of his comm-link shattered the graveyard-shift stillness of the security offices. Queeblint, no doubt, demanding his immediate presence in her office for a "debriefing." Wincing against the electronic scream—the damn thing was designed for Wormat ears and produced an ear-piercing howl even at the lowest possible frequency setting—Rourke stabbed at the AC-CEPT contact.

The sound died and the comm-link screen cleared, but instead of an angry Vost, Rourke found himself staring at the mottled visage of Haffveniir Riic.

"To you be hailing, most supreme arsonist Rourke," the Lling female squawked on seeing him. "Been you setting fires to burning of most recent late?"

Riic worked in Personnel, a senior data entry clerk in the records division. They traded favors on occasion, with Rourke giving her access to the security computers in return for additional vacation hours and sick leave. It helped to have friends.

"Not funny, Haffveniir." Rourke gave her a scowl. "This doesn't look good."

"Be getting more worser even. You troubles soon be having of nature most serious and problems dire." Her command of English syntax was atrocious, but she prided herself on an extensive if somewhat garbled vocabulary. "Know who be you fornicated?"

"Ambassador Konstantin Vetch. And I interrupted the fornicating."

"Is word-bonded, this Vetch, to Authority chief counsel. Chief counsel be Wormat elder. Power filling maximum his vents." The clustered wattles fringing her lower jaw were crimson with agitation, the crest inflated and almost purple in hue. She gaped, her wide lipless mouth hanging open. "Be here to telling you that access requests of records of one Rourke, Kenneth Christian, reaching proportions major. Line forms rear, as you say."

"Who's asking?"

"All names. Peklo district manager. Queeblint. Legal department. Protocol department. Wormat Embassy. Col delegation. List long. Very long." A swallow traced its way down her slender neck. The four small manipulators behind her skull waved for emphasis, like a baby's arms attached to the back of her head. "Fornication of magnitude most serious about to be done to Rourke, Kenneth Christian."

"Great."

Haffveniir turned her head to stare at him with one yellow eye, black pupil irising in and out hypnotically. "Sorry you be getting news megadire from this one so humble. But figure you tip be welcoming. Yeah?"

"Yeah." He nodded. "Thanks, I owe you one. Meet me at the Good Sport after your shift. I'll pick up the tab."

"Hearing that sounds like fine to me. Perhaps being I getting there sooner than you and on my own starting. And my ears open will be to any information more about Fireman Rourke. All luck be good." Haffveniir blinked once slowly, then swung down to disconnect.

Rourke sank back into his oversized chair. It was worse than he had imagined. Not only was Vetch an ambassador—clout enough to cause serious trouble—but he was bonded to an Authority lawyer, a Wormat. There were few beings in the galaxy more frightening than a pissed-off Wormat armed with the law.

Rourke cataloged the other names Riic had mentioned. Queeblint and Protocol checking his records was expected. The Wormat interest had been explained, as had the ominous attention from the company's legal department. But what the hell had he done to the Col? Nothing except fail to pay a life debt.

He considered placing another call to the union, but after the last five dodges Rourke figured that the Worker's Representative Association was intending to maintain a low profile during his case. They evidently wanted nothing to do with what looked like a major political morass.

No doubt about it, the Vetch incident was shaping up into a serious error—a Category Five.

During his long and varied career Rourke had made his share of mistakes. Over the years he had developed a ranking system, pigeonholing various faux pas into categories ranging from one to five, based on severity. The higher the number, the greater the mistake.

Category Ones were the most common: little errors in judgment made on a daily basis—eating anything from the employee commissary, drawing to an inside straight, or playing the slots down at Coqui's Gambling Emporium. Minor irritations that were immediately forgotten.

Learning experiences always rated at least Category Two. These were slips great enough to cause acute but temporary discomfort, like his brief stint as an asteroid miner, which had ended in financial ruin and forced him into the merchant marine to duck some outstanding debts and leave the debtors behind him. His first marriage had been a definite Cat Two—painful but not fatal. And the pain always faded with time.

Enlisting in the service was a Three. His patriotic fervor en-

hanced by half a case of Mayfield Stout, Rourke had printed a
contract that had earned him four standards of bloodshed and
strategic insanity along the Oolaan–Human border. A valuable
lesson: patriotism always resulted in mistakes of magnitude three
or better.

Repeat stupidity defined Category Four. Reenlisting was one
of his more notorious Fours. So was his second marriage. Both
blunders had damn near cost him his life. In fact, potential fa-
tality was common in Fours.

And then there were Fives.

A Five transcended all other mistakes. Not just an error and
far more than a learning experience, a Five was a pivotal point,
a collision with fate that permanently altered the path of his life.
Looking back, Rourke could see them like bomb craters spread
out along his serpentined past. But he could see them only in
retrospect.

That was the worst thing about a Category Five—one never
saw them coming.

His first Category Five had occurred almost forty standards
back, a damned eternity, except when his mood was right and
certain channels in his brain snapped open. Then all Rourke had
to do was stare blindly out into space and it came jolting back
through him: the crowds, the dust, that single suspended moment before impact.

The ancient and time-honored sport of baseball had survived
countless centuries of social change. Certain alien cultures considered the game Humanity's only worthwhile contribution to
the galaxy. It was played on hundreds of worlds and colonies,
from the red dust of Malacar to the domes of Stuart's World.
Teams of Humans or Vost, Wormat, Eng, or Lling were pitted
against each other in ritual combat, testing their biological ad-
aptations for racial superiority.

At fifteen Rourke was already exhibiting the potential of a
professional pitcher. He was lean, lanky, with big hands and
long fingers—living proof that Mother Nature could still generate athletic perfection equal to the cloning labs on Earth.

Two to one, top of the ninth, his team clinging to a slim lead.
Rourke had pitched well, allowing only two hits, a home run in
the seventh and a single in the ninth that the center fielder's
throwing error had transformed into a triple. The tying run was
ninety feet away. He stood on the mound and massaged the ball

in his glove as Arramson took a long, leisurely stroll out from the dugout.

"Feeling okay?" the coach asked.

Rourke nodded.

Arramson was a big man, his jaw fringed with a stained beard, his eyes hidden in his wrinkled face. Rourke sometimes fantasized that the coach was actually his missing father, imagining that he had not really been abandoned on Hardcore but that the man had needed to conceal his identity for a while because of some deep dark secret. There always seemed to be fatherly concern in his wizened features.

"You own this guy," Arramson said, jerking a thumb toward the plate. "Keep 'em high and inside." The coach started to walk away, stopped, and turned back. "And Casey. Forget about 'em." He gestured toward the scouts in the stands drawn by rumors of Rourke's blinding fastball and phenomenal control, then trotted back to the bench.

The suicide squeeze was a brilliant gamble. Rourke pitched him tight, but the Wormat got the bat down, and the ball came off in a dribbling arc.

Rourke was down from the mound in a heartbeat. The catcher also committed, throwing back his mask and charging. And the first baseman was halfway down the line, all converging on the ball as if drawn by a magnet. Rourke reached the white orb first, scooped it up, and leapt over the crouching catcher, stumbling toward the plate.

The Wormat runner had momentum and size, hurtling toward home like an incoming shuttle.

"No! You stupid shit," he heard Arramson screaming as he braced himself for impact. "No!"

The last thing Rourke saw was the creature's grinning maw as they collided.

He woke up in the hospital, coming out of surgery. They repaired his knees and shoulder well enough that he was able to do his time in the military and the Bureau, but his dreams of a baseball career were over. The rhythm was gone, he had a slight hitch in his stride, and his control had vanished.

Another learning experience: Sacrifices done for team goals were often hazardous to individual goals. Translation: Only fools threw themselves on live grenades.

As with all Category Fives, Rourke could close his eyes and see the moment of decision, that instant where he might have pulled up, or tried to tag the runner instead of facing him at the plate, or let the first baseman take the ball. And he was almost certain he would have done it differently.

So it was with the Vetch incident. A minor substitution—tossing in a stun grenade instead of a blinder, waiting for backup, or disregarding the call completely.

Looking back, the better choice always seemed so clear.

The blade fell at shift change.

His comm-link shrieked again; Queeblint's grim visage appeared on the projection surface. The red illumination added a satanic gleam to her triangular face, the velvet patch between her two bulbous eyes shimmering like a flame. Her antennae shifted, wavering.

"Rourke?"

"Yeah," he said, his guts suddenly cold.

"Office. Mine." Her whistling voice was shrill and tremulous as if she were low on air, her speech sac bubbling as it reinflated. "Now."

The screen went dark. Queeblint was never much of a conversationalist—Vost speech did not translate well to Patois or English—but the message was brief even for her usual style. Big trouble, Rourke knew, reading between the lines.

The office smelled like a candy store, the air rich with a cinnamon tang of pheromones, pleasant and soothing. It was the smell of grandmother's house on a vid-show, the scent of apple pie and freshly baked sweet rolls.

Queeblint was working hard to put him at ease.

Rourke stepped inside the low portal and waited for his eyes to adjust to the dim red illumination. Vosts had no use for bright light and compromised with the races that were night-blind by pumping in a steady glimmer of low-frequency radiation. The stifling heat sucked moisture from his skin, leaving beads of sweat glimmering on his arms. He wiped his brow and gave the traditional half bow of deference.

"Sit," she hooted from behind the safety of her desk, pointing toward the low bench in the conversation pit.

The pit was a concession to upright aliens; the Vost preferred cramped quarters and low ceilings. As he sat in the circular alcove, his eyes were level with Queeblint's as she lay supine behind the horseshoe-shaped work station. The desk was as complex as the bridge of a ship, controls studding the panels both above and below her triangular head. Even the walls were crammed with machinery: comm-links, viewscreens, a holo projector.

Queeblint rubbed a forelimb through the red velvet patch between her eyes, a familiar nervous gesture. The Vost was never comfortable dealing with Rourke, and her mood was darker than usual.

"About last night," he said, launching into his prepared speech.

"Silence." Red highlights flickered on the black lacquer of her chitin. "Observe. Listen. Learn." She released another jet of sweet aroma and stroked a console with one feeler. A viewscreen flickered, displaying a computer form: NOTICE OF SUSPENSION FOR THE PURPOSE OF TERMINATION.

His name was prominently displayed at several key points on the page. Rourke felt his face flush with anger.

"Now just a damn minute . . ."

Another blast of scent, strong enough to make him think he was drowning in a vat of syrup.

"Quiet. Please." She brushed her forelimbs on the contacts. A parade of violations ticked across the screen. Queeblint read each aloud, the words shrilling from the metal voice box attached to her vents. "Dereliction."

"He was asleep."

"Drinking. On duty."

"One frakkin' beer?"

"Assault."

"They were assaulting him . . ."

"Discharging weaponry."

Rourke stood up, crouched to avoid striking his head, and leaned over her desk. "I thought somebody was murdering the bastard!"

Her antennae bristled in alarm, three scarlet plumes twitching above her skull. Another gust of scent, bitter and acrid: fear. Her sac expanded, pumping out a neutralizing agent. "Calm. Please."

"Frakkin' hell, Queeblint!" He stared at the list of numbered counts covering the wall. "Are you just going to let them crucify me?"

"Discussed. Pleaded." Queeblint whistled mournfully. "Overruled."

"You haven't even heard my side." It was futile; Rourke knew that even as he spoke. Vetch was bonded to a Wormat; he had the ranking hand.

"Hearing. Two cycles."

"And until the termination hearing?"

"Suspended." Another low whistle. "Unpaid."

"Thanks for all your help." He rubbed one hand through the stiff stubble on his scalp. "You'll be hearing from my union rep."

"Get attorney."

"Any more good advice?"

"Possibly."

Rourke stopped and stared. "What's that?"

"Transfer." There was a single pinpoint of darkness in the center of her ruddy compound eyes.

"Where?"

"Factor Division."

The statement caught Rourke off guard. During his time with the Authority he had come in contact with a few members of the Factor Corps. Scattered across the colonies and stations of the Quadrite and the unclaimed systems wedged between Human and Oolaanian space, they were an elite group primarily responsible for protecting company interests against encroachment by competing firms, local political entities, and other variations of the ancient and time-honored occupation known as piracy.

An odd combination of merchant, explorer, judge, diplomat, and priest, they were expected to negotiate trading charters, arrange for loans and developmental funds, keep the unmanageable members of the Trading Corps in line, placate local rulers, and even forestall the occasional war—all with equal skill. Always patient, kind, and understanding, facing life with a smile and a hearty handshake, most factors Rourke had met had seemed banal and boring; he avoided them whenever possible.

"Never thought of myself as factor material," he said. "Are you offering?"

"No." Chitin scraped loudly against chitin somewhere behind her desk. "They inquire." Another wheezing gasp of air filled her sac. "Nothing promised. Want to meet. Talk. Tomorrow, midshift."

Queeblint raised one long slender limb and offered him a plastic card. He took the flat square. It was cold to the touch, black and gold, an access card that would allow him entrance to the main office complex down in the financial district.

He tapped the card against his fingertips. "Who wants to see me?"

"Xe'Aul. Chief. Factor Division."

Xe'Aul. It was a Quorg name. He had never trusted Quorgs as far as he could throw them.

"I'll think about it." Rourke climbed up out of the pit.

"Remember." One forelimb waved toward the form on the viewscreen. "Two cycles. Think. Fast."

"Sure." He stalked out.

Back at his desk, Rourke made a quick call to Haffveniir. She answered on the second page, her mottled face appearing on the screen, her wattles quickly turning blue with mirth.

"So soonest be you calling me, yes?" The Lling warbled softly. "More news perhaps you for the telling have?"

"Hell," Rourke growled, "I can't tell you anything new. You knew the score before I did. What I need is a favor. Can you get me any information on Xe'Aul and the Factor Division?"

It was like asking an arsonist for a light.

"Being done consider it, yes?"

"Good. Bring it—and anything else you think I might need to know—with you to the Sport tonight." Rourke sucked in a deep breath. "And Haffveniir, in case I forgot to tell you, thanks a lot."

"None problem," the Lling chortled. "All need friends— even fornicators most dire." She cut the connection, her laughing image fading from the comm.

Rourke spun around to face his computer screen, the report etched in green and black on the display. His workstation had always been a constant reminder of his minority status within the organization. The desk was standard Wormat issue, similar to human furnishings but thirty percent larger to accommodate the massive Wormat frame. Even the lighting was makeshift, a rack of fluorescents scrounged from supply. Everything was temporary: Brilliant planning on the part of his superiors; all traces of his tenure could be erased in less than an hour. And it looked as if their caution were about to pay off.

He stared at the script and the flickering cursor, certain it would take at least another shift to complete the paperwork remaining from the Vetch incident. The hand gesture Rourke made to the screen just before heading for the door was an ancient Human sign of extreme displeasure.

What he needed was a few drinks, a hot shower, a few hours sleep, some breakfast, and some time to think.

If Queeblint did not like it, she could add another charge to his termination orders.

NINE

The Good Sport was jammed.

A wave of nostalgia swept over Rourke as he navigated through the tangled press of drunken aliens filling the pub. There were not many places on Central he would truly miss after he was gone, but the Sport ranked high on that short list.

Mygrazee had pulled out all the stops for her annual postconference celebration, with the wall dividers rolled up to allow for additional seating and portable chairs and benches wedged into the aisles. Five of the six holoscreens were running—displaying two klaav matches, a baseball game, and a pair of unidentified alien physical contests—audios blaring loudly, images merging at the fringes into a blurred collage.

Stepping over a Trelar sprawled on the floor, Rourke slid into the booth beside the slouching form of Haffveniir Riic. The Lling was already well anesthetized, staring blankly at him for a moment before recognition hit.

"Welcome, Fireman Rourke," Haffveniir warbled. "Be that hearing I am sirens to approach?" Her wattled skull turned crimson with mirth.

"The only sirens you're hearing are in your head, Haffveniir. Chemically induced." Not that he begrudged the Lling her relaxation. His own conspicuous sobriety was an indication of the seriousness of his troubles. By now—under normal circumstances—Rourke would have been among the walking wounded. But, Rourke grimly reminded himself, circumstances were far from normal.

"Here then to louder them making!" Grabbing the lyki platter with one pair of rubbery manipulators, she lapped at the thick layer of narcotic sludge, her lipless mouth slurping noisily.

Rourke waved a hand at Mygrazee; the bartender detached herself from the counter and pushed her way through the patrons, moisture glistening on her slick hide.

"Another for my friend," Rourke said when the Eng was close enough to hear over the din. "Coffee for me. Virginal."

"This temperance is a little late in coming, eh, Rourke?" Like most Eng, she spoke a Patois that was smooth and accentless. On occasion she had even been known to greet him with a few ancient Germanic curses, all part of making her customers feel at home.

Myg snorted loudly as he tried to hand over his chit. "On the house. It's old Engi custom to treat the soon to be executed to free drinks. Brings good luck." She waddled away, her loose gray-green flesh sagging around the taut straps of her equipment harness.

Rourke returned his attention to Haffveniir. She was studying him closely, her enormous yellow eyes filled with drug-enhanced pity.

"What have you got for me, Haffveniir?"

The Lling shuddered, a swallow tracing the length of her slender neck. "How you wanting be it told? Straight like?"

Rourke nodded.

"Choices two. Fired. Transferred."

"That much I know. Factor Division. Any rumors as to where I'm headed if I accept the transfer?"

"Station Mael."

"A known hellhole." Rourke shook his head.

"Must very dangerous being too."

"Say again?"

"Knowing you not? Last factor. Dead. See?"

"How?"

"Most explosively. Accidental."

"Great." Rourke scowled darkly. "Just what I need, an extended stay on a station where my predecessor was fragged."

"Definite ass pain," Haffveniir said sagely.

"I still don't understand it." Rourke pounded his fist on the black plastic tabletop. "Why me?"

"Col asked." The Lling warbled as if at some hilarious joke. "Seeing how it is? Wormats furious. Peklo division, legal division, both wanting masculine parts gender yours be for trophy. All demand termination employment immediate. But Col for ask one Rourke, Kenneth Christian."

"Since when did the Col get so damned powerful?"

"Since renegotiation time contract due. Butt-scuttle be saying renewal get light of green for this gesture most magnanimous. Must be favor seriously major owed Rourke by Col? No?"

"Other way around, Haffveniir. You get this Col's name—the one who did the asking?"

"Dar Il Chedo."

"Bingo." He was silent for a minute, staring out at the crowd, trying to figure the angles quickly. Percentages were shifting, odds tilting in his favor. "Got anything on the director of factors?"

"That being one Xe'Aul. One major type political beast. Fast. Hard . . . not any way resembling Queeblint." Bending down, she retrieved a packet from the bench and flipped it to Rourke. "Be watching backside of yours most valuable being if you going working for her slime kind Quorg."

"That goes for any kind of Quorg." He opened the parcel and found a handful of infocubes, copies of personnel documents, and organizational charts from the Factor Division. "But if I play it right, I could make it worth my while. For enough credits, even a stint in hell would be bearable."

"So you going be, then?" Haffveniir glanced at him, her head tilted ninety degrees.

"I don't know. If I were a betting man, I'd lay odds that my next residence will be on Mael Station. What frakkin' choice have I got? But if the Authority wants to use me as a bargaining chip, they'll have to pay for the privilege. And I'm not cheap." He stood up as Mygrazee returned with the drinks. "Thanks for the leverage, Haffveniir."

"None problem." She arched her neck and clasped his hand with her four small limbs. "All to you luck be most good, Rourke."

"You too." He pulled away slowly, conscious of a sudden tightness in his throat and a burning in his eyes. Certain beings he would miss almost as much as the familiar atmosphere of the Good Sport itself.

"Say, Rourke," Mygrazee said, nodding toward his coffee. "You want that to go?"

"Real funny, Myg. Very frakkin' funny." But he grinned despite himself.

Rourke headed for the door, anxious to prepare for his meeting with Xe'Aul and equally anxious to be gone before the lump in his windpipe got any larger.

TEN

Fans howling in protest, the hovercab decelerated and dove toward an exit that suddenly yawned in the side of the trans-Central tubeway.

In the rear compartment Rourke cursed under his breath as centrifugal force slammed him against the thinly padded door panels and inertia tried to push him through his shoulder harness. It was no accident that he had taken the time to strap himself into the rear seat of the cab. The driver was a Lling, and as a race, the Lling tended to value speed over safety.

As the hover slid down the exit ramp, the curved alloy walls of the tube gave way to open space. He caught a brief glimpse of the skyline, a travelogue panorama of the towering structures clustered in the vast orbital's central ring, the corporate arcologies thrusting up toward the light of the core.

The exit ramp merged into the Grand Concourse, Central's main thoroughfare. The financial district was a showcase for visiting dignitaries. Flowering plants lined the median. Upscale shops occupied the ground floors of the corporate towers, specialty stores and boutiques, store fronts and brokerage houses designed to cater to an upper-level management type of clientele.

Five massive structures rose above all else, the home arcologies of the five sisters of the Quadriate—Beladyne, Huus/Deerbi, Hive Tekas, the Rowm, and the United Trading Authority—the league's largest and most influential corporations. The structures rose like massive temples, monuments to the Quadriate gods of finance, huge castles housing thousands of top executives and support staff for their far-flung mercantile empires.

Visiting dignitaries might have been convinced that the Quadriate was run by the director and the other elected officials on the operating committee. But the average citizen knew that decisions made in the boardrooms of those arcologies often determined the future course for entire planetary systems. Corporate plots and intrigues were common themes in the holos, with fictional careers rising and falling as a result of the subtle machinations of cunning executives. And though the holos tended to sensationalize their products, Rourke suspected that the truth was worse than fiction.

Line employees like himself did not usually get involved in corporate intrigue. Plots, takeovers, and career assassinations usually took place on levels far above the average grunt. But Rourke had the sudden feeling he was no longer average.

Rourke had spent the evening preparing for his meeting with Xe'Aul, and as he stared at the arcology towering above him, he felt the fear return. Xe'Aul was not a being to be taken lightly. The infocubes had given Rourke an image of the Quorg as a consummate corporate political infighter, skilled and ruthless, whose rise to the top was littered with the careers of his foes.

After examining the merits of a variety of bargaining tactics, Rourke had finally decided on the "wise fool" approach. Haffveniir had given him some serious leverage, but Rourke knew from painful experience that leverage was never enough to guarantee success and that revealing one's strengths too early often allowed an opponent to turn defeat into victory. His strategy was simple: play dumb until Quorg had committed, then start raising the ante. Planned stupidity had served him well many times in the past.

And if that did not work, he was not above begging.

The hover slewed up to the curb and stopped, pressure venting from the air bag. The cabbie kept the passenger door sealed until Rourke's credit chit had cleared and the financial transaction was complete, then kicked open the panel and waited long enough for him to get one foot on the curb before accelerating away in search of another fare.

Inside the cavernous lobby of the arcology his footsteps echoed like gunshots on the smooth expanse of pale flooring. The place was a study in muted elegance, spacious and broad, radiating an aura of wealth. Rourke walked to the lift tube, pausing on the platform to dig the access card from his pocket and slip it into the slot on the security panel. A lev-bubble formed around him.

Without command, the bubble rose from the ground and shot skyward up the clear plasteel tube.

* * *

It was a long ascent. The tube twisted up through the center of the arcology. Floors flashed by: brightly lit internal malls, residential zones and work environments, long chambers filled with employees huddled over glowing data terminals. Each level was separated by clusters of hothouse plants and stone terraces.

Somewhere in the upper strata of the complex the lev-bubble was diverted to a landing station. The gleaming sphere came to rest on a pad and then vanished. Rourke found himself at the end of a short corridor, facing an enormous pair of ornately carved doors. The panels swung wide as he approached.

Low-ceilinged and dimly lit, the reception area maintained the atmosphere of tasteful elegance. On one low wall was a hologram of scattered star systems, specific clusters highlighted in brilliant primary colors like paint splotches thrown by an idiot child. Alien furnishings were arranged in small groupings: Vost benches, massive Wormat settees, and other items whose users' forms could only be guessed.

A Vost neuter hung in a sling in the center of the receiving desk. Its chitin was polished to an ebony brilliance, contrasting sharply with the vivid patches of yellow velvet between its two enormous compound eyes. A trio of antenna plumes pivoted at Rourke's entrance, vibrating gently as they sampled the messages his subtle Human pheromones offered.

"Rourke, Kenneth Christian," it said before he could speak. Its voice was a soft whistling, its Patois far superior to Queeblint's, "You are expected." Forelimbs danced across the keyboard studs. A door yawned beyond the desk. "Go right in."

Instant access was a sign of power as obvious as the flickering arc from a high-voltage circuit. Suddenly he was generating enough juice to avoid spending idle time languishing in a waiting room. Rourke logged the fact into his mind and adjusted his program accordingly, raising his price by ten percent.

Stepping through the door, he entered the lair of the beast.

Impossibly, the office seemed as vast as the lobby of the arcology, its depths lost in soft shadow. It was the largest single room Rourke had encountered in his five standards on Central, a not-so-subtle statement on an orbital construct where space meant power. The thickly padded floor was terraced into multiple levels. Portable screens of lacquered wood created small alcoves and cubicles. Open frames held a variety of art pieces: statues and carvings from a dozen different races.

A massive bio-designed workstation dominated the central level of the room, an oval chunk of hardware and steel inlaid with blood-red wooden panels. Squatting in the shadows behind the workstation was an aged Quorg as massive and immobile as the desk. The jeweled facets of his eyes glimmered in the dark gray backdrop of his misshapen, asymmetrical skull.

An Eng stood in the shadows behind the desk. Moisture gleamed on the creature's skin, slick and oily against the fabric of a dark jumpsuit.

"Sit down, Ser Rourke," the Quorg said, raising one thick limb and pointing toward a polished wooden bench that sat like an altar before the massive workstation. "Please, make yourself comfortable."

As he sat on the hard wooden bench, Rourke struggled to keep from laughing at the irony of the statement. There was nothing comfortable about the office, nor was there anything but cold calculation in the eyes of his Quorg host. The Eng was studying him as if he were a specimen in a scientific experiment.

"I'm Xe'Aul," the Quorg continued. "Director of factors for the Carstan Sector. This is Nebuun, one of my primaries."

His voice was a sibilant whisper, like the low register of a woodwind instrument, without the heavy lisp usually caused by the several meters of ropy tongue coiled in the average Quorg's bulging throat. Noting the flaccid sac hanging below the creature's jaw, Rourke realized that he had undergone some type of corrective surgery. No doubt Xe'Aul was far from average.

"Did Queeblint inform you of the nature of this meeting?" Xe'Aul asked casually.

In his mind Rourke heard the soft buzz of cards being shuffled. The game was on, hands being dealt. He managed a cool smile, feigning blank confusion.

"I was told that you wanted to speak with me about transferring." His subtle word choice implied that the Factor Division had contacted him—he had something they wanted.

"The chance for a transfer," Xe'Aul said, correcting him gently. "There is an opening in my department. Factor, Mael Station. I'm interviewing potential candidates. You were recommended."

"I find that strange." Rourke shrugged. "I've never expressed any interest in being a factor."

"Some of my best employees were reluctant when first approached. They had to be . . . convinced . . . about their own abilities." He regarded Rourke with one ruddy eye. "You, for example, speak fluid Colese and have had experience dealing with the Col. The Col are a major influence on Mael Station.''

"I hope you haven't been misled." Rourke shrugged. "My Col is far from fluid, and my experience with the Col people is limited."

"You are too modest."

"No." Rourke grinned. "I'm just not stupid enough to believe that my Colese makes me a prime candidate for the job."

"Quite perceptive, Ser Rourke. Another of your hidden talents." Xe'Aul paused as though gathering his thoughts. When he continued, he spoke carefully, framing each word. "I think we should speak frankly, you and I. What would you say is the primary business of the United Trading Authority?"

"Let me guess. Trade?"

"Among other things," the Quorg purred, ignoring Rourke's sarcasm. "But trade is certainly important. Tell me, Ser Rourke. Do you know the secret of the trading art?"

Rourke had no answer.

"Accommodation, Ser Rourke." The Quorg leaned forward, shadows receding from the lumpy features, revealing the gray wrinkled skin hanging loosely alongside the slitted mouth. "The willingness to provide for the client that which he thinks he requires.

"Now, there are times when a client's need is met solely by the product and the price. But that does not require a trader, only a clerk." He made a disgusted sound at the back of his throat. "A trader knows that price is a poor foundation on which to build a relationship. A lower price and the buyer is gone. No, Ser Rourke, if you want to keep a client happy, you must be accommodating."

The Quorg shifted in his desk. Rourke had the sense of a vast bulk moving, of weight settling. The desk creaked with the strain.

"Believe me," Xe'Aul continued, voice hissing and whispering in the dark, "many deals are made which have nothing to do with the goods being exchanged. Sometimes these additional favors are monetary, but more often they are of a more personal nature. Like providing female companionship for a drunken diplomat far from home and feeling lonely. Do you understand?"

"Yeah," Rourke said, cringing at the memory of Vetch spread out on the sensor field, the two hookers standing beside him.

"Excellent." The Quorg burbled softly. "Because you and I, my dear Rourke, we must accommodate each other."

"What did you have in mind?"

"I need a factor for Mael. The Col have asked for you." One of the creature's five rubbery limbs traced a pattern on the desk top. "Accepting the position would help me to accommodate the Col."

"I hate to point this out, but I don't know anything about being a factor."

"A minor detail. You will be factor in name only. Nebuun will accompany you and see to the daily operation of the port. You will be required only to keep the Col happy. But whatever they demand of you, you will clear with Nebuun before accommodating them."

"So I help you. What's in it for me?"

"A continuing future with the United Trading Authority."

"Mind if I ask about the financial considerations for the position?"

"Not at all. They should be familiar. They're identical to those of your present job."

"Then I'm afraid I've been wasting your time," Rourke said. He stood and smiled sheepishly. "I'm really very happy in security. I'd need some serious incentive to leave."

For a moment the Quorg stared at him. Then a feral grin spread across his features. He laughed softly. "You please me. You have the potential to become an excellent factor."

"I don't—"

"Sit down, Rourke." Xe'Aul's digits touched the keyboard at his side. The viewscreen on the wall flickered, resolving into the block script of a bureaucratic form: Rourke's termination orders.

"You see, Ser Rourke? I'm quite familiar with your . . . security work. In truth, you should already be standing in the unemployment lines. But life is funny, yes? One moment bound for termination, the next a prime candidate for the job of factor. I'd hate to see an argument over money ruin a promising career move, but it's your choice."

"I think you're overestimating the strength of the termination case," Rourke said. "I've consulted with the union and have been assured that I will not be fired."

The Quorg snorted derisively. "I've heard different. In fact, I am certain that the union has been ignoring your calls. But you can believe what you want. And if you want to defend yourself at a hearing—alone—so be it." Another spattering of clicks from the keyboard. "I only wonder if you've thought about all the ramifications of your pending termination."

Another flash of static on the viewscreen, and an unfamiliar court document appeared. Rourke winced. After the events of the past few cycles he had developed an aversion to terminal displays—they always seemed to predict doom and gloom for his future.

"Recognize this?"

Rourke shook his head.

"Well, the Pleasure Guild and the Peklo industrial complex have decided that you owe them civil damages. A specious case. While you are still employed by the Authority, they can't sue you personally. However, if your employment should end, it could prove to be quite expensive."

"And a transfer to the Factor Division would ensure my continued employment?"

"Exactly so."

Rourke was silent for a moment, as if actually considering the offer. He had to admit that it was a smooth piece of negotiating, and the Quorg seemed certain of his answer. But it still seemed that he had the advantage—the Quorg needed him more than he needed the job.

"Look, why don't we skip all this talk about the firing rap? We both know you need me, so you're going to make sure I beat it. But if you want me in your department, you'll have to give me some serious financial incentive."

Xe'Aul inhaled deeply. "Rourke, what makes you feel you are so valuable?"

"Simple." Rourke paused for maximum dramatic effect. "I'm the only candidate with the personal recommendation of the Col."

The Quorg's laugh was like the wind through dry grass. "I believe you will make an excellent factor."

"If you're willing to pay for my services."

"Oh, I'll pay. But how much?" Another demonic chuckle.

Xe'Aul pressed another contact. The image on the viewscreen jump-cut from block text to a holograph of a room. Rourke felt suddenly ill; it was a shot of the interior of his suite.

"In my research," the Quorg said, staring at him over the tips of his steepled digits, "I've learned a great deal about your life, Ser Rourke. If you ever leave the Authority, I'd recommend a career in politics. You have remarkable latent diplomatic talents. Consider for a moment your apartment. Slightly above what I would expect for a Level One security operative.''

The scene shifted to the bedroom, showing Rourke sleeping peacefully on the suspensor field.

''You have no idea how particular the Authority is about its budget. Can you imagine how they will react when they learn that you are occupying a suite that has been 'closed for repairs'?''

Rourke saw no need to speak.

''Your wages will be attached. Rent, food, utilities. The charges will be extremely great. I calculate it would take you thirty standards at seventy-five percent withholding to pay the debt. And then there would be the interest . . .'' His voice trailed off to silence.

''Thirty standards.'' Rourke swallowed hard. His leverage had suddenly dissipated like an early morning fog.

''Thirty-three point two to be exact.'' The Quorg's jeweled eyes sparkled. ''Of course, this is the kind of thing that they're not likely to find on their own. I had to do quite a bit of digging—and I knew where to look.''

''So they don't know.''

''Won't find out, either, unless someone tips them off.''

Rourke took a deep breath. ''You wouldn't turn in one of your employees, would you?''

''No.'' The Quorg shook his lopsided head. ''We look out for each other in the Factor Division. I treat my employees like family, like my own young.''

Rourke was an experienced poker player and knew when to fold a hand. ''I guess you found your man.''

''I thought I had, so I took the liberty to have the necessary documents prepared.'' Swiveling in his chair, Xe'Aul produced a contract and handed it to Rourke. ''Straight transfer; you maintain all benefits and seniority. All charges are dropped. And the housing item will be our little secret.''

Printing the ident, Rourke slid the papers back to the Quorg. ''When do I leave?''

''Immediately. There's a hover waiting to take you to the shuttle docks. I've booked you passage on a flight to Mael Station shipping out at shift change.''

''No time to pack?'' Rourke spread his hands helplessly.

''I've already arranged for your things to be shipped. Packing started as soon as you left for this appointment.'' He consulted his timepiece. ''They should be finished by now.''

"Damn sure of my answer, weren't you?"

"Ser Rourke, in my position I've grown accustomed to getting what I want." He touched a switch, and the door swung open behind Rourke. "Good-bye, Ser Rourke."

Rourke stood and walked from the room. He rode the lift down in a trance, numbed by the speed of the exchange, marveling at how quickly his leverage had evaporated. He knew one thing for certain: He didn't ever want to play cards with the director.

By the time he hit the front doors, Rourke was laughing out loud. It was all one big ironic joke. From ex-security operative to factor in a matter of seconds, a skillful sleight of hand without benefit of mirrors or wires.

All Rourke could do was whistle in admiration.

Xe'Aul waited until the doors had swung shut behind the Human. Then he turned slowly to face the Eng.

"So, Nebuun," he purred softly. "Say what you think."

"I think you are a fool." The Eng made a wet noise with his mouth. "To trust such a position to one such as this. Little more than a common felon. And a Human at that. I believe you have taken leave of your senses."

"No, Nebuun. I am not crazy. But my choices are limited. You know how it has been lately. Corta has been dogging my heels since the Betal debacle. I cannot afford to lose another contract. Especially not Mael. Ancestors help me if I lose the musk concession."

"But a Human?"

"If he keeps the natives happy, then he is worth the risk. Besides, you will limit his impact. Am I understood?" The purr suddenly held a frigid edge. "Our fates are entwined, dear Nebuun, yours and mine. If I fall, you will fall with me. Think about that. Watch the Human closely. The Col want something. It's in the wind, and they think they can get it from this man. Hold him tight, Nebuun. We might both still come out of this intact."

"As you wish, Ser Director." The Eng bowed stiffly. "Now, if you will excuse me. I believe I have a flight to catch."

The Eng walked quickly to the door and stepped between the panels before they were fully opened.

Xe'Aul watched the creature depart. In the sudden silence of his office, his hunting sense tuned in, receptors on his skin listening/feeling/tasting for the approach of prey and other predators.

It seemed to the Quorg that he could sense the killers outside waiting, Corta and her minions encircling him, hiding in the cover of their own offices, seeking a moment of weakness to rush in and take not his flesh but his power and position.

And just as surely ending his life.

ELEVEN

Rem Il Leera stood motionless before the door to Dar's private chamber, unable to will her symbiote to raise a limb and press the entry contact.

Her mind was a whirling chaos of thoughts and emotions, equal portions of hope and fear blending with a mixture of too few facts and too many fictions. Scattered impulses leaking into her leera's nervous system made the muscles vibrate like tightly drawn wires.

Tongues had been buzzing all shift with whispers of a surprise elevation—the time of merging was said to have come at last to Rem the Forgotten. Idle gossip only, she thought bitterly. Nothing more. Too many such rumors had come and gone, too many standards had passed as she watched her peers chosen one by one while she remained a leera. Time had carved the lessons deep into her psyche, forcing Rem to accept her lot in life, convincing her that dreams of elevation were for the young and that fulfillment could be found in any station. Not happiness but perhaps satisfaction . . .

. . . Until the next flurry of rumors swirled, and Rem dared to hope again.

The portal beckoned. Beyond it lay, if not elevation, at least answers. Somehow, Rem found the strength to manipulate the lowbrain. Numb leera digits touched the diamond-shaped contact. The door slid open.

The sleeping chamber of Dar Il Chedo was an architectural showcase, a flagrant pronouncement in stone and wood: the

Authority was a powerful friend deserving of a permanent association. Rem knew the place the designers had mimicked—the southern vista at the Great Chasm of Dhalgri, holographic perfection re-creating the vast fissure complete with its misty depths and jungle-studded cliffs. She could not stand within the electrically woven network of flowers and vegetation, waterfalls and breezes, without imagining a gaping wound on Verrin where this landscape had been carved free, a barren gouge of exposed strata and blasted rock.

As she crossed the threshold, Rem sensed a vague uneasiness permeating the room, a subsonic discord emanating from her master. Dar stood on the edge of a small terrace, staring out at the chasm, Relhr's fading light painting everything a bloody red. A pair of valthins rode the updrafts and thermals, their leathery wings dark against the twilight sky.

The chedo appeared not to have noticed her arrival, an impossibility given the animal's keen senses. Yet Dar ignored her presence almost as if he—the chedo of legendary control—needed time to compose his thoughts and master his emotions. Another entry for Rem to add to his growing catalog of recent odd behaviors.

At last he faced Rem, and she could read the pain and sorrow in his symb's haunted eyes. Then control returned and the telltale candor vanished, replaced by cool precision.

"Dar Il Chedo," Rem said, fighting the slight tremor that had crept into her leera's voice. "You sent for me?" Her symbiote slipped automatically into the ritual of greeting, touching forehead, lips, and breast, raising its chin, and exposing its throat to his talons.

"Yes, Rem." Resignation tainted his words. One midarm swept toward the railing. "Come stand beside me. There is much we must discuss—and little time."

Overriding her leera's instinctive flight reaction, she forced the creature to move closer. Its claws clicked softly on the polished golden octagons of heredia wood. The railing was warm to the touch, almost alive. Her beast's hearts were pounding hard both from fear and from the demon of hope that Dar's strangeness had reawakened in her soul.

"But for the certainty that we are aboard an orbiting construct, we might be home," Dar said, pointing toward the city that clung to the side of the canyon. Layers of tapering angular structures clustered among the vegetation, visible only to the trained eyes of a native. "Nassony. Just as I remember it. Though

I was little more than a novice when I last trod its streets." His chedo inhaled deeply. "Do you smell the bakeries?"

"Yes." The spicy scent of nut cakes made her symb's guts rumble with hunger.

"Such realism. The mind knows it is an illusion, a fantasy of mirrors and electronics, but the trick is so well devised." Both turreted eyes swiveled to stare at Rem, the sharp leera features reflected in the black orbs. "Should we not wonder what other tricks these clever aliens are weaving around us?"

"It is a thought to make the wise mind fear."

"So it is said, little one. And only a fool accepts without question the gifts of enemies or friends, even the gifts of masters." His beast grimaced as if suddenly remembering old wounds. "No doubt you have heard the news."

'I have heard whispers."

The chedo chuffed explosively. "How could it be otherwise in this rumor mill? Nothing is so impossible to control as the tongues of one's subordinates." Dar hesitated and then continued, making no effort to mask his sorrow. "The whispers are true, little Rem. Your time of elevation has come at last."

Rem felt as if her mind had been split by a sharp blow. One portion was overwhelmed by sheer joy, the ecstasy of a dream finally realized. Yet another part of her intellect was baffled by the growing tension in Dar. She formed her response carefully. "It is an honor—"

"No," Dar snarled, a sudden flare of anger radiating from his symb. "Make no mistake. It is not honorable. It is a perversion, an act forced upon me by events beyond my control."

Turning away, the chedo looked back across the mock chasm, its eyes fixed on a point in the projection's hazy distance. Muscle clusters along its face and neck quivered and spasmed, evidence of Dar's intense emotions seeping into the chedo's lowbrain.

Rem was too stunned to speak, terrified of his open rage and afraid that any wrong word might destroy her chances for merging. Elevation was offered but once to each level and, if missed, was generally not tendered again. Fear of rejection overshadowed everything else.

"You do not understand yet," he said after a moment. "But you will. And I hope you can forgive me for what I must do, for what I have failed to do. I should have seen to your elevation many standards ago. I have used you badly, Rem. But not without reason."

"I would never question your motives, Dar Il Chedo." At her

urging, her leera tipped its head back and presented its throat, the movement slow and exaggerated, its neck forming a nearly impossible angle.

The chedo cradled her beast's jaw in its talons. "That has always been your greatest flaw, little one. A habit you must now discard." A gentle pressure forced her leera to relax. "From this point forward, all motives must be suspect—mine, as well."

Releasing her, the creature turned its attention to the polished banister, sinking sharp claws into the smooth surface. The talons flexed and relaxed in slow succession, four sets of bony daggers shaving away small fragments of gleaming wood.

"I know you have questioned some of the tasks I've required of you lately: the visit to the Human, the late excursion into the Authority Personnel Office, our meeting with Ouerrabbi. You considered those more than just minor inconveniences. But you did as I asked."

"The Chedo commands—and I obey."

"And if I ordered you to dive from these cliffs?"

"Where would you have me land, my Chedo?"

"On Jurrume."

"A very long jump."

"Longer than you know." The talons continued to tear at the railing, the rhythmic scratchings punctuating the silence. "What have you heard regarding your elevation?"

"Very little. It seems to have taken everyone here by surprise."

"Excellent." His symbiote bared its fangs, its yellow teeth gleaming behind a rictus of taut lips. "Then there is still hope that your arrival on Jurrume will be equally surprising."

"Jurrume?"

"You will leave immediately. Gral Il Chedo is to be your sponsor."

"Then surely he must know I am coming," she said indignantly. "Have you not asked him to honor me with his guidance and wisdom?"

"He knows nothing—and every precaution must be taken to assure that his ignorance remains complete until you land. I will give you a holographic message requesting his sponsorship. You will give it to him when you meet."

"What if he refuses? What—what will I do?" she stammered. The move was too unorthodox, too odd for her to comprehend fully.

"He cannot refuse. I am to be one of his merge partners."

"I still do not understand." Her leera shuddered, bewildered by the confusion leaking into its system. "Why would you want to keep my elevation a secret?"

The turreted eyes returned to stare at Rem. A moment of silence passed. Muscles twitched on the angular face. "How do you capture a girga?"

"What?" She was thrown by his strange question.

"Answer me!"

"Get close." Her mind was racing. "Stay quiet. Conceal the hand that grabs until the last possible moment."

"Precisely." The chedo nodded stiffly. "The same tactics apply to other prey—even traitors."

Stunned, she made no attempt to hide her shock, letting the breath rush from her beast with an audible sigh.

"Tell me," Dar hissed. "What do you know of Gral?"

"There are stories," Rem answered cautiously. "Tales of certain improprieties. Such fables are common among all hetta and raas. No doubt Gral's retainers spin their own legends about you."

"Every lie contains a grain of truth. That's a Human philosophy, though I know you discount their intelligence." The yellow fangs gleamed again. "Have you an opinion of your new sponsor?"

"He lacks your control. But Gral is a chedo and worthy of my respect."

"Most certainly he deserves respect—but so does a wild chedo. And for similar reasons. They are both dangerous." His voice lowered to a whisper. "Do you have any enemies, Rem?"

"There are some who are gladdened by my failures."

"But are there any who would destroy you in an effort to better themselves, any who view your destruction as necessary to their own advancement? That is the true measure of an enemy." The words rumbled from deep within his beast's throat. "I believe Gral is my enemy, Rem. My enemy, your enemy, even the Prime Triad's enemy. He will destroy us all."

Blasphemy, she thought, and her leera flinched away from him. Rem tried to conceal her reaction, turning the lurch into an exaggerated attempt to gain a better view of the chasm. Dar was not fooled.

"You think my time of hardening has come early," he said softly. "I wish it were so. Insanity and death would be preferable to what I see in the future."

"And what is that, my Chedo?" Concern surfaced momentarily amid the storm of emotions clashing inside her mind. "What do you see?"

"War. Col against Col." The dark eyes glazed for a moment, as though seeing the horrors of battle. A sudden tremor wracked the chedo's frame but was quickly stilled.

"But why?"

"No doubt you know of the Oolaanian offer and the Prime's refusal?"

"I have heard as much." The Prime would never accept alien machinery with such strings attached, demands that would sully the purity of the Col.

"Word has reached me that Oolaanian ships still navigate Col Space. I can only assume that someone dares to negotiate with them despite the Prime's orders. It must be Gral—he is the guardian of the gate."

"Why would Gral do such a thing?"

"Surely you know what is said of him. Some say he is the Filitaar."

"Idle whispers." It was Rem's turn to flash leera fangs. "The same is said of you."

"Yet I think Gral believes."

"Have you proof of his treachery?"

"No. If I had, I would go to the Triad and be done with it. Gral is too clever. I have nothing tangible—yet. But I know he plans something—just as a hunter knows the prey he pursues through heavy foliage. A flash of wing, a cry, a faint scent, nothing that can be held in one's grip, but taken together they create an image of the beast. So it is with Gral."

"In my dealings with him I have seen nothing."

"The eyes of our beasts are easily fooled." One limb gestured toward the holograph. "We stand here watching night creep across the Dhalgri Gorge, a place half a galaxy distant! The illusion is seamless. But if we reach out, will we not touch the walls? Tear down those walls, we will find the machines responsible. And what else might we discover? What other secrets have the Vost or Trelar hidden behind this comfortable facade?"

Rem said nothing, silently wondering how long Dar had been concealing such deep-seated, dangerous paranoia. Rivalry between merge partners was to be expected, was in fact a precursor of the internal war they would wage during the merger—the struggle for eventual mental dominance of the Triad. No doubt, if questioned, the closest aides of Harn Il Chedo would report their own tales of their chedo's tension and moodiness. Still, Dar's fears were far beyond those of mere rivalry.

Dar turned to face Rem, his chedo's eyes smoldering in the darkness. "The time has come to learn what Gral is hiding."

"So you would send me to Jurrume as a spy?" she asked, incredulous.

"I have no choice. If I were to go, he would only tighten his security. But if you visit Jurrume under the pretense of elevation, Gral might not be so careful."

"I do not consider my elevation a pretense," Rem said stiffly.

"Nor would I if there were an alternative." A snarl escaped his chedo, mingled with a ragged breath filled with rage and despair. "See how Gral perverts everything he touches?"

"I do not see Gral in this chamber." Rem looked down, noting that her beast had sunk its small, blunt claws deep into the wooden railing. "What you ask of me is against the Coda."

"As it must be. Every strategist assumes that a certain amount of predictability exists in his enemy; therefore, I must counter with seemingly random factors, unanticipated actions for which he has no planned defense. Gral thinks he knows me. He will not be expecting a response that violates the Coda."

The chedo reached across to the small trickle of water that spilled beyond the edge of the terrace, a real fixture woven within the holograph. Tiny droplets flashed and gleamed on the seamed flesh of its dark palm.

"Once you are on Jurrume," he continued, his chedo's eyes avoiding her beast, "you will do all that is required, the tests and the rituals of purification. And while you are being the perfect initiate, you will peer into the guts of his stronghold and divine for me what Gral is planning.

"You will be alone, without support. You can trust no one or make any attempt to contact me. Once you have proof of his treason, get off-planet. Go to Mael Station. The Human, the one called Rourke, will be the new factor on Mael. Ask him to arrange for safe passage out of the system. Rourke cannot refuse. He owes a life debt."

"Conspiring with aliens is expressly forbidden by Triad dictate." Her tone was frigid.

"Another of my erratic variables." The chedo exposed its fangs grimly as if to tear flesh. "As for how to conduct your investigation, I can offer few suggestions. I would say to trust your instincts, but I doubt you have such reflexes, little Rem."

"I will not be part of this abomination!" Rem forced her leera to turn and face him, stiff-spined and rigid-bodied, voice filled with bitterness. "I have served you well, Dar Il Chedo. I earned my chance at elevation long ago. Still, I came here expecting disappointment. After so many standards of rejection, one becomes accustomed to the pain. But you have found a new way to injure me, with your talk of plots and treason."

"Surely you must see—"

"No, my Chedo." She cut him off, all sense of propriety forgotten in her growing rage. Her leera was trembling, the baubles in its horns jangling softly. "I will go to Jurrume, but I will see nothing. I go not as a spy but as an initiate to be tested and purified. Not to obey you but because it is my right. And I will do nothing while on Jurrume to jeopardize that right."

Enraged, Dar whirled, one clawed limb swinging up, talons extended. The chedo's maw worked soundlessly as he struggled to choke back an attack scream and divert a killing blow. The bladed fist wavered above her beast's skull. Rem became aware of a low keening as her leera moaned in terror.

Gradually his control returned. The claws dropped slowly.

"Go, then," Dar hissed. "Gral waits. Be happily blind and receive your elevation. But you will be chedo among the dead." He turned away.

In silence, Rem headed for the portal. At the door she stopped and looked back. Dar was a dark shape against the fading glow of Relhr.

"If the All Knowing has any compassion," she said, her voice quavering, "when my time of merging comes, the memory of this moment will not survive."

Dar did not reply.

TWELVE

A hovercraft and driver were waiting for Rourke outside the UTA arcology. At the port terminal, a skeletal cargo lighter shuttled him out to a freighter-class transship bound for Mael.

For the first few minutes of his forced commute Rourke tried hard to be angry at his fate, but it was futile. His emotions lay buried beneath a thick layer of conditioned acceptance, an indifference hardened by a lifetime of sudden reversals. Besides, he had learned earlier that luck never stayed good forever. Nor, thankfully, was it eternally bad. The secret to survival was to swim like hell when the current was favorable, drift when it was not, and fight only when one's life was at stake.

So he drifted from vehicle to vessel, watching silently as the streets of Central were replaced by the catwalks and gantries of the docks and finally gave way to the black velvet palette of space.

The cabin was small and universally outfitted, which meant that nothing fit him comfortably. There was a suspensor, a folding table, an autobar, and a small entertainment console.

It took Rourke less than a minute to stow his gear, another minute to test the suspensor field and find that it was adjustable within his tolerance limits. Crossing to the entertainment unit, he stabbed the power stud, hoping to find some decent gambling programs or a few Human-class vids. The console did not respond, its screen remaining dark and silent. He pressed the switch three or four more times before admitting defeat and then moved to the autobar. A few experimental selections revealed that the only beverage available to him was water, a tepid fluid that tasted of iron and was regrettably nonalcoholic.

Rourke was just heading toward the door, looking for the steward, when there was a knock on the portal.

"Come in," he snapped.

The door obeyed his command and slid open. Nebuun, his newly appointed guardian, filled the portal with his sagging bulk, his musty stench wafting in on the thick, close air.

"I see you have settled in," the Eng said, scanning the chamber and noting that Rourke's gear was already stowed.

"Yeah." Rourke nodded. "But I hope you're not paying full price for the private cabin. The entertainment unit is on the fritz, and the bar is dry."

"Exactly as I ordered it."

"What the hell do you mean, 'Exactly as you ordered it'? It's a ten-day run; what am I supposed to do locked up in this room, inventory my fingers and toes?" Rourke stammered.

Nebuun grunted softly. "I have no desire to know the number or condition of your digits. Besides, you will be too busy studying to need any other forms of activity."

The Eng dropped the load of gear he had been carrying onto the small table. Rourke glanced at the pile of material: infocubes with Vost labels, a portable cube reader, a few books.

"What's this?"

"Company manual. Col language tapes. A full dossier on Mael Station and its operations." Nebuun shrugged. "The usual informational package given to a new employee. It's all in Patois. Not Human, but I figure you'll get the feel of it quickly. If there's anything you don't understand, just ask."

"That's very nice, but we both know I'm not the typical new hire employee. I got the distinct impression from Xe'Aul that I was going to be a figurehead."

"And I seem to recall that I was put in charge."

"But—"

Nebuun shook his head slowly. "Only a fool puts an uninitiated person in a position of such authority. You will find, Ser Rourke, I am many things, but fool is not one of them. And I do not intend to spend the rest of my life on Mael Station wet-nursing a sniveling Human. You may know nothing about being a factor now, but by the time I am through with you, you will be able to handle a position on any station in the Quadriate."

"Now, just a damn—" Rourke spluttered.

The Eng ignored him. He stacked the pile of materials quickly, organizing them as he spoke. "Begin with this orientation unit. It covers the history of the United Trading Authority. Then I suggest you go through the operations manual to get an idea of how a station functions. After that, you had better familiarize yourself with the organizational chart for Mael Station. Be sure to memorize the names of those individuals who hold positions of authority. And if you get bored, brush up on your Colese—you're going to need it."

Nebuun finished arranging the gear and headed for the doorway. "You probably will have time to get the first part of the manual committed to memory before our first jump. I'll quiz you on it over dinner just to see how much you've retained." He turned to grin at Rourke, his lipless mouth gaping and his slick pebbled skin wrinkling around his protruding eyes. "I've never had many dealings with Humans. Be rather interesting to study your learning capacities."

"Yeah," Rourke said belligerently. "Well, what if I don't want to participate in your little experiment? What are you going to do, fire me? I don't think the Col would like that too much. Nor would Xe'Aul, either, for that matter."

"I'm afraid you've overestimated your value to me, Ser Rourke." The huge amphibian clucked his tongue. "And if you refuse to cooperate, your value drops to zero. Xe'Aul has given me specific instructions regarding your disposition should you become a liability. Not only will I fire you, but I will personally escort you to Peklo and turn you over to their judicial system. I'm sure they have some most creative punishments for assaulting ambassadors. Wouldn't you agree?"

Rourke had no ready answer.

"I'm glad that we had this little discussion. Now that we understand each other, we can work together better as a team." The Eng gave Rourke a loose salute, a jaunty snap of one webbed hand. "Good luck with your studies. I'll see you at dinner."

He stepped out into the hall, the portal sliding shut behind him.

For a moment Rourke stood staring at the portal, thinking of a few choice words and how good they would have sounded echoing in the small chamber. But he could not quite bring himself to say them out loud. Instead, he poured himself a cup of water, stepped to the small fold-out table, and picked up the first cube. It was cold in his fingers, surprisingly heavy.

Muttering under his breath, Rourke slotted the cube and activated the reader. He sank back onto the suspensor field, massaging his temples, trying vainly to erase the dull ache that was just starting to spread across his forehead.

A mechanical voice swelled out of the speaker, tinny and monotonous, the Patois flawless and unaccented.

"Welcome to the United Trading Authority," the programmed message began.

It was going to be a long trip.

BOOK TWO

THE GULF

One of the principal qualifications for a political job is that the applicant know nothing much about what he is expected to do.

—Terry M. Townsend

THIRTEEN

Deep within the labyrinth of the mothership, the main reasoning center of the Ssoorii Unity studied the skeletal cloaking shell that framed the newly discovered jump nexus. Black on black, the webbed pylons were an octagon of darkness against the starry reach of the galactic arm.

Lacking true visual organs, the reasoning center could see neither the containment structure nor the slight space/time warp that marked the gravitational anomaly of the nexus. Rather, it waded through the flood of data pouring in from a thousand remote sensory elements, fashioning a gestalt of reality from the stream of information sluicing into its lobes.

Details emerged from the flood. An engine failure that had temporarily delayed a shipment of minerals and inorganics, a collision between two spinner mechanisms leading to the loss of a significant fraction of Unity mass, a malfunction in an anchor pylon gyro—these would cause additional delays in the construction of the shell. There were other factors that counterbalanced the delays: increased efficiency in the transmutation process, a larger than anticipated supply of nickel iron requiring less purification, a greater supply of hydrogen in the dust belt to be used for power.

The reasoning center took those facts and wove them into the projection of the immediate future that the Designers had conceived. Each string of data subtly edited the Unity's decision template, narrowing its options, refining its actions and reactions.

Already the projection had been altered drastically, as whole probability structures had been nullified by earlier decisions. The refusal of the Col Prime Triad to negotiate had slashed away an entire path and eliminated a possible though highly improbable solution. The appearance of the Col collaborator, Gral Il Chedo, had collapsed other template branchings. And accepting his offer of capitulation in return for the Unity's assistance in overthrowing the Prime had sheared still more routes from existence.

The reasoning center made no judgments regarding the validity of its decisions. To do so would have required an understanding of the Grand Design far beyond its capabilities. A combat element, the Unity saw only the small segment of the future laid out before it—a task to be completed, an objective to be achieved. Nothing more. Even the discovery of the Unity installation on Jurrume by the strayed alien craft and the subsequent elimination of the two aliens on the station had caused no dread or regret. Such difficulties were but intersections on the pathway, crux moments anticipated by the Designers, requiring the Unity's thought and action within its prescribed parameters.

And once they were passed, the shape of the future was irrevocably changed.

Had the reasoning center been given to comparison, it might have thought of those paths as diseased growths that needed to be cut away from a healthy organic structure. But it did not have the capability for such thoughts. It only reacted to data, which it measured against remaining future probabilities.

A dispatch from the home system arrived via the Gulf, routed through a network of shielded relay units spaced along the dark sweep of the dust belt. Entering the mothership's communication node, the particle stream was immediately translated into chemical data and channeled through other lesser-priority inputs directly into the reasoning center.

It was a simple string of surveillance information. Human ship movements. An enemy battle group had been removed from the present theater of interaction. Present whereabouts . . . unknown. Exact destination . . . unknown. Probability of insertion within Mael system . . . high.

A few hundred microspans elapsed while the reasoning center fit the data into the template. Routes changed. Options collapsed. Probabilities were recalculated.

Finally the reasoning center dispatched its orders. Two corporal freighters and their escorts turned in formation and left the main group, heading for the planet Jurrume to assist units already in place with the manufacture of biological combat elements. Previously inactive fighter units were calved from the mothership and elevated to full-alert status. Additional heavily masked surveillance craft were dispatched to bolster the sphere of observation points already in place throughout the quadrant.

The command was simple: Prepare for enemy contact.

The task complete, the reasoning center went back to its study of the future and the present, neither worrying nor judging, simply waiting for Humanity to appear.

FOURTEEN

". . . camaii musk is a by-product of the camaii, a mammalian ruminant that roams through the central plains of Jurrume in vast herds." The voice filled his small cabin, a monotonous vibration that was more background noise that lecture.

Stifling a yawn, Rourke switched off the cube reader and rolled out of the suspensor field. He stood and stretched slowly, trying to work some feeling back into muscles numbed by three cycles of inactivity. His joints cracked and popped explosively.

So far the trip had been an exercise in boredom. Though three cycles out of Central, the freighter was still nine cycles away from Mael. They had made two jumps, through the Galad and Arduun nexuses, gut-wrenching flexes that had left him weak and ill for a few miserable hours afterward. According to the infocubes, one jump still remained, at Noram, and then an eight-cycle run on impulse before they reached the station.

Rourke had passed most of the time in his cabin studying the cubes or trying to sleep. Not because of any sense of duty he had suddenly developed regarding his upcoming position as factor but because Nebuun seemed determined to turn him into a functional manager before they reached Mael. Twice a shift the Eng came to the cabin and grilled him on his knowledge of the station, its internal workings, and its staff. And Rourke had to admit that the Eng's methods were working.

From the dossier, Rourke had learned that Mael was a mid-range star system. Ten planetary bodies, a large asteroid belt, and a G-type star. Mineral assays had detected large deposits of a wide range of ores, not as concentrated as those of Peklo or Hardcore but sizable enough to support serious exploitation. Several of the planets had definite reformation potential and would have made good agricultural complexes.

Mael might have been mainstream instead of a backwater if not for two major drawbacks. The first problem was that fate and creation had conspired to deprive the star system of a jump point within its economic sphere. Travel time to the nearest nexus averaged eight cycles, almost twice as long as for most other planetary systems. The extra fuel required by the impulse engines during the long insystem transit chewed up profits and created a cost prohibition that had discouraged settlers, keeping the system relatively undeveloped compared with similar colonies such as Bacchus and Malacar.

The second serious glitch preventing major Quadriate exploitation of the system was the fact that Mael had already been claimed by the Col Empire.

To call the Col holdings an empire was to be charitable. Though they controlled six small systems along the edge of the gulf, as a spacefaring race the Col were technologically backward. They might not have had space flight capability at all if not for the greed of a few unscrupulous Eng traders that had passed through their home system four centuries earlier and sold them some used impulse ships. Even now, after conquering five uninhabited systems, the Col still lacked jumpspace hardware and bought most of their ships secondhand from the Quadriate.

The Col had essentially a single commodity to sell to the Quadriate: camaii musk. In fact, if not for the two fist-sized glands above the genitals of the camaii bull, chances were that Mael would have had no Quadriate presence at all, the United Trading Authority would have set up shop in some other system, and the Col navy would still have consisted of those five original Engi hulls.

But the plains of Jurrume, the fourth planet in the Mael system, were black with herds of camaii. Vost pheromone consumers prized the pungent odor derived from the glands of the sturdy ruminant, and the trade that had developed between the UTA and the Col had proved lucrative to both parties. Col herders and ranchers harvested the musk. The United Trading Authority purchased the raw product, refined it, and shipped it back to the Quadriate for resale. And everyone was happy.

Everyone but himself, Rourke thought bitterly. He would have been much happier back on Central with a cold brew in his hand and a warm, willing female on his arm. He might even have settled for both items on board the ship. But the beer tap dispensed water, and if there was a Human female on the freighter, she was staying well hidden.

Besides himself and Nebuun, there was apparently another passenger on board the ship. Rourke had not yet encountered the being, but he had heard it moving through the corridor on one occasion, a faint musical jangling marking its passage from cabin to dining chamber and back again. There had been something oddly familiar about the sound, but when he had looked, the passageway had been empty, the door on the cabin at the end of the hallway sliding shut.

Now, though, as Rourke stood and stretched, he heard the sound again, a faint tinkling as if of bells passing by his door.

Maybe what he needed was some company and conversation to thaw his mind. He took a moment to splash some water on his face and pull on his coveralls. Then he stepped out into the passageway and headed for the dining chamber.

The commissary was a small alcove in the center of the craft. It had been designed primarily for Lling and Vost; the lighting was dim, and the temperature hot. There were no Human furnishings. And he had learned during his previous visits that there was nothing in the dispensing units specifically tailored for Human consumption. But the compatibles were passable, bland and tasteless yet filling. Rourke had a feeling that he needed to get used to such fare. He doubted there would be better on Mael Station.

As he stepped into the chamber, Rourke mentally adjusted his optics to Vost specs. The darkness evaporated, the shadows replaced by a soft red glow. A quick glance around revealed four empty tables, stools fastened to the bulkhead, dispensing units racked on the far wall . . .

. . . and his fellow passenger standing before one of the food machines.

Recognition hit Rourke in stages.

Slender frame and scaled flesh, wedge of feathers spreading across the jutting breastbone, bony fan spreading behind the conical skull like the fingers of an enormous hand. A Col, he thought.

Silver vest and tunic, hawksbill mouth edged with black lacquer, glittering trinkets dangling from her horns.

The Col. The leera who had visited him in his apartment back on Central.

"It's you," Rourke said, almost shouting. "You're Rem Il Leera."

At the sound of his voice, the leera whirled, food packets

flying from her grasp and clattering across the floor. A gasp escaped from the back of her throat, a rattle of distress. She bolted for the door, trying to go around him.

"Wait a minute." Rourke grabbed her by the shoulder. He felt cold flesh beneath his fingers, sharp smooth scales. "You are the one, aren't you? The one who came to see me? From Dar Il Chedo?"

"Please," the creature hissed. "Let me pass! You are mistaken."

"The hell I am. You're Rem Il Leera."

The Col pulled away from Rourke and stood staring at him in silence for a moment, her mouth gaping in distress as she breathed in ragged gasps. "Yes," she said finally. "You are right. I am Rem. But you must forget me, forget we have ever spoken. The visit I made, it was a mistake."

"What do you mean, a mistake?" Rourke snapped. "The main reason I'm on this tub heading for Mael Station is because your boss, Dar Il Chedo, asked for me personally. Life debt, remember?"

"Listen to me carefully, Kenneth Christian Rourke." Her voice lowered to a tight whisper. Her eyes were wide and bright with fear. "Forget Dar Il Chedo. If he should try to speak with you, do not listen. If he demands action, do not obey. Forget your life debt. You owe the chedo nothing. Nor do I."

"But—I don't understand."

"You should consider your ignorance a blessing," she said solemnly. "I must go."

The leera stepped around him and through the doorway, hurrying down the passage. Rourke stood and watched her vanish into her cabin, his mind whirling with confusion, a feeling of cold unease growing in the pit of his stomach.

Inside the cold confines of the sleeping compartment, Rem Il Leera sagged against the portal. She fought to control the nausea churning in her symb's guts, driving her mind probes deep to quell the leera's distress. But she could do little to ease her own fears.

The Human was here, on board this very ship, bound for Mael and carrying with him proof of her foolish complicity like the seeds of a dreaded plague. What would Gral do if he learned of Dar's plan? What would he do if he thought her a spy? She could not imagine. But surely it would mean an end to her dreams of elevation.

For the millionth time Rem cursed Dar's insanity and her own blindness, wondering if perhaps she had not been infected herself. Certainly her judgment had been dulled by his presence, her intellect blunted by his hypnotic power.

It was fear of his narcotic control that had caused her to refuse to see the chedo a last time before leaving the embassy.

Two confused leera clerks with an anxious summons had appeared unescorted at her door, another breach of etiquette, unsettling and disquieting for all involved.

"Rem Il Leera," one of the leera standing in the threshold had said. Her symb's breast feathers were bronze, a single trinket hanging in its fan giving her seniority over her medal-less companion. "We are sorry to disturb your tasks, but Dar Il Chedo wishes to speak with you."

Rem had ignored them, concentrating on packing her few belongings.

"The chedo requests your immediate presence," the intruder had insisted, its voice rising an octave.

"No." Rem had turned her symbiote's attention to stripping a closet of cloaks and tunics, struggling to keep her own emotions under control.

"But—" the youngling had stammered, incredulous at her refusal.

For a moment anger and pain had overwhelmed her intellect. Her symb had whirled, muscles tense, posture threatening. "Go back to him! Tell Dar there is nothing further to discuss."

"You cannot be serious."

"It will take more than the two of you to drag me to him. Let Dar send hetta soldiers—if he dares. Now go!"

The leeras had retreated, babbling in confusion.

Rem had stood for a moment, her symb trembling with fear and fatigue. Then she had returned to her packing, shoving her gear into a bag and straining to hear the steady tramp of soldiers approaching down the corridor.

The hetta had never appeared as she had spurred her leera across the tile portico and out the compound gates.

An embassy vehicle had waited to take her to the shuttle port. As she slid inside, Rem had looked up to the top of the building and caught a final glimpse of the chedo. He stood like a sculpture on the edge of the serrated parapet, gazing down at the hover. He was still staring intently as the vehicle rounded a curve and she lost him among the crowded structures.

Rem had hurried through the glass and steel corridors of the terminal expecting at any moment to hear her name rumble over the loudspeakers or feel a touch at her back—a contingent of hetta and leera come to tell her that Dar had changed his mind and withdrawn approval of her elevation. But no one had tried to stop her flight.

There was a seat on a shuttle in her name, a berth on a freighter bound for Mael. Yet even after she had felt the first reality flex on the initial jump, Rem had been unable to relax. She was eleven cycles away from arriving unannounced and uninvited at the door of a rival chedo. The thought filled her with dread.

How would Gral respond? Would he refuse to sponsor her? And if so, what would she do? Return to Dar? She could not face him again, could not stand by and watch him fade slowly in the throes of his madness. Would she be cast adrift, clanless and purposeless? Her mind whirled with confusion.

Three cycles of traveling had failed to reveal a solution to her quandary, yet Rem thought that the time spent alone in her cabin contemplating the wisdom of the Coda had brought her the strength to accept her fate with grace and eased her anxieties.

But now she knew that her inner peace was a lie. Her encounter with the Human had demonstrated beyond a shadow of a doubt that she had left nothing behind on Central. Dar had a long reach, and she had no more control over her fate than did a leaf caught in a windstorm.

No. Her fear had not died—it still lurked deep in her soul. And, Rem suddenly realized as she sagged against the cold steel door, it was growing stronger with every passing cycle.

FIFTEEN

"We will try it again," Nebuun commanded. "Perhaps this time you will do better."

Sagging back onto the suspensor field, Rourke shook his head and tried to clear away the cobwebs. They had been at the reader for three hours. His mind felt like pounded meat, numb and raw. His eyes burned with fatigue.

"You go ahead without me," Rourke muttered, closing his eyes. But his refusal was halfhearted. Since his chance meeting with Rem in the commissary, he had been taking his studies much more seriously.

Rourke had spent a great deal of time analyzing that exchange, but he had been unable to interpret the Col's erratic behavior toward him or the meaning of her cryptic warning. He might as well have been trying to decipher the intentions of an Oolaanian combat force, a task that had scrambled the brain of more than one Human military strategist. Something had occurred that had freed him of his debt to Dar Il Chedo. Exactly what had transpired was still a mystery.

Despite his confusion, Rourke had seen no need to burden Nebuun with any fears about his relationship with the Col. There was only one thing keeping Rourke from a prison camp on Peklo—the continued belief by Xe'Aul and Nebuun that he still had value to Dar Il Chedo. Doing anything that might cast doubt on the strength of their supposed friendship did not seem wise.

"I cannot continue without you," Nebuun said. "And I cannot allow you to rest. We will be docking in a very few shifts. You must be ready to assume the position of factor."

"So I won't know everyone's name and job at first. It's no big deal. I'm quick. I'll get them in a few days. Trust me."

"Listen to me." The Eng was very firm in his refusal. "You cannot have a few days. You are no longer a line employee. You are the new factor. There are protocols. Not knowing the identities of your subordinates—this is a thing not done by management. It is a demonstration of weakness, of inability. You must never show such weakness. Do you understand?"

Rourke shook his head. "The only thing I understand is that you are going to drill me until I get them right. Correct?"

"I have no choice." Nebuun stabbed the contact.

Another face appeared on the display screen. It was a Lling: old face, old flesh. Rourke searched his memory.

"Ianiammallo," he said after a moment. "My office manager."

Stone-faced, Nebuun pressed the contact again.

Later, in the darkness of the forward observation deck, Rourke sat alone and watched as the freighter approached Mael Station.

The station was built around a core that had once been a fairly standard Vostian construct. The hexagonal torus was still faintly visible beneath the cobbled additions that encrusted the original design like diseased barnacles. Makeshift platforms and temporary docking facilities that had long since become permanent jutted out at odd angles. Lesser objects hung in semidefined orbits around the station: rat warrens of tanks and tubing, cargo buoys, tug stands, knots of debris and litter. Everything had the burnished patina of hard use and long exposure to cold and radiation.

Rourke had spent time on a Vostian station right after fleeing the war. He remembered his stay as an eternity of backaches, barked shins, and a continuously bruised skull. Vost were notoriously egocentric and built their structures for their own comfort: low-ceilinged chambers joined by narrow passageways, erratic twists and turns seemingly without rhyme or reason. Combined with the necessarily cramped structural demands of any orbital habitat, the average Vost unit was a claustrophobe's nightmare. There was no telling what modifications previous owners might have wrought on the used can, but Rourke was willing to bet that the interior corridors were going to be, in the oft-quoted words of his sainted grandfather, "tighter than a bovine's butt in fly season."

"Attention." The pilot's sterile voice echoed in the small chamber. "Now on final approach. We will be docking shortly. All passengers please return to your cabins and strap in. Thank you for your cooperation."

Rising to his feet, Rourke promptly smacked his skull against the low, curving bulkhead. Then he jammed his knee into the door frame while trying to squeeze into the corridor. Both were bad omens.

Better get used to it, he thought cynically. He glanced back for one final look at the tangled mass. In the white light of Mael, the structure resembled nothing so much as a frontline ruin left after an Oolaanian raid.

Home, sweet home.

Rubbing his throbbing knee, Rourke hobbled off toward his cabin.

SIXTEEN

There was a sign painted across the upper arch of the docking tube, block Patois script, lettering slightly darker than the stained metal corrugations:

WELCOME TO MAEL STATION
A DIVISION OF UTA INDUSTRIES

Stepping from the exit port of the freighter, Rourke glanced up at the inscription and smiled. An alien comic with a marker had crossed out "division" and replaced it with an Engi glyph that, roughly translated, meant "diseased brothel." Others had left explicit warnings about guarding one's credit chits and posterior while on company property. Rourke decided it was good advice.

"Something amuses you, Ser Rourke?"

Nebuun's liquid voice jerked Rourke out of his reverie. He had almost forgotten that the Eng was following him down the tube.

"Well, I—" he started to say, stopping as he noted the disappointment in the Eng's gaze. He glanced back up at the graffiti and shrugged. "No. Guess I was mistaken. I don't see anything funny."

"Good," Nebuun said. "Then you will not mind if I ask that the entrance sign be repainted?"

"Of course not. I don't care what . . ." His voice trailed off as he suddenly realized where the conversation was heading. He was the damned factor of Mael Station, and this was exactly the kind of decision he was going to have to start making on his own very soon: maintenance, shipping, personnel—a thousand different demands both minor and major.

"In fact," he ventured hesitantly, "maybe we ought to have them all repainted."

"An excellent suggestion." The big amphibian tried to keep

his voice neutral, but the beginnings of a smile danced around the edges of his huge mouth. "I have done my best with you. I can only hope it was enough. Remember, follow my lead. Think before you speak."

"Right." Rourke nodded. "I'm a factor now."

"We shall see."

Metal jangled softly behind them, the sound coming from inside the ship. Medallions ringing against hard bone. A shape appeared in the airlock. A Col: Rem Il Leera. Seeing them, she paused on the threshold, bags slung over her thin shoulders, her widely spaced eyes narrowed to slits.

For a moment the Col seemed torn by indecision, uncertain whether to turn and go back into the freighter or move forward. She sucked in a deep breath, and her hesitation seemed to pass. Head lowered, she slipped between them and hurried on, her rapid footsteps punctuating the sudden silence.

"An exceedingly odd race," Nebuun said. "Most unpredictable."

"Yeah," Rourke agreed. "Most unpredictable."

By the time they reached the end of the tube, the Col was far down the dock. Her slight figure was briefly illuminated each time she passed beneath one of the overhanging clusters of sodium lights, the yellow glow turning her silver tunic to gold. She seemed to be headed toward the insystem shuttle gates, weaving through the crowds of seasonal laborers disembarking from another transport.

She did not look back.

There was a grizzled Wormat waiting for them at the end of the docking tube, an old boar dressed in bloused pants and leather harness. His brown fur was streaked with gray, and a network of ceremonial and battle scars crisscrossed the leathery hide on his broad chest. One of the two tusks curling alongside his snout was broken at the base, a jagged protrusion of yellow ivory against the black of his lips. The pink stub of a savagely chewed ear was visible through the stiff fur on his scalp, probably a reminder of some past dalliance with a flirtatious Wormat female.

Rourke matched the alien's features with the holographic faces contained in the infocubes on which he had been so heavily drilled: Thunder-of-Rushing-Waters, the head of security.

"Welcome to Mael Station, Ser Rourke," the Wormat rumbled, his voice as deep and loud as his namesake, his Patois heavily accented. He extended one limb in an odd gesture, and it was a second or two before Rourke realized the creature was attempting to shake his hand. "I am—"

"Thunder-of-Rushing-Waters," Rourke said, clasping the beast's massive paw. "You're the head of security, I believe. A pleasure to meet you." Rourke glanced quickly at Nebuun and thought he saw approval in the stoic features.

"The pleasure is mine." Obviously flattered, Thunder bowed quickly. "And you must be Nebuun," he said, turning toward the Eng. "Your reputation has preceded you. I only hope you will find Mael Station up to your usual standards."

"So far," the Eng said, "it seems most adequate. Admirable, considering your recent difficulties."

"Well, since I've been temporarily in charge during the interim period, I'll take that as a compliment." The Wormat gestured toward the entrance at the far side of the dock. "There's a tram waiting to take us to the factor office. We had to establish a temporary location after the accident, but I think you'll find it adequate. If you'll follow me."

"No customs check?" Nebuun asked stiffly.

"Well," Thunder stammered, his nostrils flaring indignantly, "considering your relationship with the United Trading Authority, I assumed we would be dispensing with those formalities."

"I do not think that is advisable." The Eng looked at Rourke. "What is your opinion, Ser Rourke?"

Rourke knew damn well what his opinion was, but he also knew what was expected of him. "You're probably right, Nebuun. Don't want to set any bad precedents."

"As you wish, Ser Rourke."

They joined the crowd at the customs office, taking a place at the end of the line. It took the better part of an hour for them to be processed.

As the Wormat had indicated, there was a tram waiting for them outside the docking facility. It was a low, squat electric platform, mag-leved, riding on a cushion of force generated by two metal strips on the corridor flooring.

The interior of the station was every bit as cramped as Rourke had expected. The corridors were low and broad, hexagonally shaped. He was thankful for the tram because he would have been unable to walk upright. His back ached with the thought of lugging his bags along the passage; his body was bent at an angle to avoid striking his skull on projecting sensors and piping.

Lighting strips running the length of the upper panels cast a dull green glow, turning his skin bluish under the odd illumination and giving everything the appearance of being viewed through seawater. The air was warm and heavy, thick with the scents of grease and ozone and a pungent unidentifiable odor vaguely resembling recycling-plant sludge laced with anisette.

"Camaii musk," the Wormat said in answer to his unspoken question. "Even the food smells like it. But you get used to it after a while. Anyway, if you think it's bad in here, wait till you get to Jurrume."

They rode along the main concourse, past shops and warehouses, offices and small cafés. A few individuals moved along the walkways, hurrying to and from their assigned tasks, members of the group of a thousand employees the UTA maintained on the station or perhaps some of the additional four or five thousand migrants drawn by the harvest season. Most seemed to be Vost, Eng, or the occasional Wormat.

Rourke saw no other Humans.

At an intersection the Wormat turned the vehicle past barricades of blinking lights and snarls of plastic tape glowing in the dim illumination. There was a stench of old smoke and scorched plastic. The lights beyond ended abruptly, and Rourke had the sense of staring out into the darkness of the gulf beyond the edge of the Mael system.

"This is the sector where we had our little problem," Thunder said. "It's still closed. Haven't even started the cleanup. Been too busy trying to reconstruct records and untangle the processing mess. Bad time to have a disaster—just as the harvest is coming on."

"Of course." Nebuun gave Rourke a pointed glance. "But it will be a priority consideration of the new factor. Am I not correct, Ser Rourke?"

"Absolutely," Rourke replied, settling into his role as hand puppet. He could say yes with the best of them. He glanced back down toward the darkened sector. "Figure out what caused the blast?"

"Methane explosion. Robot welder arced a main line in the recycling unit one level below. Luckily, it went off during the graveyard shift; otherwise we could have been looking at many more than just a single casualty."

"Always heard that working overtime would kill you. Guess this proves it."

"You bring up a curious point." Thunder turned to stare at him. His small eyes were black, without whites. "Galagazar was a competent manager but not overly motivated—if you know what I mean. Hardly ever worked the graveyard shift."

Rourke looked back down the scorched corridor, a strange chill passing through him. He did not like coincidences. Never had. "Picked a bad time to get ambitious."

"Exceedingly bad."

They drove on to the offices in silence.

SEVENTEEN

The temporary factor office was housed in an empty storage unit in the center of the warehouse district.

Stepping off the tram, Rourke scanned the area to get his bearings. On his left, row upon row of featureless repositories lined both sides of the passage, stretching all the way to the curve. More equally blank units extended beyond the office, huge semicircular portals etched with identification numbers. White spotlights gleamed above each doorway. He could feel the throb of music from the station's small Fantasyland, its neons a dim glow in the distance.

"I remind you both," Thunder said as he led them up to the door. "This is only a temporary situation. Just until the old office is repaired."

The door slid open, and they stepped inside.

Two things occurred almost simultaneously. First, all work in the office ceased. Second, a warning pulse started hammering inside Rourke's skull.

The work stoppage he could have anticipated. Llings were notoriously curious beings, and there were three of them seated at a trio of workstations in the center of the enormous chamber. At the sound of the door, they had frozen, their huge luminous eyes trained on the entrance and their wattles flushing red and purple with excitement. They went back to their duties after a moment, hurrying to look busy and stealing surreptitious glances when they thought no one was watching them.

The warning pulse was another matter entirely. His internal security net had detected a number of low-frequency transmission sources.

Closing his eyes, Rourke ran a quick internal check. All systems were green. No doubt about it, someone was very interested in the daily activities at factor headquarters. The place was wired.

Question was, Why?

Rourke could think of a dozen reasons why someone would want to bug the factor office, none of them good.

Next question: Should he tell anyone about his little discovery? No, he decided quickly. At least, not until he'd had a chance to do some checking around. Best to know the teams and the players before he started blowing whistles.

"Are you all right?" Nebuun asked, evidently noting his momentary distraction.

"Just more tired than I thought." Rourke shook his head and mentally deactivated the pulse. "Nothing that about ten hours of sleep won't cure."

"Ah, yes. The rigors of travel." The Eng nodded knowingly. "I, too, am fatigued."

Thunder led them over to the workstations, past a brace of empty desks and towering stacks of infocubes. A bank of comms formed a makeshift wall. The screens were up and displaying a variety of images, some from deeper within the station, others from downworld, vistas of blowing grass and red dust. The floor was snaked with power cables. Racks of fluorescents flooded the area with bluish-white illumination but left the far edges of the room in darkness.

Nearing the Lling, Rourke noted that two of them were young, barely past their last molt. The dark feathers covering their torsos were full and gleaming with highlights like a thin sheen of oil on the surface of a puddle. The third Lling was much older than the others, well beyond breeding age. Her frame was thin to the point of being skeletal, her flesh loose and sagging. But Rourke sensed the keen intelligence in her eyes as she studied him.

"Veearionar and Leearionar," Thunder said, pointing at the two younglings. "Your office assistants. Don't worry about try-

ing to tell them apart. No one else can. Not even by the quality
of their excellent work.''

The two Lling warbled softly and preened, black feathers
flaring with pride, wattled heads turning crimson. Whirling on
them, the ancient hen made a spitting sound, and they dived
back into their tasks, slender necks bent to the keyboards, the
small manipulators behind their skulls stroking the keys. The
elder returned her attention to Rourke, her green eyes measuring
him. Apparently, she did not like what she saw.

''Ser Rourke, Ser Nebuun,'' Thunder continued, trying to
stifle a rumbling laugh. ''May I present Ianiammallo, your office manager. As you can see, she runs this place—and with an
iron fist. Makes me think there is Wormat blood in her past. But
she gets the work done. By my blessed ancestors, I don't know
what I would have done without her these past twenty cycles.''
He gestured toward the hardware arrayed on the scarred plas
flooring. ''She put this office back together. Secured replacement gear. Rounded up the techs. Reconstructed the hard-copy
records lost in the fire. And still managed to keep the flood of
harvest data under control. All I've done is print documents and
move furniture.''

''Huh,'' Ianiammallo said, still staring at Rourke. ''Thunder
a being fool most grand. You being fool most grand?''

''Yes, Maun Ianiammallo,'' Rourke answered, searching his
memory and finding the proper term of address. ''I'm a grand
fool. But I learn quickly. And I can move furniture as well as
anyone.''

''We soon seeing shall be.'' The ancient nodded toward her
processor. ''Much work needing done to be now. No time
speaking for with fools.''

''You are right, Maun. But perhaps next shift, after I have
rested, you will brief me on your methods of operation.''

Ianiammallo's expression softened slightly. ''It will being as
you say. Now, though, work.'' She spit again toward the younglings, punishment for some imagined infraction, and then bent
back to her keyboard.

Rourke stole a quick glance at Nebuun. The Eng was watching him closely, the phantom smile still hovering at the corners
of his lipless maw.

Thunder escorted them past a pair of portable partitions, steel
frames stretched with thin layers of opaque plas, creating two
separate cubicles. Each was furnished with a workstation and a
brace of comms, a few portable chairs and benches. Lighting

racks had been secured to the partitions, and there were bioluminescent strips attached to the upper panels of the desks.

Standing between the two cubicles, Rourke switched on his
internal scanner. The security pulse resumed its steady throbbing, pounding inside his skull. Transmissions were emanating
from both of the makeshift rooms as well as the general work
area. There would be no secrets kept anywhere in the temporary
complex.

"I had these brought in as soon as we learned you were coming. I hope you find them adequate." Thunder pointed to the
cubicle on his right. "That is your office, Ser Rourke. The workstation is a Wormat unit. I'm afraid we have nothing on station
specifically designed for Humans."

"Don't worry about it." Rourke grinned. "I've learned that
there is very little in the whole damn Quadriate designed for
Humans."

"I hope you are as understanding about your sleeping arrangements. The suspensor field is also of Wormat design."

"I've slept on worse."

The Wormat chuckled softly and ushered them toward the rear
of the warehouse.

The conference chamber was beyond a floor-to-ceiling partition erected at the far end of the storage area. A door panel laid
across stacks of plastic cartons served as a table, next to which
were a pair of low benches.

The benches were already occupied. Two Vost, two Eng, and
a Lling male watched as they entered the room. Rourke felt their
eyes studying him, measuring him.

Rourke put names to the faces, surprised at how well Nebuun's coaching had prepared him for the initial meeting. The
two Engs were elder females, past breeding age. One was Yevaan, head of maintenance—he identified her by the white scar
that split the hemisphere of her lower jaw. The second Eng was
Vuuni, the senior trader. Her skin had the dry texture of someone who had spent a great deal of time exposed to the arid winds
of Jurrume.

He separated the Vost by the colors of their velvet. Kiintaart,
the head of personnel, was a red, the scarlet patch between its
eyes like an inverted flame. The head of supply, Fenlint, was a
yellow, its velvet the color of wheat.

The Lling was Abbanimeer. He was in charge of transportation. He sat motionless at the table, his wattles the deep purple

of a bruise, beak open, manipulators hanging limply beside his skull.

Thunder took his seat at the table. All eyes watched Rourke expectantly. He glanced back at Nebuun. The Eng gave him an almost imperceptible nod, his face blank, his mouth a flat line across his broad jaw.

Rourke stepped to the end of the table, searching his memory for the introductory speech that Nebuun had composed and hammered into his skull during the journey from Central. It was a short monologue, as stylized and ritualistic as a religious litany.

Protocol, Rourke thought cynically. But the words rolled easily from his tongue.

"I wish to thank you for taking time away from your busy schedules to meet with me," he said. "I also want to tell you how pleased Xe'Aul is with the progress you have made during this harvest season, overcoming what many consider a major setback. You have performed well despite the loss of your factor. We both are expecting continued success now that the factor office is occupied."

He looked around the table, making eye contact, trying to keep his expression pleasant but commanding. "In the coming shifts I will be meeting with each of you to discuss your departmental needs. And my door will always be open to each of you should you need to speak with me." He nodded toward Nebuun. "Nebuun will be observing the station for a time and making suggestions to increase operating efficiency. He is to be obeyed as though he speaks with my voice." He paused a moment for emphasis. "Are there any questions?"

Rourke had not wanted to ask for questions, afraid that he would be opening himself up to exposure as a fraud. But Nebuun had been very insistent. It was part of the ritual. Besides, no one would dare risk a foolish inquiry—many careers had foundered on far less.

As Nebuun had predicted, those gathered around the table remained silent, their expressions unreadable.

"Very well. That is all for now. You may return to your duties."

The supervisors stood and left the room.

Thunder remained behind. "I had planned a tour of the facility," he said. "But considering your fatigue, perhaps it should be postponed."

"An excellent suggestion." Rourke did not bother to check

with Nebuun for his approval. He would have to be making his own decisions soon enough. "Maybe you'll be free next shift."

"I'll make time, Ser Rourke." The Wormat gestured toward the door. "If you'll follow me, I'll take you both to your hotel."

Rourke fell into step beside the boar. Nebuun stayed a stride behind as though in a position of deference.

"I can't tell you how glad I am to relinquish my temporary status as factor," Thunder said as they walked toward the front of the building. "It will be a pleasure to return to work that I understand."

"From what I can see, you've done an excellent job filling in. Your efforts will be noted in my report. Who knows, maybe it will mean a promotion to factor."

"If that happens, I'll personally slit your throat." Thunder grinned at him. "We Wormats must snarl occasionally. Genetics, you understand. I want no job that demands a permanent smile."

"Too bad. The Authority is missing out on an excellent candidate for factor."

The Wormat wrapped one massive arm around Rourke's shoulder and brought his snout close. His breath was hot and smelled of raw meat.

"Ser Rourke," he rumbled congenially, keeping his voice low so as not to be heard by Nebuun. "You'll find that I am not the typical UTA employee. I am not much for protocol. I have a bad habit of speaking my mind. And I've always had more respect for actions than words. Many believe these character flaws will be my downfall. To speak frankly, I have not yet decided whether you are what you appear to be—or whether you are simply the slickest scavenger I have ever met. But if you can handle a pugil stick anywhere near as well as you handle your tongue, it'll be a pleasure working for you."

For a moment Rourke was silent. His mind raced furiously. A pugil stick was a padded baton used by Wormats in the mock combats that they favored for mandatory stationbound exercise. Even though it lacked an edge, in the iron grip of a Wormat boar a pugil, Rourke suspected, could still inflict serious damage, and the thought of stepping into a ring with Thunder left him cold. But refusing an invitation from a Wormat was not a healthy option, either.

Swallowing hard, he managed a hearty smile. "Give me a few shifts to settle in. I'll prove to you I can take a beating as well as anyone."

"We shall see, Ser Rourke." Thunder laughed explosively and slapped him hard on the back. "Yes, indeed. We shall see."

The hotel was near the core, a boxy structure that extended vertically through four levels. The front was open, skeletal catwalks rising above them, small sleeping units on the bottom, suites on the upper levels.

"Another temporary measure," Thunder said as he stopped the tram in front of the entrance. "Been too busy to clean out Galagazar's apartment. Haven't even had a chance to ship his remains out. I figured I'd leave that for you. After all, it didn't seem to be a priority."

"Don't worry," Rourke said, picking up his bag and stepping off the platform. "You've done more than enough."

"Yes, indeed." Nebuun levered himself from the back bench and exited the vehicle. "My report will be most favorable as well."

"You're already registered." The Wormat handed them each an entry card. "Rest well, Ser Rourke. I'll meet you here at first shift. Give you the grand tour."

"I'm looking forward to it."

"So am I, Ser Rourke. So am I."

The tram pulled away, Thunder's roaring laughter echoing in its wake.

Nebuun gave Rourke a curious glance, then shrugged and led them to the lift. After he inserted their cards into the operations panel, the platform lurched upward. It was a mechanical. No lift bubbles on the frontier.

Clearing his throat, Nebuun looked up at Rourke. His sloping face was very serious, wrinkles outlining his protruding eyes.

"I must tell you, Rourke," the Eng said softly. "I am pleased by your performance to this point."

"Played it just like you told me to." Rourke sucked in a deep breath. "Fooled them for now. Most of them, anyway. But what about tomorrow—when I have to start acting like I know how to run this place?"

The Eng fluttered his throat sac slightly. "If you continue to handle yourself as you have done so far, there will be no problems. I am here to help you with your decisions. You must simply give the illusion of control."

"And what happens when you are gone?"

"Do not worry about that, Ser Rourke. I cannot leave Mael until you are ready." His voice sounded strained, almost as if he considered himself a prisoner. "Too many careers depend upon your performance."

"I'll do my best."

"Yes, Ser Rourke." Nebuun nodded gravely, his features puzzled. "I believe you will try. You have proven to be a quick study. And a capable diplomat, as well. You are obviously quite intelligent. It makes me wonder how you get yourself into such situations as the one you left behind on Central."

Rourke shrugged. "Bad luck, I guess."

"Let us hope you have left your luck behind, as well."

Rourke said nothing.

The lift stopped, and they parted company, moving off toward separate rooms.

The suite was a luxury unit—a small sleeping chamber, a sitting area, and a hygiene closet. Rourke quickly stowed his gear and then took a shower. Under the stinging needles of hot water, he reviewed his situation.

On the good side, the port seemed capable of operating under its own inertia, which meant that it would probably be pretty difficult for him to screw things up too badly. Also in the positive column was the fact that Nebuun liked how he had handled himself up to that point. Rourke figured that the better he performed now, the less the impact when they finally discovered that he was no longer on the Col A list.

But there were some serious negatives. Someone was monitoring the factor office. He had a bad feeling about the explosion that had killed his predecessor. And he had agreed to a pugil bout with a Wormat who could probably tear his head off with his bare hands. In fact, if the monitoring and the Wormat were connected, he might have just put himself in line to be the next accidental death on Mael Station. Not a comforting thought.

One thing was certain: an investigation was in order. A very private investigation. At least until he figured out whom he could trust.

By the time he had dried off and made his way back into the bedroom, Rourke had already sketched out a loose plan of action and was mentally composing a list of the personnel files he wanted to see and the places on the station he wanted to inspect—beginning with the damaged recycler and the gutted factor offices.

He palmed off the light and slipped onto the suspensor field.

Despite his worries, fatigue pressed down on him like a leaden weight. His eyes fluttered heavily.

Just before succumbing to exhaustion, Rourke activated his security net. A warning pulse started throbbing—another low-frequency transmission source. His rooms were bugged as well.

Welcome to Mael Station, he thought cynically.

Deactivating the alarm, Rourke rolled over, closed his eyes, and drifted off to sleep.

EIGHTEEN

Like a stone, the cargo shuttle fell toward the mottled surface of Jurrume.

Bracing against the uneasy anomaly of a controlled fall, Rem's leera clung tightly to the arms of the flight couch. Rem was vaguely aware of the dizzying plunge but ignored the nausea churning in her symb's guts. Her mind was occupied with other matters, concentrating on the dark possibilities that loomed in her immediate future, fears far beyond the simple worries of failing alien technology and pilot error.

In a very few spans she would be landing, an interloper without escort or introduction, in the domain of Gral Il Chedo. It was an act to make her wonder again if Dar had not somehow infected her with his madness.

She had almost turned back at Mael Station.

Inside the cavernous shuttle hanger, her footsteps echoing, equipment humming in the distance, Rem had felt her symb's hearts racing as she approached the flight counter. Each breath seemed to catch in her beast's throat; each step was an effort. Her mind whirled with conflicting emotions—fear and anger and despair. She was poised on the razor's edge of flight and kept moving only through inertia; it was easier to stumble on than to try to stop.

An enormous Eng male squatted behind the counter. He turned at her approach, a slow movement like a clockwork device. His jaws were masticating rhythmically, strands of dark fibers protruding from his lipless maw.

"Your pardon, please," Rem said. Her leera's voice sounded distant and alien, the voice of a stranger. "I am to go to Jurrume. I believe passage has already been procured for me."

"Name?" The Eng continued chewing the mass. Juices oozed from his mouth—white, milky sap.

"Rem Il Leera."

"Spell it." More sap dribbled down the pebbled green jowl.

Rem spelled her name carefully, using Patois lettering. The Eng entered it onto the keyboard with a single digit, one letter at a time, and then depressed the ENTER function. Lights flickered on the display screen, reflected in the crenellated yellow foil of his eyes.

"I show a reserved seat on the next available flight. Prepaid in your name." He spun an ident plate toward Rem. "Print here to prove receipt."

Rem willed her leera to raise one limb but stopped before touching the glowing plas surface. A wild thought swept over her, a crazed yearning for peace and solitude: the imagined comforts of home remembered through a skein of incarnations, the chance to leave her uncertain present behind.

"Is it possible," she said, uncertain if she was really speaking or if some demon was controlling her voice, "to change my flight? To choose another destination?"

"That depends. Where you would go?"

"Verrin." The name of her homeworld trembled in the air, spiritual, magical.

"That is not possible," the Eng said, strings of sap stretching between his wide jaws as he spoke. "You are Col. You should know as well as I that no flights from this station go to Verrin, not through the Restricted Zone. Nothing goes to Verrin except through Jurrume."

"Of course." Reality flooded in to extinguish the small flame of hope that had burned so brightly only a moment before.

She forced her leera to close its eyes for a moment, fighting for control. When she looked again, the Eng was watching her, staring at her symb's upraised limb hovering above the ident plate. Releasing her hold, she let the limb fall and felt the plas surface distantly, flat and warm beneath the leera's digits.

"The next shuttle leaves in a quarter span." The Eng pointed toward a waiting craft. "You can board now if you want."

"You are most kind." An automatic platitude, cold on the tongue.

Rem shouldered her bag and walked to the shuttle. Another cramped interior. Another acceleration sling.

Another step closer to Gral.

Grav generators rumbled, their grating vibrations jerking Rem back to the present.

The shuttle penetrated a thin cloud layer. Below, Rem could see the cold gray gleam of an ocean, its wrinkled surface like the hide of a beast stretched over the globe. Soon the craft was close enough that she could distinguish individual waves, long breakers crested with white froth, rolling beneath the stinging lash of the wind.

A ragged coast appeared on the horizon: splintered rocks and serrated ridgelines, green with dark growth. The shuttle raced toward the mountains, arced over them, and left the sea behind.

In a few moments the coastal range gave way to rolling hills and then flat tableland. Thick forest became sparse woodlands, the stands of scrub separated by vast stretches of brown grass. Plumes of dust marked herds of camaii moving along the plains. Dirt roads were carved across the landscape, the ruddy slashes connecting small herder outposts, isolated domes, wellheads, wind generators, evaporative units, and the abstract geometries of holding pens and stockyards.

For a time the panorama remained unbroken, a vista of gold shimmering beneath the hollow sky. Then a distortion rose out of the vastness—the conical shell of a long-dead volcano thrusting up into the heavens, its steep flanks dark above the amber grasslands. As they drew nearer, the mountain gained size and definition, towering above the tableland. Ancient lava flows formed frozen rivers of black rock and red cinder across the prairie.

Gral Il Chedo's compound was an enormous cluster of domes and spires capping the volcano. Built on the ruins of a heretic monastery, the gray ferroconcrete structures followed the contours of the rock, descending the sheer slope in angular levels, using the strength of the stone as a foundation. Gun emplacements and tracking sensors studded every flat surface, and additional batteries dotted the prairie around the base of the mountain.

Staying well clear of the compound, the shuttle banked hard, following the dark line of a broad highway etched across the plain—the road along which huge trucks hauled loads of camaii musk from the interior. The roar of the gravs grew louder, vibrating through the craft. Ahead, Rem saw the outlines of the main Authority landing field, a sprawling complex almost in the shadow of Gral's fortress. The grasslands had been scorched bare, and alien architecture jutted from the blackened soil. An angular network of landing pits and runways stretched into the distance, the tarmac red from the pulverized cinder that had been used in its construction.

The shuttle banked again, dropping into the final approach, and the ground rose up to meet the craft. There was a sudden shudder as the gravs deadened impact, and then they were down, braking retros screaming, clouds of red dust swirling up to blot out the sun.

There was no one waiting for her on the tarmac.

The other passengers—Vost and Lling shift workers returning from a holiday on the station—exited the craft and headed across the field in a loose group, bickering and joking among themselves. Rem stayed behind at the bottom of the ramp, waiting in the shadow of the shuttle, uncertain how to proceed.

Logic said that she should go to the main office and ask them to contact the compound about sending an escort. But pride negated that option. She could not bear the humiliation of a public refusal. If Gral declined her sponsorship and cast her adrift, so be it. But she would not allow aliens to sit in judgment of her sins.

To the south, the volcano towered, Mael's red light painting the surface of the Col citadel with blood.

Stifling a shudder, Rem urged her symb to pick up her bags and turn away from the Authority complex. No one tried to stop her as she crossed the runway. By the time she had reached the broad dirt road that seemed to lead to the mountain, her leera had settled into an easy, mindless stride.

And Rem lost herself in the steady rhythm of its feet.

NINETEEN

Alexis Weiss arrived at Mael Station on a Vost freighter inbound from Atabar. The ship carried a full cargo of consumables and three hundred migrant laborers hoping for seasonal work in the musk harvest.

She was the only Human on board.

The customs officer was a young Lling female, one of a dozen clerks trying to process the flood of new arrivals. She looked up from her screen, one small limb out to take the next identity chit, and stopped, stunned by the incongruity of a Human face among the flood of Vost, Eng, and Wormats that had preceded Alexis.

"Human," Alexis said in answer to the CO's unspoken question.

"Knowing that," the Lling warbled peevishly. "Knowing what is Human. Thinking just that oddness great must be. Seeing none Humans beings through this port in many standards. Then being we see two Humans in shifts as many. Oddness that. Yes?"

"There's another Human on Mael?" Her question was carefully phrased, simple curiosity masking her true interest. There were not supposed to be any other *Homo sapiens* on Mael.

"Most certainly. Factor. Newly come to Mael last shift." The Lling slid the chit into the processing unit, a block of text rolling up onto her display terminal. She slipped easily into her prescribed litany of questions. "Nature your being this trip?"

"Business," Alexis said evenly. "Scouting locations for a possible manufacturing habitat. Certainly hadn't expected to meet any of my kind this far out."

"Lucky that, yes." The Lling glanced at her sideways, head canted as she inputted arrival data into the processor. "Luckier still, maybe." Her wattles flushed crimson with humor. "Him male-type Human. Name Kenneth Christian Rourke. Maybe him turning trip business type to pleasure, yes?"

"If only it were that easy."

"Ah," the Lling said as if she understood perfectly. "Mating rituals."

It took Alexis almost an hour to get through customs and two more hours to locate lodgings.

Most of the dorms and hotels were booked, jammed with seasonals, but she managed to find a luxury suite in a core establishment that was too expensive for migrants. The universal furnishings were almost unusable, but she had slept on worse, and the room had a private comm, an essential item for Alexis to initiate her groundwork.

When she scanned the place for surveillance devices, she found it refreshingly clear.

Her gear was stowed in less than ten minutes. Ten minutes more and Alexis had the miniprocessor concealed in her bags assembled and patched into the comm. Activating the seeker program and the analysis core, she stood for a moment, watching the lights flicker on the screen, digits and letters scrolling by as the unit interfaced with the station's central storage through a back door opened in the comm system.

Then she switched out the lights, rolled onto the suspensor, and closed her eyes, willing herself to sleep instantly.

An hour later Alexis was awakened by the chirping of the processor. She squatted on the floor before it, reading the screen:

INTERFACE: COMPLETE
EXTERNAL COMMUNICATION LINK: COMPLETE
SECURITY ACCESS: COMPLETE
LOCAL CLEARANCE: COMPLETE

The list ran the length of the screen. Insertion and attachment had been achieved without detection. She now possessed a security clearance and a pass code that would give her access to all station records. The pass code was a fictitious accounting number assigned to the United Trading Authority's internal audit department. It would not be readily questioned.

Alexis flicked across the processor's menu and selected the GLOBAL RECORD SEARCH function. Her first entry was the ship identity sequence from the pirated sensory scan the Bureau had received from Galagazar. Then she typed in two names after the prompt: Galagazar and, after a momentary hesitation, Kenneth

Christian Rourke. She did not like random variables, and the presence of an unknown Human on the station seemed more than a coincidence.

At the touch of her finger on the contact, the processor dipped back into the information stream, the screen glimmering with phantom messages.

Her immediate task complete, Alexis returned to the suspensor and her dreamless slumber.

TWENTY

A rhythmic pounding echoed through the suite.

Rourke was instantly awake. He lurched up from the grip of the suspensor, eyes wide, momentarily baffled by his strange surroundings. Then the geography slotted into his skull: Mael Station, morning shift. With a groan, he rolled to his feet and staggered toward the door.

Thunder filled the doorway, leaning against the jamb. His blunt muzzle split into a lupine grin when he saw Rourke; his broken bottom tusk was a yellow stub against his black lips, and his small golden eyes were bright with humor.

"Good morning, Ser Rourke," the Wormat rumbled. "I trust you slept soundly."

"Yeah," Rourke grunted. "Like a dead man." He rubbed the sleep from his eyes. "What time is it, anyway?"

"One point two." Thunder smiled at Rourke's uncomprehending stare. "First shift, second interval. Station time. You'd better get used to it."

"Right. That mean I'm late?"

"I am not early." A laugh came from deep within the Wormat's broad chest. "I waited for you out front. When you did not appear, I decided to wake you personally."

"All right, then. I'm awake. Give me a minute to dress. I'll be right with you."

"As you wish." The Wormat bowed low, chuckling again. "I'll await you out front."

The big boar vanished out the doorway.

Stepping into the hygiene unit, Rourke splashed some cold water on his face. He rubbed his stubbled jaw, decided he could go another shift before depilating, and went back out into the sleeping chamber.

As he pulled on his coveralls, Rourke switched on his internal net and scanned the suite. The transmission sources were still in place. He avoided looking toward them, not wanting to let anyone know that he was aware of the surveillance. There was a slight advantage in secretly knowing he was being watched. Very slight, but Rourke needed all the angles he could get.

At the door, Rourke stopped for a moment, suddenly aware that he was unarmed. Factors had no use for weapons, so his Spencer Pinpoint was back in Queeblint's desk on Central.

But Factors did not often die in their own offices, especially not because of random methane explosions. He made a mental note to secure a sidearm as soon as possible.

And as he stood at the edge of the railing and looked down at the big Wormat waiting in the tram, Rourke hoped he would not need a weapon before his grand tour was complete.

The mag-lev bounced softly as he slid onto the front seat beside the Wormat. Rourke glanced over at Thunder. "We have time for a quick breakfast before we get started? I'm starving."

Thunder nodded. "Fear not, Ser Rourke. I'll see that you are fed. But I hope you won't mind if we make a brief stop first. I guarantee it will not take too long."

"You're the tour guide," Rourke said with a shrug. "Lead on."

The cart lurched away from the building, Thunder rumbling ominously as they accelerated along the narrow passage.

A featureless unit, white fascia painted with pale blue stripes.

Thunder swung the tram into the low entryway and down the ramp leading to the parking structure. Pulling onto an empty recharging pad, he switched off the mags.

"Come on," the Wormat said mysteriously. "This will help you work up an appetite. Make you want to eat compatibles."

"Wait a minute." Rourke's instinctive trouble radar was up and operating, sending little warning messages to his brain. "What is this place?"

"You'll see soon enough." Thunder turned and headed for the double doors.

Against his better judgment, Rourke climbed out of the cart

and followed the Wormat, bending low to keep from striking his skull on the projecting trusses overhead.

As they approached, the doors slid open. Heated air spilled out, ripe with the stench of alien body odors: sweat and pheromones. It was a gymnasium smell.

"What in the hell?" Rourke stopped on the threshold.

"I believe you promised me a pugil bout," the Wormat said, his broad grin exposing more yellowed teeth.

Rourke's guts did an elevator plunge. The place beneath his arm where his Spencer used to hang seemed suddenly very hollow and empty.

"Yeah," he said slowly. "I recall saying something about going a few rounds some day, just to see how long I could last. But I don't remember agreeing to do it first thing this morning."

"There is no time like the present, Ser Rourke." The Wormat laughed softly.

"You're serious, aren't you?"

"Quite. You see, Ser Rourke, I am a Wormat. Despite my civilized appearance, you must remember that my race evolved from pack animals. I am afraid I am still driven by certain genetic imperatives, one of these being the need to establish the physical superiority of the dominant male in the pack. And Mael Station is my pack."

"Are you telling me the old factor, Galagazar, had to beat the hell out of you to be your boss?"

"No." Thunder shook his shaggy head. "Galagazar was an Eng. He would have stood no chance against me in any physical test. When the differences between two races are great enough, it is easy to sublimate primitive urges." He grabbed Rourke by the arms and squeezed, testing the musculature. "But you are a Human. Yours is a warlike race. You have been a soldier. I can tell by the way you carry yourself, the way you move. Your very presence is a physical challenge to me. And so, sooner or later we will have to face each other. It might as well be now."

"All right," Rourke said, trying to smile. "Let's say, just for the sake of argument, that I don't win. What happens then?"

The Wormat looked almost stunned. "Ser Rourke, you can't possibly defeat me. But you need not worry about any further difficulties with me. I will have established my physical dominance, which will enable me to accept you as a leader because your presence will no longer pose a threat."

Rourke was silent for a moment, uncertain whether to scream

for help or run. "Anybody ever tell you that you're crazy?" he asked finally.

"Of course! Insanity is a prerequisite for off-world service. Sane Wormats see challenges in everything. They'd spend all their time fighting duels. Never get anything done. Now," he said, wrapping one arm around Rourke's, "if you'll follow me. I've reserved a combat chamber."

The big Wormat ushered him into the building.

The combat room was a padded chamber roughly four meters square. The padding was slick and spongy beneath Rourke's feet. There was no Human combat gear, so he was swaddled in a Wormat suit. They had taped fabric into the interior of the helmet to keep it from slipping down over his eyes. He gripped the pugil stick tightly; it was a heavy weight in his hands. The ends were made of leather stuffed with foam, deceptively soft. His heart pounded furiously, and cold sweat beaded his back and face.

Across the chamber, Thunder was a solid block of muscle and bone. Brown fur covered every portion of his body except for the black hide on his chest. His arms were enormous, corded as if sculpted from polycarbon fiber. He held the pugil stick as if it weighed nothing, swinging one end back and forth hypnotically.

"You know the rules?" the Wormat asked softly, his eyes intent on Rourke.

"Yeah." Rourke nodded slowly. "Three falls and you lose. Everything else is fair."

"Precisely."

"One question. What's keeping me from taking three dives?"

"Pride, Ser Rourke. I can see it in your eyes."

And then the Wormat was moving, faster than Rourke could have imagined. One shoulder dropped, a long thick leg sliding out to advance his weight. He whirled, the pugil stick swinging around in a blinding arc at waist level.

Rourke had a fraction of a second to react. Dropping the tip of his stick, he tried to parry the blow and succeeded only in slowing the impact as the baton caromed up into the center of his chest. Even through the two layers of padding, the blow drove Rourke back against the wall, paralyzing his diaphragm and knocking the air from his lungs.

He managed to raise his pugil in time to deflect a second blow, baton striking against baton, jarring his wrists. The third stroke caught him on the top of the skull and sent him sprawling face first into the corner, the loosely fitting helmet twisting around to block his vision.

For a moment Rourke lay prone, waiting for the Wormat to finish him off. If there was going to be an accidental death, the Wormat's opportunity had come. But Thunder went back to his corner to wait.

Rolling over, Rourke stared up at the bioluminescent strips on the button-tucked ceiling. He wondered if the Wormat had ever hit an opponent hard enough to drive him into the padding above. He had a feeling he was going to find out before the ordeal was over.

"The honor of the first fall is mine," Thunder growled. The creature was not even breathing hard.

Rourke staggered to his feet, taking a moment to catch his wind. Then he assumed a defensive posture, holding the pugil with both hands, angled in front of his body.

"Ready?" the Wormat asked.

Rourke nodded quickly.

The creature's second advance was slow, the pugil held loosely in both paws and carried parallel to his broad chest. Rourke matched his movements, keeping low, pacing the Wormat.

One experimental lunge with the stick; Rourke met and parried it. The Wormat tried a second, flicking the baton out to touch and withdraw. Rourke kept his eyes locked on the Wormat, searching for patterns in his movements, subtle clues that might telegraph his attack.

Then the baton flicked down, a sweeping hook under Rourke's attempted block, catching him squarely in the groin. Nausea flooded his guts as his knees collapsed. He never even felt the blow that drove him flat onto the floor.

"Second fall." Thunder said, laughing out loud. "Obviously, your tongue is your best weapon."

"Too bad," Rourke groaned, holding his genitals and trying to suck a breath through his gasps of pain. "I think I just swallowed it."

"Do you wish to concede?"

The thought had most certainly crossed his mind, but he could not ignore the contempt in the Wormat's features. It spurred him on. Maybe it was impossible to defeat the brute, but he sure as hell was not going to give him the pleasure of an early surrender.

Rourke shook his head and managed to get to his knees. "I believe you said three falls."

"Excellent." Thunder's grin reappeared, his contempt held at bay for the moment. Evidently he did not care so much that Rourke was able to fight, only that he was willing to try.

The Wormat came at him from the side, pugil stick thrust forward like a lance, shoulder open. Rourke stepped back, moving in against the wall, holding his stick level with his own chest and trying to look as defensive as possible, hoping to draw the Wormat into a quick attack.

Thunder took the bait, twisting the pugil stick vertically and then slashing downward, aiming it at Rourke's skull. Rourke ducked, and the club head slammed into the wall. He drove his stick hard into the exposed chest of his opponent. Thunder staggered, shifting his weight to his rear leg and bringing the pugil down in a vicious arc for another skull shot. Dropping one shoulder, Rourke let the impact glance off his back. He rolled with the force, seeming to collapse beneath the assault and swinging his own stick as he fell, his baton coming in hard behind the Wormat's bent knees.

Thunder fell like a wind-blown tree, sprawling flat on his back, the pugil stick skittering from his grasp.

Rourke grinned—wolfishly, he hoped. "My fall."

"Granted." Thunder sprang back to his feet. "And a clean shot, too. I may have to reassess my judgment regarding your skills." He picked up his stick with one hand and spun it quickly. When he looked back at Rourke, there was a new respect in his eyes—not fear, but an acceptance of the fact that the Human had proved to be a decent opponent.

"You will not drop me again," the Wormat said simply. It was a statement of fact, not a prediction.

"I wouldn't be so sure. We Humans might be tougher than you thought."

"Arrogance does not become you, Ser Rourke." Thunder chuckled savagely as he advanced, warily sliding one foot forward, keeping his pugil out as a blocking mechanism to protect his side, his legs slightly bent and his weight dispersed.

Rourke moved out to meet the Wormat. They exchanged a few tentative strikes, blocking and parrying. And suddenly Rourke saw an opening as the Wormat's side was exposed. He lunged, driving the stick in hard on the soft target.

Thunder dropped his arm as the stick slammed into his ribs, rocking back to lessen the impact, pinning the pugil against his side. He twisted, slamming Rourke into the wall. Two sharp blows caught Rourke in the face, driving his skull back into the padding. The shaft thudded against his chest, knocking the wind from his lungs, and he staggered forward, head down, gasping for breath.

A shadow sliced across the padding below him. In the last instant before impact, he realized it was Thunder's pugil slashing down on the back of his head.

Then the padded floor rose up and struck Rourke in the face.

When he awakened, he found himself stretched out on a bench. Cold water beaded his face. An anvil chorus was pounding inside his skull. Thunder loomed over him.

"Ah," the Wormat said. "Evidently you did not get enough rest last night. You needed more this morning, as well."

Rourke sat up, his head spinning and his brain feeling as if it were loose and sliding around inside his cranium. Touching his cheek, he found it puffy and swollen. He moved his jaw experimentally and was pleased to find that it was not broken.

"I take it you won," he said through his swollen lips.

"I have not lost in ages," Thunder replied. "But I must give you some credit. It had been quite some time since I had given up a fall. You should feel exalted at such an honor."

"Oh, yeah." Rourke nodded. His skull felt as if it were about to split. "I feel *much* better knowing that."

"Do not become too confident, Ser Rourke," Thunder rumbled. "Next time I will take all three. I have my reputation to protect."

"I got news for you, Thunder. There won't be a next time."

"Of course there will." The big Wormat clapped him soundly on the back with one furred paw. "At last I have found a formidable opponent. I do not intend to waste the opportunity. And you must exercise. Some type of regular physical conditioning is required of all stationbound personnel. I have already scheduled a room for us every third cycle." He stood. "Now, if you will get dressed. I believe you wanted to get some breakfast before we begin the tour."

"Yeah. Breakfast."

"One other thing," the Wormat said, his eyes dancing with mirth. "It's an old Wormat custom. Loser buys."

He was still laughing as he headed for the hygiene unit.

TWENTY-ONE

"Damn compatibles," Rourke muttered glumly. "Nothing like 'em to ruin a good appetite."

The substance in the bowl on the table in front of him was the color of dried blood, thick as pudding and filled with unidentifiable lumps. Fighting his gag reflex, Rourke spooned some of the cold, salty gruel between his swollen lips. It was an effort to swallow.

"Ah, yes," Thunder said through a mouthful of breakfast. "Another victim of demon economics."

The big Wormat crouched on the opposite side of the low table, busily carving gobbets of meat from a raw slab nearly five centimeters thick. He stabbed one chunk with the end of his knife, thrust it into his mouth, and washed the mass down with a slug of liquid from a steaming mug.

"You see," he continued, wiping the juices from his chin with the back of one hairy fist, "the Human population base on Mael is too small. In fact, you're it. Which means there's simply not enough of your kind around to justify stocking traditional Human consumables. Kindred population is something you ought to consider before you accept your next post. Lots of advantages to having others of your species around, not the least of which is better meals."

"Thanks for the advice," Rourke said, stirring the slop with his spoon. "But I think it's going to be a few standards before I'm offered another position."

"Then I'm afraid I see many, many kilos of compatibles in your future."

Rourke nodded sourly and choked down another gelatinous gob. A drink from his mug failed to kill the taste.

The cafeteria was located on the main radial passage. A large establishment, it spanned two levels. Tables and benches filled the square rooms, arranged in the precise designs that spoke of Vost management. There were few patrons, mostly Vost and

Lling gathered in small groups, talking softly among themselves.

Thunder had selected a table on the upper level, beside a clear plas panel where they could look down on the traffic flow in the broad corridor. Pedestrians hurried along the passage. Trams and cargo platforms zipped past on the twin silver rails of the mag-lev track. A line of seasonals stretched from the entrance of an employment office.

"So," Thunder continued, his voice drawing Rourke back to their conversation. "You are expecting a long tenure here at Mael Station. Kiintaart will not be pleased by such news."

Rourke scanned his memory and attached a face to the name: Kiintaart, the scarlet Vost in charge of personnel. "What'd I do to piss off the Vost?"

Thunder grunted softly. "Took its job."

"Kiintaart was expecting a promotion to factor?"

"The Vost has great plans for its future. Mael Station is but one step along the path toward becoming a corporate director. It was so certain of the promotion that it had already selected new office furniture." Another chunk of bloody meat disappeared into his mouth. "Your appointment was a most unpleasant surprise."

"Not just for Kiintaart," Rourke grumbled under his breath.

The news that someone had coveted his new position was not too startling. In fact, he had already considered such a possibility as a motive for bugging his office and hotel suite. Kiintaart had just become a prime suspect.

"Who else wanted the job?" he asked casually, glancing at Thunder.

"No one." The Wormat shrugged. "There are no other viable candidates on station."

"That doesn't answer my question."

"There is a great deal of difference between wanting and receiving, Ser Rourke." The boar grinned, black lips drawing back from his fangs, curled tusks gleaming with saliva. "Yevaan might want to be factor, but she has spent eighteen standards as head of maintenance. She knows her time for promotion has long since passed. As for Vuuni, the Eng is a downworld trader at heart. She is happy on Jurrume. Probably go crazy trapped on station."

"What about the other Vost, the head of supply?"

"Fenlint? Competent . . . dependable . . . plodding. No chance, and knows it. Abbanimeer is just the opposite. Too crazy—too volatile. If the Lling were not such a wizard with fleet operations, his attitude would not be tolerated by the home office.''

''That just leaves you,'' Rourke said evenly, meeting the Wormat's gaze.

Thunder's laughter was a breathless rasp. He shook his massive head. ''No, Ser Rourke. As I told you last shift, I have no desire to be a factor. Which is good, since the UTA has no intention of making me one. You've seen my personnel file?''

Rourke nodded.

''Then you know I was once head of security for Malacar. My being transferred to Mael Station was a demotion, Ser Rourke. In truth, I was lucky I was not fired.''

''What'd you do?''

''I broke one of the cardinal rules.'' Thunder carved another slice of meat, his knife scraping on the plate. He kept his gaze on his task, as if pure concentration would hide his anger. ''I got involved with local politics, chose sides in a dispute between two rival client factions. But I learned my lesson. In the UTA or any other Quadriate trading company, there is no god but credit and no morality that does not involve a profit.''

''I'll keep that in mind.''

''That attitude should already be instinctive.'' The Wormat cocked his head and smiled, trying unsuccessfully to appear innocent and naive. ''After all, you are a factor.''

''Yeah.'' It was Rourke's turn to grin. ''But I'm new at this.''

''I suspected as much. Explains Nebuun's presence.'' The alien picked up his mug. ''How'd you get this appointment, anyway?''

''I lit an ambassador on fire.'' He laughed at Thunder's puzzled stare. ''It's a long story. One I intend to save for some graveyard shift when I've got a very parched throat and you're buying.''

''Sounds like a most interesting evening.'' The Wormat returned his attention to his meal.

Rourke studied the beast for a moment. Common sense said he should be afraid of any creature as big and powerful as Thunder, especially after his pugil stick lesson. But despite his throbbing bruises, he found himself instinctively trusting the Wormat.

Still, his instincts had been wrong before, and there were a lot of questions yet unanswered.

''What can you tell me about the old factor?''

''Galagazar?'' Thunder frowned. ''He was a good enough

manager, but I didn't care for him. There was something unsettling about him. Something wrong. Just a vague sense that he was not entirely honest. Nothing I could identify, you understand. Believe me, I tried. Personnel records, accounting, arrest records—everything was clean. But I always came away from a meeting with the Eng feeling like I needed to be dusted for vermin. And I wasn't the only one who felt that way.''

''Guess you weren't too sorry about his death.''

''No. Nor was anyone else.''

Rourke was silent for a moment, carving patterns in the congealing soup with the edge of his spoon. ''You sure it was an accident?'' he asked finally.

''That's what it says in my report.'' The Wormat fingered his broken tusk absently. ''What makes you think otherwise?''

''I don't know.'' Rourke took a deep breath. ''I just don't like coincidences. You said it yourself: Galagazar didn't routinely work overtime. The explosion just seems too convenient. I mean, it could have been staged, right?''

''Certainly. But that would have been murder—and murder requires suspects and motives. There are none on station.''

''What about Kiintaart? You said the Vost wants to be factor.''

''Not enough to commit murder. Besides,'' Thunder said, sopping another ragged morsel in the pool of fluids on his plate, ''Kiintaart knows a thousand ways to destroy a career. Killing a rival would be unnecessary.

''As for the rest of the department heads, none of them have stones enough to kill.'' He popped the ruddy chunk into his mouth and swallowed without chewing, his throat muscles rippling beneath his thick fur. ''Except me. And if you're thinking I might have done it, remember that I am a Wormat. If I decide a being deserves to die, I'll do it with my bare hands and not try to hide behind any subterfuge. I may be civilized, but I haven't forgotten the joys of justifiable senticide.''

Rourke studied the Wormat for a moment and decided he was telling the truth. Thunder had not killed Galagazar. Maybe no one had murdered the Eng. Maybe it had only been an accident.

''I don't know,'' he said, shaking his head. ''I guess I'm just trying to make too much of a simple coincidence.''

''That's the way I see it. But if anything turns up that changes my opinion, you'll be the first to know. Now, if you're done with your meal, we had better get moving or we'll be finishing this tour during the graveyard shift." Thunder pushed his plate aside and rose to his feet. "I'll get the tram. You pay the bill."

Before Rourke could protest, the Wormat was gone.

TWENTY-TWO

Through the gathering shadows of dusk, Rem Il Leera stumbled toward the mountain.

Above, the citadel glowed like a flame, its gray structure painted red by Mael's last gleaming. Rem had left the paved surface of the musk highway when it had seemed to veer away from the mountain. It had been an easy decision, made even simpler by the fact that the automated transports rumbling along the highway had not offered interim transportation. The narrow dirt road she was following wound and dipped across the flatlands, a pale slash in the darkness curving up the flank of the dead volcano. Cinders crunched beneath her symb's raw feet.

Rem had long before stopped looking back to measure her progress. A glance toward the landing field only made it seem as if the distance from safety were growing. The lights of the complex glimmered in the bottom of the shallow valley, soft and warm. Ahead, the mountain appeared no closer; her universe was reduced to the road and the darkening sky beneath the brooding face of the citadel.

It had not occurred to Rem as she marched from the landing strip that she might die along the road in the darkness. That thought had arisen in her mind much later, as the shadows had deepened and Mael had begun its inexorable slide into the horizon. She did not know what creatures lurked in Jurrume's long night. But there were strange scuttlings through the tall grasses on either side. And wild cries echoed in the distance, howls and barkings, the sounds of predators moving through the gathering twilight in search of food.

If the beasts did not get her first, there was a killing bite to the wind that whipped across the plain. It carried the sting of blowing sand and the stench of carrion and dark water, the frigid taste of ice. Her leera was slowing down, its limbs and muscles stiffening in the cold. Her bags hung from its back like dead flesh, their straps cutting deep grooves into the leera's thin shoulders. Dawn might come and find her huddled along the road, her symb gnawed to ribbons by scavengers.

In truth, Rem did not think that it would be a terrible tragedy if her time as an outcast were cut short. Still, her leera continued to stagger forward one slow step at a time.

When she was a young raas, there were outcasts beyond the gates of her home crèche.

The memory came to her suddenly, and she was raas again, feeling the lumbering mass of flesh and thick bone, the raw power of muscle and brute strength.

With the dawning, the crèchemaster would gather her charges and instruct them to bring up the scraps left from the night's meal. Rem remembered the heavy weight of the slop pails, the sewage reek, the contents rimed with an orange film of congealed grease. She could still hear the rattle of chains as the huge gates swung open and the first light of morning spilled across the portico.

Gray phantoms crouched on the stones beneath the high arch; others were sprawled on the grassy swale that stretched between the wall and the encroaching jungle. Some were seen only as shadow movements within the waxen leaves. Rags shrouded their thin frames. Bones jutted against emaciated flesh.

Placing the buckets against the wall, they would collect the pails left from the previous morning.

And one morning, with the mists still rising from the grass, Rem had bent to pick up one of the pails from beside a slumbering form, and a skeletal hand had darted out to clutch her raas symb's huge clawed fist.

She tried to jerk free, amazed at the strength the cadaverous leera possessed. The rags fell away from its face. An image of disease, scabrous patches peeling and raw on its twisted features.

"Please," came the supplicating voice, a rustle like the wind through dead leaves. "I beg of you. Give me peace!"

"I am sorry," Rem hissed, her symb shuddering as it recoiled from the beast. "I did not mean to disturb you." Her raas backed away without urging, snorting and squealing with terror.

"Please . . . please!" The leera writhed toward her, crawling on its belly, its claws grasping toward her flesh. "Peace . . ."

Whirling, Rem had fled, back across the swale and into the crèche, the pitiful mewling following her through the cold stone corridors.

It was only later, as she lay in her straw bed, that Rem realized the true peace the creature had demanded.

And now, staggering along the cinder road, she at last could understand its wish to die.

The sound came to her distantly, a faint whining as if of lazy insects swarming in a shaft of golden light. The thought filled her with warmth, made her think of Verrin and better days, when the sun on her symb's flesh was like a drug and the feel of its life surrounding her was like a spring wind through tall grass.

Part of her mind recognized the insanity of her confused thoughts, realizing that the cold and the growing dark were settling over her like a cloak. Her beast kept lurching forward, its breath like ice in its lungs, its muscles burning, its limbs tremoring with strain.

Again the sound swirled around her, louder now, sweeping toward Rem on the cold breath of the wind. She forced her leera to raise its head, hoping to see the jungles of Verrin instead of the barrens of Jurrume, praying that this was all some sort of terrible dream. But there were no jungles, no buzzing creatures flitting through warm shafts of morning sun. There was only the pale slash of the dirt track and the darkness of the mountain blocking the sky.

And then she saw the thick line of dust rising up from the road.

It was a few moments before her sluggish mind was able to interpret the corresponding stimulus of the road and the dust and the sound. A gestalt formed in her mind; a vehicle was approaching.

Rem forced her symb to stop in the center of the road, driving her probes deep until the beast stood swaying and trembling on the cinders. Phantom twinges cramped its legs, as if it were still walking, still trying to stumble forward.

The vehicle was a low-slung armored hover. It roared toward her, turbines whining, gravel spraying out along both sides of the roadway. A rack of floodlights spilled cones of brilliant illumination across the prairie. Rotating sensor units and antennae were silhouetted on the armored turret. The thick barrel of an energy cannon protruded from the front, with smaller weapons arrayed below it. A red circle appeared on the center of her leera's slender chest, a sighting laser finding its mark.

She was not far from the hover when it reversed thrust and slowed its armored mass. The vehicle skidded to a stop less than ten body lengths from where she stood.

For a moment there was only Rem and the armored crawler, facing each other, an insane standoff on the alien road.

"Hold and identify!" The command crackled across external speakers, echoing across the plain.

"I am Rem Il Leera," she said. "I have been sent by Dar Il Chedo. I bear a message for Gral Il Chedo."

Silence stretched as the occupants relayed information back to the citadel. Then the speakers blared again.

"Your arrival is unauthorized. You have no clearances. Explain."

"I bear a message from Dar Il Chedo. I come at his request and following his instructions."

There was another pause while the soldiers awaited the orders that would decide her fate. She thought of the clanless outcast before the gates of the crèche and wondered if she would feel the shot that took her symb's life.

But they did not fire.

The rear of the craft yawned, the clamshell doors swinging wide. Hetta troopers thundered out, huge shapes in the darkness. They stood beyond the arc of light from the floods, and Rem lost them in the glare. In her symb's blindness, she heard movements surrounding her, crunching steps on the stones, creaking harnesses, the clatter of weapons being cocked and leveled.

A pair of soldiers approached from the crescent of darkness, weapons slung at their sides. Rough hands searched her and rifled through her bags. Then she was being pushed forward and up the steps into the hover.

The rest of the troop slipped back inside. The doors swung shut. Turbines howled as the hover rose.

Pivoting in the roadway, the vehicle accelerated toward the mountain.

The armored carrier slid along the road, the wail of the turbines vibrating through her skull. The interior was dark and hot.

Gradually her symb's eyes adjusted to the dim illumination.

The troopers surrounding her were hetta regulars. Not the showpieces who lined the corridors of the Col embassy on Central, beasts whose function was to accessorize the trappings of diplomacy, but combat veterans, blooded and scarred in the heretic wars. Gone were the traditional dress uniforms; the gaudy outfits had been replaced by drab garb the color of summer grass, functional and practical, studded with weaponry kits, explosive charges, and ammunition. The weapons they clutched in their huge manipulators were heavy alien fighting devices, wickedly lethal.

Only a fool could doubt their ability to kill.

How long they drove Rem was uncertain, but gradually she became aware that the hover was slowing. Finally the craft stopped and settled down with a hiss of pressure escaping from the air bags. The rear doors swung open, and she was ushered out into a vast cavern and marched quickly across the interior of a huge flight hangar.

Gral's compound was located in the inside of the enormous caldera at the summit of the dead volcano. The jagged rim of the huge crater served as a bedrock foundation for a massive ribbed dome that spanned the depression from side to side.

A ferroconcrete wall lined the interior of the crater, leveling out the ragged edges and providing a solid attachment for the central dome. Walkways and lift tubes formed hard angular lines against its rounded curves. Massive cable trunks snaked out to each, carrying the energy needed to power the plasma weapons and the force fields, like the root system of some enormous plant cluster burrowed deeply into the hard soil.

Below the dome, a secondary network of scaffolding supported clusters of movable lighting, gantries, and cranes clinging to the webs of steel. Mechanics and techs were busy working on the single-occupant fighters and shuttles squatting on the ferroconcrete flooring. They did not look up as Rem was escorted to a yawning exit.

After stripping Rem of her belongings, the soldiers led her to a small holding cell. She was thrust inside without ceremony or explanation.

The walls of her prison were gray stone. The ceiling was mirrored glass.

And after a time Rem knew that she was being watched.

TWENTY-THREE

Vaz Il Tran was deep in prayer when the warning Klaxons erupted, the call to general quarters audible even in the soft silence of the compound's small temple.

He ignored the intrusion. His time on Jurrume had acclimated him to the periodic wail. Such sirens were an integral part of the daily routine of Gral's troops, the lumbering hetta hammered into machinelike precision by the constant pressure of practice and drill. It was easy to shut out the sound and concentrate on the mechanical precision of his daily oblation, forcing his symb to draw the multirazored blades of his oribi between its belly plates and flense the soft flesh underneath. Blood oozed slowly down the swell of its abdomen and dripped into the cup resting beneath him on the floor.

It was a clean offering, untainted by pain or protest from his docile tran. The mantra of honor was an unending circle of rhythm spinning through his thoughts; Vaz allowed his beast to feel nothing except the waves of pleasure he sent sparkling across its cortex. The creature would have raised the gleaming oribi to its throat and drawn it deeply across the corded flesh had he wished it, but that was a pleasure reserved for another time: the day of his own elevation.

He did not notice the messenger until the touch on his symb, a slithery sliding of scale against scale, abrupt and startling. For a second Vaz lost his mental grip on his beast's muddled low-brain. Pain savaged his intellect as the raw scream of severed nerves flashed up from its flayed gut.

"Excuse my intrusion, blessed Tran," the small creature squealed, its voice a thin reedy sound in the stillness.

"I am at prayer," Vaz said, struggling to control his beast. The creature twitched, whining softly. "Surely you have eyes to see." His anger was a concentrating force, helping him quell the tran.

"The chedo calls." A simple statement. A request not to be denied.

Vaz tightened his grip. "A moment more to cleanse my symb and make my offering."

"The chedo's orders were clear. You are to come immediately."

"As the chedo wishes." Vaz rose from his kneeling position and took only a moment to don his robe of office. The fabric clung to the sticky slickness of his beast's swollen abdomen. He followed the messenger out into the corridor.

Pain was a thin high note sounding clearly in his brain.

The observation chamber was dimly lit; Gral Il Chedo was a vast shape in the darkness, motionless and silent. Another figure stood beside the chedo—Kars Il Jujun. The killer watched Vaz intently, optical clusters erect, muscles tensed.

"All blessings, Lord Prefect," Vaz Il Tran said, pausing on the threshold.

Gral stirred, a slow shifting of his symb's bulk. Light glittered from its eyes. "Come in, Vaz. There is a matter which requires your attention."

Vaz entered, bowing low, limbs held in the traditional sign of tran deference. The room seemed very close, thick with the stench of Gral's beast and the radiant hatred of the jujun. Its hide gleamed softly in the indirect light filtering from hidden fixtures. A clear panel angled from floor to ceiling before the chedo, as though some enormous pressure had squeezed the chamber and forced it to slide away from them. Most of the cells displayed below were dark, but one gleamed with illumination, a square of light on which to focus his attention.

The cell held a single occupant—a leera perched upon the single bench, as motionless as a statue. Its colors were not those of the Gral holding. Vaz searched his memory for a reference to the beast's brocaded silver and black, found it, and recoiled mentally: Dar Il Chedo.

"The leera is a far distance from home," Vaz said, studying the creature. The leera was poised and collected, as if waiting for a meal at a fine table—a strong display of control in what had to be most distressing circumstances to its symb.

"Farther than you can imagine," the chedo grumbled. "Do you know the beast?"

"No."

"That is Rem Il Leera, Dar's aide and confidante. The famous Rem the Forgotten."

"Where is the rest of her party? Her attendants? Her soldiers? Surely they must be upset at such treatment."

"She is alone."

"Alone? Such a thing is not done." A murmur of discontent burbled in his symb's guts, mingling with the thin song of its pain. Vaz did not bother to ease its fears; sometimes instinct had a purpose and made one's thoughts clearer, but only in moderation. "Why has she come?"

"For sponsorship."

"You knew she was coming and did not tell me?" Vaz turned to face the chedo, his beast's voice even and controlled. No anger or shock. A simple question.

The jujun lunged forward, enraged by the lack of respect. Its energy weapon was clutched in one fist, pointed at Vaz.

"Hold, Kars!" Gral commanded.

The jujun froze, but the rictus of rage on its blunt features remained, fangs bared, optical stalks lowered.

"There are many things I see fit not to share with you, Priest," Gral said carefully. "But this was not one of them. She is as great a surprise to me as to you."

"And you are sure she is here with Dar's blessing."

"We speak of Rem the Forgotten, she of the unbending will and steady resolve. Would she have come without his permission?"

"No." Vaz sighed softly. "But I still do not understand."

The Chedo unclenched one massive fist. A crystal rested on the horned flesh, bright and gleaming. "This will explain far more eloquently than my thick tongue."

His chair swiveled slowly, the dry hinge squealing in protest. A touch on a hidden panel, and a cube view rose from the dark square of the small table at his side. Thick fingers, moving more delicately than Vaz would have imagined possible, fit the cube into the proper slot. The wall screen flashed into being. A chedo reclining in a luxurious office, walls of green and brown. Dar Il Chedo.

"Greetings, brother," his voice intoned, the prerecorded message unwinding its tones through the hidden speakers. "It has been too long since we have shared thoughts."

The message was brief. Rem was due her elevation. Would Gral be her sponsor and guide her through the rigorous tests of elevation? The implication of the cube was clear. Gral could not refuse his request. But the Dar Il Chedo was mistaken.

"She must go back," Vaz said before Dar's image had faded completely from within the crystalline screen.

"How odd it is to see that you and Kars share an opinion. But she cannot. Dar has released her from his household." The chedo shrugged. "If I refuse, this one will be cast adrift."

"The weight will be Dar's burden. He sent her without introduction, without escort, without even a whisper of his intent. How can he expect otherwise?"

The chedo's bulk shifted as it scratched itself with pleasure. "Those are poor reasons to refuse a simple request."

"Perhaps." Vaz's beast swallowed nervously. "But valid. Sound enough to act upon. You cannot accept her as a novitiate. Not now. Not when all approaches fruition."

"But don't you see? That is the very reason I must accept. We can ill afford close scrutiny at this time. A refusal might bring other, more pointed inquiries."

Vaz shuddered in exasperation. Sometimes the chedo seemed so dense, so unreasoning, so far removed from Col philosophy. Could one be so ignorant and still be Chosen? It was a thought bordering on heresy.

"Do you not understand, my Chedo? This one, this Rem the Forgotten—" Vaz waved one limb toward the distant screen. "She could be a spy."

A whine of mirth escaped the chedo, a sound more bestial than civilized. It made Vaz burn with sudden anger, and he had to fight to keep the blush of irritation from suffusing his symb's blunt features.

"Conspiracy does not become you, Priest. You are too much the amateur. Of course the leera is a spy."

"Then we are discovered?"

Another humorous rattle. "I think not. Dar knows nothing. Suspects something, perhaps. An intuitive sense of wrong. But he is as much out of his element as you are in these matters. He has fears, but they are probably nothing more than the tremblings of one who sees the time of merging coming on like a battle and fears the rape of his unwilling mind. We are most certainly not discovered. One does not send a spy to confirm what one already knows. Spies are dispatched to listen and learn, to bring back confirmation. Dar is digging, but he does not know for what it is he searches."

"Then we must send this one away." Vaz's symb inflated its

crest, its agitation showing through his control. "Lest she find what he seeks."

"No, Priest. My refusal would only compound his suspicions. It might also arouse the curiousity of my other merge partner, Harn Il Chedo. I ask you, if our roles were reversed, were I sending one to him, would Dar refuse? No. Not Dar, the paragon of the Coda. He would welcome his duty with anticipation and overlook my flaws of decorum. If I refuse, he will simply send other spies, more difficult to detect, more difficult to control. I am satisfied with this one. We shall keep her."

"I respectfully—"

"Enough! I tire of your respect and your words. Limit your counsel to the affairs of my soul and leave the business of revolution to those with more experience, or next time I will not stop Kars when he attacks."

The chedo rose to his full height, his massive armored body towering in the small chamber. His breath was rank and filled with the stench of raw flesh.

"We will accept his request and sponsor this leera most graciously. That will serve only to confuse his suspicions, for why would we welcome a spy into our midst if we had something to hide?" He leaned against the glass, staring down into the cell as if contemplating a pounce and a quick meal of rangy leera flesh.

"Mark my thoughts, Tran. They will serve you well if you continue in this business of treason and treachery. There is nothing more useless than a known spy."

"Yes, my Filitaar," Control returned: caution and precision. "What is to be done with this leera?"

"Trials and elevation of course. She is to be treated like any other initiate. If she is truly a pilgrim, then she shall earn her elevation. And if she is a spy, she will reveal herself. Our job is simply to make certain she sees nothing incriminating."

"And if her eyes are too sharp?" Vaz stared at the chedo. Its grin was chilling.

"Then she will fail her tests. It will not be the first time that an initiate has fatally proved its inadequacy during the rigors of elevation." A rumble thundered low in his symbiote's thick throat. "And none will mourn her passing more than me."

"As you wish, my Chedo. So it shall be." Vaz bowed low. There was an odd logic in the beast, something beyond the mundane thought that was stifling the progress of the Col. No doubt the spark the tran had seen when they had selected Gral for his Chosen role.

"Go now, Priest. Say your prayers for our success and plan your rituals. Tomorrow you must be the perfect tran."

Vaz bowed again and slipped from the room.

When the tran had departed, Gral turned toward Kars. The big jujun was still glowering, his beast's square face and blunted features twisted as if in pain, needle fangs exposed behind the serrated plates of its mandibles.

"You disappoint me, Kars," the chedo growled. "I expect better control from one of your rank."

"The priest showed disrespect, my Filitaar." The dark planes of the jujun's face shifted, sliding back into a mask of stone.

"I do not care about respect. Not now. Not when we are so close to completion."

Kars said nothing.

"The time of my division rapidly approaches. While I am in transition, my fate will depend on your judgment and your control. We cannot succeed without the priest. Kill him in a fit of anger, and we have lost everything. Do you understand?"

"Yes, my Filitaar."

"On your bond, Kars. His life for yours."

"I swear it shall be so."

Gral stared at him, measuring his contrite gaze. "When the priest is no longer necessary, then you can have him. Not before."

"I will count the days, Chedo."

"As will I."

TWENTY-FOUR

She was still being observed.

Sitting motionless in the center of the narrow cubicle, Rem sensed the presence of the unseen sentries beyond the mirrored walls. Their gaze was like a faint pressure on her leera's skin, as unsettling as being awakened by a strange touch in the night, and she tightened her grip on the lowbrain to keep its anxiety in check.

Reflections of her symbiote filled every surface of her prison, replicated again and again until the very universe seemed to be populated solely by a thousand pious leera squatting with their scaled limbs folded into postures of calm repose. Indeed, she could not have been praying any more fervently had she been within the green arches of a homeworld shrine instead of the close confines of the argent holding cell. But there was little comfort in the logical devotions, and she was uncertain how much longer she could conceal her terror behind a placid facade.

Analyzing her fear, Rem realized it was not caused solely by the simple act of confinement. She had spent many long spans in transit cabins of similar dimensions, and her symb had long since lost most of its instinctive claustrophobia. Her dread arose from the reception she had received upon arriving on Jurrume; the military greeting had been far from anything she had anticipated.

The long trip from Central had allowed her ample time to construct numerous scenarios of her future meeting with Gral Il Chedo. She had envisioned elaborate dramas of debate and discussion, filled with the trappings of protocol. Most had ended in wholehearted acceptance, Gral welcoming her into his household, followed by a time of feasting and celebration before the rigors of her elevation. A few had ended in failure—the chedo refusing her sponsorship and sending Rem away—but even the tragedies had been fraught with dignity, her departure and subsequent exile ripe with the bittersweet glory of legend.

Nothing she had imagined had prepared her for the reality of Jurrume's dark plains, the hetta troops in combat armor, and the threatening muzzles of alien energy weapons. It was as if she were a wanted criminal, a heretic or murderer come to spread destruction on the surface of the planet.

It was as if she were a spy.

The thought brought a fresh wave of terror boiling up from her intellect, and Rem struggled to contain the flood of emotion. In the clear plane of the cell walls, her symb held its composed posture. Only close inspection revealed the slight tremors in its rigid limbs.

As abruptly as it had begun, her imprisonment ended. Pressure hissed somewhere beyond the walls. A seam appeared in the panel directly in front of Rem, a crack widening across the center of her reflection, separating head from body. A prophecy, perhaps? A small shudder traced its way up her symb's spine.

Figures filled the dimly lit corridor beyond the panel: hetta soldiers standing at attention and among them the massive figure of a jujun. Their uniforms were stiff and spotless, their weapons ready.

The jujun made no attempt at greeting or formality as it stepped forward into the threshold. Its optical clusters scanned her briefly as though to confirm that she was still submissive, unarmed, and defenseless.

"You will follow me," the creature said stiffly, a hint of disdain in its voice.

Without looking back, the jujun turned and stalked down the corridor. Rem forced her symb to stand, ignoring the pain in its stiff joints. She hurried after the jujun. The hetta fell into position beside her, matching her stride, leather harnesses creaking softly.

They went up a short lift, through a series of tight corridors, up a second lift, and finally up into a small chamber somewhere near the top of the compound. Though the interior was dark, no one moved toward the light panel.

"Wait here," the jujun commanded, and then retreated back into the corridor. Before the doors slid shut, Rem saw the hetta assume guard positions along either side.

After a moment her symb's eyes adjusted to the dim illumination. Humped shapes became furnishings. Black walls became curved transparencies scattered with stars. She was standing on a private observation deck above the rim of the caldera. On one side was the vast wasteland of the plains. On the other side the caldera fell away, its steep interior sides layered with terraced structures and equipment.

Rem stood in the darkened glassine bubble and stared silently at the night sky. The view was frigid, as cold as the sense of betrayal that had hardened like a stone in the center of her mind.

"Beautiful, is it not?"

A voice at her back caused Rem to whirl in surprise. She had heard no one approach, yet a chedo stood at the top of the spiral staircase leading from the lower levels.

"Yes, Chedo," she answered hesitantly, afraid to offend.

The creature was alone, without leera or jujun to speak for it, without guards or escort. A breach of etiquette as great as her own solitary arrival. Perhaps it was a conscious move, a subtle effort to ease her discomfort, but such an action did not seem to fit her image of the warrior Gral Il Chedo. He moved closer, his beast's lanky frame a dark silhouette against the stars. His symb was larger than Dar's, its musculature defined and sculpted beneath the combat armor.

"I did not mean to startle you. But aren't we always startled by the unexpected?"

"My fault, Chedo." Rem bowed her head quickly, her mind burning with the veiled reference to her own unannounced arrival. She forced her symb to raise its head and expose its throat. "I was lost in thought."

"Understandable, Rem Il Leera. Your immediate future is filled with many situations worth pondering." A neutral response, yet it contained a subtle phrasing, a hint of suspicion. Or was she being too critical? Searching for trouble in every word or gesture?

"I am Gral Il Chedo." He moved close and reached out, claws tracing a line across her symb's throat in the traditional gesture of greeting. "I wish to welcome you to Jurrume. I hope you were not overly offended by the zealous nature of my troops. But surely you must understand. This is a border post, gateway to the Col homeworlds, and certain precautions are necessary."

"Of course, Lord Chedo." Rem nodded, the bangles in her horns clinking against the bone, the vibrations ringing in her skull. "And is it not thought in the Coda that conformity is the duty of the visitor?"

"So it is." His turreted eyes glittered. "I trust you know why you have been sent to me."

"Yes, Lord." Elevation. She dared not let her symb utter the word. "I only hope that I am worthy, that I am prepared."

"Do not fear," Gral said, chuffing softly. "Many have thought you ready for elevation for a very long time. Yet despite our urgings, Dar seemed unable to part with you." He paused for a moment and studied Rem closely. "One can only wonder what finally motivated him to raise your status now."

Rem said nothing.

"Ah, well," the chedo continued, turning his attention back to the external view. "Is it not always the way? One plods along in the same rut for many standards, and suddenly the trail turns. We often feel unprepared, but what can we do but follow and try our best to meet the new challenge?

"So it was when I was first sent to this system. 'Build a fortress,' the Triad had commanded. 'A wall to stop the alien in-

fidels from encroaching.' I did as ordered, carving a citadel
from the rock. Steel and alloy, yes. And other materials not
seen—the flesh and blood of many raas and hetta killed during
construction. But the wall was built, and the Triad was pleased.''

He turned to stare at Rem. "Such is the way, is it not? Our
superiors give us a task to complete. They care not whether it
costs us our lives to perform.''

Another veiled insinuation? Her symb's heart thudded in its
breast. She stroked the lowbrain softly with a calming flow of
simple pleasure.

"Dar has given you no easy task," Gral said slowly, his beast's
hooded eyes narrowing. "Elevation is a dangerous process. The
rigors of the tests of worthiness, leaving your flesh behind to
calve, then merging with the minds of those chosen as your
partners. These are not trials to be taken lightly. But if you are
willing to take such risks, then it will be my honor to act as your
sponsor.''

"Then my prayers have been answered," Rem said, forcing
her leera to bow low.

"For now. But I suggest you continue with your daily devotions. Elevation is a poor time to renounce the All Knowing.''
His symb's throat throbbed with mirth, and Rem began to relax.
Surely her imagination had been running wild, conjuring threats
from simple conversation.

The chedo moved across the room and touched a panel along
the wall. A chime sounded somewhere down the corridor, and
almost immediately the door to the corridor slid open. A young
leera appeared, slight and slender, her scales still bright from
her recent molt. Two hetta stood behind her in the entrance. The
jujun and the rest of the troop had vanished back into the compound.

"You must be tired after such a long trip," Gral said. "Our
facilities are humble, but our hospitality is generous. I have had
a room prepared. Go now and rest. The tran will call for you
tomorrow.''

"I thank you, Lord Chedo.'' Her limbs slipped into the rhythmic gestures of the rite of gratitude.

Gral stopped her with an upraised paw, claws retracted.
"There is no need for such formalities here. You are an initiate
for elevation, and as such you are without a master. You serve
no one now. Not me.'' He paused for a moment of silence.
"Or Dar.''

No doubt now. He knew.

"As you wish, Lord Chedo." Rem bowed her symb's head and let the young leera usher her from the room.

In silence, Rem followed the leera, her two hetta escorts marching several paces behind. The leera took them into what was obviously the living compound, past ranked barracks for the troops and dormitories for the civilian staff. The corridor was broad and painted green; the olive color was the only element that served as a reminder of Verrin.

"You will stay in the green passages," the aide said as they walked. "Those have been deemed safe for the uninitiated and untrained. All others are dangerous and off limits. Don't venture into these areas, as the chedo would not like to have to send his condolences to Dar."

It was an order, Rem had no doubt.

The room where she was taken was small and sterile. A sleep net clung to one wall; a wash and waste unit occupied the other. There was a terminal and a stool for reclining. No windows, no viewscreen. The walls were white and unmarred.

It might have been another prison cell.

Again the guards assumed positions outside the small portal.

Rem spent a moment examining the furnishings. It took only a moment. The sleep sack was adequate, the stool too firm. Finally she sat down, uncertain how to proceed.

She should have begun her meditations, slipping into the routines of control and exercise. Soon she would need all her skills if she was to complete the tests of elevation. But Rem found herself unable to concentrate, her mind wandering through the maze of her emotions.

Prior to her landing, Dar's ravings about Gral and his treason had seemed only that—mindless chatter caused by some deepset insanity. But now that she was on Jurrume, Rem was not certain who was insane. Surely Gral was not normal. There were many unsettling elements about Gral's citadel, an undercurrent of violence that seemed to bode preparations for war.

Yet perhaps it was all in her imagination. Maybe she was reading doctrine into innocent preparations. Indeed, Jurrume was a fortress, designed for warfare, specifically created to establish a perimeter between the aliens and the Col. Perhaps such expenditures—such an alien attitude—were necessary. Her head spun with uncertainty.

The door slid open. A raas laborer entered, bearing greens

and soil. Those small items of tradition were soothing, a bit of ritual to which Rem could cling gratefully.

Gral had not lost all semblance of propriety.

Rem accepted them gratefully, and once the raas was gone, she lost herself in the ritual of welcoming.

From that small start it was easy to forget her fears and shift into the meditations of control.

TWENTY-FIVE

A security pulse flickered through her brain.

Eyes locked onto the display screen of her microprocessor, Alexis Weiss activated her anterior scan and moved one hand slowly toward the weapon lying in her lap. A single heat signature appeared in the doorway of the sleeping chamber—mammal, low and squat, watching her silently.

"Hello, Khurrukkatey," Alexis said without turning. She moved her hand back to the keyboard. "About damn time you got here. I see you're still trying to sneak up on people."

"And I see you are still reading other beings' mail." Chittering softly, the Rath entered and stood behind Alexis, staring over her shoulder at the entries scrolling across the display. "Find anything interesting?"

"Ninety percent trash—but isn't everything?" Punching the hold key, Alexis glanced up at the Rath: narrow conical skull covered with short black fur, delicate ears laced with blue veins, dark protruding eyes. The slender tendrils wreathing the pointed snout wriggled nervously, tasting the air. She did not bother asking how the Rath had gotten into her rooms. Unauthorized entry was the creature's specialty.

"How long you been on station?"

"Half shift." Khurrukkatey waddled over to the suspensor and palmed the switch; the spongy field elevated her as it ballooned up from the floor. "Came in on a freighter from Yowni. Unregistered cargo."

"Any problems?"

"None. Security system is archaic, mostly prewar vibration sens-net in combination with antiquated visual units. I could probably blind it with a fart."

"Data system is better protected, but not much."

"Nice setup you got here." The Rath rolled onto her back and sighed contentedly. "Much more comfortable than the heating pipe I'm calling home. Maybe next time I'll take the front job. Being a target might be worth it if you get luxuries like these."

"I wouldn't know." Alexis slapped the side of the processor. "This hasn't allowed me much time to sleep."

"So what do you got?"

"Nothing solid." The woman shrugged. "Which is odd. Every information dealer I've ever encountered has had some kind of a fail-safe, something that would spill his sources and point some incriminating fingers if he suddenly met an untimely end. I scanned the old factor's records for a blind drop or a trip wire, some secret files which might have been automatically released by his death. But if Galagazar left anything behind in the data, I haven't found it yet."

"Maybe it's not in the comm system."

"My thoughts exactly. Could be a hard source: infocube or tapes. Got three places for you to check out." Alexis ticked them off on her fingers. "Old factor office, his apartment, and a shuttle called the *Eariimuus*. The old office was burned out in the fire that killed Galagazar, so it doesn't look too promising. But give it a scan, anyway. And I want you to check out every square centimeter of the apartment."

"Yes, master." The rodent scratched her belly fur lazily, her hind leg spasming with a reflexive twitch. "What about this ship, the *Eariimuus*? That's a Lling name, isn't it?"

"Very observant, Khurrukkatey. I'm impressed. The sensory scan sent to headquarters by Galagazar was made by the *Eariimuus*. The pilot was a Lling by the name of Bezhjenzarthra. Odds are he spotted the Oolaan and sold the images to Galagazar, who was trying to broker it to us. It's possible that the flight data from the *Eariimuus* might just lead us back to the Oolaan—if it still exists. Anyway, it's worth a try. The shuttle is in a parking orbit near the station. Think you can get aboard?"

"No problem." The Rath bent her star-shaped maw into a twisted mockery of a smile. "I'll turn the ship inside out. If there's anything hidden, I'll find it."

"One other thing," Alexis said. "If the Oolaan offed the

factor because they knew he was trying to sell them out, they're probably combing the same places looking for his evidence. Watch your tail.''

"Always. I'm rather attached to it." The Rath waved the hairless member in the air. "So while I'm out risking life and limb, what'll you be doing?''

"Playing corporate hack. Going to meet with the new factor, feel around, see if he knows anything.''

"Any chance that the Quadriate is part of this setup—maybe dealing with the Oolaan?''

"The thought has crossed my mind. Hard to believe, though, especially considering the race of the new factor." She met and held the Rath's curious stare. "He's Human.'

Khurrukkatey snorted, a wet rattling in her snout. "That doesn't mean he's innocent. In fact, I can't imagine a better cover for an operative. Factor has total access to all station records and communications. If he's on their payroll, the Oolaan already know we're here.''

"True. But if he's not with the Oolaan, then maybe we've got an inside track.''

"Either way, you better pinpoint his orientation fast.''

"I know.'' Alexis nodded slowly. "Because if it's the wrong one, I've got to take him out. And soon.''

TWENTY-SIX

By the time the tram coasted to a stop in front of the factor offices, Rourke felt as if he had inspected every square centimeter of Mael Station.

Thunder had dragged him from the core to the external radius, top to bottom, through a seemingly endless array of warehouses and recyclers, power plants, hydroponic farms, and residential and corporate structures. He had even roamed the darkened corridors of the maintenance level, peering into ducting and twisted mazes of pipe, watching robotic work units pursuing their mindless tasks.

"Well, you've had the grand tour," the Wormat said, glancing at Rourke. "And I suppose if I were to drop you off somewhere on the other side of the core, you'd be able to find your way back here. Right?"

"In about five standards," Rourke answered sarcastically. "With a map and a compass."

"That's about what I thought. Too much to absorb in one shift. But you're smart—you'll learn soon enough how to find your way around."

"What about a tour of Jurrume?"

"Have to arrange that with Vuuni. She knows the dirtside. Just not my area of expertise."

Rourke nodded and stepped out of the tram. "Guess I better get inside. Got a feeling my day isn't over yet."

"That's why you get the big salary." Thunder surged the mags, and the tram rose from the deck. "You need anything, give me a call. Even if you're just looking for a drinking partner. I'd really like to hear about how you lit an ambassador on fire. And if I don't see you sooner, I'll meet you at the gym in three cycles."

"What if I get lost?"

"Don't worry." The Wormat grinned broadly. "I'll find you."

A touch on the throttle and the cart sped away, mags whining softly. Rourke watched until the vehicle disappeared around the bend before heading inside the building.

Entering the factor offices, Rourke caught a glimpse of his reflection in the front doors. Purple bruises surrounded both eyes, and one side of his jaw was swollen, the distended cheek an angry shade of crimson. He looked like a Lling with severe emotional problems.

The security pulse started hammering in his head as soon as he stepped into the structure. Kiintaart's surveillance net was still operational. He wondered if the Vost was learning anything of value. What was the bug looking for, anyway? Evidence of incompetence to use against him in a bid for his job? If so, it probably would not take long, even with Nebuun holding his hand.

Veearionar and Leearionar warbled a greeting to Rourke as he crossed the cavernous warehouse/office. Then Ianiammallo darted out from the back, and the two younglings dived for their desks, their wattles turning pale with terror.

The old Lling glared at Rourke. If she was startled by his

bruised features, she kept it hidden beneath a cool mask of disgust. She spread her stubby wings and fluffed her feathers as though her long-dormant nesting instincts had suddenly gone berserk.

"You being are most late," she barked.

"Sorry, Ianiammallo. But it's a big station. A lot to see." Rourke shrugged and gave her his most disarming smile. "Besides, I knew you had everything under control. After all, you did without a factor for twenty cycles."

The flattery had no effect on the old Lling.

"Not being now so. Now being items many awaiting print of yours. Placing these on the desk you for be to finishing. Hurry now. Yes?"

"Yes. Hurrying. Where's Nebuun?"

"Office being yours. Work doing being of yours, too." She made a spitting sound just loud enough for him to hear and then turned away, her wattles flushing to magenta as she stalked toward her workstation.

Rourke shook his head. He might have convinced Thunder that he was a sentient being, but Ianiammallo obviously still had serious doubts. And he had no idea how to change her mind. There was probably some nasty little ritual necessary to overcome her racial conditioning, like climbing into a padded box and letting a Wormat beat him senseless with a leather club.

The thought left him cold.

Nebuun was hovering over his desk, sorting information on a trio of display screens. He glanced up as Rourke entered the cubicle. As he noted the bruises, his rubbery features slid into an expression of extreme disapproval.

"I see you spent some time in the gym with the Wormat," the Eng said sourly. "I had hoped you were smarter than that."

"Believe me," Rourke replied, gingerly massaging his jaw, "I hadn't intended to get in the ring with him. But Thunder can be very persuasive."

"You are supposed to be more persuasive. Remember, you are the factor of this station." The pearlescent flesh on his throat sac rippled as he swallowed angrily. A sigh rattled from deep in his chest. "At least you are still standing. Can I assume your wounds are superficial?"

"I'll live."

"Then sit down and let us get to work." Nebuun gestured toward the displays. "There are many items requiring your print.

We will go through them individually so that you understand the purpose of each."

Sliding onto the hard bench, Rourke braced himself for a long siege. The Eng pivoted the screens so that he could see the Patois text.

"This is a Form 2003SJ97," the Eng began. "It is a standard requisition form required when purchasing . . ."

Half a shift later they were still at it, Nebuun bringing up the documents and describing their purpose in meticulous detail, Rourke imprinting the plas identity panel and fighting to keep from sliding into a catatonic stupor.

Ianiammallo appeared in the doorway of the cubicle. Her feathers were fluffed, her wattles a cold blue.

"There is being one here wishing the factor to be seeing," she announced stiffly. "Name Weiss is. From Genam Corporation—"

"Wait a minute," Rourke said, interrupting her garbled tirade. "Did you say Weiss?"

"Most so assuredly."

"But that's a Human name."

"Is Human type being." The Lling made a spitting sound. "And a being not having appointment. Shall it be I am sending in or away?"

Rourke was quiet for a moment, silently figuring the chances of two Humans meeting on an isolated station such as Mael. The odds were long enough to qualify the event as a major coincidence, and that made a little voice start to whisper warnings in the back of his mind.

Ianiammallo cleared her throat loudly. "Which is choice yours?"

"I could use a break," Rourke said, glancing at Nebuun. "How about you?"

"Yes." Nebuun pushed himself away from the desk. "A moment of rest would be most welcome."

Rourke turned back to the Lling. "Show Ser Weiss in."

"Sera Weiss," Ianiammallo said, coolly correcting him. "Is female type Human." She marched off toward the front of the building.

"I thought I was the only Human on Mael," Rourke said as he watched the Lling strut away.

"You were." Nebuun shrugged his thin shoulders. "But evidently your solo status has changed."

* * *

"Ser Rourke?" the woman said, standing on the imaginary threshold of his cubicle. "I am Alexis Weiss."

Blond hair, brown eyes, slender well-toned body moving gracefully beneath the severe cut of a business suit. Rourke estimated her age to be somewhere near thirty. Her voice was soft, her smile warm and seemingly genuine.

Still, the little voice in his skull kept whispering words of caution.

"Please come in, Sera Weiss." He waved her into the room. "Sit down and make yourself comfortable—if you can." Rourke gestured toward the hard benches. "You'll have to excuse the condition of my office. Had a fire a few cycles back. Forced us to set up temporary quarters. They're not pretty, but they're functional."

"No explanations are necessary, Ser Rourke." She sat down on one of the benches, a fluid motion, controlled and precise. "In fact, this is more comfortable than many of the places I've visited during this trip. And there's the unexpected pleasure of encountering a fellow Human. My research department must have fouled something up—they told me an Eng by the name of Galagazar was in charge of Mael Station."

"He was. Unfortunately, Galagazar died in the fire which destroyed the factor office."

"I'm sorry to hear that." She was suddenly very sober. "Perhaps I should come back at a more appropriate time."

"No, Sera Weiss. That won't be necessary. We were just about to take a break." Rourke nodded toward the Eng sitting beside him. "Nebuun is here from the home office, helping me get settled. And if it wasn't for the occasional interruption, I think he'd work us both to death."

"If you'll pardon my noticing," the woman said, her smile returning, "it looks as if he's already had resort to force to get your attention."

Rourke felt his face flush red. He reached up and touched his swollen jaw. "I had a little accident in the gym this morning."

She raised one eyebrow.

"My sparring partner is a Wormat," he explained. "And don't bother telling me how stupid I am for getting in the ring with a boar. Nebuun has already pointed out the error of my ways."

"I wouldn't think of it, Ser Rourke. It's not my business to pass judgment."

"So, what exactly is your business?" He leaned forward, resting his elbows on the desk.

"I'm with Genam Corporation. My official title is field analyst. Basically I'm a scout, sent out to search for promising locations where the company might want to establish a branch operation."

"Is Genam a Human Alliance corporation?"

"No." She shook her head and her blond hair shimmered. "Our charter is with Marlboro, an independent colony. Genam is primarily a manufacturing operation, raw materials into a variety of items from parts to finished products. The Mael system is being considered as a possible expansion site."

"Mael doesn't seem like a very good place for a manufacturing plant. Hell of a long way to the nearest shipping nexus."

"True." The radiant smile flashed again—even, white teeth behind bow-shaped lips. "But my company has had surprising success with plants in less than ideal systems. Cheaper material costs. Cheaper wages. Sometimes these offset the negatives. Anyway, that's what I'm here to find out.

"Of course," she continued, her serious mask reappearing, "our presence would in no way intrude on any business arrangements which presently exist between your company and the Col. We aren't a trading firm—and have no intention of becoming one."

"I see. Then what exactly do you want from us?"

"Information. Access to your data concerning this system. Mineral assays, planetary surveys, and the like. Anything that you think would help me make my preliminary report. No sense in my company duplicating work yours has already done."

"I assume," Nebuun said carefully, "your company is willing to pay for our assistance."

"I'm prepared to negotiate. And Genam is also prepared to pay your firm for acting as our agent in negotiations with the Col should Mael prove to be a prime location."

"A most interesting proposition." Nebuun stared at Rourke expectantly.

Rourke's mind raced. Obviously the Eng was waiting for him to say something intelligent. But what? He had little experience in those types of negotiations. Taking a deep breath, he plunged ahead blindly.

"You realize," he said, trying to keep from stammering, "I'll have to run this by the home office and wait for their response. It might take a few shifts."

A faint hint of a smile appeared on Nebuun's rigid mouth.

"Certainly." The woman pursed her lips. "In the meantime, would you mind if I looked the station over? Just to establish what kinds of facilities you already have in place. Existing amenities can play a decisive role in making a final selection."

"Not at all. Feel free to visit any of the public areas." He paused for emphasis. "Of course, if it's a restricted sector, you'll have to contact this office for permission."

"That goes without saying." Reaching into her case, the woman withdrew an infocube. "This will give you the details of the proposed project." She placed it in his open palm. Her fingers were soft and warm.

"I'll forward it on to UTA corporate headquarters immediately," he told her.

Weiss stood and straightened her clothing, brushing imaginary wrinkles from the immaculate fabric. A dancer's thigh was outlined beneath the cloth.

"I'll be anxiously awaiting a response. Thank you for your time, Ser Rourke." She glanced at Nebuun. "It was a pleasure meeting you both."

"The pleasure was ours, Sera Weiss." Nebuun bowed slightly. "I hope you have an enjoyable stay on our humble station."

"I'm sure I will." The woman walked to the door and stopped, glancing back at Rourke over one shoulder. "I don't suppose I could interest you in dinner tonight. After all, we are both a long way from home."

"I'd like that. But it'd have to be late." Rourke gestured at his desk. "As you can see, I've got work to do."

"I don't mind eating late." Her smile was as warm as Sol. "Give me a call when you're finished. I'm at the Inn of Peaceful Rest."

She walked away slowly, the curves of her body fluid and intriguing.

"Excellent," Nebuun said when the woman was gone.

"My sentiments exactly."

"I am referring to your conduct," the Eng said stiffly. "You handled the situation extremely well. You should always defer to the home office when in doubt. Seek their advice. If you do, you will have a long and distinguished career with the United Trading Authority."

"Don't worry, Nebuun." Rourke winked at the Eng. "One

thing I don't have to learn is how to pass the buck. Avoiding decisions has always been a specialty of mine."

He looked toward the front of the building, catching a final glimpse of Weiss as she stepped out the door.

Though her story had seemed genuine and Rourke had no doubt that an identity check would reveal a seamless persona, his little mental voice insisted on crying wolf. There was something vaguely unsettling about the woman, something beyond mere sexuality. Her presence had conjured up images within him of the cold, hard operatives he had known from the Bureau of Human Affairs.

Or maybe it was just his imagination working overtime.

"Now then," Nebuun said, assuming his position at the keyboard. "Shall we get back to work?"

Sighing loudly, Rourke returned his attention to the new form that had scrolled up on the gleaming display.

TWENTY-SEVEN

"Coordinates achieved as ordered, my Jujun."

Pivoting the helm chair, Kars Il Jujun, Hautrun of the forces of Gral Il Chedo, scanned each of the external screens. Every visual was the same: scattered stars and empty space. No ships in sight. Nothing to justify the covert journey to the edge of Col Space. Still, it was not his place to question the chedo's orders, and Kars knew his place very well.

Behind the jujun, Gral stood stiffly, watching the proceedings in silence. His chedo's maw gaped in satisfaction. He was pleased, and Kars allowed himself a moment of pride.

Then the creature at Gral's side moved suddenly. Fluids gurgled as its front leg swelled and canted the triangular body forward. Moisture seeped down the thick membrane straining to contain its gelatinous guts. To Kars it was a monstrosity, a thing that seemed more manufactured than spawned.

The jujun would never know how close he was to the truth.

"All engines, full stop," Kars commanded emotionlessly.

His symb's features were as smooth as polished stone. "Weapons systems on full alert. Maintain communications silence. Observation, I want immediate notification of any approaching object—vessel or otherwise."

"As you wish, my Jujun."

The orders went down the line, with the hetta crew members quickly performing their assigned tasks. As its thrusters deactivated, the ship fell silent. The only sounds were the hiss of life-support systems and the subliminal hum of the screens.

They did not wait long.

The first sign of the approaching craft was a thin line of radiation that flickered on the edge of the detection spectrum. Observation had barely a moment to note the anomaly and report.

"Unknown reading on Screen Three," the hetta said. "Pulse-type radiation—"

"I have incoming, my Jujun," the weapons officer stated flatly, overriding the observation officer in midsentence. "Target one thousand mega-lengths and closing."

"Impossible!" Kars hissed, his control momentarily shaken by the incongruity of the data. "Observation. Confirm."

"Sighting confirmed, my Jujun. Permission to broadcast on Screen Four."

"All screens, immediately. Bring all weapons systems to bear on target. Prepare to fire on my command."

"Acknowledged as ordered, my Jujun."

The forward screens flickered and consolidated as the image of a single craft spread across the forward bulkhead. A war vessel, weapon pods spread, ports opening as it bore down on them. Kars leaned forward, his symbiote's mouth gaping in disbelief. Hanging in space less than a thousand mega-lenths distant, the ship was almost on top of them, a wicked mass of steel and energy fields.

"Scan confirms enemy ship has all weapon systems activated and targeted," the observation officer reported.

Kars whirled, glancing back at Gral. The chedo touched his symb, claws pressing into the flesh of its shoulder.

"Hold position, my Jujun," Gral said softly, his symbiote's gaze locked on the screens.

"As you wish, my Chedo." Kars had no options. Besides, if it was a trap, they were already dead. He cursed himself for allowing the chedo to participate.

"Hold position," he snarled. "Do not fire!"

"Enemy closing, my Jujun. Collision course."

The enemy craft was seen now as a partial structure, so massive that it eclipsed half the galaxy.

"Maintain position, helm."

For a moment the bridge was silent, watching as the ship grew in the screens. Then it seemed to flex, folding in upon itself. A heartbeat later it had disappeared from all sensors. A shuddering wave of energy rumbled over them, a harmonic vibration caused by a propulsion field passing so close to their hull.

"Enemy ship no longer in visual," the observation officer reported, a hint of awe creeping into its voice. "All detection fields show negative for contact."

"I want full detection at maximum range, observation. Weapons, maintain alert status."

"Maintaining as ordered, my Jujun," came the reply.

Kars turned back to Gral. "We have lost them, my Chedo."

"Do not fear, Kars," Gral rumbled. "You did well. It is our enemies who should fear."

"You are pleased?" the communicator asked. Its voice was a high-pitched atonal whine.

"Yes." Gral's chedo flexed its claws contentedly. "A most impressive demonstration. We will take as many of these craft as you can deliver. And we will require appropriate instruction in their operation. How soon can we expect them to arrive?"

"Shipments will begin as soon as the jump nexus shield is completed."

"How soon?" Gral insisted.

"Thirty cycles. No more."

"Very well," the chedo grunted. "But do not think that these insystem warships will fulfill your obligation. I was promised jump technology. I will have jump technology. Am I understood?"

"We have not forgotten our agreement, Gral Il Chedo." Liquids gurgled internally. "When the jump point is properly prepared and shipments can begin, you will have jump ships of your own."

"I had better."

A long silence stretched between them, broken by the bark of the observation officer.

"Craft incoming, my Jujun."

Kars turned and saw the angular shape of the warship bearing down on them.

"Status," he snapped.

"Its shields are down. Weapons inactive, my Jujun."

"Receiving hailing frequency, Jujun," the communications officer cut in. "Requesting permission to dispatch shuttle and retrieve our passenger." The hetta nodded toward the Oolaanian.

"Permission granted. But maintain present alert status."

"As you wish, my Jujun."

Kars pivoted the command chair and glanced up at Gral. "They are coming for the communicator, my Chedo."

"Very well." Gral glanced at the Oolaan. "Take this message to your superiors. I will be out of contact for several cycles. You will direct your inquiries and problems to Kars. He speaks with my voice until my return."

"It will be as you request, Gral Il Chedo," the Oolaanian intoned.

"Go, then."

Fluids surging in its legs, the Oolaanian left the bridge.

"Watch them closely, Kars," Gral whispered. "I do not trust these allies the All Knowing has sent us."

"I will watch them, my Filitaar," Kars replied.

And silently he vowed to kill them, each and every one, if they dared betray his chedo.

TWENTY-EIGHT

The woman was waiting in the lobby of the Inn of Peaceful Rest, sitting on the curved edge of a padded Vostian bench.

Her sunlit smile greeted Rourke warmly. He acknowledged her wave with a quick nod and headed in her direction, silently cursing the low ceiling that forced him into a simian posture, back bent and shoulders hunched.

"I see you found the place," she said as he approached. "Maybe I should have warned you that this was a Vost establishment. You could have worn a helmet."

"Or knee pads," Rourke growled, collapsing onto the bench beside the woman. Her shoulder was warm against him even through the fabric of his coveralls. "Hell, I should make them both part of my standard uniform. Damn few places where I can stand upright in this station."

"Yeah," she nodded, her blond hair falling gracefully. "I hate Vost constructs. Lack of headroom won't kill you, but it gets on your nerves after a while. Just one more little irritation, like the lack of decent food and"—she patted the bench—"the fact that none of the furniture fits your butt. It's enough to make you stop every so often and examine your reasons for being on the frontier, just to make sure that the reward is worth the sacrifice."

"That only works if you're here by choice."

She glanced at him, eyebrows raised, pale gold arcs above sable eyes.

"It's a long story," Rourke said, laughing softly.

"Sounds like prime dinner conversation. Got a good restaurant in mind?"

"Doesn't really matter. Compatibles here seem to be universally bad. But I passed a Wormat place on the way over, dive called the Golden Tusk. Wormat alcohol is passable. And we'd be able to stand. At least until the drinks kick in."

"Lead on," she said, pulling him to his feet.

She linked one arm through his, and they headed out into the passageway.

The Golden Tusk was crowded, the dimly lit interior warm and close. The decor was neo-Wormat classical, with plastic chairs and booths sculptured to look like wood, green plastic vines twining through plastic trellises, plastic fruit and plastic birds. The air was heavy with the competing reeks of Wormat sweat and camaii musk. Muted conversations in the Wormat dialect rumbled softly, like guttural static filled with clicks and burrs.

Rourke ordered a pair of ales from the ragged bartender while Alexis grabbed an empty booth near the door. As he picked up the foam-capped mugs, a drunken voice nearby slurred from Wormat to Patois; it was loud enough for him to hear the comment clearly.

"Damn Humans."

Ignoring the drunk, Rourke headed for the table. But he felt a cold stare following him.

"Damn . . . stinkin' . . . Humans," the speaker rumbled

again, louder now, the threatening tone cutting through all other conversation.

"This might not have been such a good idea," Rourke said, putting the mugs on the molded wood-grain plastic and sliding into the booth. "One of the natives seems to be a little bent by our presence."

"So I heard." She smiled at him. "Do you always have this effect on Wormats? I mean, you tangled with one earlier today. And now this. I sense a pattern."

Rourke heard the heavy scrape of a chair on the floor and saw a massive shape approaching from the bar.

"This doesn't look good," he whispered. "Think we can make it to the door?"

"Not a chance." Alexis shook her head. "I hope you learned some tricks in the gym this morning. 'Cause I think you're going to need a few."

A huge paw dropped onto his shoulder, blunt claws digging into his flesh. Rourke was spun around, and a snout, topped by red-rimmed golden eyes narrowed to slits, was thrust into Rourke's face.

"You deaf, Human?" The Wormat's breath was sour with raw flesh and wine.

"No," Rourke said carefully. "I heard you. Everyone heard you."

"Then if you aren't deaf, you got to be stupid. Is that it, Human? You stupid?"

"Evidently—or I'd have known better than to come in here."

"By my ancestors' tusks!" the Wormat bellowed. "What does it take to make these stoneless Humans fight?"

The partisan crowd roared with delight. Alexis pursed her lips, her eyes scanning the nearest patrons. Sizing them up, Rourke realized suddenly. Picking her targets.

"I'll be damned," the Wormat slurred, looking at him closely. "Somebody already got to this one. A Wormat, too, I'll wager, by the size of the bruises. Don't look like it's your lucky shift, Human."

"Why don't you just tell me what this is all about?"

"What this is all about, Human, is payback. Understand?" The boar wavered drunkenly. " 'Bout ten cycles back, damn near got my boat rammed by a Human battlewagon coming out of the Malacar nexus. Didn't bother to hail and see if I took damage. No apologies. Nothing. Just headed on their way. So right then and there I swore that the next Human I saw was going to answer for that insult.''

"And that would be me,'' Rourke said, mentally selecting his own target, the soft flesh of the boar's throat.

"Like I was saying,'' the Wormat rumbled, drawing back one boulder-sized fist, "just not your lucky shift.''

Time slowed, individual seconds ticking by as Rourke ducked and the hammer blow glanced off the side of his skull. The plastic trellis behind him exploded. Driving his fist up and out, Rourke felt warm fur and soft giving flesh and heard a roar of pain.

Then he was flying, twisting through the smoke-filled air like a rag doll.

Just before he crashed into the tables, Rourke caught a glimpse of Alexis. The woman was standing in the center of the floor, a leg kick driving one attacker into the wall and a rigid forearm chopping a second across the windpipe. A third was already crumpled at her feet.

Then Rourke slammed into the tables among a snarling ring of angry Wormats, and events were suddenly compressed into a single gestalt of pain.

Sirens wailed.

Curses and struggles faded into an angry silence. The crushing weight of an unconscious boar was rolled from Rourke's prone form, and he could breath again, sucking air into his lungs and still trying to lash out with his fists at the Wormat who peered down at him.

"Hold on, Ser Rourke,'' a familiar voice rumbled. "I'm on your side.''

The furred muzzle split into a wide grin. One tusk was broken at the base. One ear was a chewed pink stub. Thunder.

"Am I ever glad to see you.''

"Can't imagine why,'' the Wormat said, jerking him to his feet.

Around them, the bar looked as if someone had detonated a small tactical nuke. Tables were overturned, and chairs had been reduced to fragments. Half a dozen furred bodies were sprawled amid the rubble. Others stood back behind a line of Wormat security officers holding stun batons.

Alexis Weiss was leaning against the wall. Her hair was tousled and the sleeve on her coveralls was torn, but she did not seem to have sustained any serious damage. She grinned at him.

"This has been one hell of a day," Rourke muttered, wiping at something wet on his chin. His hand came away bloody.

"I tell you, Rourke." Thunder wrapped one massive arm around his shoulders. "If I'd have known this was your plan for the late shift, I'd never have taken you to the gym. Could've just met you here. Would've been more fun. No pads." He laughed loudly. "So, you want to tell me what happened?"

"Seems one of your fellow Wormats made a vow to beat the hell out of the next Human he saw. Can you guess who that was?"

"Got a fair idea. Which one of my brothers is the guilty party?"

Rourke scanned the crowd and finally spotted the boar in a heap beneath a table. There was a massive lump on the beast's thick skull. Minor justice, but Rourke grinned despite the pain.

"That's him," he said, pointing to the unconscious figure.

Thunder walked over to the boar, bent down, and checked the pulse beneath his arm.

"Well," Thunder said, "he's still breathing. I'll break the good news to him later. As for the rest of you—" He glanced around the bar. "Allow me to introduce you to Kenneth Christian Rourke. Ser Rourke is the new factor of Mael Station."

A stunned silence settled over the crowd.

"In the future," Thunder continued, "I'll expect you to treat him with the respect due his position. Otherwise you'll have to deal with me. And I guarantee you, I can be most unpleasant. Now—" He jerked his head toward the door. "—why don't you all go find some place quiet to cool down before I find a reason to start taking identity chits."

He did not have to ask twice. The place was empty in seconds. Only the wounded remained. Thunder moved from body to body, checking for signs of life or serious injury, stripping out identity chits and passing them on to a subordinate.

"Looks like you acquitted yourself admirably, Ser Rourke," Thunder said as he worked. "Must have been toying with me at the gym."

"No." Rourke shook his head. "At the most I took two of them out."

"And the others?"

Rourke nodded toward Alexis. She said nothing.

"The woman did this?" Thunder grinned at her appreciatively. "Then I suggest you take some lessons."

"I might just do that." Rourke rubbed his jaw thoughtfully,

remembering how the woman had stood, the killing stance, arms up, legs bent. Bureau tactics.

"Well," Thunder said, rising to his feet. "I need to get the wounded down to the tanks before they start waking up. Do me a favor. Stay out of trouble long enough for me to get this bunch processed. All right?"

"Don't worry. It's dinner and then straight to bed. I've had enough excitement for one cycle."

"Maybe," Thunder rumbled, looking from Rourke to the woman and back again. "And maybe not."

Still grinning, he grabbed the legs of the nearest downed Wormat and dragged him outside to a waiting tram.

Rourke limped over to Alexis. His shoulder felt as if it had been dislocated and something had spent a few minutes gnawing on his leg. He grimaced in pain with each step.

"So, Ser Rourke," Alexis said, her eyes sparkling with laughter, "what can I expect for an encore? Do you light yourself on fire?"

"No. I light other people on fire." Her puzzled expression brought a smile to his lips. "Maybe I'll get the chance to tell you about it some day. As for tonight's encore, dinner and sleep. Still hungry?"

"All I did here was work up an appetite."

"Good. I'm buying." He started toward the door. "I think I saw a cafeteria down the passageway."

"Not this time." Alexis slid an arm around his waist and helped him limp up the stairs. "You picked this place, remember? Now we'll do it my way."

They bought compatibles from a small restaurant near the Inn of Peaceful Rest and took them back to her rooms, where Alexis doctored the food with spices from a kit she produced from one of her bags. Old Earth herbs: basil and parsley and rosemary, oregano and lemon peel.

Over the fragrant bowls and stout glasses of Wormat ale, they spoke of their pasts. She told Rourke stories of growing up on a frontier colony. He spoke of events on Central and before, warmth flooding him as she laughed at his tale of Vetch and the prostitutes.

And finally, when the food was gone and the ale had been reduced to a few warm swallows, Rourke met her gaze and watched her silently for a long moment.

"You have a question, Ser Rourke," she said. "I can see it in your eyes."

"It's not what you think." Rourke smiled and nodded toward the door of the sleeping chamber. "Although I must admit, the thought has crossed my mind."

"So if that's not what you're thinking . . ." She studied him over the rim of her mug. "Then what is it?"

"I was thinking about the way you handled yourself down at the Golden Tusk. It was quite a show. And I was wondering where a field analyst would learn to fight like you do."

"I'm a long way from home," Alexis said with a shrug. "And sometimes knowing how to defend yourself comes in handy."

"Your instructors—whoever they were—should be damned proud. You learned your lessons well."

"Ser Rourke," she said, reaching out and gently taking his hand. "You're about to learn that I can do many things very well."

And then Rourke forgot all about how she had moved in the bar. He stopped listening to the small voice in his head whispering its plaintive warnings. There was only the feel of her in his arms and the warmth of her skin beneath his lips.

It was only later, as he lay beside her in the suspensor field, that Rourke realized how skillfully she had ended his fumbling interrogation.

Whatever doubts he had felt before were gone. She was a Bureau operative. But that certainly only raised new questions in his mind. Why had she come to Mael? What was she looking for on the desolate station?

Rourke did not have a clue. But he had a sneaking suspicion that he was already deeply involved.

BOOK THREE

IN SYSTEM

No battle plan ever survives contact with the enemy.
—Army War College maxim

TWENTY-NINE

In the vast darkness of the Gulf the core of the Ssoorii Unity was expanding rapidly. Incoming shipments of raw materials were being converted immediately into biological substance, living mass expanding to fill every twisted crevice within the mothership.

Most of the new growth was linked to the main reasoning center: analytic structures for processing and collating the ever-increasing flow of data pouring in from countless external sources, memory units to store and retrieve the information for subsequent use, semisentient subsets designed to model and chart specific projection variables.

While the majority of those subsets were known to the reasoning center by technical labels, a few had alien names: Gral Il Chedo, Vaz Il Tran, Kars Il Jujun. Those few did not function as a part of the Unity. They thought in primitive patterns, modeled after their namesakes, and allowed the reasoning center to test theoretical scenarios. Their responses helped predict the success or failure of the myriad possible options envisioned by the Designers.

But this additional mass was not without a price. Reasoning times had been slowed by a now-tangible interval, several thousandths of a microspan. And the interval grew exponentially when factored into the total decision-making process. Additionally, because incoming messages now had to be shunted through an enlarged battery of analytic subsets, communications lagged.

Thus it was almost a full hundredth of a span before the news of several enemy presences within the proscribed sector reached the main reasoning center.

There were three separate infiltration points, two confirmed and one probable. All data had been obtained from station sources.

Point one: Human; Kenneth Christian Rourke; newly appointed factor for Mael Station.

Point two: Human; Alexis Weiss; field analyst with a Human business entity known as Genam.

Point three: an unconfirmed sighting of Human warship at or near the Malacar nexus.

Slowed by its new mass, the reasoning center took thirty-thousandths of a microspan to analyze the data and insert it into the Designers' projection. Future probabilities shifted as a dozen possible scenarios collapsed into stunted fragments.

A course of action emerged. Orders went out for increased patrols along the Malacar vectors. Station sources were commanded to retrieve all possible information concerning the two Humans on the station. Two new semisentient subsets were created.

Their names were Alexis Weiss and Kenneth Christian Rourke.

THIRTY

The dawn pipes called softly through the sterile corridors of Jurrume, their thin, reedy wail announcing the birth of a new day.

Rem was awake long before the trilling flutes began their morning song. She was too excited to sleep.

As she sat and listened to the familiar tune, memories drifted up from the deep chasms of her mind, stray images that had somehow survived the rigors of her previous elevations.

Once, while a lowly raas back on Verrin, she had been privileged to witness the ceremony of dawn at the Great Temple of Selkirk. She remembered how the first light had streamed through the window of the world, reflected in the thousand prismatic facets of the Eye of the All Knowing. The glare spilled out from the huge jewel in sharp daggers, piercing the shapes of the priests as they waved their glowing censers, illuminating the clouds of smoke billowing up through the predawn pallor. The throats of a thousand pipes welcomed the gleam of Rehilr.

Compared with the pageantry of the temple, Jurrume's simple

ritual seemed as nothing, an afterthought designed to meet minimum spiritual requirements. Yet the frail song swept through Rem like a searing flame and left her mind trembling with anticipation. Her day had finally come, and the softly ululating notes were the opening chords of a song that would end in her blessed elevation.

Sensing her excitement, her leera rumbled and purred. All the discomforts of the purification fast faded like wind-blown smoke as Rem stroked its pleasure centers, her probes caressing the clustered neurons so that the creature shivered with delight. Soon they would separate, Rem withdrawing her essence from the skull cavity that had been her home for so many long standards. She was uncertain whether guilt or pity fueled her sudden compassion. Regardless, the lowbrain did not question her motives, accepting her ministrations gratefully, its small mind blissfully ignorant that elevation was, for itself, a death sentence.

There were some who might have argued that elevation marked the end of Rem as well as her symbiote—aliens and even a few heretics among her own race who viewed the coming tests as little more than a trial of deprivation and pain leading to oblivion.

The process began with a series of tests designed to determine worthiness. Those who survived the trannish rituals were allowed to withdraw their essence from their symbiote's flesh. Once free of the beast, the small lump of organic matter that was the Col essence calved, producing two smaller masses. These were taken by the tran to be attached to a pair of young raas males to begin their own life journeys. The remaining portion of the old intellect was then merged with two other Col essences. From that joining came a single, newly formed entity. And unless one proved to be vastly stronger than the other two intellects, each was but a portion of that new mind, past memories fragmented and co-mingled into a strange gestalt of self. The new entity was then united with a young symb of the next highest caste.

Rem was not among the insane minority who saw the process as nothing more than death. Elevation was the one true path to growth. And just as the seed was irrevocably altered in its striving to become a tree, so, too, was the mind as it was raised to a higher order. A portion of her thoughts would be carried forward. That was all the immortality she required.

It was the way of all things, a dance of living and dying. She could understand it rationally. Still, the flesh had served her well. And Rem continued to stimulate the pleasure center with gentle prods.

Before the song of the pipes had faded from the corridor, there came a soft tap on the portal. A hesitant touch, the knock of an awestruck acolyte.

Rem took a moment to compose herself, withdrawing her probes from the leera's pleasure zone and settling the beast into a posture of meditation.

"Enter and be welcomed," she called, her emotionless voice concealing her manic joy.

A hiss of pressure, and the door slid open. A young leera waited in the corridor, freshly molted, its skin gleaming with oil. Its eyes were wide with the awe usually reserved for the famous or the Chosen.

And in that moment Rem realized that she was finally among the Chosen, destined for elevation to chedo.

She remembered her own awestruck moments, when she, too, had been young, ministering to those rising above her level. She thought of her own tongue-tied awkwardness as she aided the Chosen in their ritual mornings. And now, at last, her time had come. She could barely contain her excitement.

"Good dawning," the acolyte said softly, its beast's voice breathless and hurried as it stumbled through the prescribed litany. "I bring greetings from Gral Il Chedo. He hopes this morning finds you pure and focused, rested and prepared."

"It is so," Rem replied, the words thrilling and sweet to her mind. "I am ready."

"Then let us make the flesh as pure as the mind."

Rem followed the acolyte out of the small chamber and into the corridor. Two other leera waited, one with a glowing censer, the other with a fragrant branch of lakka flowers. Rem wondered for a moment where such beautiful blooms might grow on the cold plains of Jurrume. A hothouse, perhaps? She forced her beast to incline its head. The acolytes blessed her symb's skull. The blossoms were soft against its flesh, and the smell of incense was a burning reek in its flaring nostrils.

Behind the acolytes an honor guard of hetta soldiers waited in tight formation. Though there was no disguising their deadly capabilities, the hetta had dressed in full formal gear, their alien sidearms replaced by ceremonial weapons. They fell into step behind Rem, and their throats joined in the song of Annunciation, a vibrating chorus that rumbled down the corridors.

Rem's beast assumed the traditional gait of elevation without prodding, falling easily into the stride reserved for sacred occasions. It was a skill drilled into the lowbrain by spans of practice, many days spent on the fields of youth while the tutors berated and cajoled their novice charges. And many nights spent practicing in the privacy of dim chambers where all young leera dreamed of the day when they, too, would make their own march of elevation.

The cleansing chamber was in stark contrast to the sterile, functional design of the rest of the compound. The low curved ceiling approximated the contours of the bathing caves of home; the lighting was dim and red as if torches burned in the recesses. Three pools glimmered in the twilight. A smell of sulfur and mud boiled up from the steaming liquids, their surfaces skimmed with a froth of gases. Thick moss formed a soft carpet beneath her leera's feet.

Rem stood quietly while the acolytes stripped her and led her into the first scalding caldron. The mud was thick and viscous, as hot as summer sunlight. Her presence tripped some unseen device; jets of gas and steam boiled up as she stepped down into the pool. The ooze roiled, and churning particles scoured her leera's tough hide.

In the second pool the waters were clear, blood-warm and slippery with oil. Rem forced her symb to sit and submit to the ministrations of the acolytes, the beast protesting angrily as the young leera abraded its hide with stiff bristled brushes, digging between the overlapping scales and scraping away dead skin and mud. When they had finished, its flesh tingled and burned. It had been ages since she had felt so much life in her ancient symbiote.

The third pool was clear and sweetly scented, slightly warmer than body temperature. Softening agents and medicines gently soothed the irritated hide like a gentle blanket wrapped about her symb. It was hard to make her leera stand and leave the waters, where comfort held it as securely as the grip of deep mud.

The acolytes robed her in the pure white vestments of the initiate. The fabric was soft and shining, glimmering with subtle highlights that seemed to display a myriad of colors when glanced at through the corners of the eyes, yet it was the purest, most brilliant white when examined directly. There was open envy in their features, awe and desire. She knew their feelings, having succumbed to them herself many times as she dressed others who had been Chosen. Over the passing of the standards, those feelings had grown so intense that she had found herself hard pressed to control her emotions and had avoided attending the ceremony whenever possible.

It was pure bliss to let them pamper her so and to see the longing they tried so hard to contain.

Dressed and prepared, they led her to the temple.

Considering the sterile confines of her sleeping chambers, Rem was expecting the temple to be a marginal structure. A storage chamber, perhaps, or some cramped corner of a hangar smelling of grease and dust. Surely the sensibilities of such soldiers as these brooding hetta required little in the way of spiritual icons. They carried their gods on straps across their broad backs and placed their faith in their ability to kill. A temple would have been redundant.

So it was with some surprise that she noted that the tunnel they were following had begun to widen, the low ceiling sweeping up in a gradual curve to meet the perimeter of a broad stone archway. Sweet scents washed forth from the gateway, smells of green and growing, of life and prey. Her symb mewled, its guts rumbling hungrily.

"This way," her youthful guide urged, his voice cutting through Rem's reverie. "The chedo waits."

Leaving the hetta at the gateway, her leera escort led Rem through a short side passage to a small contemplation chamber. The close atmosphere reeked of chedo, and her symb hesitated. It was still not comfortable with Gral's scent. Unlike the familiar stench of Dar, Gral's pungent odor still held the threat of the unknown.

Gral Il Chedo waited in the dimly lit adit, his chedo form kneeling on the bare stone. Hearing them approach, Gral finished his devotions and rose, turning to face them. His lean symb was dressed in a tight-fitting scarlet uniform of simple military style, his jet fur dark against the red fabric. His only decoration was a single command insignia over one breast.

"My Chedo." The escort bowed. "She has been prepared as ordered."

"Good," Gral ran his talons across the youngling's exposed throat, lightly caressing the scaled flesh. "You have done well."

The chedo turned his attentions to Rem, studying her in silence for a moment, his gaze calculating and then fading to warmth. "This one says you are prepared. Are her eyes as keen as she imagines?"

"I am ready, Chedo."

"So it always is among the faithful," he said to no one in particular. "Always so anxious to suffer the pain and cast off the flesh." He inhaled deeply, his chedo's chest expanding, the fabric of his uniform stretching as the muscles bulged.

"Let us go," the chedo said finally. "It is not good to make the tran wait." He nodded toward the escort. "Lead on."

Bowing, the young leera led them back out into the tunnel. In the cavernous entryway the hetta had formed an honor guard, their huge frames standing at attention against the polished stone. As Gral appeared, they stiffened, muscles rigid, optic clusters locked on his movements as though waiting for the command to attack.

The small phalanx of acolytes moved forward, forcing their symbs into the stylized gait of ritual processions, upper limbs rigid and legs kicking high into the air. Each step made the bangles in their horns ring joyfully.

Before following them, Gral turned to Rem. His claws touched her throat gingerly, a faint trace on her flesh.

"May the All Knowing think kindly of you during your trials, little one. And may the blessings of the All Knowing be on you and your flesh." Then he was moving away from her, his claws clicking against the stones.

Rem waited until they had entered the temple proper before proceeding. Her symb was nervous, its lowbrain skittish. She drove her probes deep and forced the flesh to comply, matching the stylized march of the acolytes.

Through the archway of polished stone, and suddenly she was bathed in a magical light that spilled down from a seemingly blue sky high above. Her symb gazed in wonder at the panorama that spread before them. It was as if somewhere within the stone tube they had leapt across the cold vastness of space and touched down on Verrin.

The stone tunnel ended in a series of low steps leading down to a green paradise, the rock giving way to rich black loam. The vast green growth of a Verrin jungle arched high above them, trees and creepers twisting, blossoms dotting the verdancy with bright shards of color. Small creatures flickered through the dense foliage. Girga and huuthans, chittering cabansas.

There was a small clearing, an oval of space within the thick tangle where the edges of the brush had been cut into a sheer wall. Gleaming censers sat on brazen tripods around the vale, curls of smoke wisping up into the steaming air. In the center of the clearing was a raised dais, a tran altar carved from Verrin stone, slick and black as if a chunk of dark water had been carved from the sea and had somehow solidified.

On the dais, the tran waited, resplendent in his robes of divinity. His beast's narrow, hatchet face was strangely blank, its proboscis retracted into a tight coil. As he watched Rem approach, she thought she saw a small flicker of hatred and fear burning for a moment within his beast's eye clusters. Then it was gone, extinguished like a spark in a pond.

Reaching the foot of the dais, the acolytes knelt slowly. The leader raised her symb's head and began to croon the Song of Offering. Her liquid warble made Rem's symb shiver with delight.

"Exalted One," the leera sang, her voice loud in the clearing and making the animal life fall silent with sudden fear. "Living representative of the All Knowing. We bring you one who begs an audience. He is upright and just and is well beloved of the All Knowing, foremost in the mind of the One whose thoughts conceived the Universe and the Col. We ask that you would hear his words."

"So be it," the tran said. "Come forward, pilgrim." His eyes lingered on Rem for a moment, then turned to Gral as the chedo approached.

At the foot of the altar Gral's symb knelt stiffly, its muscles tense, its flat features rigid, its gaping mouth locked in a rictus of defiance.

"Exalted One, I thank you for your indulgence." The chedo spoke as one accustomed to command often speaks when forced into deference, words clipped and short, phrasing flat and even. "I come to you with a request, a boon to be passed from your ears to the mind of the All Knowing."

"Speak, then. I am listening."

"What I ask is not for myself but is the wish of one who has spent her life in honor and duty, following the wishes of her lord, asking nothing in return until this time. Even now others must speak for her because she would not be so bold as to ask. But her readiness cannot be denied, and the time has come for someone to raise a voice in her name."

"And what boon would she require?"

Rem had heard the litany a thousand times, had memorized each phrase and mouthed each word in the silence of her tiny room, waiting for this moment to arrive. Yet now each syllable seemed new and fresh, and her emotions stirred within her like a storm.

"She would ask for elevation, Exalted One."

The tran was silent a moment, a heartbeat of indecision. Those new to the ritual would have noticed nothing, but Rem spotted the flaw and paused to wonder.

"And you believe this one to be ready for such an honor?" The tran spoke carefully, enunciating each word as if mouthing a foreign tongue. A look passed between tran and chedo, an unspoken question.

"I do."

Another flicker of distress in the cold eyes. Another hint of anger quickly quenched. Confusion welled within Rem.

"Do you speak for her as a sponsor in good faith and free of coercion?"

"I do."

"And what is this one called?"

"She is Rem Il Leera."

"Rem Il Leera," the grating voice boomed. "Come forward."

Rem approached the altar as if walking under water, her limbs leaden and heavy, everything about her seemingly like the fixtures of a dream. Responding to some inner programming, her symb went forward almost unassisted and found its place at the foot of the altar, kneeling slowly and tilting its head, exposing its jugular to the blunt claws of the tran.

"You are Rem Il Leera?"

"I am." Her voice was alien, strange and husky.

"Do you know why you have been called here?"

"I do."

Unexpectedly, the tran raised its bulk from the dais and waddled down the steps to the foot of the altar.

"Before I ask if you are prepared for elevation, I want to be certain you know what faces you. Do you understand?"

"Yes, Exalted One," Rem stammered, uncertain how to respond.

"Get on with it," Gral whispered threateningly.

"As a priest, I must do my duty to all." The tran stared at him placidly, yet the flicker of cold annoyance was still there. Was Gral so blind as not to see this defiance? Rem wondered, glancing at him. But the chedo only gritted its teeth and waited in silence.

The tran looked back to Rem. "No doubt you feel yourself ready for elevation. All admit you have been ready for many standards. But by delaying your rite, Dar Il Chedo has done you a grave disservice. The tests you face were not meant for the elderly. Withdrawal and merging are trials for those in their prime, strong and secure and able to withstand hardship. I tell you this truthfully, Rem Il Leera. For one of your age, elevation is most likely a sentence of death for the intellect as well as the flesh.

"Suicide is no honor. It would be no dishonor to decline. No one would think less of you if you returned to your chedo and lived out your life as a leera. Have you considered that option?"

Rem stared at the tran uncomprehendingly. Was he really suggesting that she refuse her elevation? In all her standards she had never witnessed such an aberration. A small flame of rage flared within her. She was no youngling needing to be coddled, nor was she ripe for her time of hardening.

"There is only one course open for the righteous," she said stiffly. "I am ready to take the path that awaits me. As for my flesh, while I am not as strong as some, my standards have given me wisdom most will never attain. And like all who believe in the All Knowing, I choose to place my faith in thought over any fleeting strengths of the flesh."

"Reflect carefully on what you are saying," the tran whispered.

"I've had all my life to think. Nothing you can say will change my mind."

"I am a priest—not an executioner," the tran insisted.

"Enough," Gral snarled. "Ask her the question and be done with it!"

"As you wish." The tran looked back at Rem and drew a deep breath, as if admitting defeat. "Rem Il Leera, you have heard the words of this chedo. He is a just and upright thinker. He deems you ready for the rigors of elevation and the challenges of the chedo form. Do you accept his sponsorship and accept the honor of elevation?"

"I do," Rem said firmly.

"Then it shall be as you both desire." The tran raised his limbs and laid his cold digits on her symb's skull. "This flesh has served you well and faithfully. Now it will serve you even unto death. From this moment forward you will allow your leera no nourishment, no liquid, no blood, no matter of any kind which would sustain its life. Nothing shall be allowed to pass through its lips. Nothing through its skin, nor through any other orifice until death separates you from its grasp.

"I charge you with the duty to make its passing painless and quiet, for it is known that the ability to make one's flesh die with peace and dignity is the ultimate skill of the mind. All others are second to this capacity. Do you understand?"

"I do."

"Then go now with the blessings of the All Knowing. Spend your time wisely contemplating the Coda and preparing yourself for the first of the many hurdles of your elevation."

Rem found the strength to stand.

"Thank you, Exalted One," Gral said, inclining his head slightly.

The acolytes burst into the chorus of the Song of Joy half a beat late; they, too, were disturbed by the priest's strange behavior. The song followed Rem out of the corridor and into the hall.

Back in her room, Rem settled into the posture of Purest Thought and tried to concentrate on the first trial. It would be the rite of the girga, and she knew it would be difficult. Already the purification fast had left her beast rumbling with hunger. The mental image of a girga struggling in her grasp filled it with primal ravenings. But she fought the urge down and settled into the thoughtful ritual.

And after a while she forgot the odd meanderings of the bloated tran and was able to set her gaze securely on the future.

In the dim confines of the contemplation chamber the tran stood rigidly, its ample flesh motionless, its multiple eyes locked on the face of the chedo towering before it. Gral stared at the being, barely able to contain the killing rage and keep it from flooding into his symb.

"Explain yourself," he demanded, spittle arcing from his chedo's fangs.

"I had hoped only to discourage the leera," Vaz stammered. "To convince the creature to leave of its own accord. I thought it a practical solution."

"You fool! Your words did not dissuade her. She is Rem the Forgotten. Rem of the Coda! Her faith is legendary." The chedo balled the claws on forelimbs and midlimbs, snatching futilely at the air. "Did you really think she would listen to such drivel?"

"I thought it possible."

"You thought wrong. All your words did was fuel the fire of her suspicions."

"I am sorry, Filitaar. I had only hoped to—"

"Silence!" The angry chedo paced, prowling around the priest. "If you ever dare to challenge my authority again, I will have your flesh torn limb from limb and your essence burned to ashes. Do you understand me?"

"Yes, Filitaar."

"Go, then. The time of my division is near. See to your equipment. And do not dare darken my chambers with your presence again until all is in readiness—or I may not be able to control the urges of my flesh."

"As you wish, Filitaar."

The priest hurried from the room, thundering howls of chedo rage spurring his flight down the narrow passage.

THIRTY-ONE

The insect whine of a personal tram echoed down the concourse as the cart flashed past the charred facade of the factor offices.

In the darkness of the burned-out structure, Khurrukkatey the Scrounger held her breath until the sound had faded into silence. Only then did she move toward the melted windows and steal a glance out into the corridor. It was blessedly empty.

Though her heart gradually resumed its normal rhythm, the Rath did not relax as she returned to her search. Relaxation was not possible, not while she was subject to the whims of Mael Station's erratic security force.

Compared with most of the security operations Khurrukkatey had encountered in her illustrious career, Mael's team was strictly amateur. The staff consisted primarily of hypertrophic Wormats armed with stun batons. Dangerous but certainly not in the same league as Phura combat troops or Oolaanian biologicals.

Yet it was that amateur nature that made the squad so dangerous. The Rath had learned long before that predictability was the key to successful covert operations. Knowing enemy routines allowed one to steal into secure areas on the heels of vigilant guards and vanish moments before they returned. Thus every mission began with surveillance, studying the opposing force to pick out habitual routes and prescheduled timing.

Khurrukkatey had spent almost two full cycles—five shifts—trying to determine the patrol patterns of station security. From hidden vantage points near the office, the apartment, and the *Eariimuus*, she had watched a few officers come and go, drifting by at odd times, in pairs or alone. Her frustration mounted with each passing shift.

Finally the truth dawned on Khurrukkatey. There was no pattern because there were no regular patrols for those areas during the harvest season. The small force was too busy down in Fantasyland breaking up fights and arresting drunks. The handful of officers she had seen were making rounds on their own initiative, their visits random and unscheduled.

And there were few things Khurrukkatey feared more than unpredictability, especially when she was engaged in searching unfamiliar structures for unknown materials.

The Rath had chosen to make her move during the off-shift period when Fantasyland was crowded and most of the security units were busy trying to keep order. Still, despite the empty condition of the corridors, she came in through a vent in the rear of the structure to avoid being seen.

For three-quarters of a shift she systematically dissected the charred wreckage, scanning for hidden compartments, secret panels, or anything that would offer a clue to the nature of the Oolaanian involvement within the Mael system. But her efforts were in vain; the ashes yielded nothing.

She was on her way back to the ducts when a glint of light on the paneling caught her attention. It was a reflection, the gleam of her dim flash on a crescent-shaped fragment embedded into the wall. Moving closer, Khurrukkatey saw a deep scar in the panel. A five-centimeter-long claw was hooked into the torn insulation and jagged plasteel.

Prying the talon free, Khurrukkatey studied it for a moment. Chitin, Phura chitin. And where there were Phura, there were Oolaan.

It was a small but satisfying victory. Weiss would be pleased.

Chittering softly, the Rath placed the find in one of the pouches on her belt harness and slipped into the duct. In minutes she had left the charred smell of the office behind and was scrambling toward her next target.

THIRTY-TWO

He awakened to the smell of freshly brewed coffee.

Opening his eyes, Rourke rolled to his side on the suspensor field. A myriad of aches and agonies accompanied the simple motion and brought the events of the previous evening flooding back to him in stark images of pain and pleasure: snarling Wormats with upraised fists and, later, the caress of smooth flesh pressing against him, soft and warm. He stretched slowly, trying to loosen his stiff muscles.

Alexis came in from the sitting room, stooping to avoid the low ceiling, a steaming cup in each hand. The oversized shirt she was wearing made her seem small and vulnerable, almost childlike. It was hard to reconcile her present guise with his memory of the night before and the woman who had dropped four enraged Wormat boars with her bare hands. A few hours sleep had made the incident seem like a dream.

Was she really as dangerous as he had imagined? Yes. Rourke was certain she possessed lethal talents, though that was hard to believe of the woman who had touched him so tenderly in the darkness.

A more troubling question was whether Alexis was dangerous to him personally. Only if he was foolish enough to interfere with her mission, he decided after a moment.

But what was her mission? Why would a Bureau operative come to Mael Station? Rourke had no clue. Based on the little he knew about the Mael system, there was nothing there of interest to the Human Alliance.

Did it have something to do with the old factor's death? That was a possibility. If Galagazar had been murdered and if Alexis really was with the Bureau, the two incidents were probably connected.

Which brought him back to square one. Was Alexis really with the Bureau of Human Affairs?

Maybe. Or maybe he was just jumping at shadows.

"Colombian," the woman said, handing him a cup and then sinking cross-legged onto the floor.

"Are you kidding?" Rourke inhaled deeply, letting the aroma scald his nostrils pleasantly.

"I never joke about coffee. It's one of my biggest vices. I take beans, a small grinder, and a brewing unit on every trip. That's the mark of a professional traveler. You always bring along a small piece of home to remind you of what you've left behind."

"I stopped doing that years ago."

"You're not a professional traveler." Alexis shook her head. "You're a nomad. There's a big difference. Nomads never go home."

He nodded and sipped from his cup. The dark liquid traced a warm path down his throat as he swallowed.

And the ghosts of his past reared up inside of him: wives and friends, his parents, the old house on Telenor, corpses littering the trenches on Atasca. His hand trembled as he set the cup down on the small table beside the field. The woman looked at him with questions in her brown eyes.

"In a few cycles you'll be gone," he said simply. "Taking your coffee with you. No sense getting readdicted to a substance I kicked long ago."

"Spoken like a true nomad." Her laughter was soft and musical.

"What time is it, anyway?" Rourke rubbed his eyes, welcoming the pain from the fresh bruises. It helped push his past back into the distance.

"Three point eight."

"Only gives me two-tenths to stop by my place, clean up, and head for the office. I'd better be going." He stood and pulled on his coveralls, his joints protesting noisily. "You need a tour guide for today?"

"You offering?"

"No." He shook his head. "Too damn much work to do. Besides, I couldn't find my way around this place if my life depended on it. But I'm sure I could find someone willing to show you the sights."

"Don't bother." She shrugged. "I need to survey the entire

station, not just see the tourist attractions. A guide would only slow me down."

"Whatever you say." But her explanation did not ring true. The little nagging voice in his head was back, whispering softly.

"So, shall I expect you for dinner?" she asked, changing the subject. "Or am I another addiction you'd rather avoid?"

"I think it might be too late to avoid that little problem," he said, and felt incredibly foolish before the words had left his mouth. Realizing how true the statement was only increased his embarrassment.

"At any rate," he stammered, "I'll . . . be here."

To spy on the spy, Rourke asked himself silently, or to sleep with the spy? A little of both.

"I'll be waiting," Alexis teased. "Unless I get a better offer while I'm looking around the station today."

"Not a chance. Or maybe you're into aliens?"

"Didn't you know?" She kissed him lightly and patted his paunch. "I'm partial to fat old men."

Before he could respond, she darted into the hygiene unit. She grinned at him from beyond the half-closed door. "See you tonight."

Then the door slid shut, and he was alone with his doubts.

By the time Rourke reached the lobby, his suspicions were back up to full strength, overpowering his confused emotions.

He left the Inn of Peaceful Rest and walked down the concourse in the general direction of his hotel. As soon as he was certain no one was following him, he slipped into a comm-link booth and punched in Thunder's code.

Rourke was uncomfortable making the call in such open surroundings, but unlike the comm at his hotel suite, the public unit, he was certain, had not been wired. A few moments later the Wormat's grim visage appeared, his cinnamon-brown fur a distinct olive green in the scrambled color tones of the dilapidated screen.

"Ah, Ser Rourke," the Wormat purred. "I did not expect to hear from you again so soon. To what do I owe the pleasure of this call? Not more trouble, I hope."

"I don't know yet," Rourke said cautiously. "But I was hoping you could do a little security work for me. Maybe get me some answers. Find out if we're in trouble."

"That's part of my job." Thunder cocked his good ear forward intently. "What's the problem?"

"You got anyone on staff who can tail a person without being spotted?"

Thunder nodded. "One, possibly two."

"Good." Rourke took a deep breath to steel his nerves before plunging ahead. "I want someone on Alexis Weiss at all times. I want to know where she goes, what she does, everything. And while you're at it, I want you to run an in-depth check on her, every detail of her life. You find anything suspicious or if she does anything suspicious, I want to know about it immediately."

"I'll put someone on the woman immediately." The Wormat paused, fingering his broken tusk. "Can you tell me what this is about?"

"Not yet." Rourke shook his head. "Hell, it may be nothing. But if it's what I think, we might be in for big problems."

"I understand."

"Get me a report as soon as you can. And one more thing. I want this to be our little secret."

"As you wish."

The Wormat's face vanished as he broke the connection.

When Rourke arrived at his office, Nebuun was waiting. The Eng was still huddled over the terminals, almost as though he had never left.

For a heartbeat Rourke considered telling the Eng about his suspicions regarding Alexis and his orders to the Wormat, but two small details made him hold his tongue.

One: The security pulse throbbing in his head confirmed that the office was still tapped. He damn sure did not want to share his troubles with whoever else was listening.

Two: He had no solid evidence yet. And Nebuun struck him as the sort of being who wouldn't believe his butt was on fire unless he had pictures.

"You are late," Nebuun said, glancing up at him.

"Sorry." Rourke shrugged. "Guess I'm still running on ship time."

"You are a factor now," the Eng persisted. "Promptness is a small matter. But the success or failure of a career often hinges on such small matters. A bad example can quickly spread throughout the operation like a plague. Am I understood?"

"Yes." Rourke did his best to appear contrite. "It won't happen again."

"Good." Nebuun nodded toward the terminals. "Can I assume you had your fill of desk work last cycle?"

"That'd be a damn safe bet."

"Then perhaps you would welcome an opportunity to work outside the office this shift."

"Depends on what you have in mind."

The Eng shoved a stack of hard copy toward him. Rourke glanced at the paperwork. It appeared to be a list of household items and furnishings.

"The home office is attempting to expedite the settlement of Galagazar's estate. To do so, his personal effects must be inventoried." Nebuun stared at him placidly. "Do you think you are capable of performing an inventory, Ser Rourke?"

"I think I can handle it."

"Excellent. Ianiammallo will provide you with a card key to the residence and instructions on how to locate the place. Please try and have the work finished by the end of the shift. I would like to get a crew started on the packing. After all—" a smile bent the edges of the Eng's rigid mouth "—the sooner his things are cleared out, the sooner you can move in."

And the sooner the company can stop paying rent on my suite, Rourke thought silently. But he managed a grin of appeasement. After all, getting away from his desk was worth something.

"I'll get right on it." Picking up the stack of papers, Rourke headed for the front door.

THIRTY-THREE

Khurrukkatey entered the apartment through the building's recycling unit, clambering up the slick interior of the drop shaft by wedging her body across the narrow space and using the overlapping seams as claw holds.

The Rath had no illusions about being the first to search the place. Slipping into the basement to bypass the security net, she had found a black box already wired into the junction. It was a professional job, with the subloop feeding a permanent green signal into the main computer. The hardware was generic and completely untraceable, and after checking it for function, she decided to leave it in place.

She spent longer than usual scanning the apartment for signs of life. The Rath did not want to interrupt anyone. Once she was certain the rooms were empty, she pushed open the small square hatch on the recycler and wriggled out through the narrow gap into the kitchen. Her equipment harness kept snagging on the metal frame, and she had to stop several times to work it free. By the time she fell out onto the floor, she was panting and gasping for breath.

One glance around confirmed her suspicions—she was definitely not the first unauthorized visitor to have entered the apartment in the past few cycles. Someone had conducted a very thorough search. The contents of every cabinet and drawer had been emptied onto the floor. Alien foodstuffs formed a multi-colored slime on the tile. The charnel-house reek made her eyes water.

The rest of the rooms were the same. Whoever had done the work had been brutally efficient. Every furnishing had been upended, every piece of art shattered, every padded surface razored and gutted, with white batting thrusting out like pale streamers of furred intestines. Even some of the wall panels had been removed, exposing bare wires and insulation.

They had come through the front door, burning out the lock internally. Quite logical, because only a Rath could have entered through the recycler. Then the front door had been pushed shut and the windows mirrored so everything would look normal from the outside.

Khurrukkatey chittered softly, a sound of pure admiration. Chances were good that they had not left anything behind. Still, she had her orders.

The Rath began her search in the front room.

Three times during the long trek to the apartment Rourke lost his way among the twisting internal corridors.

Direction was a major problem in every Vost construct he had ever visited. Bugs tended to build their orbitals the same way they built their free-form dirtside structures. On planetary surfaces Vost tunnels followed the contours of the soil rather than a standard geometric design. Their stations tended to have the same lack of internal organization. The terms "radial" and "axis" seemed to be arbitrarily assigned. Passageways doubled back randomly, merging into tangled snarls or emptying into vast open areas filled with small living quarters or crowded with shops.

The factor residence was near the core, in an upscale, low-grav sector.

Rourke found it on his third sweep along the passage after twice driving past the front of the building. The neighborhood was definitely reserved for station personnel who had achieved permanent status—nothing like the transient sectors with their boxy sleep cubes and bars and strip and gambling joints.

Pulling the tram onto a parking strip, he shut down the mags and walked to the front entrance, knees and back bent to clear a lower than usual ceiling.

The facade was a series of interlocking octagonal geodesics formed from mirrored plasteel. His reflection stared back at him from a thousand glittering facets, hunched and stooped. The universal card slid easily into the slot with a soft click. A pair of the geodesics hinged back soundlessly.

Inside, the small lobby was tall enough for him to stand upright. Air-purifying vines covered with flowers swept up two of the three walls, the creepers firmly rooted in clear troughs of crystalline hydroponic solution. Brilliantly colored aquatics swam in the fluids. The air was fragrant, free of recycled impurities and the taint of ozone from the trams and dock vehicles. A spill of water tumbled down the face of the third wall, musical notes tinkling from strategically placed shards of metal.

A series of ramps ascended into the upper levels, with vines spilling over them to form archways filled with the soft perfume of the radiant blooms. No doubt there were Vost living in the unit, as well. They must have thought the smells a symphony. In fact, the entire gardening scheme had the touch of a Vost gardener.

His footsteps echoed loudly as he went up the narrow rampway.

To Khurrukkatey the approaching footfalls were like thunder crashing against her delicate ears.

Heart pounding, she checked her wrist scanner. A single heat signature was coming up from below. Upright, so it wasn't a Vost. The body temperature was all wrong for it to be an Eng. And it wasn't big enough to be a Wormat.

Human.

Her mind raced. Weiss? No, she thought frantically. Too tall. Too heavy. Who, then?

"Spray and dung," she swore under her breath as the identity slotted into her brain. The only other Human on station was the new factor!

Khurrukkatey bolted for the kitchen. Scrambling over the scattered debris, she dived into the recycling chute, twisting and turning frantically, trying to squeeze back through the narrow opening to safety.

The recycler slammed shut behind her as she dropped into the chute—and did not fall.

She realized with growing horror that she was stuck in the shaft.

Her equipment harness had somehow gotten snagged on the recycler's external lock. She tried to force the small hatch open but was unable to counter her own body weight as she dangled from the harness.

The Rath hung suspended in the shaft, her breath racing. She dimly heard the footsteps on the ramp outside the apartment growing louder. There was a sudden silence, followed by a sharp pounding. Moments later metal screeched as the apartment door was forced open, frozen rollers grating across the guide rails.

With a strength born of terror, Khurrukkatey jerked on the harness, straining against the fabric. The belt tore without warning, the recycler door clanging open as her weight was released.

And Khurrukkatey was falling, tumbling uncontrollably down the narrow chute.

Rourke had found the apartment by matching the Patois numerals on the door with the code on the card key in his hand. The first time he inserted the card into the lock, nothing happened. After reinserting it several times without success, he resorted to more technical methods—several sharp blows on the top of the box with one fist.

A dark powder flaked out of the card slot. Rourke looked down at his hand and noticed the smears of fine black soot, stark lines on his palm and fingers as well as on the glossy surface of the card. The lock had been fried.

Alarms started clanging inside his head.

Rourke switched his optics to infrared and scanned the room beyond the wall. Nothing inside was hot, so he tried pushing on the door. The panel moved slightly, scraping on the rails. He shoved harder and succeeded in opening it wide enough for him to squeeze into the darkened interior. Groping along the wall, he found a light switch, blinking his optics back to standard visuals as the illumination panels flickered to life.

Chaos greeted his eyes. The place had been trashed, furnishings overturned, cabinets emptied, shelving units stripped.

Something clattered in one of the back rooms, a metallic clanging.

Rourke dropped into a defensive crouch and scanned the debris for a handy weapon. His hand closed around a broken table leg. A second sweep with his infrared vision still revealed no heat sources. He crept toward the doorway into the next room.

It must once have been a kitchen. But now the place looked as if the recycler had exploded. The door to the recycler was standing open. Rotten food littered the floor, empty canisters and containers, plates and utensils.

Another crash, this one distant, boiled out from the depths of the recycler.

Rourke stepped over the debris and approached the chute. More noises rattled up from below, as if something alive were thrashing around in the litter at the bottom of the shaft.

And then Rourke was sprinting for the front door.

By the time Rourke reached the service level, whatever had been in the recycler was long gone. Among the garbage at the bottom of the shaft, he found traces of blood and a few tufts of dark hair. There was nothing else.

Pocketing the fur, he returned to the upper levels, stopping to pound on every door he passed until he finally found someone at home. The groggy Vost who answered his deafening knock must have thought Rourke a vision from hell. Rourke reeked of the recycler. His clothing was stained and soiled.

"I want you to call Thunder-of-Rushing-Waters," he commanded the wary neuter. "Tell him that Casey Rourke needs him at the factor's residence immediately. And tell him to come alone."

The Vost assented without argument. After it had taken a good look at Rourke, there was probably no one on Mael it wanted to call more than the head of station security.

Back at the apartment Rourke took a minute to scan the place and confirm that there was no one still hiding in any of the rooms. In the kitchen he found another tuft of the stiff brown fur caught in the metal frame of the recycler chute. There was a piece of fabric wedged in the hinge, part of a belt pouch.

As he stood up, a glittering fragment on the tile beneath the recycler door caught his eye. The glossy black crescent was five centimeters long and sharp as a blade.

It had been more than ten standards since he had last seen a similar shard, and at the time Rourke had been half a galaxy away from Mael, but his guts still turned cold as he recognized the gleaming claw.

A Phura talon.

He closed his eyes, and suddenly legions of Phura once again boiled out of Atasca's trenches, flames gouting from their weapons as the ships of their Oolaanian masters roared overhead. When Rourke reopened his eyes, he was trembling, cold sweat beading his face.

It was a long time before he had the courage to bend down and retrieve the glittering chitin dagger.

THIRTY-FOUR

Thunder came alone.

Rourke heard the Wormat ascending the ramps at a trot, his heavy footfalls causing the entire housing structure to vibrate. He paused outside long enough to examine the lock, then stepped through the open doorway, bending to keep from clipping his good ear on the lintel. For a moment the boar stood in the frame of light spilling in from the corridor, puffing from the exertion of his run. His gilded eyes narrowed to slits as he scanned the wreckage.

"By my ancestors' graves," he muttered softly.

"Yeah," Rourke said. "One hell of a mess."

Thunder moved slowly through the apartment, stepping carefully over the debris. In the kitchen he squatted down on his haunches and fingered a broken piece of pottery with one blunt digit.

"This was no simple burglary," the Wormat announced finally. "Whoever did this was looking for something." He took a deep breath, wrinkling his snout at the stench. "From the smell and the way this food has decayed, I'd say this happened five, maybe ten cycles back.''

"That's the way I figure it, too." Rourke glanced over at the Wormat, their eyes meeting. "Except there was someone inside this place when I arrived.''

"You get a look at them?"

"No." Rourke shook his head. "Didn't see anyone. But I heard something crashing around in here.''

"Suppose you start from the beginning.''

"Okay." Rourke reached back with one hand and massaged the tense muscles in his neck. "Home office wants to finalize Galagazar's estate, so I came over here to do an inventory. Once I got here, I tried the card key, but the door wouldn't open. That's when I noticed the lock had been fried.''

"Saw it on my way in. Very professional." The Wormat tugged on his good tusk. "You check the security net?"

"Junction's been hot-wired to a subloop in the service level. Everything's permanently green.''

"So after you spotted the lock, what did you do next?"

"I managed to shove the door open. As soon as I was inside, I scanned for life, but there didn't seem to be anyone home. About that time I heard something crash in the kitchen. I raced in here and found it empty, just like the rest of the residence. But the recycler door was standing open, and I could hear noises coming out of the shaft, like someone or something was thrashing around in the trash at the bottom.

"By the time I reached the service level, whatever was down there had fled. But I found traces of blood." Rourke dug in his pocket and produced the tufts of hair. "And this fur. There was a matching clump caught in the door of the recycler.''

"It does not make sense." Thunder took the tuft and examined it closely.

"Whether it makes sense or not, that's what happened.''

"I do not doubt your story, Ser Rourke. But this is an old break-in. I would stake my reputation on that fact. And whoever did the work was very good." His sweeping gesture encompassed the room. "Look at this place. By the time they left, they had either found what they were searching for or were certain that it wasn't here. I do not believe they would have returned.''

"I don't think they did. This was someone else.''

"Please explain.''

"Simple. If you've gone through all the trouble to bypass the net and burn the lock, why in the hell would you crawl in through the recycler?'' Rourke jerked a thumb at the open hatch. ''Whoever I interrupted didn't know about the first break-in until they were inside. But I'd bet they were both looking for the same thing.''

''Any idea what that might have been?''

''I don't have a clue.''

''But there are other things, other facts you have not shared with me.'' The Wormat looked at him closely. ''I think it is time you told me everything you know.''

''Yeah,'' Rourke said softly. ''Maybe you're right. But I want to warn you, I've got damn little evidence, and some of this is going to sound pretty crazy.''

''Why don't you let me be the judge of that?''

''As you wish.''

Taking a deep breath, Rourke spilled his story.

When Rourke had finished, the Wormat was quiet for a time as if digesting the information.

''I'm afraid you have left me with more questions than answers,'' he said after the silence had grown uncomfortable. ''For example, how did you know the offices and your rooms were wired?''

''Simple enough.'' He tapped the back of his skull. ''I've got an implant, a personal security net. A little something donated to me by a former employer. One of its functions is to scan for surveillance devices.''

''You have certainly had a most interesting past, Ser Rourke. Perhaps that explains your suspicious nature.''

''My suspicious nature has kept me breathing on more than one occasion.''

''And I'd wager it has gotten you into trouble almost as often.'' The Wormat smiled slightly, a flash of yellowed teeth. ''However, I think your instincts are correct in this case. It does look like someone murdered Galagazar. But I am not so certain that it involves the Human Alliance or that Weiss is with the Bureau of Human Affairs. There is another possibility.''

''Such as?''

''There are a number of Quadriate corporations interested in the musk trade.''

''You figure this for some kind of a corporate takeover?'' Rourke asked, shaking his head in disbelief.

''Ser Rourke,'' Thunder said patiently, ''you are a relative newcomer to the Quadriate. Obviously you have never experienced a business transaction of this nature. While they are rare, let me assure you, corporate conflicts can be quite violent.'' He touched a rope of scar on one wrist as if remembering the bite of a distant blade.

''Many aspects of the present scenario are consistent with a hostile takeover. Certainly it would explain the surveillance devices in your office and hotel suite. As for Galagazar's death, it's possible that he discovered the plot and had to be silenced. Or he might have been involved in the plans and attempted to double-cross them. It would not be the first time that such things have happened.''

''But what about Weiss?''

''Perhaps she's exactly what she claims to be, a corporate rep.'' Thunder shrugged loosely. ''Her visit might be nothing more than an untimely coincidence.''

''I might be willing to buy your explanation, except I hate coincidences. And your story doesn't explain this.'' Rourke shoved his hand into his pocket, his fingers closing around the cold sharp angles of the Phura talon. He pulled the claw out and thrust it toward the Wormat. ''I found it over by the recycler. Ever seen one before?''

''No.'' The boar shook his head.

''It's a talon from a Phura warrior.''

''Are you certain?''

''Yeah,'' Rourke said, his voice quavering. ''Once you've seen a man disembowled by these, you don't forget what they look like.'' He swallowed hard. ''The Phura are a slave species of the Oolaan. Puppets, really. If the Phura are around, the Oolaan aren't far away.''

''So you think it was a Phura that you interrupted earlier?''

''Not a chance. A Phura is too damn big to fit in that recycler. They must have done the first search. Probably broke the claw carving up some of the paneling.'' Rourke rubbed his jaw, stubble rasping against his hand. ''But however it got here, that claw is proof of Oolaanian presence on station.''

''And you think Weiss was sent by the Bureau to find out why the Oolaan have come to Mael?''

''Exactly. And I don't blame them. Fact is, I'd like to know myself.''

''So what's your plan?''

''Your guess is as good as mine,'' Rourke stammered. ''Why're you asking me?''

"I am asking you," the Wormat said, carefully enunciating every word, "because you are the station factor."

"Yeah, well, remind me someday to tell you how I got this job. I'm sure you'll find it fascinating."

"However you managed your promotion, it doesn't alter the fact that you are in charge." The boar stared at him. "What are your orders?"

"All right." Rourke nodded firmly. "Let's get a team up here to check this place over. Send a second team down to the old factor offices and have them go over it again."

"What shall I tell them to look for?"

"Anything unusual or suspicious—anything they can't identify." Rourke gestured toward the heaped debris. "Based on the condition of this place, they'll probably find a whole lot of nothing. But it's obvious that Galagazar knew something he shouldn't have known. I figure he was killed to keep him quiet. And whoever took him out is afraid he left some kind of evidence behind. Maybe we'll get lucky and stumble onto it. I'd feel a whole hell of a lot better about this mess if we at least knew why everyone is suddenly so damn interested in Mael Station."

"Perhaps the evidence is not in a physical form. Galagazar was the factor; he had unlimited access to the computer system."

"Good point. Get somebody to do a global record search. Same instructions—anything unusual."

"Consider it done. Shall I maintain the surveillance on Weiss?"

Rourke nodded. "And have that fur analyzed. I'd like to have a long chat with whatever was crawling around inside the recycler."

"So would I."

The Wormat was silent for a long moment, surveying the broken furnishings and rotting food. Finally he glanced back at Rourke. "Are you going to notify the home office?"

"Standard operating procedure, isn't it? When in doubt, call your boss." Rourke grinned.

"If you are wrong about this, it will cost you dearly."

"You think I'm wrong?"

The boar glanced around the apartment a final time and shook his head.

"Neither do I."

"Well," Thunder said as he stood up, his joints cracking.

"I'd better get some bodies up here. I'll let you know if we find anything."

"Good. Now, if you'll excuse me, I think it's time I had a little chat with Nebuun."

Pocketing the Phura spike, he headed for the door. The chitin was cold and hard against his thigh.

THIRTY-FIVE

Soft footsteps in the corridor, a hesitant touch on the door—they were all that announced the presence of a timid messenger outside Gral's rooms.

Gral Il Chedo glanced up at the door and then toward the clock on the wall. The device was an alien design, a band of darkness that grew along a horizontal bar of light, with the length of the shadow marking spans and quarters. The darkness had almost eclipsed the light.

It was time to begin.

"Enter," Gral called, affixing his symb's print to a final document, a minor task requiring his chedo's clawed fingers more than his mind. As the door slid open, he stuffed the text into a slot and cleared his desk.

A young leera stood in the corridor. She was a being on the cusp, the path not yet chosen for her future elevation, her life's direction still unknown. Gral could hardly remember a moment when his direction had been a mystery. He had always seemed to be plunging along this road, this path from darkness to light, as surely and inexorably as the clock on the wall.

"I am sorry to disturb you, my Chedo." The leera bowed in deference, awestruck to be in the presence of the one they called the Filitaar.

"Do not be afraid, little one," Gral purred softly. "Your wisdom enhances my being."

"As yours does mine." Another bow, this one with the traditional exposure of throat to claws.

"What message do you bring to me, Leera?"

"I am sent by Vaz Il Tran to tell you that all is in readiness."

"Very well." It was Gral's turn to nod. "You have done your duty. Return to the priest and tell him I am on my way."

"It shall be as you wish, my lord." The leera kept its head down and backed quickly from the room.

So the moment had finally come. In the lower chambers, the priest was waiting with his chemicals, his equipment, and his prayers, ready to initiate the forced calving necessary for Gral's plan to succeed.

Gral felt giddy, drunk with an odd combination of elation and fear. Surely his excitement was as great as that of Dar's leera, Rem, who waited in her room for her own transformation. Greater perhaps, for Gral's elevation would be much more than an individual accomplishment. It would be the culmination of a racial struggle, the transitional point when the glorious future planned for the Colby by long-dead leaders would become reality.

Gral stood for a while, examining his reflection in the mirrored stone. A chedo, that was all. Yet there was something about his presence, a tangible power that radiated from him. Was he truly the Filitaar for whom they had so long waited? Gral did not know, but there were many who had faith that his line marked the end of an era, the end of decades of darkness and submission to alien powers.

And if he died in the attempt to bring glory to his people, at least he would die pure, without allowing his essence to be merged with the impure minds of Dar and Harn Il Chedo.

On the wall the clock struck a new span. The bar of darkness vanished in a gleam of bright gold.

Gral smiled, donned his robe of office, and moved out from his chamber into the corridor.

Kars was in his chambers.

The door slid open at Gral's approach; the hetta troopers were like stone guardians carved into the wall, immobile. Their eye stalks were rooted in place, focused on a point in space somewhere beyond the chedo's shoulder.

If the jujun had been sleeping, Gral could detect no sign. The creature was standing at attention before Gral entered, limbs raised in salute, head back slightly to expose the throat, but even that traditional gesture held a note of readiness, as if the jujun might have attempted a defensive move had Gral tried to take his life. To kill without reason was Gral's right, and he knew that if he desired it, the act would not be denied. But it was reassuring to know the jujun was always prepared.

Ambush came only to those who were complacent. Kars was always on guard.

"Welcome, my Chedo," Kars said, his symb's voice a guttural bark. "I am honored by your presence."

"As I am by yours," Gral replied. "It is time."

"All blessings be to the All Knowing and his Filitaar." The jujun saluted, a fanatical devotion evident in his every move.

"You are in charge until I return." Gral slipped the command insignia from his breast and placed it on the jujun's uniform. "You are my strong right limb. Keep my enemies at bay while I am gone."

"I will not fail you, my Chedo." There was a deadly earnestness in the jujun's expression, a mad intensity.

But Gral found the madness pleasing. For it was on the backs of fanatics that empires were built.

"May the All Knowing guide your thoughts in my absence, Kars."

"How can it be otherwise when the Filitaar himself guides me with his words?"

Gral turned away and headed for the door. He could go to his division in peace, his command secure.

And pity the fool who stumbled into his domain unwittingly while he was gone.

Gral dismissed his guards on the upper level and descended to the laboratory alone. His solo walk was a concession to the traditions of elevation—the initiate always entered the temple alone.

The laboratory was in an old storage room that once had been used to hold bulk grains for the raas diet. The tran had converted the chamber into a magical place, part hospital, part temple, the aisles crowded with equipment and machinery. The scents of change chemicals and electricity filled the warm air. As he stepped inside, Gral felt a charge surge through him, as if he were bathed by an invisible energy radiating from the gleaming hardware, cleansing his being.

Vaz Il Tran waited for him before a small makeshift altar, limbs raised in prayer. Incense burned beside him in two glowing braziers. Offerings waited on the small stone slab.

He finished his benediction and turned to face Gral, another blessing instantly on his symb's rigid lips, the beast's spindly arms moving in the prescribed manner.

"Are you ready, my Chedo?" the priest asked, a traditional question that did not need an answer.

Gral nodded.

Vaz helped him disrobe and led him to the table. The metal was cold to the touch, and Gral's chedo recoiled nervously. He forced it to lie prone.

Another blessing and another shrill prayer. Gral watched the tran's motions with a growing sense of anticipation.

It was an odd combination, this insistence that prayer and science be fused into a comprehensive unit. Which was an act of purification and which a preparatory action required by the medical realities of the division process? The two were joined so well as to be indistinguishable. Gral heard the prayers and felt the sting of needles in his chedo's flesh. Tubes were inserted into every bodily orifice. Monitor plates were pasted to his symb's skull and chest. Catheters and blessings, heart monitors and invocations merging into a single unity of motion.

Then there was a pause and the tran laid its skeletal digits upon Gral's chedo. The creature's eyes glittered and burned with blessed fury as though infused with Kars's fanatical madness.

"Go with the thoughts of the All Knowing."

Gral could not reply. Tubes blocked his symbiote's vocal cords, but he forced it to nod and then watched as the bony fingers touched a contact and the medicines flowed into his chedo's veins.

There was the rush of acceleration, the light focusing to pinpoint clarity.

Before beginning to withdraw, Gral checked his symb's internal systems. All vitals were normal: breathing and heart rates, pulse and pressure. The lowbrain was dull and placid with drugs.

The moment of truth—the point when all experimentation and coaching ended and success hinged on his trust in the tran's abilities.

He began to withdraw slowly, pulling his essence out of the cavity he had carved so long ago in the brain of the chedo. Gral retracted each probe with infinite care, monitoring to see that there was no adverse change in the beast's condition as he released his hold and the life-support machines assumed control.

It was a long process.

Gradually, he realized that he was free. He had no sense of flesh surrounding him, only the vague sensations of space and exposure and intense vulnerability.

After a time he sensed the presence of the tran and of several others, the smaller forms of leera acolytes. It was hard to control his instincts, hard to keep from flowing toward them and seeking out their living flesh for his own. But he stayed his urges and waited.

Movement.

It was an undefined motion, for he no longer had a reference for direction, no up or down, no left or right. His was a universe of darkness, of impulses that he had long before forgotten how to interpret.

Something touched his lower hemisphere, a contact flooding him with energy. He recognized the curved surface of the life-support table, the device that would strengthen and nourish him during the coming ordeal, providing the sustenance that would prevent his essence from encapsulating and sliding into hibernation. Extending pseudopods, Gral searched for the network of veins that he knew spanned the table, permeable membranes rich with oxygenated blood. Finding one, his essence surrounded it and began to feed greedily.

Gral relaxed, letting the rich fluids fill him, his essence swelling slowly. Soon, when he was strong enough, he would begin to divide.

One would become three.

Then in due time, three would be one again.

And the Filitaar would rise to lead the people into the universe.

THIRTY-SIX

"Who else knows of this matter?" Nebuun asked calmly, his rubbery features assuming an emotionless expression.

"Thunder-of-Rushing-Waters," Rourke answered. "No one else."

They were alone in the small room where Rourke had brought the Eng after demanding that they have a private conversation. Annexed to the rear of the warehouse, the chamber had been used to store building materials: precast panels and lengths of plasteel beams. Rourke leaned against a stack of corrugated metal sheeting; Nebuun was seated on a carton of plastic rivets.

"Good," the Eng said, nodding decisively, his enormous head and sloping shoulders moving as a single unit. "The Wormat knows how to keep quiet. But I still wish you had come to me first. I should have been told as soon as you knew the offices were being scanned."

"I'm sorry about that." Rourke shrugged. "But I don't really think it matters much, does it? I mean, would you have done things any differently?"

"No." Nebuun tried to smile. The stiff cartilage that formed his lipless mouth bent slightly, and his aural pits were misshapen by the strain. "For a novice, you have handled the situation remarkably well. Once again you demonstrate latent abilities, which makes me think that there is hope for you yet."

"So what now?"

"We continue on the course you have set and wait for the Wormat to make his report. Though I must admit, the thought of leaving the surveillance devices in place is most distressing."

"Fragging the bugs would be simple, but it wouldn't serve any purpose. They'd probably just replace them with something more sophisticated, and they'd know we were on to them. Better to have them think we're slow. Maybe they relax a little too much on something else and we get a break. Besides, if we watch what we say in the office, they don't get anything valuable, anyway."

"You are right. Still, the thought of someone listening to my every word—it leaves me feeling vaguely unclean." The Eng rubbed his webbed digits across his skeletal thighs, loose flesh sliding, moisture glistening beneath his palms. He stood slowly, using both arms to lever his soft round body upright. "I wish to be informed the moment you have additional information."

"You'll be the first to know. In the meantime, what do we tell the home office?"

"Nothing."

"Say again?" Rourke shook his head as if to clear his hearing. "You don't think we should report any of this?"

"At least not until we have more specific information."

"You can't be serious."

"I assure you, Ser Rourke, I am very serious." The Eng took a deep breath. "Indulge me for a moment . . . please?"

Rourke gave him a slow nod.

"Can you tell me what information you would include in your report to Central?"

"Fact one," Rourke answered, counting the points off on his fingers, "the factor offices are bugged. Two, someone apparently murdered the previous factor. Three, we have a Human spy on station. Four, there is a good possibility that there are also Oolaanian operatives on Mael. I miss any of them?"

"No. You were quite thorough." Nebuun took another deep breath, fluids rattling in his thick chest. "Now, let us examine each of these—problems. Shall we?" He paced across the dusty floor, his sandaled feet leaving wide prints. "Are we incapable of dealing with the presence of surveillance devices in our own offices?"

"No, but—"

"Please." Nebuun silenced him with a wave of one hand. "I want you to listen carefully to what I am saying. You must understand my reasoning in this matter. For soon it will have to be your reasoning, as well. Do you understand?"

Another nod.

"Good. The first thing you must remember is never to contact the home office with problems that you can solve yourself. To do so is both foolish and dangerous because it suggest incompetence and invites needless intervention. Keep in mind that in a Quadriate corporation, a cry for temporary assistance is often interpreted as a need for permanent replacement.

"Now then, in regard to your suspicions that Galagazar was murdered. Do you have proof of your allegations?" The Eng raised one hand again, stopping Rourke before he could utter a sound in reply. "You do not.

"Burdening the home office with unsubstantiated allegations can lead to grave consequences. If the allegation is shown to be false, then you have done nothing except prove your inability to function as a station factor. And you must not forget the possibility that the home office will see your premature report as a request for assistance. As we have already discussed, this is a career-ending scenario. Are you still following me?"

"I'm right behind you. But what if the situation is beyond your abilities?"

"In that case, contact your superiors. However, you must be very certain before you take such a drastic step. Do you presently possess enough information to make that decision in this instance?"

"No." Rourke rubbed his jaw. "Not yet. But what about the presence of Human and Oolaanian operatives on station? Isn't that something Central should know?"

"Why? What would you have them do? Ask the Quadriate to send ships and troops? Evacuate the station? Arrest the woman?"

The Eng raised his thin arms helplessly. "We are not at war with Humanity. Nor are we at war with the Oolaan. And as far as we know, the woman has broken no laws. How could we justify her arrest?

"And if the Quadriate does respond with ships, who would pay for the deployment? The station and ultimately the United Trading Authority would be charged for the support. How would we feed the influx of additional population? Where would we house additional personnel in a station already jammed with seasonal laborers? And what about the disruption to the harvest? It would be a disaster."

"Suppose the Oolaan are planning their own disaster?"

"That is what we must find out for ourselves. But you cannot go to Central with idle speculation. Nor with which should be handled internally by station personnel."

"Correct me if I'm wrong," Rourke said, scratching his head, "but aren't you the same person who told me to call my superiors when in doubt?"

"If you cannot discern between a crisis and a problem," Nebuun said, his face very sober, "you will never survive as a factor."

"All right. You've made your point. We'll handle it from this end. And we don't call the home office unless we're forced to."

"You are learning, Ser Rourke. I find that very reassuring." The Eng reached out and touched Rourke's shoulder, turning him toward the door. "Now, I suggest we get back to the office before Ianiammallo has both of our heads."

THIRTY-SEVEN

The brazier of coals cast a feeble glow into the soft gray darkness. Waves of heat curled up from the metal bowl as lines of red and orange wormed over the coals.

Keeping her symbiote's eyes fixed on the embers, Rem Il Leera diverted its attention away from the hunger burning in its guts.

"It is a simple test," the tran explained, crouching across from her on the cold stone floor of the small chapel. "A measure of control. There are girga in the temple. You must capture one and bring it back to me unharmed. Its flesh must be pure and unmarked. No drop of its blood shall you spill.'' His symbiote's clustered eyes were hooded and dark, its pupils gleaming. "Do you comprehend the task?''

"I do,'' Rem whispered.

The dawn cry of a girga echoed distantly. Rem's symb trembled. Saliva flooded its mouth.

The tran looked up toward the oval of sky visible through the far window. Pale fingers of light were washing across the darkness, waves of color as Mael's gleam touched the magnification panels that formed the temple dome. Hands fluttering like small birds, the tran sprinkled incense on the coals, the particles sparkling and crackling. A coil of blue smoke twisted up from the flames, weaving itself through the priest's sonorous blessing.

"Go, then,'' the tran said finally, his prayers complete. "And may the thoughts of the All Knowing be your guide.''

Rem forced her leera to bow, pressing its face against the smooth round stones. When she allowed the beast to stand, its legs were rubbery and cramped from a night spent postured on the floor of her chamber. Another wave of hunger swept through the beast, so intense that it turned to nausea. Fighting the urge to retch, she prodded her leera toward the arching doorway.

On the top of the steps that led down to the green chaos of the temple, her symb caught the scent and groaned with yearning. Rem made the beast freeze, standing motionless, sucking air into its lungs in huge gulps, the scent of prey enflaming its nostrils. The need to hunt was like a demon whirling in the lowbrain.

She seized upon that need, shaping and focusing the desire, using it like a probe to reach down into the lowbrain and release hidden reserves of energy. Adrenaline flooded the leera, strength squeezed from pockets of fat, carbohydrates burning in the chemical fires of its skewed metabolism.

When Rem finally allowed the leera to descend the steps, it moved like water, flowing across the stones, silent and quick, vanishing into the tangled roots and vegetation.

Dark, dank soil smelling of humus and rot.

Green leaves and vines knit across the sky like a thick canopy. Shafts of golden light lancing down through the dense foliage.

The images punched into Rem's psyche like a coded command. Ancient structures moved within her mind as sedimentary slabs of denial and guilt canted up to release a flood of memory. Rem cringed with recognition, but she could no more avoid the oncoming anamnesis than an insect could avoid impact with the windscreen of a speeding vehicle.

She had hunted girga many times when her leera had been young and full of spirit. They had been communal affairs, Rem and Kren and others of her brood sneaking out in the darkness and slipping down to the temple grounds.

Until the early pallor before dawn they had stalked the flying reptiles and other prey, creeping through the jungle, the gestalt of life coiling around them. Recently elevated, they were still far too clumsy, far too uncontrolled and unfamiliar with their new leera forms, to actually succeed in killing anything. And as the light became a tangible presence, they would hurry back, breathless and trembling, trying desperately to reach the sleeping units before the priests made first-shift rounds.

Pleasant outings, pleasant memories. Until the last time she had ventured out into the temple grounds at night.

There had only been the two of them on the final hunt: Rem and Kren. The others had grown tired of the game and had found other pursuits. When she spoke of hunting, Rem saw a look in their eyes she could not understand, a hint of guilt and pain. It was as if their youth had somehow evaporated, drawn out of them like moisture from summer grass.

They went out in the cool darkness, Kren leading, her leera a wriggling glyph in the thick shadows. Rem followed, whispering through the stands of yaw grass and creeper, the dew wet on her symb's flushed skin.

It was dawn when Kren spotted the girga; the sun was already over the horizon.

"There!" she whispered, pointing to where the winged rodent rested in a clearing. The girga was ancient, a tattered creature crouching on the ground in a shaft of early light, letting the sun's warmth seep into its old bones.

"You take this side." Kren's symb rumbled softly, its eyes small and intense. "I'll come at it from beyond the far edge. Wait for me to get in position." Kren slipped away silently, only the movement of the grass marking her leera's passage.

The girga must have been near death, so old that its once keen senses were dulled, its reflexes nonexistent. It did not detect Rem's approach. She kept her symb low, bellying across the mossy soil, its muscles trembling.

Rem was very close when she saw Kren's leera charging from the brush. The girga spotted her at the same instant, whirling toward Rem, a single flap of its broad wings raising it from the ground. It sailed toward Rem's hiding place in a flat graceless arc.

Something roiled up from deep in her leera's lowbrain, a surge of insanity that slipped through her awkward control probes. For a moment she was the beast, her leera leaping, its taloned legs reaching, yearning. Claws snagged flesh. Screams of pain shattered the morning silence. Warm fluids pulsed and ran, a thing in her jaws convulsing and shrieking and dying.

She came back to her senses abruptly—a momentary flash of disassociation as if a veil had fallen away from her mind.

There was blood in her leera's mouth and warm gobbets of raw flesh in its jaws.

The girga was a torn, shredded mass. Throat open and gaping, purple arterial flow oozing down across leathery flesh.

Her leera was snarling, its threat rumbling across the glade.

Kren's beast stood a few paces away, frozen, eyes wide with terror. Then she was running, stumbling away through the underbrush, her symb mewling with fear and confusion.

Rem forced her beast to vomit again and again until all that surged up from its guts was thin streams of bile. But even the bitter gall did not erase the taste of blood from its mouth.

She crept back to the sleeping unit, afraid of what Kren had told the others. But her companion had kept silent.

Still, when Rem looked into their eyes, she knew a confession was unnecessary. She had learned a lesson they each had been taught: how close to the surface the beast really was and how easily it could be released.

Rem did not go hunting again.

There was a narrow tunnel through the foliage, carved out of the green by the regular passage of some small animal. Rem wriggled through the gap in silence, her symbiote as quiet as a shadow, its body sinuous and strong. Above, a girga howled for its mate, the harmonic cry slicing through the jungle din.

Freezing, her symbiote stared up into the treetops, searching for the silver flicker of girga wings against the green, like metal foil flickering in the light of the sun. Another cry, and she spotted the girga fluttering away, dancing across the tangled foliage to a perch several mega-lengths distant.

The symb hurried on beneath the cover of the leaves. Its breathing was inaudible, its feet moving like separate entities, symbiotes of her symb, selecting the placement of each step with sentient care. The rhythm of the hunt pounded against her intellect, blood lust threatening to break her grip and loose the savage primitive that lurked in her leera's lowbrain. Keeping her probes driven deep, she rode the waves of brutal emotion that surged up from her symb, balancing on the fine line between civilization and animal madness.

The base of the tree, its knurled bark creased with fissures, was a dozen body lengths in circumference. Her symb pressed itself against the fibrous surface and stared up into the green canopy, momentarily hypnotized by the flash of the girga's wings high above, where the curve of the dome merged with the leaves.

As it waited for a killing opportunity, a new scent snagged its nostrils, a smell both threatening and chilling—the spoor of a chedo boar. Her leera froze, its senses tuning in on the threat.

Rem's mind raced. Was this a part of the test? A ruse, perhaps, designed to shake her control? Certainly it would be much more difficult to manage her symb while fighting the combined drives of hunger and fear. Curling her thoughts around the symb's fear, she made it small and dense, urging the beast to abandon its winged quarry and seek out the chedo.

The symb's nostrils wrinkled as it sucked air in small gasps, searching for the spoor. It caught a ghost drift, the scent waxing and waning, and gazed around uncertainly.

There. Down low.

Dropping to the ground, the creature pushed its face into a dense thicket, its nose burning. Thorned branches scratched against its hide, snagging the now medalless fan of horns that flared from the back of its skull.

The spoor filled the thicket, the heady fearsome stench of male chedo. Rem countered the leera's fear by touching the centers in the lowbrain that controlled the creature's maternal instincts, overpowering its sense of self-preservation with the mindless need to defend its young. Falsely buoyed, the leera pushed deeper into the brush.

A damp hot gust of wind, thick with the smell, boiled up around Rem. It was all around her, yet she still could not see the beast.

The air swirled again, dry leaves twisting up from a moss-covered grating embedded into the soil.

Rem allowed her symb to approach the vent; it snuffled as it moved forward cautiously. The stench drifted up from the grating like the hot breath of a demon buried deep beneath the roots of the transplanted jungle.

She examined the grating. It was a rusted metal grid that capped an oval vent, some type of air shaft or heat-exchange duct rising up from chambers far below the compound. The tube was a narrow ferroconcrete cylinder, just wide enough so that her leera could have squeezed inside it. There was no way a chedo could have fit into the pipe, which meant that the creature had to be in the lower chambers and she was safe. Her fear gradually subsided.

And as her terror ebbed, Rem realized there was a familiar tang to the stench. After a moment, recognition dawned. It was the smell of Gral Il Chedo that wafted up from the depths, familiar and yet somehow altered.

Sitting at the mouth of the vent, Rem let her leera sample the air, tasting the spoor and separating its components. There was a medicinal taint to the rank aroma. Change chemicals, she realized suddenly—the smell of the medicinals used by the tran during an elevation.

Change scent! Rem recoiled from the pit as though something had struck her leera. What could it mean? Surely there could be no legitimate reason for change smells in the chamber below her?

And then the chedo's bestial howl shattered her thoughts. It was a scream of confused agony, raking across her symb's taut senses.

The sound broke the spell. Rem staggered back, losing her mental grip on the leera for a second. Her symbiote responded as fear of the chedo scent flooded back into its lowbrain. The beast bolted, Rem suddenly a helpless passenger.

Another cry reverberated through the jungle. The leera sprang upward, scrambling for the safety of the heights.

"You have done well," the tran said, holding the girga in his forelimbs. "Unmarked and pure. It is pleasing."

"Thank you, my Tran." Rem forced her beast to bow.

It had taken her an eternity to regain control of her leera, because first she had needed to get her own confused state mastered. But finally she had succeeded and was able to complete the hunt, bringing an unharmed girga to the tran.

"You have proven your mastery over the demons of blood and flesh," the tran continued. "Go, now, and prepare yourself for the next trial."

Rem stood and bowed again. As she backed away toward the entrance, she stopped, almost inquiring of the tran what it knew about the chambers below the complex.

But a memory of Dar Il Chedo rose unbidden within her mind. She heard his warning again: *Trust no one.*

And what if it had been nothing? Suppose it had been a fantasy conjured by her imagination, fed and fueled by her beast's hunger and lack of sleep? The thick of the green, the dense collage of smells layered like fine sediment. Had it somehow betrayed her leera's senses?

The tran stared at her, its clustered eyes gleaming, a question painted across its furrowed brow. "What is it, novice? Does something trouble you?"

Rem stood speechless, wanting to speak, yet her voice was lost, her symb's tongue as thick as a rope in its dry mouth.

"Nothing, my Tran. A moment of meditation."

The tran said nothing, watching her as if searching the smooth planes of her leera's features for hidden secrets.

"Go now, novice. Meditate in the peace of your chamber and conserve your strength. You will need it tomorrow. Another test awaits."

"Yes, my Tran."

Rem bowed and turned, hurrying from the room as if afraid the priest might question her further.

Her symb's hearts did not stop pounding until long after she had reached the sanctuary of her tiny room.

THIRTY-EIGHT

When she returned to her hotel suite, Alexis Weiss found Khurrukkatey the Scrounger in the sleeping chamber, curled onto the dark hemisphere of the suspensor field. The Rath was busily chewing tangles from her snarled fur, her curving incisors clicking softly. She did not look up as Alexis entered the room.

"Not shy about making yourself at home, are you?" Alexis grinned down at the bedraggled rodent.

"When you sleep in a pipe," Khurrukkatey said through a mouthful of hair, "you got to take your comforts where you can find them. And speaking of finding things, I found a few little biological friends in here when I made my preliminary sweep."

The Rath pointed to a dozen small objects arrayed on the

bedside table—copper-backed insect carcasses, their shells gleaming. Examining them closely, Alexis could see the surveillance hardware embedded in the metallic carapaces and the puncture wounds where her seek-and-destroy units had carried out their prime directive.

In many ways the science of information gathering had become a microcosmic battlefield, silent, brutal carnage waged in draperies and beneath furnishings, inside walls, and in tangled jungles of spun insulation. Semisentient organic listening devices secreted themselves into selected locations. Visual units sought hidden vista points. Programmed jamming units bred and multiplied, spreading out through stations and other structures, mutating as frequencies and transmission sources fluctuated. And hunter-killers sought them out, destroying and devouring the defenseless bugs.

"This all of them?"

"All I could find. And before you even ask, I didn't eat any of them. Frakkin' metal gets caught in my teeth." Khurrukkatey chittered softly. "But the place is secure. No transmissions are going out. Your jamming net is still operational, and you've got greens on all ten hunter-killers patrolling the suite. So we can say what we want. They may be trying to listen, but they aren't hearing anything."

"Nice and generic," Alexis said, fingering one of the mangled beetles. "Not a single identifying mark."

"Like everything else in this case. One thing's sure, though: Someone has taken the bait. Got you figured for a spy."

"And they're stepping up their activities. I was tailed all through the station. Two followers, at least. Maybe more."

"You like being a target?"

"Not particularly." Alexis shrugged. "But that's the way this one goes down. My job is to make them think we know more than we do. Put the pressure on them. Force a mistake. Yours is to find out what we don't know—and fast. Confirmation window is closing rapidly. The task force is going to hit this system hard in three cycles with or without Quadriate permission. We need confirmation soon."

"You don't have to remind me," the Rath muttered. "I know the timetable. Unfortunately, I'm not having much luck in the information-gathering department. In fact, I feel a little like one of our dead friends on the table." She bent to lick a raw oval on her hind quarter.

"What the hell happened to you?" Alexis asked, suddenly noticing the cuts and bruises dotting the Rath.

"Took a fall down a recycler. I was searching the factor residence when your friend Rourke showed up."

"He see you?"

"No. But it was close. And in my haste to vacate the premises, I got careless. As you can see, I paid for it with pieces of my hide."

"Hurt bad?"

"Thank you for your concern," Khurrukkatey replied sarcastically. "But I'll live—at least until I tell you I lost some evidence when I fell. Then maybe you'll kill me. Right?"

"Depends on what it was."

"Phura talon. Found it embedded in the wall at the burned-out offices. Didn't realize it was missing until I got back here. And I don't figure it to be important enough to risk going back for it. By now that apartment must be crawling with station security."

"Don't worry about it," Alexis said. "Just confirms what we suspected, that the Oolaan were involved in the factor's death. Find anything else?"

"Nothing." The Rath pulled a clump of hair from between her teeth, her lips drawn back from her star-shaped mouth, her delicate digits searching out the offending strands. "Both the office and the apartment had been thoroughly trashed. But your hunch about the missing pilot was correct. Whoever gutted the residence and the office stripped the shuttle, as well."

"I was hoping you'd say that." Alexis smiled at the Rath's puzzled expression. "Before I went out today, I spent some time working the shuttle angle. Let me show you what I found."

It took Alexis less than five minutes to reassemble the hidden components of her microprocessor and another five to call up her data. Khurrukkatey leaned over her shoulder, stubby whiskers tickling her neck.

"Now, like I said before," Alexis explained, leading the Rath through her logical progression, "Galagazar was a broker. He didn't go out and find information. He sold information that came to him, either data that he had ready access to or items supplied to him by paid observers."

"You figure the pilot was a supplier."

"Exactly. And the records support that theory."

Alexis tapped the keys and called up a screen. Dates and times filled the display—an appointment book.

"Galagazar was smart enough to know that he couldn't sit on information about the Oolaan," she continued. "Not if he wanted to stay alive. So I assumed that whoever brought him the Oolaanian data must have been one of the last people he saw. I scanned his contact records, everything from his appointment calendar to his comm-link listings. Guess who came by for a little visit a shift and a half before Galagazar went to meet his ancestors?"

"The pilot."

"Any idea where the pilot was coming from?"

"Jurrume."

"You're pretty good at this." Alexis grinned at the Rath. "The pilot made his legitimate living hauling musk up from Jurrume during the harvest. A pretty simple run between the main landing field and the station. Only his last run was aborted on the inbound leg to Jurrume. Mechanical difficulties."

"You don't think there were any 'mechanical difficulties'?"

"No." Alexis shook her head. "I think that was an excuse. The pilot saw something—something that scared the hell out of him, like maybe an Oolaanian corporal unit. But on the way back to the station he decides that he might be able to turn a profit on his sighting. So he goes to talk to the factor as soon as he's docked. The rest is history."

"That would mean that the Oolaan is somewhere along the flight pattern for incoming shuttles." Khurrukkatey wrinkled her snout. "Why hasn't anyone reported seeing it?"

"Because our pilot didn't fly the normal route."

Her fingers danced across the keyboard again. The display screen changed, a continental map of Jurrume appearing, neon green lines on a dark background.

"Company records show that the standard flight path was closed temporarily due to a storm front. Three inbound shuttles were diverted.

"Our pilot was diverted first, but when he relayed back that his mechanical difficulties were the result of damage sustained in severe turbulance, the others were sent in by a different route."

"Do we have his exact flight path?"

"No." Alexis shook her head. "That information was on the shuttle. No doubt the Oolaan destroyed it along with anything else they might have found. However, we do know that it was a coastal route. And the visual feed that Galagazar sent as a teaser shows a corporal unit entrenched in a small bay.

"Which means," she finished, highlighting a two-hundred-kilometer-long section of coastline on the gleaming map, "the Oolaan must be somewhere in this area."

"I see," Khurrukkatey grunted. "Why do I have the feeling I'm headed for Jurrume?"

"Hope you brought warm clothes."

"It's a permanent condition." The Rath smoothed her dark fur. "How do I get there?"

"I'll enter your ID into the station personnel records as a seasonal laborer and arrange for you to be part of the next down-world rotation. That'll put you on the surface. After that, you're on your own. How much time will you need?"

"To get there, do the search, and get back? Give me three cycles."

"Can't," Alexis said grimly. "Headquarters wants this pinned down before the battle group begins its sweep."

"All right. Suppose I go downworld and broadcast my find-ings within two cycles? We could use the stealth unit; a single burst would be almost untraceable."

"Agreed. I'll keep my receiver tuned and open. If I don't hear from you by the deadline, I'm coming in after you."

"Didn't know you cared."

"I don't," Alexis said with a grin. "But someone's got to get that confirmation."

"Don't worry. You'll hear from me." Stretching lazily, the Rath rolled off the suspensor field. "I'd love to stay and chat, but I'd better go find a nice quiet pipe and get a few hours sleep before heading for Jurrume."

"I'd let you sleep here," Alexis said, nodding toward the suspensor, "but Rourke will be here soon. I need to get your identity input and clear out this gear before he arrives."

"You figure his angle on this yet?"

"I don't think Rourke knows anything. He just seems to be a poor unlucky bastard who's in the wrong place at the wrong time. But I'm keeping close to him just in case I've misread the situation or he stumbles onto something we can use."

"Well, I leave you to your . . . interrogations."

"We both have jobs to do."

"Right," Khurrukkatey chittered. "Only some jobs are more pleasant than others."

Still chittering, the Rath waddled over to the heating vent and slipped inside. For a few seconds the soft scrabble of nails on metal echoed faintly.

Then there was only silence.

THIRTY-NINE

It was well into the third shift before Rourke was finally forced to leave the office.

Ianiammallo and the twins had gone home at the shift change. Even Nebuun had called it quits, proving that the Eng did occasionally need to sleep. But Rourke had stayed behind, indenting forms and balancing figures, trying to keep his thoughts focused.

Phantom images of Phura warriors and Oolaanian tac-fighters hovered at the edges of his mind. Every time he stopped concentrating on the details of the task before him, they came whirling in to haunt him. Rivers of flame choked with burning corpses, the smell of ozone and charred flesh, the screams of the dying and wounded—ghostly visions poured out of his subconscious and left him trembling and bathed in a chilling sweat.

But eventually there were no more forms, nothing left to balance. And Rourke fled from the empty warehouse as though running from a graveyard.

He stopped by Thunder's office on his way to the hotel.

The office was small and cluttered. Weapons studded the walls, standard-issue gear mixed with exotics taken during crime seizures. Among the arsenal, Rourke spotted an old Spencer Pinpoint. It was fitted with Human grips.

Thunder was seated behind his workstation, his cinnamon fur gleaming like copper wire beneath the overhead lights. He looked up at Rourke's entrance and grunted softly.

"Nice to see you, too," Rourke said, settling onto the bench in front of the workstation.

"No offense intended." The Wormat grunted again. "Just assumed you'd be asleep by now."

"Don't think I'll be getting much sleep tonight." The thought of closing his eyes filled Rourke with dread. The Oolaanian phantasms were still circling, waiting for him to relax.

"That'll make two of us. I'll be here all night trying to sort through all this." Thunder patted a stack of infocubes. "Preliminary data from the residence and the factor office."

"Anything yet?"

Thunder nodded. "Some. Mostly minor stuff. Best estimate is that the residence was searched at or around the same time the recycler blew. And now that we have a better idea of what to look for, we've found some damage in the office consistent with that at the residence. So it's safe to assume the explosion was no accident."

"Which means Galagazar was murdered."

"No doubt about it."

"So, was the fire supposed to conceal his murder or destroy evidence of the search?"

"Both." Thunder pulled at his tusk. "And maybe something else. Like you said, they were looking for something. I don't think they found it, so they were probably hoping to destroy it in the explosion."

"Plausible. But why didn't they torch the residence?"

"To buy time. Whoever did this must have figured that sooner or later someone would discover Galagazar had been murdered. They wanted to ensure that the discovery would come later." The Wormat leaned forward, his eyes intense, his good ear twitching. "When they didn't find what they were looking for in the office, they were forced to search the residence. Probably went through once without damaging anything, checking the obvious hiding places. When nothing was found, they went through it again. Tore a few things up, stuff that could be repaired or overlooked. By the time they made the third or fourth pass, they were probably stripping panels from the walls.

"Which meant they eventually had to make a decision. Torch the place to cover their tracks or leave it and hope no one came sniffing around for a while." Thunder stabbed his own chest with a blunt finger. "Another fire would have attracted my attention. This way they bought themselves almost twenty-three cycles."

"Smart," Rourke said. "I wonder how many other places they've searched in that amount of time."

"I'm one step ahead of you." The Wormat pointed to a pad of paper. "Already compiling a list of places to check out. Places Galagazar frequented. I'll put somebody on it next shift."

"Anything else I should know?"

"Yeah. Found some matching hair strands in the burned offices. Same as the stuff you picked up at the residence."

"Identify it yet?"

"No. But there's a chemist down in quality control who doubles as my taxonomist. She's running it down. Probably have it classified in the next couple of shifts."

Rourke nodded. He was quiet for a minute, staring down at his hands. Finally he looked up without moving his head.

"What's happening with Weiss?"

"Nothing." Thunder chuffed softly. "My people were on her the whole time, but she didn't do anything unusual. Saw the sights. Made some notes. Very visible. Almost like she wanted to be seen."

"Maybe that's her angle; maybe she's a diversion."

"But whose?"

"It's got to be the Bureau." Rourke took a deep breath and drained it slowly through his clenched teeth. "And that's bad news. Because any time Humanity and the Oolaan collide, people get killed. People like us."

"Then we'll just have to make sure they collide someplace else."

"I just hope we aren't already too late." Rourke stood slowly. "Well, Weiss is waiting."

"You want me to cancel the surveillance for tonight?" The Wormat grinned, black lips skinning back from his fangs.

"Why don't you do that," Rourke said as he headed for the door. "I got it covered."

The Inn of Peaceful Rest was quiet.

Outside the door of Weiss's suite Rourke hesitated for a moment, stooping in the low corridor, a container of compatibles cradled in one arm. He held a large plastic jug of Wormat ale in his other hand, his finger looped through the plastic ring molded into the thick neck of the bottle.

When he pressed the call panel, it was warm to the touch. He heard the buzzer echo distantly.

"So you finally made it," Alexis said as the panel slid open. Her smile seemed warm and genuine. "I'd almost given up on you."

"Had to work late." He held up the food container. "Hope you haven't eaten."

"No." The woman shook her head, light flashing in her hair.

"Good. I brought enough to feed a small army."

"Smart man." She took the containers and led him toward the table. "What we don't finish tonight we can save for breakfast." Her laughter was soft and breathless.

They ate sitting on the floor, using the Vost bench as a table. Rourke concentrated on his meal, listening distantly to her quips about her tour of the station.

"You're quiet tonight," she said after a while. "Something wrong?"

"Distracted," Rourke answered. "There's been some trouble on the station."

"What kind of trouble?"

"Not sure." He stirred his stew absently. "Don't have all the details yet. And what we do know is confusing. But it looks like someone might have murdered my predecessor."

"Sounds serious. You think you're in any danger?"

"Could be the whole damn station is in danger. That includes you."

"Is that a warning?" She raised one eyebrow, her brown eyes studying him.

"Maybe." Rourke shrugged.

"Why would I be in danger?"

"Because," he said, watching her closely, "there are some on station who don't think you're a field analyst for Genam."

"Please don't tell Genam." Alexis shook her head and laughed. "They might stop sending me my paychecks." Then her laughter faded. "You're not joking, are you?"

"Afraid not."

"Anyone bother to check with Genam?"

He nodded. "Uh huh. And they swear you're one of their best employees. But that's the way a cover usually works. I know. I've been undercover a few times myself."

"You think I'm a spy, then?"

"It's been suggested."

"Any particular organization, or am I free-lance?"

"Bureau of Human Affairs."

"That would make sense." She took another mouthful of food. "After all, I am Human. I mean—you don't doubt that part of my story, do you? You've had firsthand experience."

"No." Rourke managed a smile. "I don't have any doubts that you're Human. It's just what you do for a living."

"Is this where I'm supposed to tell you that you're wrong?" Alexis took a long drink of her ale, her eyes sparkling at him over the rim of her glass.

"Something like that."

"Why bother? You wouldn't listen." She set her glass down carefully. "So I have a better idea. Let's talk about why I think you could be a spy."

"All right. I'm listening."

The woman paused to pour herself another glass of ale. The golden liquid gurgled from the jug, splashing into her cup.

"First of all," she said, "let's consider your background. You've had both military and security experience. Some people might consider that to be basic training for a spy. Makes you look suspicious.

"And in addition to your background, you happen to be one of a very few Humans employed by an alien corporation. You have been placed in a powerful position, which allows you access to a tremendous amount of information—a job for which you readily admit you've had no experience."

"I told you how I got this job," Rourke said stiffly.

"An incredible story. The part about the ambassador was a nice touch. Inspired, really."

"You can check it out."

"And you called Genam, didn't you?" She held his gaze, her eyes dancing.

"So you're denying—"

"Look," Alexis said, silencing him. "I'm not going to convince you any more than you're going to convince me. So let's just agree we'll both be careful and move on to other things." She raised her glass in a mock toast. "Agreed?"

"Agreed." He matched her gesture. "But I have a feeling we'll be having this conversation again. And soon."

The woman only smiled.

Several hours later Rourke lurched upright on the suspensor field, the fragments of a nightmare fading slowly from his mind. The woman stirred beside him but did not open her eyes.

As he sat on the field, shivering and sucking air into his lungs in ragged gasps, Rourke spotted something on the floor directly below him. Even in the shadowy darkness he recognized the object.

A tuft of dark brown fur.

After slipping the strands into the pocket of his coveralls, Rourke crawled back into bed.

But there was no sleep to be found in the soft contours of the suspensor.

FORTY

In the quiet darkness of her small room, Rem Il Leera crouched on the floor and tried to ease the turbulence in her brain.

Damn him, she thought bitterly. Damn Dar and his madness. For as surely as a diseased blade transmitted illness, Dar had infected her with his paranoia. His words had contaminated her mind, and a fever raged in her intellect, a pyrogen of suspicion and guilt that filtered the input from her symb, turning innocent actions into conspiracy and odd smells into proof of high treason and blasphemy.

Rem attempted to force her symb into the ritual of peace, but the litany seemed a mockery. Her mechanical prayers were powerless against the combined force of her weakened state, the darkness, and her enflamed imagination. Each time she let the beast close its eyes, the stench of change chemicals burned in its nostrils again and the agonized howl of Gral's chedo echoed in its ears.

Perhaps some time spent meditating in the temple might soothe her torment, she mused hopefully. Maybe a moment amid the green and growing would cleanse her of Dar's fears.

Or did something else call her to the depths of the jungle? Something far more dangerous than idle speculation.

Driving the thought from her mind, Rem urged her beast to its feet. The leera padded from the cubicle, its stiff muscles aching with each step, the lowbrain complaining bitterly.

The passage was dark and seemingly empty, but Rem sensed the hetta standing against the wall as she stepped out into the corridor.

At her appearance, the shadow came to life, the hetta moving out to block her way, materializing as though oozing from the gray stone. It stood solid and immobile in the corridor. Highlights gleamed on its burnished harness and the barrel of the weapon it held across its broad chest.

"I cannot sleep," Rem said. It was not a lie. "I wish to meditate in the temple."

The guard considered that for a moment, weighing the request against the heft of its orders. Evidently, what she had asked for was not forbidden.

"Very well," the guard said evenly. "I will take you there."

"I know the way," she protested.

"You will follow me."

Without further discussion the hetta turned and marched down the passage, its leather harness creaking softly as it walked. Rem had to hurry to match its long stride.

There were only a few guards in the passageways, stationed at long intervals at intersections and doorways. They did not acknowledge Rem or her escort but stood like statues in the dim light, weapons at the ready, eyes alert for danger.

At the entrance to the temple, her hetta guide stopped.

"I will await you here," it said, standing at attention against the wall.

"Thank you." Rem forced her symb to bow. "Your respect for my privacy is most welcome."

The hetta did not respond.

Rem hurried on, her symb's quick footsteps echoing inside the sanctuary. When she looked back, the hetta's chameleon hide was already beginning to take on the hue of the gray and black striated stone behind its back.

Pausing at the top of the grand staircase, Rem stared out at the moon-silvered jungle. Did she really believe that peace waited for her among the leaves and vines? No, she realized suddenly. There was only one way to quiet her fears. She had to go into the pit, down the vent into the chambers below. Only in hard proof would she find the answers that would give her comfort.

Part of her knew that what she was about to do was insane. She was risking her future to satisfy the demands of another's paranoia. But the need was beyond her control. Relaxing her hold, Rem let her symb proceed down the steps.

The pale beams of a simulacrum of Verrin's single moon filtered down through the dappled leaves. She followed the spoor her leera had left during the earlier test. The track twisted through the jungle, over rocks and logs, through dense thickets; the sharp thorns of a hidden acania traced paths down her symb's tormented hide. A riot of sound washed over her: songs and chitterings, rapid scuttlings, the brutal cries of hunter and hunted.

Then a smell reached her symbiote—the scent of chedo and the acrid burn of change chemicals.

Rem spurred her beast deeper into the tangled brush. The ground was soft and spongy, thick with dead leaves and small writhing creatures that wriggled and died beneath her symb's groping pads.

There. Her leera touched something metallic and regular: the grating.

The smell of chedo surrounded Rem as though it were heavier than the air and had collected into a sphere of subliquid density. Her symb snorted and chuffed, twitching nervously. She drove her probes deep, overriding its impulse to flee.

Kneeling, the symb gripped the center of the grating and strained to lift it. The screen came up slowly, metal scraping against ferroconcrete; a soft rasp, but to her leera's heightened senses it sounded like a shriek. For a few tense heartbeats Rem waited, expecting to hear the approach of hetta through the brush.

When she was certain no one had followed, she leaned out over the vent. Though she could not see the opening in the darkness, she sensed the yawning depth. Far below, light glimmered, a crescent of illumination from the subterranean chambers. It seemed as if the sky and soil had somehow traded places and she was staring up a tunnel into Verrin's soft night. A cruel illusion; her home was not beneath the cold soil of Jurrume.

May the All Knowing have mercy on me, Rem thought fervently as she commanded her symb over the side and into the corrugated gut of the vent. Claws scrabbled, seeking and finding slight purchase.

Rem glanced back up into the arching jungle. Far above she saw the dim light of Jurrume's pale moon.

Then, steeling her nerve, she urged her symb down into the pit.

The interior of the tube was rough, its grainy surface abrading the hide from her leera's shoulders and hips, scraping knees and elbows as the beast descended, searching blindly for holds in the pitted ferroconcrete. To keep from striking its horns against the tightly curving walls, the leera had to stare up toward the dim circle of sky. It was as if Rem were lodged in the gullet of an enormous beast, one whose hot breath reeked of chedo and medicines, herbs and plastics and holy incense.

She had barely begun the long descent when she was stopped by soft sounds from the jungle above. Was that the stealthy crackle of footsteps? Had she seen a shape momentarily eclipse the moon?

Her symb froze, senses intent. But all she heard was the pounding of her beast's throbbing hearts and the rush of blood through its veins. She spent a moment whispering the mantra of courage, trying to condense and compress the fear in her symb's lowbrain. It seemed to have little effect, but after a while she was able to continue, her leera moving its limbs cautiously.

The tube went straight down for thirty body lengths. She passed two small junctions, vents coming in from other areas. But they smelled only of sewage and waste—the scent of chedo was strongest in the main bore.

As she neared the bottom, the light grew more distinct, a gilded aura that revealed the speckled composition of the tube walls. Small clusters of luminescent algae and other one-celled plants grew on the rough surface. Clots of phosphorescence clung to her symb where it had brushed against the glowing flora, organic star clusters and constellations painted on its scales.

Finally her leera's foot touched another metal grating, this one a fine mesh. Rem halted, listening to the noises rising up through the screen: the rhythmic click of valves, the gurgle of fluids coursing through pumps, the electric hum of energized machinery.

There was nothing that indicated the presence of flesh except the smell of chedo.

Twisting painfully, the leera reversed position in the tube, head down so it could scan the area below the grating. Rem could see cobbled flooring and the angular shapes of a number of strange machines, their flat surfaces littered with gleaming instruments. In one corner there was a small stone altar.

Again she waited in silence, straining to hear anything that would indicate there was life in the chamber. Was that soft susurration the rasp of air through damp nostrils? She could not be certain.

Her symb sampled the pungent air. There was the signature of a chedo, Gral's beast. Others had been in the chamber—raas and tran—but their smells were old and cool. Only the chedo stench seemed fresh. Had he just left the room? Or was he still present, waiting in ambush for Rem to appear?

It was not too late to turn around and climb back up the tube. No one had seen her yet. If she left now, no one would know of her transgression. She could replace the grate, go back to her room, and return to her rite of elevation.

But it was as if Rem no longer controlled her own flesh. She had unknowingly and unwittingly given it to Dar back on Central. If she let her beast close its eyes, Dar appeared. She could see him standing against the montage of Dhalgri. She could still hear the pleading in his voice.

Love or insanity—she did not know which dictated her actions. But she forced her leera to slide its claws through the thin mesh and open the latches that held the grate in place.

The panel swung open, and the symb lowered itself gently. Legs gripping the interior of the tube, the beast slid forward, slowly easing its head into the chamber.

Not a living area, Rem decided immediately. A laboratory, perhaps, or a medical facility. Certainly the machines she could see were medical in nature, trannish devices scattered abstractly around the long narrow room. She had seen such units before in tran infirmaries where the sick and injured were brought for healing.

Though the scent of chedo was strong, Rem did not see any signs of flesh. Nothing moved except the machines. Satisfied that it was safe, she allowed her beast to reverse position, gripping the bottom of the grate and rolling slothlike until it hung by its upper limbs. A moment more and the creature released its hold, dropping to the floor. It landed on all four feet, tensed and ready to spring back up the tube at the first sign of a threat.

Rem waited to see if her movements had attracted any attention. When no one appeared from deeper within the complex, she prodded her leera into an upright stance.

The beast sampled the air. Plastics, free monomers released from warm machine covers and lengths of turgid tubing. Medicines, like the interior of a hospice. And change chemicals. She was certain of it.

Following the odors, Rem crept down the narrow aisle between the racks of hardware, past an array of distillation units and ventilation pumps and other large blocks of technology whose function she could not discern.

At the end of the row of machines was a small table. The scent of change was strong, drawing her like a beacon. She padded closer, torn between fear and curiosity.

The table was low, its surface curved like a basin. A large spherical mass rested in the bottom of the bowl, a lump of milky tissue, highlights gleaming from its pulsing membrane.

Rem stared at the object, sick fascination turning to horror as she realized what she had found.

A Col essence.

She had seen many essences in her time. Withdrawal was the climax of the elevation ceremony. Those who had survived the trannish trials were allowed, amid the prayers and chants of the celebrants and witnesses, to separate their small physical beings from their old flesh. The essences then calved, producing two smaller masses, which were each taken by the tran and attached to raas younglings to begin their own life journeys. The remaining portion of the old intellect was then merged with two other mature Col essences to form a single new entity and united with a symb of the next highest caste. Such was the cycle of life for the Col.

But this was an abomination. Somehow the essence had been extracted from its flesh and maintained in a state of flux, the substance kept fluid by the machines attached to it via the life-support table.

Snorting softly, her symb backed away from the quivering mass. Perhaps the sight of an essence recalled for the beast its own elevation, the moment of first contact as Col matter had spread across its face, forcing entry into its airway, acids boring an opening into the skull so that her symbiotic intellect could attach itself to the leera's confused lowbrain.

A surge of terror roiled up from the symb, and Rem momentarily lost her grip. The beast bolted, whirling to crash against another table.

And suddenly Rem was staring down at the slumbering form of Gral Il Chedo.

How long she remained motionless beside the table, Rem did not know. Gral lay as though dead, unaware of her presence. Tubes protruded from every orifice, fluids gurgling in cloudy segments separated by waste and air. The chest rose and fell slowly, the breath whistling through partially obstructed nostrils.

She examined the skull more closely. The bulges where Gral's intellect should have been—flesh swollen by many spans of experience and growth—were flaccid, sagging against the bone like melted wax. Through the yawning mouth, she could see the opening in the septum where the essence had entered and exited.

Understanding seized her brain like a fist. Gral's flesh was not dead. It still lived, sustained by the same machines that fed his essence on the other table.

Then the chedo stirred, a spasm passing through the beast.

Perhaps her leera's scent had roused it from the depths of its drug-induced slumber. Or maybe it was the soft mewling that had escaped her symb's throat, a keening whine of panic. The chedo's claws flicked out in a blind arc, talons scoring a path across her beast's ribcage.

The leera collapsed, sprawling onto the floor.

Roaring, the chedo struggled to rise. Tubes were torn free. Fluids sprayed through the air. An alarm wailed, its shriek harmonizing bizarrely with the screams of the beast.

The sound would bring help. Rem drove her probes deep and got her symb moving, stumbling and crawling toward the duct.

Footsteps echoed in the corridor.

Her flesh leapt, snagged a hold on the grate, and dragged itself up into the tube. Reaching down, it fumbled to grasp the wire panel.

On the table, the chedo was upright. Its blind eyes rolled back in its skull. A white froth of saliva dripped from its gaping mouth.

Somehow Rem managed to close the grate and snap the latches before the door slid open and a brace of leera hurried into the room. She hung motionless in the tube, praying for invisibility.

The leera attendants surrounded the bed, grabbing the thrashing chedo. They forced the beast to a prone position, struggling to get restraint straps secured.

Rem detected the urgent approach of another being. Not leera—the footfalls were too heavy. And not hetta, for there was no telltale creak of leather. She knew its identity even before the creature spoke.

"What is it? What is the problem?"

"I am not certain, my Tran," one of the leera answered. "A transient mental image, perhaps. A dream."

So, Rem thought grimly, the tran itself is part of the abomination. How deeply did the corruption penetrate? Beyond Jurrume? Into the upper echelon of the priesthood? Perhaps even Dar had not realized how far the taint of blasphemy had reached.

"Can you control it?"

"Yes, Tran." There was the sound of liquids being purged, equipment being adjusted. "An additional dose of drugs should return the beast to a sedative state."

"Do it, then." The threat in its voice was unmistakable.

Rem heard the tran move toward her hiding place. Unable to glance down, she could not see the creature as it passed below her, but she could sense it sniffing the air, searching for anything odd. She clutched the lowbrain tightly, holding her flesh rigid, not daring to let it breathe.

After a long moment the tran returned to the chedo.

"See," the leera orderly said, its voice simpering. "Already it is calm and deep in slumber."

"Excellent."

Another few minutes passed while they spoke in hushed tones, examining the gear. And then, finally, the creatures departed.

Rem was moving as soon as the door had slid shut, scrambling quietly toward the surface.

By the time she reached the top, her leera was trembling with exertion. It staggered from the tube and fell prone onto the moist soil, where it lay motionless, gasping for air. Its muscles burned with lactic acid and adrenaline.

And suddenly an enormous shape materialized from the darkness.

Rem stared up in shock at the face of a hetta, the massive beast blotting out the moon. Her symb had a chance to make one short, startled cry before a huge paw was clamped across its mouth. There was something clutched in the thick digits, a piece of fabric soaked with a cloying fluid. An astringent stench flooded her leera's nostrils. It struggled for a moment, trying to breathe.

Then there was only darkness.

FORTY-ONE

Railing against the sensory limits of his self-imposed exile, Gral Il Chedo tried vainly to interpret the fragmented images he had gathered during the past few moments of chaos. A single suspicion emerged from the montage of struggling life-forms and high-frequency vibrations that had surrounded his essence.

Something had gone terribly wrong.

Gral had suspected trouble soon after his limited senses had first detected the presence of a solitary leera in the lab. The beast's sudden appearance in a quadrant of his amaurotic universe that had never before produced such a signature had been a glaring departure from the routine of his essential existence.

Though withdrawal had reduced Gral's life to basic elements—dark and light, heat and cold, animate and inanimate—he had developed a system for measuring time. Specific intervals were segmented by the patterns of life that flowed around his essence. Rhythmic surges in the veins that fed him, regular changes in the chemical content of his nutrient fluids, the thermal fluctuations of the life-support table—all those things became the fractions of his internal clock. But by far the most dependable of his time-pieces were the routine visits of his leera orderlies.

The ability to detect living flesh was the strongest sense possessed by a Col in the essential state. It was a primitive instinct surviving from a time long before the establishment of the tran and the ritual of elevation, when the essence had been forced to hunt and subdue a beast on its own, a solitary and dangerous pursuit. Using that instinct, Gral had quickly learned to recognize the leera who visited his bedside. He knew when they would come and when they would leave.

Clusters of the leera visits were grouped into larger units by the occasional appearance of the tran as the hunched being came to stand and stare and pray over him. Though Gral could not see the priest, he could imagine the creature bowing low, brow plates overlapped with concern, a meditation whispering from taut lips. Gral found no comfort in thoughts of prayer, but there was peace in the clockwork progression of his life's new routine.

Until the solitary leera had appeared.

Gral first sensed the creature as a blot of heat in the upper corner of the imaginary cube he used to map his dark cosmos. Then he lost the presence in a swooping dive to the lower left as the glowing silhouette dropped below the horizon formed by the edge of the life-support table.

The leera reappeared, slowly approaching him. For an instant Gral toyed with fantasies of attachment and control. But the fantasies faded as he realized that the beast did not conform to previous patterns. The timing of the visit, the singularity of the presence, the hesitant movements—all those formed a disturbing gestalt: that being had no business in the laboratory.

What had gone awry? Was his symb dead or dying? Had he been discovered? Would other presences appear at any moment? Other hetta? Other tran? Minions of the Prime who would switch off the machines and leave him to harden on the cold steel?

Panic welled in him, a terror he had not known for centuries. Gral waited, trembling.

The presence loomed over him. Gral felt a whirling maelstrom of emotions as the creature stared down at his essence: fear and hate and disbelief and rage.

Suddenly the leera retreated, scrambling away as if from a fire. A single sharp tremor touched him, a shock wave jarring the life-support table. Then high-frequency vibrations began pulsing across his membrane. He sensed his chedo thrashing and struggling, the distant flesh a bulge of warm color rippling on the horizon.

Vanishing up into the same quadrant from which it had come, the intruder disappeared. Moments later, three more presences entered his sensory field in the area Gral had defined as the front entrance of the chamber—leera orderlies followed closely by the waddling shape of the tran.

All four gathered around his chedo flesh, individual forms merging into a single enormous signature. The high-frequency pulses subsided. The thrashing of his beast faded to stillness.

When they came to him, Gral tried to warn them, struggling vainly to tell them about the intruder. But he had no way to communicate with the creatures. His voice was in the chedo on the other table, a distance as wide as a galaxy for his essence to cross.

And then they were gone, drifting out of the room, leaving him to rant and rave in silence.

For a time Gral considered attempting to return to his flesh. But eventually reason regained control, and he began to formulate a theory to explain the visitation.

The intruder was a spy, of that he was certain. Probably operating alone or with little support. Most likely Rem.

Could she conceivably get a message off-world? Possibly; after all, she had succeeded in penetrating the laboratory. Safest to assume she was more capable than he had imagined.

Did she have support nearby? Possibly, but it was doubtful she had enough firepower to match his own loyal forces. Only the Triad could raise such an army, and it would take at least three cycles to reach Jurrume. Which meant Rem was too late.

In another cycle Gral would have attained enough mass to calve two segments of adult size, mindless segments, which could be substituted for the essences of Dar and Harn Il Chedo at the time of their eventual merging. And once he had returned to his flesh, Gral would destroy all evidence of his crime. The word of one addled leèra would never stand against that of Gral Il Chedo, Chosen of the Triad.

No, Gral would not crawl to his flesh and retreat. He would stay the course and continue feeding for another full span.

And when he was back in his flesh, if the leera still lived, he would personally handle her execution.

FORTY-TWO

Rem awakened slowly, drifting up from the darkness as if her consciousness were a silver bubble rising through a warm, viscous liquid. Jumbled memories assaulted her: the dark jungle, crawling through the tight confines of the duct, the abomination in the chamber, the hetta rearing up to block out the night sky. Terror gripped her mind, fear lacing her confusion.

Her symb was still not aware. For a few panicked moments she was trapped in its skull, unable to see or hear, certain that the beast had expired and that she was caged in dead flesh, too late or too slow to escape the prison of its bones. She sought out and found autonomic responses: respiration, heartbeat. The slow course of blood through veins was a gentle, reassuring thunder.

The drug wore off in measured stages. Her leera's senses gradually returned, tuning in one at a time as if someone were flicking switches from a remote location.

Sight came back first as light without focus resolved into a glimmering sphere above where her symb lay, a point of brilliance on a dark expanse. A spotlight, she realized suddenly—an angular fixture anchored to the rusted beams of a curved ceiling.

Rem kept rising up through the drug-induced lethargy, her intellect synchronizing with the leera's fuzzy lowbrain. She sorted through the erratic data filtering in from the beast's external senses, individual bytes like the tesserae of a vast mosaic that she was too near to see clearly.

Chemical taste in her symb's mouth, antiseptic and astringent, like the residue of a strong drink from the night before.

A cold hard floor beneath her leera. Stone, not plas. Solid and smooth and chilling.

The smell of dust overlaid on the ozone tang of electrical gear.

Voices. Soft, urgent whispers like the buzz of insects in the night.

"Kill her now and be done with it." An odd speech, leera words delivered in the guttural tones of a raas, a juxtaposition as jarring as the content. "Every moment we delay is a moment closer to discovery."

"No, we must keep her alive for now. She's been inside. She's seen Gral. I'm certain of it."

Rem recognized the new speaker. It was the hetta guard who had subdued her symb. She remembered his huge manipulator, the thick smell of the cloth against her leera's face, and the pressure on its neck. Rem tried to make her symbiote turn its head, but the beast's muscles were still detached. Only the eyes moved, making the room sway and giving her a distorted image of shapes beyond the perimeter of light.

"Impossible!" The raas/leera snorted with disgust.

"I saw her when she came out. And the stench. Change scent. Don't you smell it on her beast? Or are we all imagining that?"

"We've been trying to get into that lab for thirty cycles. Nothing—not a single gap in his security. Yet this one crawls inside through an open grating? I refuse to believe it."

"It would not be the first time chance has been the deciding factor in the downfall of a tyrant," her advocate insisted. "The ducting is old, the chambers below part of the original structure that predated Gral's arrival. I doubt he is even aware that it exists."

"Make no mistake; Gral knows every part of this citadel. If she found a way in, it's because she's a plant. She was supposed to find a way inside, to draw us out. And you fell for it."

"You weren't there," the hetta said stiffly.

"If I had been, we wouldn't be having this discussion. She'd be dead already." There was a chilling certainty to that flat pronouncement.

"Enough!" A third speaker, one with authority enough to silence the others, one accustomed to giving orders and being obeyed. "First we question her. Then we'll decide what to do with our guest. Wake her up."

Footsteps approached Rem. A shape loomed—the hetta guard. Kneeling, he squinted into her eyes and grunted with satisfaction.

"She's already coming around."

"Bring her up the rest of the way," the leader commanded.

"There is no time to be gracious. We must be finished here before they discover she is missing."

The hetta produced a canister from his equipment pouch. Rem heard a hiss of discharged pressure, and felt a moist spray misting her leera's muzzle, the burning chemicals searing its nostrils. Then the beast was gagging and choking, swinging erect, its muscles spasming. The contents of its stomach came surging up again and again, thin greenish puddles forming on the cold stone floor.

The spasms passed quickly, and the nausea faded. A rag was pressed into her leera's hand. She took it gratefully and completed the job, letting her symb dab gently at its horned beak, wiping away the stomach acids that dribbled down its serrated maw.

As her beast cleaned itself, Rem examined her surroundings. A gray cavern, light in the center, the edges lost in shadow. A sense of vast space and disuse.

Rem was not certain what she had expected. A torture chamber? Perhaps a tran medical unit with inquisitors and devices designed to make her confess her sins. Gral sitting in judgment, his components still separate, intellect and flesh resting beside each other on a pair of life-support tables.

Instead, she was in the center of a dusty warehouse somewhere on the fringes of the compound. Plastic cartons and fiber boxes formed walls and furniture. Hardware was stacked in a compact pyramid: portable viewscreens and data units. Weapons were racked against a wall of plasteel catalyst canisters.

There was no sign of Gral. Only a hetta and two raas laborers seated on boxes beneath the cone of light spilling down from an overhead fixture.

"Bring her over here," one of the raas said, the one with command, with power thick in its rumbling voice. The hetta obeyed, guiding her gently toward them.

Another oddity—a raas commanding a hetta. Nor did it make sense that the raas spoke so clearly. The brooding laborers were not supposed to have a mature Col intellect; their essences were just slightly more sentient than their symbiotes' sluggish low-brains, able to comprehend and understand little beyond simple tasks.

But then, nothing made much sense anymore.

Rem let her symb sit down on a box, feeling their eyes watching her.

"Where am—" she started to ask.

"Where you are is not important," the raas said, cutting her off in midsentence. "Nor is it important that you know who I am—yet. What is important is that you answer my questions. Understand?"

And maybe we will decide not to kill you. She understood perfectly. She allowed her symb a slight nod.

"Good." The raas shifted its enormous grublike body, and twin rows of manipulators folded across worn yellow breastplates. "Who sent you to Jurrume?"

"Dar Il Chedo," she said softly.

"For what purpose?"

"My elevation."

"It has been a long time, but I do not remember any test of elevation which required one to climb through a tight vent into a subterranean chamber." The hard slabs of its chitinous face slid to reveal an oval mouth, the walls of the dark cavern studded with nubs of crystalline teeth. "Gral thinks you were sent to spy on him. And as unlikely as it might seem, after the events of this past cycle, I find I must agree with him."

Rem had no answer.

"You were inside his lab tonight," the raas continued. "I want you to tell me everything. How you got in. What you saw. What happened. Leave nothing out, no matter how insignificant."

Again the unspoken threat: Your story might just save your life.

So Rem told them of her excursion into the lower chambers.

When Rem had finished, they were silent, weighing what she had relayed to them.

"If what she says is true," the hetta guard said finally, "we may be too late. He is farther along than we had suspected."

"Something must have spooked him."

"Or she lies," the other raas hissed.

"She is telling the truth. Aren't you, little one?" The chedo term of endearment sounded strange coming from the mouth of this raas who led hetta and commanded leera. "She is not a plant. If she was, Gral's troops would already be here. She is an accident. A bit of luck sent to us by the All Knowing. And we are going to use her wisely."

"How?" The dissenter seemed choked with disbelief.

"This one has found a way inside. A way only she can use. One does not throw away a tool that might be necessary later."

"But she is not one of us!"

"Need I remind you that Taj did not survive regression? We

have no leera flesh. Is there anyone else among us who can fit down that tube?''

The dissenter remained silent.

"And you will help us. Won't you, little one?'' The leader turned his gaze back to Rem.

"You are not—with Gral?'' she asked haltingly.

"No.'' The faceplates shifted again, scraping against each other, a rasp of hard-edge chitin. "You need not seem so surprised. Dar is not the only being with eyes sharp enough to spot a traitor.''

"Then who sent you? Harn? The Council of Chedo?'' And a final inquiry, not so much spoken as breathed into the dusty air: "The Prime?''

"It would be best that you did not know. Suffice it to say that we work against Gral. In that we are most definitely allied.''

Rem nodded.

"You will help us, then?''

"What would you have me do?''

"For now, go back to your cubicle. Tell no one of this meeting. Continue with your tests. One cycle, perhaps two. We will come for you when we are ready.''

"But—'' She had so many unanswered questions.

"I can tell you nothing more. And I caution you. If Kars Il Jujun should hear of anything—if one suspicion should cross his mind—he will not hesitate to kill you.'' The raas lowered his voice carefully. "I assure you, death at his command will be most unpleasant.''

But certainly no more fatal than at your orders, Rem thought cynically. She swallowed hard and fought the nausea that surged in her beast again.

"Tark will take you back to your rooms.'' He nodded toward the hetta.

The big soldier stood. There was something in his hands, a black hood. The raas must have seen the questions in her leera's eyes.

"A temporary precaution,'' the raas said, refering to the hood. "The blindfold will be removed when you reach the compound proper. It would not be wise for you to know too much. Kars can be most persuasive when extracting information. What you do not know, you cannot divulge, even to the most skilled of torturers.''

"I understand.''

"Remember, do nothing until we contact you.''

Rem nodded.

"May the thoughts of the All Knowing continue to bless and keep you."

The hood dropped over her leera's head and shut out the light. Her symb recoiled under the firm grasp of the hetta, but he pushed the beast forward, guiding it gently toward the distant doorway. Their footsteps scraped on the dusty stone floor.

Behind her, Rem heard the hissed whispers begin again, the harsh cutting sounds of argument fading to silence as she moved away.

FORTY-THREE

Rourke abandoned his futile search for sleep just before shift change. Rolling off the suspensor, he struggled into his coveralls and sat down to slip on his shoes. When he looked up, the woman was watching him silently.

"Can't sleep," he said, tightening the Velcro straps across his arches. "Might as well be working."

"See you for dinner?" She shifted position on the field and propped herself up on one elbow. The sheet fell away, exposing one small breast and a dark brown areola.

As he stared at her, Rourke felt something stir inside him, a need beyond simple lust. Love was an emotion he had thought long dead, killed by two wives and ten standards of solitude. But evidently it had only been dormant, waiting for the proper catalyst to bring it back to life.

And though certain that he was a damned fool for even considering Alexis as a lover, Rourke knew from painful experience that his emotions often overrode the protests of logic.

"I guess so," he said finally. "But I might be—"

"Late." She finished his statement with a smile. "I know the drill."

She took his hand and pulled him close. Her lips were soft and warm against his, and Rourke found it very difficult to pull away. She held his gaze, a distant sadness in her brown eyes, as if she, too, felt the same strong attraction.

Rourke could not help wondering if it was all just an act.

"You know," she said after a long silence. "What we were discussing last night. I can't be the only one who finds your presence on Mael Station suspicious." She bit her lower lip. "If you're smart, you'll start looking over your shoulder. You might even think about carrying a weapon. Especially considering the way you handle yourself in a fight."

"I'll give it some thought." He managed a grin. "Thanks for your concern."

"No thanks necessary. My reasons are purely selfish—I'd hate to see you end up like your predecessor."

"Then why don't you just tell me what's going on?"

She looked away from him.

"You know," Rourke said flatly. "Maybe not everything, but a hell of a lot more than I do. Something's going down here. Something big and bad. And you're right in the middle of it."

Alexis took a deep breath, as if considering her options, fitting his presence into her perception of reality. He could imagine the interlocking pieces sliding across each other within her mind, fitting into place, her gestalt adjusting around them. For a second Rourke thought he had broken through to her, touched some chord beyond national boundaries. But the opening vanished, and her mask of firm resolve returned.

"If, as you suspect, I am with the bureau," she said, "then you know I can't tell you anything. Nothing except name, rank, and serial number. That's the way the game is played. Right?"

"Only between enemies."

"That's one of the drawbacks of this business. Can't always tell the difference between friends and enemies."

"I swear to you," he said through clenched teeth, "I'm going to figure this out."

"Won't do you any good. Nothing you can do will stop it. But I'll give you one more free piece of advice. Keep your bags packed. Be ready to roll when the shooting starts."

"And when will that happen?"

"Soon, Rourke. Very soon." She rolled over and closed her eyes, ending the conversation.

For a minute Rourke stood over the bed, staring down at the curve of her shoulder above the sheet, the slow rise and fall of her breathing. Then he turned stiffly and headed for the door.

As Rourke entered his suite, the comm-link was wailing, its strident tones echoing through the room, the sound level slightly higher than his auditory pain threshold. Palming the light switch, he staggered toward the shrieking unit and slapped the ACCEPT contact. For a few blessed seconds silence reigned.

Thunder-of-Rushing-Water's disheveled face appeared on the monitor. His cinnamon fur was lusterless and tangled, his small eyes puffy from lack of sleep.

"About time you showed up," the Wormat snarled grumpily. "I've been ringing your place every tenth for the past half shift. I was seriously considering sending a team up to the woman's place to see if you had joined Galagazar in the great beyond."

"Sorry to disappoint you," Rourke said, "but I'm still breathing. Which is more than I can say for you. You get any sleep yet?"

"No." Thunder shook his elongated skull and stifled a yawn. "Too much happening. The taxonomist gave me a tentative identification on the hair sample. And my source in data processing just called. Claims to have discovered something we might find interesting. I'll pick you up in twenty."

"I'll need at least thirty to get showered and—"

But there was no point protesting. Rourke was already talking to an empty screen.

He was waiting out front when Thunder arrived.

The Wormat slowed the tram, and Rourke jumped aboard. Even before he was seated, they were back out into the traffic flow, a steady stream of cargo haulers and passenger platforms whirring along the broad, low-ceilinged concourse between the docks and the warehouse sector.

Settling onto the front bench, Rourke glanced over at the Wormat. The boar looked even worse in person. His pelt was matted with sweat and oil, and his leathery face was lined with fatigue. His gamy stench proclaimed several shifts without a bath.

"You sure you're okay to drive?" Rourke asked casually. He was pretty damn certain he already knew the Wormat's answer.

"Don't worry." Thunder grinned, twin rows of yellow fangs gleaming behind his black lips. "I could find my way around this station in a coma. In fact, I've done it many times during the harvest. You just sit back and relax."

"No offense, but I haven't been able to relax since I got to Mael." Thrusting one hand into his pocket, Rourke withdrew the tuft of fur and held it out toward Thunder. "Found this last night—in Weiss's suite. I think it's the same as the clump I found in Galagazar's apartment."

"You figure her place has been searched?"

"No." Rourke rubbed at the stubble on his jaw; several millimeters of growth were stiff and scratchy against his palm. "She hasn't admitted anything. But if her rooms had been searched, I think she'd have told me."

"Means our shedding friend was there with her permission."

"That's my guess. Probably part of her team. She's visible, the target." He raised the dark brown tuft. "This one is doing the legwork. We find him, we get some answers."

"Taxonomist says the hair is from a Rath. I ran a search through the personnel files. There are three Rath presently registered on station."

"Any of them look like possible suspects?"

"Not really." Thunder steered the vehicle around a slow-moving passenger platform loaded with migrants. "One's an albino. Fur is white. One's got an airtight alibi for the periods in question. He was crushed in a work accident. Lower leg paralysis which is just beginning to heal. Been in the infirmary for the last two deca-cycles."

"What about the third one?"

"Didn't get on station until last cycle." He sucked at his teeth. "Anyway, I couldn't question her even if I wanted to—she's already downworld."

"Maybe our visitor isn't registered. Could someone get on station without passing through customs?"

"It's possible. I don't have much control over incoming transships. A stowaway could conceivably jump ship and enter the station through any number of service hatches if he were careful and if he had the hardware needed to bypass the security net."

"Any chance of coming up from Jurrume?" Rourke asked, glancing at the Wormat.

"You mean coming up on a shuttle?" Thunder chuffed softly. "No chance at all."

Rourke raised his eyebrows.

"Look," Thunder explained. "The only commodity in this whole system worth protecting is camaii musk, and I've spent a fortune in company credits ensuring that it stays safe. The holds on all outbound transships and surface-to-station cargo shuttles have been rigged with heat sensors, motion detectors, audibles—a whole friggin' array. Anything tries to slip inside a hold filled with musk gets gassed or charged. All we have to do is send in a team to pick up the pieces or collect prisoners.

"Now, it might be possible to hijack a hopper jumping from post to post on Jurrume. Too many of them to outfit. Or some-

one could jump a load once it's been transferred from our ships."
Thunder bared his fangs in a deadly smile. "But no one gets
near the musk while it's in a company vessel under my control."

"You're pretty confident that the system can't be beat."

"Designed it myself." The Wormat's golden eyes gleamed.
"Care to give it a try?"

"No, thanks," Rourke said, holding his hands up in mock
surrender. "I'll take your word for it."

Thunder veered off the main concourse, heading down a side
passage that seemed to Rourke to lead back toward the core.
The dimly lit tunnel merged with a service corridor, a tight
fissure between two structures, levels rising above until they
were lost in the darkness. Catwalks and bridges spanned the
gap. Lengths of piping and disposal chutes traversed the sheer
faces of the buildings.

"Where are we going, anyway?" Rourke asked, staring up
into the darkness.

"To talk to Phanteent," the Wormat rumbled mysteriously.
"Called me earlier. Said there were some interesting patterns
in Galagazar's data. Thought we might want to see them."

Then he was turning into an even narrower crevice, a short
adit where he parked the tram and switched off the mags.

"Follow me," he said. "We'll walk from here."

The Wormat led Rourke down the constricted alley, stepping
through puddles of moisture scummed with algae and covering
piles of litter. A ball of fur and teeth scuttled between Rourke's
legs and darted for the safety of the open space beyond the tram.
Water trickled down the side of the wall from a leak farther
above, rust and moss forming a slick delta on the plas.

"What is this place?" Rourke asked, stumbling over a fragment of debris.

"Service corridor behind data processing." The Wormat had
to turn sideways to squeeze past a stack of empty cartons.
"Phanteent uses the rear access as a home address."

"This Phanteent lives in the core?"

"Lives . . . works. For some beings there isn't any difference."

Thunder stopped at a low door near the end of the passage.
He pounded on the reinforced panel five separate times before
there was an answer—a crackle of static across a small intercom
speaker cobbled onto the plasteel frame.

"Who?"

"It's Thunder-of-Rushing-Waters."

"Other?"

"Kenneth Christian Rourke," the Wormat snarled. "The new factor. Now open the blasted door, Phanteent."

The portal swung open on oiled hinges, golden light spilling out in a precise shaft, carving an ellipse on the far wall, their hunched silhouettes like an exhibit in a nouveau gallery— "Crouching Figures on Plas." Almost crawling, the Wormat slipped inside; Rourke followed a half step behind, balancing on his hands to keep from falling.

Beyond the door there was a small room, low and wide, unfurnished except for a single bench and a rack of lockers. Paper coveralls were draped along the opposite wall, green smocks complete with hats and surgical slippers. Gold biostrips in the ceiling cast a warm yellow light. The air was cool and dry, smelling faintly of Vost pheromones, ozone, and warm electrical apparatus.

"Put this on," Thunder commanded, tossing him a paper suit. "Phanteent won't come out here, so we've got to go in there." He pointed toward an irised lock at the other end of the dressing chamber.

"Who is this Phanteent, anyway?"

"Hardware/software tech—keeper of the core." The Wormat shrugged. "Crazy even for a Vost, but nobody on station knows the data system like Phanteent. Studies data patterns as a hobby. Calls it an art form. Claims to see truth in the visual representations, images, and structures." He grabbed a smock for himself. "Phanteent is . . . unorthodox, but I figured you were more concerned with getting answers than making sure I went through proper channels."

Nodding, Rourke pulled on his coveralls. They were designed for brachiates with two arms and two legs, one size fits all, which meant that they did not fit him at all. He rolled up the sleeves and the pants legs, tucking the excess fabric into the elastic bands at the ankles and cuffs. The booties extended up almost to his knees. The snood was more like an EVA helmet. He caught a glimpse of himself reflected in the stainless-steel leaves of the hatch. He looked like a deflated green balloon.

Thunder grinned at him.

"Not one damned word," Rourke said threateningly. "After all, you don't look so hot yourself."

"Wouldn't think of it." The Wormat pulled on his hood, laughter sparkling in his golden eyes. Still grinning, he turned toward the intercom and stabbed the contact. "Ready in here."

There was a hum, and the hatch opened, the overlapping panels scissoring back into the wall. They crawled through into the data core.

Phanteent was waiting for them at the bottom of an oval shaft that extended up through the center of the core.

Wrapped in a full bag suit, the ancient Vost neuter was so old that its velvet was almost nonexistent, a faint yellow patch still visible on its forehead. Its feathery antennae were brittle and stunted as if sections had been severed and had never regrown. A cable snaked from its back, a long electric tether that wired it into a junction on the floor and from there into the mainframe.

"Welcome, Thunder," the Vost said as they stepped into the circle. Its words crackled from the intercom speakers scattered around the shaft. The being had slaved its pheromone translator directly into the core and spoke with the voice of the machine.

"Phanteent, this is Rourke." Thunder jerked a thumb toward him. "New factor. He's the one interested in Galagazar's patterns."

"Sorry," Phanteent replied. "No patterns. Not Galagazar. Patterns others."

"Nothing on Galagazar?" Rourke asked.

"Peripheral pattern." A long pause as the bug sucked air. "Exceedingly strange. Observe."

The Vost touched a control on its belt. The floor rose slowly, and Rourke realized that it was an enormous lift panel. They slid up through the shaft, past data tanks and blocks of hardware, huge slabs of infocrystal, and gold bric-a-brac circuitry.

Near the top, on a level encircled by viewscreens, they halted. Phanteent touched another control, and the screens flickered to life. A vast branching network of numerical strings appeared, a geometric construct of numbers like an abstract drawing, the gleaming digits forming interwoven squares and triangles, parallelograms, octagons, and pentagons, all gleaming in basic shades of red and blue.

"What in the hell?" Rourke asked softly.

"It's a digital representation of a data stream," Thunder said. "A pattern, if you will. Phanteent is always looking for informational strings which form coherent images when examined on a large enough scale."

Rourke raised his eyebrows.

"You see," Thunder continued, "Phanteent here could take your daily computer entries for the past five cycles and graphically represent them in numerical strings. It would create a repetitive pattern. That's what you are looking at right now, only the data string is much larger.''

''This global search,'' Phanteent said. ''All data. Galagazar's.''

''A global search?'' Rourke stared at the frozen pattern, noting the wavelike rhythm of the line entries and responses. ''Requested by whom?''

''Internal audit. Central.''

''Central has requested access to every entry made by Galagazar?''

''More. All data. Everything Galagazar. Understand?''

''Let me get this straight,'' Thunder said, stroking his good tusk. ''Someone has accessed every record which even peripherally involved Galagazar?''

''Affirmative.''

The Vost stroked its small keyboard. A single string of numbers was isolated from the image and enlarged, dominating the screen.

''Requester code.'' Phanteent glanced at each of them, its faceted compound eyes glittering. ''Invalid. No match. Not in Central register.''

''Someone fabricated a code and penetrated the station's records.'' Rourke suddenly realized that his jaw was hanging open. ''How long ago?''

''Four cycles.''

''Just about the same time Alexis Weiss arrived on station,'' Thunder rumbled softly.

Rourke said nothing.

''Other pattern,'' Phanteent continued, touching another contact. The screens flickered. A different image appeared, with similar numerical strings but a new structure, staircase lines stuttering across the circular display. ''Same code. Different records.''

''What's this one?''

''All data. Bezhjenzarthra.''

''Who's Bezhjenzarthra?'' Rourke glanced at Thunder.

''Lling contract pilot.'' The boar shrugged. ''Hauls musk up from Jurrume on a cargo shuttle. Owns his own ship. Keeps pretty much to himself.''

''Can you think of any reason why Weiss would be searching his data trail?''

''None.''

''Maybe we ought to have a chat with him.''

''My thoughts exactly.'' Thunder nodded, his good ear

twitching. "He shouldn't be hard to find. It's harvest time. He's either sleeping on station or en route with a load." The boar turned back to Phanteent. "Anything else you want to show us?"

"Nothing. But this—" The Vost swept one limb toward the frozen pattern. "—is good. Yes?"

"Is very good," Thunder affirmed.

Dipping its triangular head, Phanteent bowed. A joyful scent managed to escape the confines of its bag. Its furred paps caressed another switch on the belt keyboard. The lift sank back toward the floor.

Back in the entry chamber they stripped off their isolation suits. As he peeled off his paper trousers, Thunder coughed and cleared his throat. Rourke did not look up, but he could feel the Wormat's eyes studying him.

"I think we have probable cause to have the woman arrested," the boar said quietly. "Charge her with corporate espionage. Search her place—we might find some answers."

Rourke was quiet for a moment, concentrating on wadding the paper suit into a compact sphere.

"Not yet," he said after a minute. "I don't want to lose a potential ally. I've got the feeling we're going to need all the friends we can get."

"As you wish." Thunder stuffed his suit into the recycler chute. "But I'll have the documents drawn up—just in case. Better safe than sorry."

Then the boar palmed the door contact and crawled out into the dripping alleyway.

FORTY-FOUR

"Gotcha," Khurrukkatey the Scrounger whispered softly to herself as she raised her imaging device.

Crouching on the edge of a sheer stone cliff, the Rath squinted through the viewfinder and studied the crescent of beach curving below her perch. The sand was black, churned to gray in the oily surf. A thick expanse of dense foliage began a few spans above the shoreline; tangled vines and evergreens covered everything and even clung to the flanks of the steep granite cirque.

And in the center of the beach there was the enormous humped shape of an Oolaanian corporal unit.

The central mass of the Oolaanian was a huge, swollen oval gorged with fluids and organic matter harvested from the encroaching forest. Many of the closest trees had been stripped bare, the undergrowth uprooted and devoured by questing pseudopods. Swathed with sand and debris, the Oolaanian's external membrane had been hardened so that it appeared to be nothing more than a curious rock formation rising from the beach. Branching tentacles plunged deep into the roiling waters, drawing moisture and minerals into the bottomless gut of the immense biological factory.

Focusing on the mass, she slowly squeezed the trigger on the holo unit, imagining as she did so that the box was actually the sighting mechanism for a high-frequency pulse battery. In her mind she could see the gouts of flame and feel the concussion of a barrage of thundering explosions. Gelatinous flesh spewed in guttering arcs, charred fragments festooning the cliffs in bubbling streamers.

It was a particularly satisfying fantasy.

Her journey to this isolated beach had been long and arduous, filled with many trials and travails.

On the flight down from the station Khurrukkatey had been crammed into a passenger hold with a hundred other laborers, all sweating and bickering in the close confines of the shuttle. The stench still clung to her nostrils like the smell of rotting garbage.

She had arrived at the landing field in the middle of the graveyard shift and had been assigned to work in the maintenance sheds. For the remainder of the shift she had labored in the cold metal buildings, refueling spent vehicles and overhauling lift trucks and gravs. Finally, at the shift change, Khurrukkatey had been able to steal a grav-sled and slip away, heading across the plains and toward the sea, using an intersecting network of shallow ravines and numerous rock formations for cover from overflights and prying eyes.

For an entire planetary day she had navigated the stolen grav-sled through the rugged coastal mountains, seeking out likely enemy locations, creeping up onto them slowly to avoid any sen-

tries or troopers. Most possible sites had yielded nothing beyond
surf and sand, and a few stray creatures cavorting in the water.

Until this beach with the humped back of the Oolaanian crest-
ing in its shoals.

At last her search was ended. Another few seconds of holo
recording and she could retreat to a safe area for transmission.
Her broadcast would be received almost a full shift before the
deadline. Chittering under her breath, she panned the imager
and swept the crescent of beach.

Khurrukkatey was so intent on her target that she did not
notice the small clumps of Oolaanian flesh secreted among the
rocks surrounding the beach. Nor did she see the small green
dot centered on her chest until a fraction of a second before the
energy weapon fired. She tried to dive for cover behind the low
stone shelf in front of her, but she reacted a heartbeat too late.
The crackling bolt struck her just above the eyes, the super-
charged pulse slicing away the top of her skull. Impact spun her
spasming body around, her momentum carrying her to the edge
of the cliff. She wavered on the brink for an instant, then toppled
forward, spiraling down toward the pounding surf.

The Rath was dead before she hit the water.

Inside the Oolaanian corporal unit the small reasoning center
studied the impulses it had received from its battery of remote
sensory elements.

An intruder had penetrated the unit's peripheral defenses. Such
was not an unusual occurrence; on twenty-one previous occasions life forms had blundered into the sensory net and had been
destroyed.

This particular beast had been a small creature, mammalian,
possibly sentient, and possibly armed. Defense had fired once,
reporting a single confirmed hit. Probability of resultant wound
being fatal: nearly absolute.

Two combat entities had been dispatched to search the site.
They had found blood and other organic matter. The corpse had
been lost to the denizens of the sea.

The small reasoning center considered its limited options,
studying the tiny fragment of the Designers' plan encapsulated
in its specially modified intellectual substance.

Its ruminations lasted only a few millionths of an interval.
The signal lens swung up to aim along the communication vec-
tor and fired a quick burst of encoded frequencies, notifying the
Unity of possible enemy contact.

Nonstandard task complete, the corpus returned to its basic programming, concentrating on the rapid manufacture of ground-adapted combat entities.

FORTY-FIVE

"Better order up another body bag," Thunder said, breaking the connection and pushing back from his workstation. "I think we'll be needing one for Bezhjenzarthra—that is, if we ever find his corpse."

The Wormat had been occupied at his desk for the last quarter of a shift, making calls and pulling records. And except for the few minutes it had taken him to check in with Nebuun, Rourke had spent the entire time sitting on the hard bench in front of the workstation, the polished slab the only other piece of furniture in the Wormat's sterile office.

"You really think he's dead?" Rourke said, rubbing his throbbing temples. The pain in his skull was a dull, constant ache, part fatigue and part frustration.

"Nothing else makes sense. Not based on what information I've been able to gather so far." The Wormat drummed his blunt claws on the plas surface of the workstation. "Twenty-four cycles ago Bezhjenzarthra aborted the inbound leg of a cargo run due to a malfunction and returned to the station for repairs. Remember, this is the harvest. I've seen pilots refuse to ground virtual death traps because they couldn't afford to lose the profit from a single load during the musk run. But the Lling pulls out due to unspecified damages caused by turbulence. Rather odd, don't you think?"

Rourke nodded.

"Since then, his shuttle has been in a parking orbit around the station. And except for one short visit when he first arrived, no one has seen him on station. There's been no contact with him at all. Nothing going in, nothing coming out. No answer to my hailing frequency. Do you know what it's like to be trapped in a shuttle for five cycles, much less twenty?"

"As a matter of fact, I do." Rourke closed his eyes, and for a moment he was back aboard the single-ship with the little Col. He shook his head to clear away the memory. "You think he's still aboard the shuttle?"

"Maybe, or maybe his pieces have been stuffed into the nearest recycler. Either way, I doubt he's still breathing. But there's one way to find out." Thunder spun one of the pivoting screens toward Rourke. Gleaming Patois text filled the display. "It's a writ of search and seizure. All it needs is your print to make it legal."

"My print?"

"You're the factor. He whose word is law."

"Right." Rourke touched the ident panel. The printer spit out a hard copy.

"I'll get right on this," Thunder said, tearing the document from the dispensing unit.

"I'm going with you." Rourke stood up and walked over to the Spencer Pinpoint hanging on the wall, one of a number of weapons on display. He picked it up, curling his fingers around the grip, feeling the familiar heft of the sidearm. "This functional?"

"It was last time I checked."

"You can have it back when this is all over."

Sliding the pistol into the pocket of his coveralls, he headed for the door.

They took a cargo lighter out to the shuttle. The lighter was little more than a metal frame built around a pressurized pod and a brace of maneuvering jets. Thunder piloted it skillfully, explaining that he had started his career with the company as a stevedore. Old habits died hard.

Reaching the shuttle, Thunder matched velocity, pivoted the lighter, and jockeyed the docking rings into position. A touch on the thrust lever and the vessels mated, metal clanging, the lighter jarring softly. There was a low hum as the corrugated docking passage extended from the pod and attached itself to the shuttle's external hatch.

Thunder went first down the tube, pulling himself along in the weightless environment, tool bag trailing in his wake. Rourke followed, the Spencer a heavy bulge in his pocket.

"Lock's been fried," Thunder said as he reached the hatch. He slapped the square mechanism: a digital keyboard and a card slot. Black soot and fragments of burned components flaked out from a gaping hole in the bottom of the unit. "Evidently, by the time they got to this point, our friends were either getting sloppy or desperate or both.''

It took Thunder less than a minute to pry the cover from the security box and bypass the fragged circuits. "I once worked as a security system technician,'' he said with a grim smile. "The old training comes in handy sometimes.''

He touched two leads, and blue sparks arced; the hatch groaned open slowly. Stale, fetid air spilled out of the interior of the shuttle. A cloud of litter and debris whirled around them, spinning in the currents created by the movement of the pressure door. Papers and tools, fragments on insulation and foam padding, clothing.

"I'll get a team out here,'' Thunder said. "But if it's anything like the apartment or the old offices, you're looking at another dead end.''

"Maybe.'' Rourke pushed a wad of cloth away from his face. It collided with a globule of liquid, hundreds of tiny spheres vectoring away from the impact. "But there has to be a connection. Some link between Galagazar and Bezhjenzarthra. We find that link, we might just figure out what's going on around here.''

"What'd you have in mind?''

"When you call for the forensics team, contact Phanteent. Tell the Vost to gather up every document it can find on our pilot. And cross-reference that information with Galagazar's records. Have everything sent to your office.''

"As you wish,'' Thunder growled. "But I've got a feeling I'd better get my reading lenses cleaned. Sounds like it's going to be a long shift.''

FORTY-SIX

At two minutes after shift change Alexis Weiss switched off her processor and began quickly to dismantle the unit, secreting the components in her bags.

The deadline had passed, and Khurrukkatey had failed to broadcast any information. There were only three explanations: The Rath was dead, injured, or captured. Of the three, death was the most likely. But the reason for failure did not matter. Alexis had no choice. It was time to move.

As she prepared herself for her journey downworld, Alexis gave thanks to the gods of chance for seeing to it that Rourke had been too busy to join her for dinner.

She had been truly disappointed when he had called to cancel, but in the back of her mind she had suspected that his absence would prove to be a blessing. Had he been with her now, she would have had to neutralize him. The simplest method would have been termination, but Alexis was fairly certain she would have done something stupid like drugging him and leaving him alive but temporarily incapacitated. Further proof that she had allowed herself to become too personally involved.

A fool's mistake.

She finished dressing almost without thinking, her body reacting to layers of conditioning. The last thing she did before leaving the room was to set the self-destruct mechanisms on her equipment. If anyone was bold enough to tamper with her gear, it would be his last mistake.

And that included the factor.

Alexis activated her sensory imaging unit before entering the lobby. The holographic projection that surrounded her body was that of a young Quorg, not yet chairbound but with ample flesh to hide her presence within the image. She walked carefully, avoiding contact with other patrons or furnishings. Accidentally merging with an object would surely blow her cover.

There was a single Wormat stationed outside the Inn of Peaceful Rest, waiting for Alexis to appear. He did not give the Quorg youngling a second glance.

She maintained her disguise until she was far down the concourse. Then she slipped into a side passage, deactivated the imager, and melted into the shadows.

The docks were bustling with activity. Cargo lifts buzzed back and forth between a brace of shuttles, stacking pallets of musk. Stevedores tightened loads and marked inventory sheets, their shouts and hurried conversations making a rumbling din. The stench of camaii overrode all other smells.

It took Alexis a few minutes to isolate a shuttle preparing for departure and work her way close to its berth without being seen. Hiding in the darkness beneath the loading ramp, she scanned the area for alarms and found nothing. Evidently, ship security was as lax as that of the rest of the station. A symptom of having lived too long at peace. Or maybe the company wasn't too particular about stowaways. Probably just put them to work without pay if they were caught.

She waited until the crew had boarded and the ramp was beginning to lift before she slipped inside the craft.

Alexis chose the rear cargo compartment, a small tapering chamber with a curved ceiling. The bulkheads were ribbed plasteel, tie-downs and straps racked along the edges of the hold. She found a small alcove behind some cables and positioned herself to absorb the forces of launch and acceleration.

And the hatch slammed shut, toggles snapping into place.

And sirens began to wail.

And she was clawing for her belt pack as clouds of gas started spewing from a hundred hidden nozzles.

The narcotic fog zeroed her brain before Alexis even got the clasp open on the pouch that held her rebreather.

The security grunt had to stoop to step into the hold, his big Wormat body almost filling the service hatch. His heavy breathing whistled through the vents of his air helmet. The portable light clutched in one paw cut a bright swath across the bluish haze that filled the chamber. He kept his stun baton elevated in the other paw, ready for combat despite the narcotic mist swirling around him.

No stowaway had ever come out of a gassed hold under his or her own power, but he did not want to become the statistic that proved the rule.

"Nothing yet," he muttered into the intercom as he sidled across the chamber, baton held across his body defensively. "Maybe it was some kind of malfunct—"

Then his beam touched the woman's face. Her features were frozen in a rictus of pain, her skin an angry shade of red. If she was still breathing, it was too shallow to detect.

"By my grandsire's testicles," the Wormat swore, dropping to his knees beside the downed alien. "Get a medical crash team down here on the double, prepped for mammalian physiology. And someone send for Thunder. Tell him I just found the Human female inside Hold Number Three!"

FORTY-SEVEN

"I think she will survive," the Eng physician said. "But you must understand, that is only a guess. Her condition is far from stable."

Standing beside the medical unit, Rourke looked down at the placid face beneath the clear plas panel of the machine. The only sign of life was the mist her breathing left on the curved crystalline surface and the twitch of REMs across her eyelids.

The station hospital was in a low-grav sector adjacent to the core. A network of expansion grates and catwalks linked the three levels. The uniform white of the walls were broken only by the chrome and plastic fixtures. There were twenty medical units anchored to one side, and most of the gear was species-specific.

Alexis was in a Wormat unit haphazardly modified to meet her physical needs. Rourke considered her present survival to be due not so much to quick medical care but to the presence of a tech who knew how to adapt the necessary machinery. If he did nothing else as factor, Rourke would make sure that tech got a substantial raise.

"How long will she be out?" Rourke asked, his eyes still fixed on Alexis's waxen features.

"I cannot say. Nor can I tell you whether she will suffer any permanent damage from the effects of the gas." The physician fluttered her throat sac rapidly, a sign of nervous distress. "My experience with mammals is very limited. With Humans it is nonexistent."

"I understand."

Rourke laid his hand on the panel above the woman's pale forehead as if trying to stroke her gleaming hair. He was torn between the desire to offer her comfort and the need to scream at her for trying to stow away on a musk shuttle. If only she had come to him for help. If only she had trusted him.

But such speculation did not change reality, nor would it help ease the grip of the deadly forces he sensed enveloping the station. The time had come for action. Pushing his regrets aside, he turned his attention back to the present.

"Just do what you can," he said. "And keep me informed. I want to know as soon as she becomes conscious."

"As you wish." The physician bowed stiffly and moved away to visit her other patients.

Rourke stood beside the unit for a few minutes longer, watching the slow rhythm of the woman's breathing, Then, finally, he pulled his hand away and turned toward the stairs. His footsteps were loud on the expansion grate catwalk.

Thunder was still on the docks, standing near the shuttle where Alexis had been found, making notes on a voice recorder while other members of his security team scoured the area for clues. Spotting Rourke, the Wormat waved one huge arm and started toward the approaching tram.

"How's the woman?" he asked as Rourke coasted to a stop before him.

"She's still breathing," Rourke answered, switching off the mags and letting the tram settle to the deck.

"That's a good sign. Some of the smaller species don't handle the gas dosage too well. Brought a Rath out of one hold about two standards back—it was dead before we even reached the infirmary."

"Still no guarantees that she'll survive."

"I wouldn't worry about it. She'll probably outlive both of us." Thunder sucked a breath through damp nostrils and spit loudly. "Outside of getting gassed—a trap she couldn't have been expecting considering the general lack of security measures on station—she didn't make many mistakes. No one saw her leave her hotel suite. And no one saw her board the shuttle. Might as well have been a ghost."

"Almost was."

"Yeah." The Wormat nodded. "And so were three members of my ersatz forensic team."

Rourke raised his eyebrows in a silent question.

"I sent them up to her suite. Just to look around," he added quickly, stifling Rourke's protest, "and see what they could find. They tiptoed in and hustled right back out again. Seems she's got the place hard-wired to a series of explosive devices. One wrong move and the occupants of the Inn of Peaceful Rest will be having dinner with their ancestors. I've told them to cordon off the area and wait. If she comes out of it, we'll let her do the disarming. If not, someone's going to earn some substantial hazard pay.

"One thing's for certain, though. She's definitely an operative for someone with some serious intentions."

"She's Bureau," Rourke said quietly.

"Possibly. But she still might turn out to be a corporate blade. Corporate operatives can be pretty cold. Very sophisticated." Thunder touched his ragged ear gently. "You've never been in a corporate war. Some of us have. Me, Nebuun, Ianiammallo. We all remember the last takeover. Some of the things we've seen, you haven't."

"Maybe I haven't taken part in a corporate bash. But I've seen my share of frontline action. And I've got a gut feeling that in a real short time we're all going to be sharing the intimate joys of a full-scale invasion."

"You thinking about calling in some Quadriate ships?"

"Yeah." Rourke nodded. "Should have done that about three cycles back, but I let Nebuun talk me out of it. Now, maybe we're too damn late to stop them."

"Who are you planning on stopping?"

"The Oolaan."

"Okay," Thunder said. "Next stupid question: Where are they?"

"Somewhere in this system. We both know it!"

"Sure we do. But outside of the claw you found at Galaga-zar's, we haven't seen hide nor hair of them." The Wormat took a deep breath and let it hiss slowly through his clenched teeth. "Now, I don't know Nebuun very well, but even though I figure he and I wouldn't see most business matters in the same way, I've got to agree with him in this situation. The Quadriate won't send a force out here unless you've got proof of a threat. Something much more solid than suspicions or gut feelings. Something they can shoot at. Understand?"

"I can get the proof we need," Rourke said grimly. "It's on Jurrume."

"Are you sure about that?"

"Yeah."

"Just because the woman tried to stow away on a down-bound shuttle?" The boar jerked a thumb back toward the dock. "That makes you think all the answers are downworld?"

"Not quite." Rourke shook his head. "Weiss only confirmed my theory. I had it figured out even before we were called down here. The clues were in Bezhjenzarthra's records."

Thunder stared at him uncomprehendingly.

"Look," Rourke said, spreading his hands apart, palms up in supplication. "We both agree that Galagazar was killed because he knew something he shouldn't have known. The Oolaan took him out to plug a potential leak. Right?"

"Granted."

"But the way I figure the scenario, Galagazar was carrying secondhand information—data he'd gotten from Bezhjenzarthra."

"That would explain his sudden disappearance."

"It's more than just his vanishing act," Rourke explained. "Bezhjenzarthra's records indicate a rather severe break from his normal operating routine during the cycle just before he went AWOL—the same cycle, incidentally, that Galagazar went to meet his maker. First, he aborted his inbound run and returned to the station empty. Second, he failed to arrange for repairs on his supposedly damaged ship, a ship so badly fragged by turbulence that he couldn't complete his run. Third, he went to see the factor as soon as he docked, a rather lengthy meeting which made him one of the last beings to see Galagazar alive."

"So you think he saw something during that last run?"

"I think he spotted the Oolaan. Some kind of a presence, a ship or something. And I'm willing to bet that if I follow his last route, I might just stumble over it myself." Rourke looked up at the Wormat. "Any chance you could get me his final flight record?"

"I'm afraid that's not possible," Thunder rumbled softly. "Oh, I can get you a pretty decent reconstruction. Good enough to do the job. But I can't get you his flight recorder data. You see—" The Wormat grinned at him. "—The flight recorder was the only item missing from his ship."

It was almost shift change before Thunder completed the reconstruction.

"What you're about to see," the Wormat said, entering a series of commands into the processor, "is an amalgamation of data collected from a number of separate monitoring sources. Shuttle field flight control, station control, and satellite traffic transmissions, even a few bytes gathered from the flight recorders of other shuttles. Everything I could find that had any relevance to Bezhjenzarthra's final run."

The wall screen display flickered and flashed, a schematic of Jurrume gleaming in neon green. He punched in another series of commands, and the image zoomed into a close-up of a single continent, its topographical contours rippling.

"Merging the information gives us this." More commands, a flight vector in electric blue slashing across the verdant margins of the continental shelf. "A fairly close approximation of the route taken by our pilot on that fateful cycle."

Rourke studied the jagged line for a moment, squinting at the screen. "Can you superimpose the path of an earlier flight over this one?"

"Yes, master." Thunder's voice was thick with sarcasm as his thick digits stabbed the keys.

Another vector appeared on the stylized image of Jurrume, a brilliant pink. Initially the two tracks were almost identical, but near the center of the screen they diverged. Bezhjenzarthra's flight path swung wide and made a sweeping curve along the coast, ending abruptly in a series of rapid turns and then an almost vertical ascent back into orbit.

"Let's see a third."

A yellow vector flickered into being, almost a mirror image of the pink line. The similarities only served to highlight Bezhjenzarthra's aberrant route.

"Shall I pull up another?" Thunder asked.

"No need." Rourke shook his head. "I found what I was looking for."

"Which is?"

"A radical course deviation." Rourke stood and walked to the wall screen, tapping the image where the three lines diverged.

"According to the records, he was diverted to a secondary route in order to avoid a storm front."

"Why he veered isn't important. The point is—" This time Rourke tapped the screen where Bezhjenzarthra's flight path deteriorated into a chaos of erratic turns. "—he ended up way outside the normal flight corridor."

"I don't follow you."

"Look, if you had something to hide, something you didn't want anyone to see, you wouldn't drop it in the middle of a busy corridor. Right?"

The Wormat nodded.

"So, the flight paths of the cargo shuttles are fairly regular. And they're common knowledge. No one would try to hide anything too close to them. But Bezhjenzarthra had to swing wide to avoid a storm." He traced a finger along the sweeping curve of the neon vector, pausing where the arc tightened into a hard spiraling turn. "Right about here I think our pilot spotted something unusual. He dropped down to take a closer look. And whatever he saw shook him so bad that he pulled evasive maneuvers for a few hundred kilometers before pointing his nose at the sky and burning for orbit.''

Thunder touched the keyboard again. A small column of figures appeared in one corner of the screen. Rourke recognized directional headings and altitude and speed readings.

''Telemetry seems to confirm your scenario,'' the boar said with a grunt.

''I think it deserves a closer look.''

''High-altitude flyby?''

''No.'' Rourke frowned. ''Whoever is down there was burned once from the air. They've probably taken precautions to see that it doesn't happen again. This will have to be a ground-level survey. Hitch a ride on the next shuttle to the surface. Then borrow a sled and head overland to here.'' He indicated a steep ridge that divided the plains from the coastland, the same area where Bezhjenzarthra's flight line seemed to indicate that the pilot had made his sighting. ''With a little luck, I should be able to complete the sweep and be back in time to catch one of the morning flights out.''

''Frankly, it seems like a real long shot.'' Thunder stroked the fur beneath his jutting jaw. ''Especially considering how much the Col frown on trespassers. Unauthorized entry onto Col land is a direct violation of our trading charter.''

''Then I'll have to be certain I don't get caught. But it's a chance Alexis was willing to take. She wouldn't have tried to go there without reason. Who knows, maybe I'll get lucky and find the proof I need to take to Nebuun. Something we can shove down their throats back at the home office.''

Thunder studied the map silently for a few seconds. When he looked back at Rourke, all traces of humor had fled from his gleaming golden eyes. ''Suppose you do find something. Suppose you succeed in convincing Nebuun. I mean, we're still a small trading station. A few ships. Fewer weapons. And we're at least ten cycles away from Quadriate support. If the Oolaan and Humanity collide here, what do you propose we do until Quadriate forces arrive?''

''I don't know.'' Rourke threw up his hands. ''I haven't thought that far ahead yet. But I figure going to Jurrume beats the hell out of sitting around here just waiting for the fireworks to begin.''

''A very convincing argument.'' Thunder stood and walked to the weaponry display on the far wall. Selecting a knife and a wide-bore energy pistol, he clipped them onto his belt. "We'd better get moving if we're going to make the next shuttle."

"I thought you didn't know anything about Jurrume," Rourke said as they headed for the door.

"I don't," the big boar replied with a grin. "But by my grand-sire's testicles, I certainly know more about the plains than you."

BOOK FOUR

MAELSTROM

From lightning and tempest;
From plague, pestilence and famine;
From battle and murder, and from sudden death,
   Good Lord, deliver us.

—Prayer Book 1662

FORTY-EIGHT

Turgid with data, its thought processes reduced to lethargic sublight intervals by a surfeit of information, the main reasoning center of the Ssoorii Unity pondered the few viable options that remained within the Designers' framework of the immediate future.

The cause of its ruminations was a momentary warning pulse that recently had been received from a corporal unit on the surface of Jurrume—a brief message detailing a possible enemy contact. Scrutiny of the communiqué had revealed a high probability that the intruder was a Rath, a species with known links to the Human Alliance. And though the being had been destroyed before it could escape or broadcast any data, the reasoning center had no choice but to classify the information as a confirmed enemy incursion.

As far as the Ssoorii Unity was concerned, the first shots of the Battle of Mael had already been fired.

That assumption sheared away two entire pathways from the already narrowed schematic of probability, leaving essentially three acceptable solutions to the operation, and the reasoning center altered its command instructions accordingly.

With all possibility of completing the nexus shield before an enemy confrontation gone, the reasoning center dispatched orders to the construction vessels to cease their present activities and begin immediate retrofitting for possible combat. It felt no regrets as it issued the commands; the need to complete the shield prior to a full-scale engagement had vanished with the now-nonexistent pathways, swallowed in the darkness of the past.

Additional instructions flickered out along shrouded routes, recalling all reconnaissance vessels and consolidating the fleet for an impending advance on the Mael Station–Jurrume complex.

Because each of the remaining future options had one common element—a confrontation with Human forces somewhere along the flight corridor between Jurrume and the station.

And two of the paths led directly to war.

FORTY-NINE

The cargo ramp descended with a hydraulic whine, vibrations drumming through the rear of the shuttle.

Standing at the edge of the platform, Rourke studied the landscape stretched before him like a painted backdrop: grasslands and low hills, a distant line of vegetation beneath a shell of cobalt sky.

A dry breeze blew across the landing field, the air still warm but laced with the chill of the coming night and heavy with the stench of camaii musk and old urine. Mael was a red ball sinking into the horizon, its ruddy light filtered through a thick plume of pulverized fecal matter that spread across the valley from an abstract array of holding pens. The confused lowing of ten thousand camaii was audible even over the whine of the approaching industrial trucks and cargo lifts.

"Smell that?" Thunder asked, sucking in a deep breath, his massive chest expanding.

"How can you miss it?" Rourke fumbled with the straps of his breathing mask, tightening them across the back of his skull, the respirator reducing his voice to a sibilant whisper. Even through the heavy filters, the aroma was overpowering. "Can't understand why this place isn't a resort."

"Scoff if you want, but that smell is the sweet scent of credit, a fortune in musk. Millions of Vost would gladly give a standard's wages for one hit of camaii half as rich as what we are now breathing."

"Think it's worth dying for?"

"Not if I had a choice." The Wormat looked at Rourke, his black lips pulled back into a sinister grin. "But if the choice has been made without my consent, I will make someone pay dearly for their presumption." He pulled his goggles over his eyes to protect them from the blowing grit. "Now, shall we go see if we can round up a couple of sleds?"

"After you."

They headed across the tarmac toward the distant cluster of domed warehouses.

The shuttle field manager was an elderly Eng named Uhn-rutte. She was past breeding age, and her skin was loose and dry, covered with wrinkles and scales. Dust coated her coveralls and the lenses of her goggles, and there were pale circles on her face where the goggles had rested.

"By slime and damnation," she swore as she stomped into the room. "Thunder, you have some nerve showing up like this! You know I've got no time for inspections, especially in the middle of season!" The Eng glanced over at Rourke and jerked a bony digit toward him. "And I've sure as slime got no use for rotten damned tourists!"

"Uhnrutte," Thunder said, puffing his jowls, "I'd like you to meet Kenneth Christian Rourke, our new factor."

"I know who the Human is," she snapped. "I'm not stupid. But he can make appointments just like everybody else. Why in Hoth's name do you think calendars were invented? For decoration?"

"Calm down, Uhnrutte." Thunder leaned back against the wall, grinning and fingering the edge of his broken tusk. "This isn't an inspection. And we're not tourists. In fact, if anyone asks, you haven't seen us."

The way she reacted to the tone of his voice told Rourke that the two beings were old friends and knew each other very well. Her anger dissipated like wind-blown smoke, the bluster replaced by calm concern.

"So what is it, then?" she asked.

"Better you don't know." Thunder studied one of his digits, examining the curled claw. "Let's just call it official business."

"All right." The Eng vented loudly. "Besides sudden blindness, what else do you want from me?"

"A pair of grav-sleds . . . and a pair of jamming shields, too."

"Now, Thunder," she said, her lipless mouth gaping in the Eng equivalent of a grin. "You know the Col don't want us using anything that fools their primitive scanners."

"I also know that you always have the herd count long before the Col make their annual preseason report. A feat that would require scouts equipped with shields."

Still grinning, the Eng walked to a wall filing unit and pressed a hidden switch. The file swung back, revealing a hidden compartment. Rourke spotted a rack of technical hardware. The Eng picked up a pair of jamming units and tossed them to Thunder.

"I hope you two know what you're doing," she said. "Besides being a violation of the operating charter, unauthorized entry into Col land is risky business, sometimes even fatal. The Col take a dim view of trespassers."

"Like I said," Thunder commented as he pocketed the cubes of circuitry, "official business."

Uhnrutte nodded. "Since I've never seen you, I guess I don't have to worry if you don't come back."

Thunder looked at Rourke for an answer.

"If we're not back tomorrow night," Rourke said, "notify the station."

"You got it." The Eng glanced over at Thunder. "If you've set me up for trouble, you fur-bearing bandit, you'll pay dearly."

"You'll have to get in line, Uhnrutte."

"Don't think I won't." She picked up her goggles. "Well, if you'll excuse me. I've got a post to run."

Without a backward glance, Uhnrutte stomped from the room. Rourke looked at Thunder.

"Don't worry," the Wormat said in answer to his unspoken query. "She'll keep her mouth shut. All you need to worry about now is staying alive."

A short time later two grav-sleds slipped away from the maintenance shed. Their silent passage along the landing strip was hidden by the gathering night. No one noticed when they coasted off the edge of the runway and down into the depths of a slight ravine that twisted out across the plains toward the distant serrations of the coastal range.

FIFTY

The second test of elevation was the ritual of fire. Rem passed without incident, but the tran did not seem pleased.

When Rem returned from the temple, a raas was leaving her cubicle, the creature huddled and bent with deference. Yet it met her gaze as it passed her in the corridor, and a flicker of recognition passed between them.

She found the message on the table, a single word written in colored wax on the gleaming surface: "Tonight."

With one pass of her leera's forelimb, the words smeared and then vanished into the surface.

Her fear was not as easily erased.

A night without sleep, without peace. Rem waited in the darkness, her flesh trembling, nauseated by her terror.

Finally the door slid open, a soft hiss in the stillness. A hetta waited in the corridor, huge and solid, a leather harness crisscrossed over his chest. He met her gaze, cold and steady. The light flickered on his weapons.

Nodding slowly, the guard turned and headed down the passage. Rem followed a few paces behind him.

Down the silent corridors, past stoic sentries, into the temple.

They skirted the edge of the thick vegetation, stopping before a small service door. The guard flicked open a panel on the wall, metal disguised as stone. A small tangle of circuitry appeared in his manipulators. He fit it carefully into the panel. The door yawned.

Then the guard was moving again, his grip tight on her symb's forelimb, his pace quick and silent.

No need for her to be blindfolded now. No need for total secrecy. The implication made her shiver.

Obviously, she would not be coming back.

* * *

Deep in a warehouse, she found them waiting. Five conspirators—two raas and three hetta—crouched over a small makeshift table.

There was the smell of blood in the air. A young leera lay on the floor near the table, limbs bound, muzzle gagged. She looked at Rem, her eye wide and filled with terror.

"Were you followed?" one of the raas asked as they approached. The leader, Rem realized, recognizing the commanding voice.

"No." The hetta shook his massive head. "It went as planned. The monitors are disabled, loop units. Crudely done. They will fool security until the next watch makes a visual inspection. Two deca-spans. Three at the most. Then the jujun will know something is wrong."

"We will be long gone by then."

"Or, more likely, dead," the other raas muttered. The dissenter. Rem could still sense the hate in his words.

The leader ignored the comment. He faced Rem, his stiff features an expressionless mask.

"The time has come for you to make a decision," he said quietly. "Are you with us or against us?"

She knew the weight her decision carried. There was no neutrality in this cold, dusty warehouse. Allies participated and lived. Enemies—she glanced toward the young leera trussed up on the floor.

"I am with you."

"Excellent." His gaze held her symb hypnotized. "We are moving against Gral tonight. We all have our roles. But yours will be of primary importance. Can you go back into the tube?"

Rem felt numb. It was as if everything she had ever hoped for was slipping away from her grasp. There would be no elevation in her future, no chedo flesh. Only death. The question was simply who would deliver the killing stroke. Her symb seemed to nod of its own accord.

"You must go back inside," the raas continued. "Once there, you will wait for a power failure. It will be brief—ten quarter spans. No more, no less. When the power stops, you will move out into the laboratory. Trade Gral's essence with the essence of this one here." He pointed toward the leera sprawled beside him. "Then back out the tube. Do you understand?"

Another nod.

"There is no room for error. Switch the entities while the power is down and be gone before it returns. The attendants will come to check on Gral as soon as the auxiliary power units kick in. They must suspect nothing. If you are caught, all is lost. If they even suspect that you have penetrated the chamber, all is lost.''

"I cannot—" she blurted.

"You have no choice."

Rem shivered, her symb ill and bewildered. "I am not a soldier. I know nothing of spying and stealth. I do not even know whose side you are on."

"We are united against Gral; that is all you need to know. And if you do not help us, all is lost. Gral wins. Do you understand me?" He leaned forward, his rough limbs grabbing her symb and squeezing tightly until all was pain and confusion. "You must help us."

"All right," she said softly. "I will try."

"You will not try," the raas snarled. "You will do as commanded, or we are all dead."

"Yes." She nodded, shivering, her symb mewling piteously.

"Madness," the other raas whispered venomously. "She cannot even control her own flesh. We would be better off using her essence for the switch and sending this one into the chamber in her place." He jerked a limb toward the captive.

"We are all mad," the leader said. "That is why we were chosen for this mission." He looked back to Rem. "Do you have a timepiece."

"No."

A nod toward one of the hetta, and a digital unit appeared from his equipment pouch. It was cold and hard in her symb's grasp. And other gear materialized: a harness that clamped over her symb's skull, with mechanical lenses to alter its vision; a thin monomer bag of black plas; gloves of a similar material.

"Night eyes," the raas explained. "You will be in total darkness for a time. These will allow you to see." He picked up the bag. "You will carry the substitute essence down to the chamber in this sack. It is impermeable to essence. The same goes for the gloves. Wear them before touching either mass. When the power is off, you will make the switch. Flesh is flesh to a monitor. They will not know what has happened until the tran examines it closely. If all goes well, we will be off-world by then."

"What about the attendants?" Rem asked. "What if they are in the chamber with him?"

"They will not be. We are hitting at vespers. They will be at prayer down the corridor. The power failure will temporarily lock the security doors. No one will get in or out. Except you. Tark—'' he indicated her hetta escort ''—will be waiting for you at the top of the vent. He will lead you to the rendezvous point. From there, we will escape off-world. Any more questions?''

She had a thousand questions but could find no words.

''Then we must move.'' The raas turned toward one of the other hetta. ''Do it now,'' he commanded.

Rem watched horrified as the soldier drew his blade and bent over the young leera. A flash of steel cut across the creature's throat. Blood gouted in a thick stream as its legs spasmed and its sphincters voided. A second slash cut away the gag, a hideous gurgling filling the room. Sensing the death of its symbiote, the jellied essences bubbled from the leera's gaping mouth.

She looked back at the raas, fighting to keep her symb from wailing in terror.

''As I said, we all have our roles to play.'' His face was cold. ''But some of us are more willing participants than others.''

In a few short minutes Rem was stumbling along in the grasp of Tark, her mind reeling in confusion, the monomer bag and its gelatinous contents drumming softly against her symb's back.

FIFTY-ONE

Resting on the nurturing table, drawing sustenance from the network of veins that crisscrossed the curved surface below his essence, Gral had nearly recovered from the strain of division when the power failure hit.

He was aware of a sudden darkness. The nerves spanning his membrane keenly detected the abrupt cessation of the engines of life that had previously throbbed around him, registering the fading temperature of lights and other heat sources suddenly deprived of energy. Within a very few moments the small signatures of his calves were the brightest spots in his black universe.

Gral waited for a time for the backup generators to kick in and the machines to respond. But the darkness and the silence seemed to stretch into infinity. His imagination switched on, doubts surging through him like high-voltage electricity. Had something gone wrong? Was this the beginning of a coup?

A clanging vibration drew his attention, displaced air currents playing across the glistening surface of his external membrane. In the upper quadrant a heat source appeared, a warm radiance.

Living flesh, leera presence.

The memory of his last secretive visitor surfaced, overlaid upon the present reality, meshing perfectly. Rem—still free and still threatening, a random factor.

Vibrations thrummed through him, transmitted through the surface of the table: a weight hitting the floor, approaching foot-steps, life radiation closing on him hurriedly.

This was no exploration visit, he understood grimly. The leera knew what she wanted, and fear or determination was driving her toward him.

Gral wasted no effort wishing for a voice. Even if he had been able to cry out, no one would have come to his rescue. The power failure had blinded his forces, silenced all alarms, and sealed the entrance to the lab. If he was to escape his enemy, it would be by his own initiative. Extending a pseudopod, he vainly searched the curved lip of the nutrient bowl for a projecting edge to use as a hold to pull his essence out of the depression.

Thoughts of the power failure were particularly unsettling. It was unlikely that a single being could neutralize the generation source and enter the laboratory at the same time. Such a coor-dinated act would require a number of operatives, and that im-plied a deep penetration into the compound and the security units.

How many conspirators? he wondered furiously. And what had they planned? His death?

No. Gral set aside thoughts of an assassination. Had the leera wished to kill him, it would have done so during the last visit. Rem had other plans. But what were they? His mind raced, his pseudopods groping frantically for purchase on the slick metal.

The leera loomed over him. Gral turned, recoiling defen-sively, hoping for a chance to gain a purchase on the beast's flesh. But Rem stayed well out of reach.

Vibrations jarred him as the impact of a smaller weight landed beside him on the table. Gral sensed a second presence, a smaller life. Not the radiant heat of flesh but the electrical impulses of thought and cohesion. A Col essence outside its envelope of flesh. It lay motionless on the table as though stunned.

Gral flowed toward the new intruder, but a sudden pressure stopped him. He turned on this new assault, flowing toward it, around it, seeking flesh to attack. Touch/taste revealed inert material, cloth fabric, woven plastics, free monomers. Gral retreated, but the pressure increased, encircling the rigid hemisphere of his essence.

His pseudopods pushed against the fabric, and understanding slotted through his brain. A bag. Not death, then, but an abduction.

Searching the pouch for an opening, he found nothing, no flaws or weakened spots in the plastic monomer. There was the rapid, dizzying sense of movement, gravitational displacement that flattened his structure and twisted his equilibrium. The universe he had so carefully constructed over the past few cycles was wiped away in an instant, all his reference points obliterated. Heat flooded over him, life radiation, flesh. So close yet separated from his probes by the tough plas membrane.

And then the leera was moving, each stride bouncing Gral against the body of his abductor. Pressure nerve clusters were quickly overloaded, intellect interpreting the impulses as pain.

He had a sense of upward movement. The small dying heat and radiant sources within the laboratory vanished, to be replaced by a cold darkness he could only assume was stone. Gral strained his minimal senses but could detect no sign of pursuit, no telltales of alarm or alert.

For the moment his kidnapping had gone undetected.

His thoughts went white with anger, rage burning in him as hot as the flame of life carried within the flesh of the leera. He was in the clutches of his enemies, and everything he had worked for was lost.

No, he realized suddenly. All was not lost yet. He simply needed an opening, a momentary lapse by his captors. They had already made one potentially fatal error—they had left him alive. Surely they would blunder again.

The theory soothed Gral, calming his rage. His chance would come. He was suddenly certain of it.

After all, was he not the Filitaar, the most blessed of the All Knowing?

And when it did, he would make certain they all died most painfully, but only after having lived long enough to regret not destroying him when they had the chance.

* * *

In the sudden darkness of his austere chamber Kars Il Jujun was instantly alert, his symb's senses focusing on the distant sounds of the compound around him.

Though there were no signs of trouble in the silence, he urged his beast up from the small workstation and moved unerringly to his weapons locker, formulating his battle orders as his symb reached instinctively for its harness. He was fastening the chest strap when the lights returned and the screens on the monitors flickered to life.

In truth, it was highly probable that the power loss was nothing more than a mechanical failure. Others might have been content to assume an innocent cause and wait for a confirming report from maintenance.

But Kars knew the strategic value of pessimism. Until it was proved otherwise, he would consider the compound as being under attack.

As soon as he had finished arming his symb, the jujun crossed back to the comm and opened a broad-frequency command channel.

"Attention, watch command." His voice was emotionless, the instructions to his subordinates terse. "This is a Stage Three alert. Initiate full lock-down procedures. Double guard posting immediately. Dispatch roving teams to secure perimeter. Instruct maintenance that I want a full report on the nature of the power failure within the span. And inform the tran that I wish to speak with him as soon as he has finished attending to the chedo."

Warning sirens began to wail through the compound even before he broke the connection.

Switching off the safety on his sidearm, Kars marched out into the passage and headed for the command center.

FIFTY-TWO

Rem had barely begun climbing up the narrow vent when the alarm sounded, the howling sirens freezing her with terror. Overwhelmed with panic, she nearly lost her grip on the low-brain; her symb's torn and broken claws scrabbled for purchase on the rough ferroconcrete. She did not try to control the beast as it scrambled toward the surface.

Every movement caused the bag containing Gral's thick essence to swing in a short arc, pounding against her leera's back. And each time the sack collided with her beast's spine, she cringed in anticipation, imagining the burn of contact as Gral's attachment acids chewed into its hide. She could feel him inside the taut plastic, squirming and twisting, seeking a way to touch her flesh.

Reaching the top, her leera crawled from the duct and sprawled onto the ground, its muscles still spasming and its digits still clutching spastically for purchase. Tark, the big hetta guard, grabbed her symb and jerked the beast to its feet, blunt nails digging into its flesh. The pain yanked Rem back to reality.

"What happened?" the hetta whispered fiercely, his voice low and threatening. "What went wrong?"

Who are these creatures? she wondered silently. To whom had she given her allegiance? Murderers and lunatics, all of them.

"I don't know." Rem forced her flesh to thrust the sack toward him as though its contents were confirmation of the deed. "I did exactly as I was told. Switched the essences while the power was out. The sirens did not start until I was in the shaft."

The hetta eyed the bag suspiciously. Inside there was an essence very similar to the one Rem had carried with her down into the depths of the vent.

"If you are lying . . ." he said. He did not bother to finish the threat. Still gripping her symb's arm, the hetta whirled and darted off through the brush, dragging Rem in its wake.

They sprinted across the green chaos of the temple, keeping low and trying to move quietly. It was unnecessary caution; the sound of their passage was drowned out by the wailing alarms.

Rem allowed herself to be led, stumbling blindly in behind the hetta, depending on him for guidance through the darkness. Tark moved surely, as though he knew the twisting trails by memory, his beast reacting to every turn of the path as easily as a tran might respond to the words of a ritual.

With every stride the bag drummed against her beast's spine. Branches and vines whipped its flesh, slashing the leera's hide, the welts stinging and burning. She expected at any moment to feel the sack of essence tearing, the touch of Gral's mass another flame on her flesh.

But miraculously the monomer held fast.

Finally the vegetation thinned and the steps of the temple appeared, marbled stone rising from the dark soil, the staircase merging with the gleaming archway above the portico.

Two hetta guards stood at the top of the steps, staring out into the jungle. When Rem and Tark stumbled into the clearing, they reached for their weapons, squat sidearms oiled and ugly in the dim light.

"Halt," one of the hetta shouted, his guttural voice echoing in the sudden stillness. "Who goes there?"

Her symb froze, reacting to a lifetime of conditioning, a beast programmed to respond to command tones.

Tark leaned close. "Stay quiet and follow my lead," he whispered. "And be ready to run if they start shooting."

Then he staggered forward and doubled over as though his beast were mortally wounded. "Come," he gasped, his voice a death rattle. "Come quickly."

"What is it?" The guards advanced slowly, weapons ready. "What's the trouble?"

"Over there," Tark managed to whisper, waving one arm and veering drunkenly back toward the jungle. "There's another one. He's hurt worse than me. And I can't lift him."

He dragged Rem along with him, one huge arm draped over her leera's shoulders as if it were supporting the weight of his dying flesh.

"Who is hurt?" The two guards followed cautiously, their footsteps crackling through the underbrush.

Tark stumbled on a few more steps and suddenly hesitated, wavering unsteadily, staring down into the dense foliage, a look of puzzlement on his beast's dull features.

"He was here, I tell you," he muttered. "Only a moment ago. And wounded to the death. He couldn't have escaped."

The guards moved closer, one on each side of him. Tark waited until they were within arm's reach before he let his symb attack. Then his blade whispered from its sheath in a single fluid motion, an arc of steel slashing up and out, carving across the exposed throat of the nearest soldier. The beast was dead before it hit the ground.

Almost simultaneously, Tark's hetta caught the second guard with a leg kick and sent the creature sprawling, the pistol flying from its grip. Hitting the ground, the weapon discharged once, the flash temporarily blinding them all.

Rem lost her hold on the lowbrain. Her leera bolted and slammed into the guard as he tried to rise. Her beast twisted, but the guard's arm looped around its throat and squeezed tightly, cutting off its breath. A point of fire seared her leera's back, the metal bite of a knife plunging deep into its flesh and being yanked free. Then she was stumbling forward and tripping over a bloodied corpse to fall face first into the brush.

For a few moments Rem lay prone, struggling to keep her beast from screaming in agony. Her wound was burning as though a flame guttered deep in her symb's back. Around her she could hear the crashing of limbs and stifled blows, the grunts and strain of mortal combat.

Finally there was only silence.

How long it was before Tark reappeared, Rem could only guess. Surely not more than a few heartbeats, yet it seemed an eternity while the pain in her symb's flesh faded to a chilling numbness and the night sounds returned to the jungle. Rem sensed Tark standing over her; an awkward silence settled over them.

"Do you yet live?" He asked after a few more moments had ticked slowly past.

"Yes," she managed. Bracing against a wave of anticipated pain, she urged her flesh to stand, but the ache was dull and muted as though the nerves in the flesh were already dead. Her mind spun dizzily, flooded with adrenaline and shock. "The wound—is it bad?"

"Worse than you can know," came the reply after another long pause. "The blade cut the bag."

"Gral has escaped?"

"No."

"What, then?" Rem asked timidly, already fearing the answer.

Another long silence. Somewhere above, a girga cried out as the smell of blood reached its nostrils.

"He has achieved attachment." There was no disguising the horror in his voice. "Just to the side of your symb's spine. The wound provided him an easy entry point."

Fighting revulsion, Rem forced her symb to twist its head until it could glance down at the curve of its own back. She could just make out the edges of gelatinous mass clinging to the hide, the membrane pulsing and throbbing in the dim light. The sudden numbness now made perfect sense. Gral was secreting his attachment drugs, the narcotic poisons subducting the pain.

"Let it not be so," she moaned, her leera's voice rising in a panicked wail, a counterpoint to the scream of the sirens. "By the grace of the All Knowing, please let it not be so!"

Lunging forward, Tark clamped his hand across her symb's maw, stifling its scream. Unable to breathe, the leera struggled in panic, writhing and squirming in his iron grasp.

"Shut up!" the hetta growled, his symb's twisted face inches from her leera's ears. "Shut up or you'll bring more of them."

"But—" she stammered between his bloody digits.

"There is nothing we can do. Not here."

"But he is consolidating. Even as we speak, his probes twist deeper. He touches veins and grows stronger!"

"As would we both if we were trapped in the essential state and given the chance at new flesh."

"But he is chedo," she rasped, as though his former status were somehow important, a rock of sanity in her suddenly chaotic universe.

"And I was jujun," he snapped.

She looked at him uncomprehendingly, remembering distantly how the others had spoken of regression. Surely regression was only a tale told to frighten younglings. No sane being would abdicate one flesh for another of a lower order. Still, there was madness in the quivering voice of the hetta.

"Flesh is flesh," Tark hissed. "Especially when one is without and in dire need. We all do what we must to survive." The hetta jerked her beast upright. "Can you walk?"

"What does it matter?" She tried to prod her beast and force it to twist away from him, but the leera lacked the strength to move against Tark's grip. "Don't you understand? How long before he penetrates the alimentary canal and starts moving toward the lowbrain? Probably only a few short spans. And once he reaches my intellect, I can't possibly stand against his strength.

"Have mercy," she begged. "Kill me now."

"No." The hetta shook his head. "Not yet. My orders were specific. Gral must be taken alive. I cannot risk his safety to accommodate your cowardly needs. You will stay alive until we reach the others. After we find Chul. Then perhaps you will be allowed to die. But not until Chul gives his assent. Understand?"

"Please . . ."

"Will you walk, or must I carry you?"

Rem stared into his cold features, suddenly certain not only that he would not help her die but that he would do everything possible to make sure she kept breathing.

"I will walk," she said finally.

"Follow me, then. And stay close."

She followed directly behind him.

And as she matched his stride, Rem noticed the weapons hanging from his belt. There was a sidearm, a pistol with a wide muzzle.

It would make an enormous hole in her symb's skull if she aimed it correctly.

Clinging to his precarious hold on the leera's back, Gral felt the rhythmic sway of the beast's hurried gait and allowed himself a moment of celebration.

Though he could not know the content of the conspirators' conversation, he was certain a turning point had been passed; another error had been made in his favor. They had not tried to divide his essence or cut him free of his victim, thus confirming that they needed him intact and justifying his actions during the first few seconds after his unexpected release.

Some Col desperate for flesh might have entered the leera hard and fast, punching through the thick back muscles and looping strings of guts, entering the esophagus to slide up into the brain cavity, striving for domination. Others might have tried external methods, oozing up the outside of the flesh, seeking entrance to the brain through the external ports of the aurical cavities or the mouth.

Both methods would have been doomed to failure. An external attack would have left him exposed and vulnerable for too long a time before achieving attachment. His essence could easily have been plucked from the flesh and stuffed into another monomer prison.

An internal assault would have wrought havoc within the leera, his rapid passage irreparably damaging vital organs. To kill the beast was to be helpless again, at the mercy of his captors.

Gral knew his only hope for escape was to drive Rem from her flesh and gain control of the living creature, a task for which he possessed no experience, no ready solution. So he had chosen to hold his position on the beast's back, driving his seekers through the wounded flesh to establish direct connections with the circulatory system, the taste/smell/touch of sour leera flesh filling him. Then he had stopped his probing, letting the blood rejuvenate and nourish him while he pondered a workable plan of attack.

And already the shape of a cunning stratagem was forming in his mind like a thought directly from the All Knowing. The twin demons—pain and fear of death—had served him well on the battlefield. They would not fail him now.

Increasing the flow of subduction poisons into the bloodstream to numb the surrounding flesh, Gral began slowly and carefully to extend his control probes, one network slipping toward the spinal cord and the other twisting through the abdominal cavity toward the throbbing warmth of the leera's twin hearts.

FIFTY-THREE

The wind was bitter cold, blowing down the narrow canyon.

Stepping carefully along the shelf of rock, Rourke narrowed his eyes against the stinging gusts and wondered for the thousandth time just what the hell he was doing climbing up the side of a granite ridge in the middle of an alien night. He was too damn old for soldiering. And the last time he had checked, he had not enlisted in anyone's army.

Still, there he was, walking carefully up through a tight gorge jammed with shattered boulders, praying to God that whatever was on the other side of the ridge had not set too tight a perimeter, and trying frantically to remember how a soldier was supposed to approach an enemy installation of unknown size and purpose.

The best approach would have been to plant his butt firmly on a bar stool back at the station. But something kept him moving up through the thin night air—stupidity or stubbornness. Right now, he figured the two words were synonymous.

Behind him Thunder moved silently, his breath coming hard, whistling softly through his damp nostrils. His presence was living proof that stupidity and stubbornness were not exclusively Human traits.

In the shadow of an overhanging projection of rock Rourke stopped to rest. Thunder sagged beside him, squatting on the stone and sucking in huge gasps of the thin air.

Below them the overlaying slabs of rock were a river of light in the gleam from Spira, Jurrume's small moon. Dark bands of vegetation slashed across the escarpment, as if the land had been shattered and the pieces of stone were afloat in a sea of black.

Rourke had chosen the stone purposefully, sacrificing the cover of the trees for the protection stone offered against seismics and other types of motion sensors. A thin defense, but so far it seemed to be working. In truth, Rourke was not sure that their luck was holding steady because of his caution or because the enemy had seen no need to set too large a security perimeter.

And the fact that they had not yet been attacked was no guarantee that his tactics were working. An ambush was by definition always a surprise.

He touched the sidearm on his belt. It would be almost useless against combat troops, but there was some comfort in the cold hardness against his palm.

"How much farther?" Thunder asked, keeping his voice low.

"Can't be sure." Rourke stared up at the ridgeline, a dark jagged line across the starlit sky. It seemed closer than it had on their last rest break. And the spot far below where they had left the sled seemed twice as far away as the crest. "Another klick. Not much more."

The Wormat nodded and rose unsteadily. "Let's get going."

Rourke moved out onto the inclined face of stone and settled back into his rhythm, one step at a time, head sweeping from side to side, trying vainly to detect enemy movement in the shadows above them.

* * *

They were just below the crest of the ridge when Rourke stumbled over the carcass. He remembered stepping out into a broad band of shadow, something suddenly soft and giving beneath his feet, and then he was falling forward, a charnel house reek enveloping him, thick fluids oozing beneath his groping fingers.

"Are you all right?" Thunder whispered urgently from somewhere slightly above and to his left.

"I think so. But whatever tripped me sure as hell isn't." Fighting the urge to retch, Rourke struggled to his feet.

Thunder sidled over and produced a small flash beam from his pouch. He rheostatted the intensity down to the glow of a single small candle before activating the light.

In the dim illumination the dead animal was little more than a large dark shape on the rocks, its decaying flesh gleaming wetly. It was a camaii, somehow separated from its herd and lost among the mountains.

There was something odd about the shape of the creature's skull. Taking the flash, Rourke bent closer to examine the head of the beast. The front of the sloping forehead had a fist-sized circular hole bored through the bone. The back of the head was splintered, as if the brains had been superheated and the cranium had been ruptured by a sudden release of pressure.

"Energy beam," Rourke said softly, his skin suddenly very cold. "Probably some type of microwave."

The Wormat grunted. "Means we're getting close."

"Must be." Rourke flicked out the light. "And I suggest we keep our heads down."

On the ridgeline the wind was howling, a steady pressure that tore at Rourke. It curled around him like a physical opponent, icy limbs seeking purchase on his clothing, threatening to lift him from the rock fissure where he had wedged his frame and hurl him back down the canyon.

But Rourke was glad it was blowing hard and cold. The wind would sweep his heat signature away from him, help mask his presence on the ridge. A definite plus. Because, based on what he could see below, he was certain the ridge top was being scanned periodically for intruders.

At first they had seen nothing, had not even bothered to look, lying half-dead on the wind-blown rock and gravel, gasping for breath like two dying aquatics. Finally, when his strength had returned and the competing spots of brilliance and darkness had faded from his eyes, Rourke slid forward, crawling on his belly though a body-wide crack in the stone face that rose sheer and sharp above them.

As he wiggled through the tight gap, twisting to free his clothing from projections on the stone, Rourke had the mounting fear that all he would find was another ridge, rising cold into the night, and that he and Thunder were simply perched on the edge of a false summit. But at the other end of the fissure the rock fell away steeply, a breathtaking plunge down into a vast expanse of darkness that gradually separated into striations of gray as his vision adjusted to the moon-dappled shadows.

The smell of a distant ocean forced its way through his filters, past the sterile scent of the oxygen from the feeder tubes. Rourke felt Thunder squirm into the gap beside him. He heard the rustle of fabric as the Wormat dug through his pouch for a pair of light-enhancing binocs. Then they lay in silence for a few moments, staring down at the darkness.

They were perched on the edge of a sheer cliff that was as sharp as a knife blade. The stone face dropped a thousand meters to the dense cover of a thick tangle of vegetation that covered the lower reaches of the slope, stair-stepping down in a series of short broad mesas to a narrow strip of rocky beach and a pounding surf.

Optics still on the light magnification setting Rourke preferred for night travels, he detected nothing on his first sweep of the canyon. His second scan was equally fruitless.

"I don't see anything," Thunder muttered softly.

"It's got to be here," Rourke said, flicking his optics to infrared. "This has to be—" He stopped suddenly.

In the center of the crescent shoreline Rourke detected a faint heat signature, a half dozen soft blotches barely visible where a cluster of rocky outcroppings extended into the sea. They would not have been visible from the air or even from a thousand meters higher on the ridge.

"You spot something?" Thunder whispered.

"I don't know." Rourke swept the beach area in wider circles. There were additional signatures, thermals running along the edges of an enormous stone formation that humped up through the vegetation. And then he noticed how the foliage, trees and vines and scrub, canted away from the stone as if thrown back by some upheaval.

The scene snapped into focus like one of the test cards the psychs liked to flash in front of shell-shocked patients. A death's-head or a girl combing her hair in front of a mirror? Which do you see, Rourke? Which one do you see?

A death's-head.

A damned Oolaanian corporal unit squatting in the valley like a stone monument. Chameleonlike. Assuming the guise of the land around it.

"There," Rourke whispered.

"What is it?" Thunder demanded.

"Oolaan."

"Where?"

"Thirty degrees left of center. Middle of the beach."

As Rourke turned to glance at the boar, he noticed a small emerald-green circle glowing on the Wormat's sloping forehead. Old training slotted into his mind, his responses conditioned by seeing one too many comrade's brains splattered on the walls of the trenches back on the front line.

Grabbing Thunder around the throat, Rourke pulled the boar down below the lip of stone just as the energy pulse slammed into the cornice where his skull had been only a heartbeat earlier. Fragments of superheated stone showered down around them.

"Perimeter defense," Rourke said, anticipating the Wormat's question. "Probably a semisentient automated system. Must have popped that camaii buck we found downslope when it stuck its head up over the ridge." He glanced over at the boar. "You care to take a second look?"

Thunder shook his shaggy head.

"Then let's get the hell out of here before they decide to come up and see if they hit anything."

Rourke slid back out the fissure to the other side of the ridge. He scrambled down the first few hundred meters at a crouch, staying low but moving fast. Thunder was right beside him.

All the way down Rourke was certain he could feel enemy weapons taking aim at a spot right between his shoulder blades.

They were almost at the bottom of the ridge before Rourke stopped to rest. Thunder fell to the ground beside him, sprawling onto his back, his mouth gaping and his chest heaving. Rourke collapsed against a boulder, staying on his feet. Both kept their gaze locked on the ridgeline, as if expecting at any moment to see a craft split the summit, searchlights and weapons cones glowing.

"So," Thunder asked between breaths, "what was that thing?"

"An Oolaanian corporal unit—a biological factory." Rourke spread his hands, trying to explain. "Look, the Oolaan don't have a rigid physical structure. They're really little more than an organized mass. Flesh without form. At least as we know it. These masses, some of them are enormous. We don't really know how big they can get. But they can restructure themselves, reorganize into smaller units with specific jobs and limited intellects. Understand?"

The Wormat nodded, a slow ragged movement of his goggled head.

"Now, a single small mass can be dropped into a biological zone, say, like the coast of Jurrume. Given time and adequate raw materials—organics and minerals and the like—a mass can replicate itself. Or grow larger. Or create more individual units. Like breeding, except it only requires a single mass."

Rourke pointed back up the ridge. "What we saw in the canyon was a corporal unit—a bio-factory utilizing the local flora and fauna to manufacture something, like maybe a few hundred thousand smaller units. And I don't think they'll be accountants. Know what I mean?"

"Soldiers."

"That's my guess." Rourke coughed and spit. "Probably what Bezhjenzarthra figured, too. When I was researching his records, I discovered that he'd spent some time on the fringe between Human and Quadriate space. Must have seen pictures of Oolaanian corporals in the holos. That's why he burnt for orbit."

"But why did he go to Galagazar?"

"Who else would you tell? Galagazar was the factor. He must have convinced the Lling to stay quiet and let him peddle the information to the Human Alliance. Galagazar was probably betting that the Humans would pay big credit for the flight records. Because the Humans would understand the significance of an Oolaanian presence on Jurrume." He turned to stare at Thunder. "You see, all you have to do is ask yourself how this Oolaanian got here. A corporal unit can't exactly book passage on a transliner."

"An Oolaanian ship?"

"More likely a whole damn battle fleet. Either way, Oolaanian craft would cause quite a stir passing through a Quadriate-controlled jump nexus. Only nobody has heard anything about Oolaanian ship movements.''

''Perhaps a back route.''

''Or an uncharted nexus.''

Thunder sat up suddenly, his eyes wide, his mouth gaping in disbelief.

''Think about it,'' Rourke said. ''A newly discovered nexus would certainly be enough to attract Oolaanian attention. They must be planning to use Jurrume as a transit port. The Oolaan tend to place their bases on planets rather than orbitals. Closer access to the raw materials that the Unities need for expansion.''

''Do you know what a new nexus in this area would mean to the United Trading Authority?''

''That's a pipe dream, Thunder.'' Rourke laughed bitterly. ''If there's a new jump point around here, it's going to end up under Human or Oolaanian control.''

''Not if we contact the Quadriate. We have proof now; they will send ships.''

''Too little, too late. They'll never get here in time.''

''What about the Col? Perhaps with their help we could hold out until—''

''I don't think so.'' Rourke gestured vaguely toward the ridge. ''Nothing that big could have reached Jurrume without them knowing about it, so they must be in this deal up to their necks. Which means our contract with the Col is about to expire.''

''That's it, then?'' Thunder looked stunned. ''We just roll over and die?''

''Die is the operative word. We might have time to evacuate a few hundred—females and children and all that rot. But this system is about to blow, and anyone still on station when it does is going to be a casualty of war.''

''But a new nexus,'' the Wormat whispered. ''That would be something worth fighting for.''

''Not fighting for, Thunder. Dying for.'' Rourke stared at him closely. ''And there's a big damn difference between the two. You fight for something if you've got a chance to win. And we haven't got a chance in hell.''

A long silence stretched between them. After a moment Rourke pushed up from the rocks.

''Let's go home,'' he said.

Staggering to his feet, Thunder fell silently in behind Rourke as they continued down the mountainside toward the thicket where the grav-sled waited.

FIFTY-FOUR

Breath burning in her symb's lungs, Rem stumbled after Tark, tethered to the silent beast by the iron grip of its manipulator on her leera's aching forearm.

The blood from the hetta's wound formed a slick sheen on its side, each stride making the gash open and close like an obscene maw drooling thick fluids just below his shoulder. Her leera's own injury was curiously painless, the only sensation a dense pressure against its spine where Gral was burrowing through the muscle tissue. She had not yet felt his touch in the beast's central nervous system, but such contact might be only a moment away. The thought filled her with helpless panic.

Distant sirens still wailed through the compound, their ululating howl drifting down from far above.

The tunnels they traveled were cold and dark, relics of an era long before Gral's coming. Filled with dust and smelling of disuse and decay, some of the narrow bores were natural formations. Others had been carved by the members of a heretic monastic order that had come to Jurrume seeking solitude in the barrens and had claimed the volcanic cone as their temple and domicile. And though the monks had departed ages earlier, portions of their original structure had been incorporated into the present citadel.

Evidently Gral had forgotten the existence of the network of passages beneath his compound. Or perhaps no accurate blueprints existed to map their trackless reaches. Whatever the reason, there were no guards stationed in the musty hollows.

Still, the apparent emptiness did not keep Rem from straining her beast's ears to listen for the sounds of pursuit beyond the muted shriek of the warning sirens.

Twice during their breathless flight across the compound Rem had found herself within reach of the stubby weapon clipped onto Tark's harness. But both times she had been unable to will her symb to grab the pistol.

She simply did not have the strength to commit suicide.

It was a startling revelation, a moment of truth that exposed her as a coward and a fraud. Perhaps Dar had been right to assume that she was not meant for elevation. If she could not kill herself now, with a future of torment and pain laid out in stark colors before her, then how could she have forced her leera to commit ritual suicide, which was the culminating act of the Rite of Elevation?

In truth, she had already failed the most important test. There would be no chedo flesh for Rem the Forgotten, only the permanent darkness of brain death.

Flesh numbed by the slow seepage of Gral's subduction poisons, Rem staggered on behind the loping hetta, his brutal momentum overriding both the narcotic lethargy and the paralysis of her despair.

The rendezvous point was a natural cavern deep in the lower levels of the compound. A single dim lantern cast a fitful glow, but viewed through the night eyes clamped to her symb's skull, the guttering beams seemed as bright as the light of Mael itself.

There was a solitary raas waiting in the shadow-filled grotto. It watched them approach in silence, its clustered eyes gleaming darkly, its multiple limbs folded across its plated breast. The leader, she surmised. Chul, Tark had called him.

"It did not go as planned," Tark said in answer to the raas's unspoken question.

"I assumed as much when the sirens began," the raas replied. "What went wrong?"

"I do not know. But we were stopped by a pair of sentries in the temple. I had to kill them both." Tark stared down at the uneven shadow-distorted floor of the cavern. "I am sorry."

"Have you brought Gral?"

The hetta nodded, his eyes still riveted on the cold stone at his feet.

"Then there is no need for sorrow."

"Perhaps you speak too soon," Tark said, his voice trembling.

Dragging Rem into the cone of light, the hetta spun her symb around, its back facing Chul. With a sudden jerk, Tark raised the robe. Rem expected a cry of disgust and horror, but there was only a long moment of silence.

"How did it happen?" the raas asked finally, his voice calm and even.

"Gral was released during the struggle with the guards. And by the time I reached the leera, he was already attached. There was nothing I could do."

Another long silence.

"Turn around," the raas commanded Rem.

She did as ordered. The raas studied her closely, searching her symb's face.

"Are you in control?" he asked.

"Yes," Rem forced her leera to nod, the movement a subtle demonstration of her command of the creature. "But I do not know for how long."

"I understand." The creature cleared its throat, a rattling cough that sounded as though its chest were filled with thick liquid. "And now you must understand something. Your physical condition presents me with a conflict of conscience. The simplest method of dealing with this matter would be to kill your leera and recapture Gral as he vacates your flesh. But you have done a great service for me and for the Col people, and I have no wish to reward such selfless behavior with an execution. Therefore, against my better judgment, I am going to let you live."

"I have no desire to live like this," Rem said, somehow managing to keep her symb's voice from trembling.

"You have never been without flesh," the raas snapped. "I have—so you must believe me when I say that only a fool prefers death to life. I speak with the voice of experience."

Rem could think of nothing to say, but her mind was filled with questions. From what ranks had these conspirators been drawn? There were rumors of prisons filled with those who had sinned against the Prime, dark tales of traitors stripped of their flesh and thrown into the darkness of disunity. Children's tales, she had always thought. Or were they? And how could such have been enlisted against Gral? Her mind swam with confusion.

"I am offering you the chance to try and reach Verrin," Chul continued. "There are tran on Verrin who can remove Gral and save your flesh. It is not an offer to be rejected lightly."

"What would you have me do in return for this favor?" she asked cautiously.

"Nothing more. You have already earned this right. All you need do now is stay alive. Fight Gral. Maintain control."

"And if I cannot?"

"Then Tark will grant your wish to die—quickly and painlessly."

Rem was silent for a moment, torn between the desire for peace and her fear of death. In the end, it was her fear that was the strongest.

"Very well," she said. "I will do as you ask."

"Good." Chuffing decisively, the raas turned his attention back to Tark. "You must take her to the alien's shuttle field and commandeer a ship as planned. Get her to Verrin alive."

"What about the others?" Tark protested.

"You must go alone."

"But—"

"Plans have changed, Tark." Chul breathed deeply. "Kars Il Jujun is suddenly faced with two dead hetta and an unexplained power failure. It will not be long before he guesses the truth and comes looking for us. And we would be too easy to find on the barren plains. So, rather than wait for him to come to us, we will attack Kars first. Perhaps in the excitement he will not notice two small beings in flight across the flatlands."

"Twenty against Gral's forces? That is suicide!"

"Need I remind you, Tark," the raas said quietly, "that we were dead before we took this assignment?"

Tark stiffened, his beast assuming a martial stance. "I respectfully request that I be allowed to fight with my team."

"I am sorry, Tark. Someone must get Gral and this leera offworld. The job has fallen to you. Do not disappoint me."

The big hetta started to speak and then stopped as if he had suddenly realized that his pleas would fall on deaf ears.

"You are to go the rest of the way down through the tunnels to the base of the mountain," Chul continued. "We will give you a quarter span to get to the entrance. Wait there until you hear the first explosion. Then move out fast. The farther you are from the citadel before the battle ends, the better your chances of escaping detection."

"It shall be so," Tark said solemnly.

The three walked toward the entrance to the cavern.

"And remember," the raas intoned as they stood in the passageway. "If capture becomes imminent, destroy Gral and give this little one the peace she so foolishly craves."

Then he turned and walked away, heading toward the upper chambers and certain death.

They stood and watched until the light from his flickering lantern disappeared around a bend in the tunnel.

* * *

By the time they reached the lower entrance, both of their beasts were winded and gasping. Rem felt light-headed, her mind swimming, and realized that Gral had entrenched himself so deeply that he was siphoning off a sizable portion of the nutrients in her leera's bloodstream before they reached her own essence. She could not stop his thievery; all she could do was force her flesh to break down its scant reserves at a faster pace, pushing it ever closer to collapse.

Tark seemed to be rapidly deteriorating. The hetta's breathing was ragged, a bubbling sound deep in its chest. The bleeding beneath its shoulder was a steady red flow, and the creature's gait was an agonized limp. It sagged against the wall and rested in silence for a moment. Finally the beast looked up and met her gaze.

"When the first blast hits," Tark said, "we'll go out through there."

He pointed down toward the end of the tunnel, a snarl of darkness that Rem suddenly realized consisted of dead branches and scrub brush used to camouflage the opening.

"Look down," he commanded. "Tell me what you see."

Rem did as ordered. At first her beast's vision detected nothing through the night eyes, but gradually a faint purplish glow became visible, a track on the floor of the cave slightly wider than the walking stance of a hetta.

"A path," she said. "Some kind of trail."

The hetta nodded slowly. "It leads through the minefield. At least it did when we laid it five moons back. Invisible unless you're wearing night eyes and standing right on top of it."

"So the mines will not be a problem. But," she said, remembering the ferroconcrete blisters studding the flanks of the mountain, "what about the gun batteries?"

"If the assault goes as planned, the sens-net for those nearest the path will be disabled."

"And if they are not?"

"Then our symbs will not have to run very far." The beast gave her a loose shrug and a tired grin. "Now get some rest, because once we start down the mountain, we won't be able to stop until we're clear of the defense perimeter."

And with that the hetta squatted onto the floor and settled into a posture of rejuvenating meditation. Soon the drone of his mantra was the only sound in the night, but Rem found no peace in the arrhythmic moaning.

FIFTY-FIVE

"It cannot be so," Vaz Il Tran insisted, his symb's voice trembling with outrage and a hint of the fear that suddenly gripped his mind. "You have made an error in your measurements."

"But my Tran," the leera orderly began, her symb keeping its eyes deferentially locked on the floor, "I assure you that—"

"Enough!" Vaz roared impatiently. "Retake the measurements. We will soon know who is right and who is wrong. And then I shall see that you are properly punished for your impertinence."

Bowing, the leera collected her equipment and returned to the life-support table where the three Col essences gleamed in the sterile glow of the fluorescent lights. As the creature began to retake the measurement scans, Vaz mouthed a silent prayer, but the mantra did little to combat the cold wave of terror washing over him.

What had begun as a routine examination after a brief power failure was rapidly deteriorating into his worst nightmare. If the leera's initial measurements were correct—and he had no real reason to doubt them—the quivering mass in the center of the life-support table was not the essence of Gral Il Chedo.

Vaz had been praying in his chambers when the blackout had hit. As soon as the lights had returned, he had headed for the laboratory in the lower levels, the screaming sirens echoing through the compound filling his mind and the tran's lowbrain with dread.

But his initial trepidation had subsided as soon as he had entered the lab; three essences rested in their curved depressions, membranes pulsing in sympathetic rhythm to the beat of the fluids coursing through the nutrient veins beneath their swollen hemispheres.

A quick check of the monitors had confirmed that all three specimens were healthy and had suffered no ill effects from the temporary outage. In fact, the two calves were thriving, growing so rapidly that they had almost matched Gral's essence in size. Vaz had ordered physical measurements simply to quantify the extent of their maturation.

And then the leera had made her announcement; the calves had indeed gained mass, but Gral had lost a substantial portion of his substance.

Which, they both knew, was physically impossible. Col matter did not vanish into thin air.

And so the small seed of doubt had taken root in his thought: What if—just suppose—the essence was not Gral's?

Finishing the second set of measurements, the leera turned to face Vaz, its features pale and troubled.

"My initial dimensions appear to be correct," the orderly whispered. "Shall I take a third series?"

Vaz was silent for a moment, trying to think, trying to keep his symb from wailing in distress.

"No," he said finally. "Repeated measurements will not change the truth. Gral is gone."

"But how, my Tran?"

"I do not know. But the defilers and despoilers who have taken the Filitaar cannot succeed. Kars will find them. Gral will be restored. It cannot be otherwise—the thoughts of the All Knowing are with us." He hoped his words did not sound as hollow as they felt in his symb's mouth.

"What can I do to help, my Tran?"

"Pray," Vaz said fervently.

And without further comment the tran hurried off to find Kars Il Jujun.

In the mottled darkness of the temple Kars Il Jujun surveyed the corpses sprawled on the ground before him. The stench of blood was thick in the steaming air, his symb reacted with nervous anticipation, the joy of combat filling its small brain.

"They were assigned to Unit Twelve," the hetta officer explained, playing his light over the bodies. "Dispatched as a roving security team on all Stage-Three alerts."

"How were they killed?" Kars asked, stopping to examine the wounds.

"This one had his symb's throat cut. The other was stabbed repeatedly and had his beast's neck broken. He put up quite a fight."

"Not good enough," the jujun observed dryly. "Have you recovered their essences?"

"Yes, Jujun."

"Destroy them both." Kars had no mercy for those who had failed, and getting one's symb killed was the ultimate failure.

"As you wish, Jujun." The hetta did not question his decision.

"What do we know about their attackers?"

"There were apparently two of them. A hetta and a leera. We found tracks and scent from both in the vicinity. And something else, my Jujun." The hetta stared up at Kars, its eye stalks erect. "We found blood from both species, as well."

"Wounded, then."

"Yes, my Jujun. And the hetta was bleeding profusely. His injuries will quite possibly prove fatal in the very near future."

"Excellent." The jujun stood slowly. "Have you determined what the intruders were doing in here?" His symb's loose gesture encompassed the green growth surrounding them.

"No, Jujun. But we have retraced their steps back to a ventilation shaft located in the center of the temple. The spoor pattern seems—"

His words were cut off by a loud argument coming from the temple stairs, hetta curses mingled with the imperious whine of Vaz Il Tran's shrill commands. Through the trees, Kars could see Vaz surrounded by a half dozen troopers, his symb's spindly limbs gesticulating and slashing the air.

"If you will excuse me for a moment," Kars rumbled, nodding toward the tran. "I must see what the fool requires."

He headed for the stairs.

"I demand to speak with the jujun," Vaz was shouting as Kars stepped out from the foliage. Spotting him, the tran broke away from the guards and hurried forward, waddling down the steps, troopers surging after him.

Kars waited at the edge of the light, dismissing the hetta with a curt wave. He studied the tran as it approached, noting the distress on its facial plates and the fear in its yawning maw.

"Gone," the tran stammered as it drew close. "He is gone!"

"What are you saying?" Kars felt a sudden coldness in the pit of his symb's stomach and an iron tension in its rigid muscles.

"The defilers," Vaz panted, his beast's voice dry as the wind through dead leaves. "They have taken Gral Il Chedo."

And then, as if to punctuate his cry, a deafening explosion tore through the compound, the concussion staggering Kars and sending the tran sprawling onto its face. The blast was followed a heartbeat later by a second eruption and then a third and a fourth, alarm bells and warning Klaxons weaving a deadly counterpoint through the thunderous roar.

For an instant Kars was stunned, overwhelmed by the sudden realization that the fortress was under attack. Then his many standards of preparation and training kicked in, and his symb was in motion, barking commands to his subordinates as it sprinted toward the command center.

FIFTY-SIX

Tark was moving moments after the rumble of the first blast in a series of linked explosions reached his beast's ears. Scrambling down the narrow adit, the hetta pushed aside the dead scrub that had been used to camouflage the entrance to the tunnel and slipped out into the night. Rem scurried after him, stumbling on rubbery legs, her symb's body numbed from the waist down by the slow seepage of Gral's subduction flow.

The tunnel dumped them out onto the flank of the mountain, halfway down from the compound. Above, columns of flame rose against the night sky, the glow, viewed through the night goggles, brighter than day. She turned away, her symb's eyes burning. Across the plain, the gleaming lights of the shuttle field seemed like a cluster of stars on the dark, rolling land.

For a moment Tark stood staring up at the compound as though fighting the urge to slip back inside the tunnel and join his fellow conspirators in their suicide mission. But duty must have overpowered his misguided sense of honor—the hetta turned and started down the slope at a trot.

Rem followed, keeping her beast's head down and its eyes locked on the faint purple track. And after a while she stopped wondering if the next step would set off a mine or the gun emplacements would open fire. There was only the trail and the night and the jarring impact of the steep descent.

* * *

Rem was uncertain how long it took them to reach the foot of the mountain. Behind them the battle still raged. She could hear the distant crackle of weaponry and the occasional throaty roar of another detonation, but the chaos seemed to be subsiding.

Tark finally halted for a short rest after they had cleared the minefield and were beyond the range of the nearest guns. The bubbling in his beast's lungs was a constant rattle, and dark fluids were dribbling from its gaping mouth. And when it started to move again, the beast staggered unsteadily, wavering on bowed legs, heading away from the distant glow of the shuttle field lights in the valley.

"Wait a moment," Rem gasped, somehow managing to induce her symb to raise a forelimb and point toward the glimmering landing beacons. "Aren't you going the wrong way? The shuttle field is over there."

"I am aware of the location of the alien landing field," Tark replied wearily. "But the musk road is this way—with its constant stream of automated vehicles. They will not notice a pair of exhausted riders. And we will reach the field in half the time. Perhaps even before Kars realizes Gral is missing."

"Perhaps." The flat statement lacked conviction.

Tark continued on, his symb's quavering steps quickly settling back into a steady rhythm.

Rem had to drive her probes deep into the lowbrain's pain centers to force her beast to match the hetta's lumbering pace.

A wide swath of black macadam, the musk road bisected the broad expanse of the plain. Tall grass and scrub formed a dense hedge on either side, the dry foliage golden brown against the dark paving. Keeping low to avoid the lights of passing vehicles, Tark and Rem lay in the prickly weeds beside the makeshift highway and watched the traffic roll past.

Monstrous behemoths, the trucks were enormous multi-wheeled and multisegmented cargo trains used to transport musk from herding outposts too close to justify the expense of hoppers but too far to drive the camaii to the shuttle field for harvest. The trucks were built for durability; a single drive unit could haul five long articulated trailers. The machines were not fast, but they maintained a constant speed, rumbling over hills and down slight grades, sensors scanning the road for obstacles and relaying information back to their small mechanical brains. Their metal sides flashed in the moonlight as they thundered by, the ground vibrating beneath them.

Tark spent a few moments letting his symb rest while he oriented himself, trying to judge the speed of the trucks and time the upcoming sprint for the last trailer.

"The trick is to move before the hauler gets too close." He panted, fluids bubbling on his thick lips. "But not so soon that the collision-avoidance system mistakes you for an obstacle and veers away."

Another truck rolled by while Tark counted softly under his breath. The beast coughed, a racking spasm. More dark liquid oozed down the plated jaw.

"Are you ready?" he asked, glancing at Rem.

Despite her fatigue, she forced her symb to nod its acquiescence.

"Then when the next truck passes that outcropping," Tark said, pointing toward a white finger of stone a few dozen megalengths down the road, "we run for it."

The hetta levered itself upright, and Rem followed suit. She could see a dark slickness coating the weeds where the beast had been lying. The smell of blood and lymph overpowered even the burn of the musk that dusted the sides of the pavement.

A truck appeared, rising up from a small valley, its blue-white lights carving the darkness, its angular shape like a demon from some black hell.

"Now!" Tark roared as the vehicle reached and passed the landmark, his symb grabbing Rem's leera and lurching out onto the road.

The drive unit swept past, a wall of air buffeting them. They were trotting, the leera on the inside between the flank of the first trailer and the loping hetta. Tark's beast was groaning with every stride, a terrible moan of pure agony that filled her numb symb with terror. Her leera's digits touched the side of the second trailer, its nails screeching and suddenly being ripped away on the edge of a razor-sharp seam in the paneling. The ballooning pneumatic tires whirred by, missing her legs by a fraction of a hand span.

Somehow Tark's hetta caught the rear ladder of the third trailer. With the other arm the beast shoved Rem's leera forward and slammed it into the lower plate on the hitching mechanism. The leera clutched frantically for a hold, seizing an angular projection and pulling itself up onto the rear platform.

A heartbeat to consolidate position. Nothing more. A fractional delay.

Yet when her beast looked up, the hetta had stumbled. For an instant Tark's symb hung suspended, its huge form airborne, dangling by one slippery manipulator.

Then the hetta was gone.

The rear trailers jarred as the wheels struck the tumbling body, the massive weight of the load grinding the flesh into the macadam, spinning fragments of the masticated corpse whirling into the underbrush along the side of the road.

For an eternity Rem clung to the articulation joint, staring at the empty space where Tark had disappeared as if waiting for his lumbering form to come loping up alongside the truck. Eventually disbelief gave way to despair. She nearly forced her symb to relinquish its hold and slide beneath the wheels.

But in the end she could not force her flesh to give up its life so easily. Too many had already died to see that Gral was brought to justice. To give up now would be to make their sacrifice a mockery, or so her cowardly mind reasoned. She let her symb save itself and climb up into the open rear of the trailer.

She had no plan, no real hope for success. Yet somewhere along the rumbling journey, as Rem searched her muddled thoughts for an avenue of escape, she remembered the Human, Kenneth Christian Rourke.

It was time Rourke repaid the life debt he owed to Dar Il Chedo.

Along the length of the leera's spinal column Gral was busily rewiring the neural connections. It was tedious work, pumping a flood of subduction poisons into the area to deaden any twinge of pain before extending a slender filament of his being and splicing it into the nerve.

The job was made even more protracted by the need for stealth and the limitations of the flesh; the beast had been ravaged by an extended fast and the rigors of the tests of elevation. Energy was in short supply. Gral sensed that the aged creature was on the edge of physical collapse. How long it could continue to support two hungry intelligences was an unknown variable.

Still, Gral was making steady progress. Already he had linked himself with most of the major nerves controlling the lower extremities and was now interfacing with the beast's internal organs. Once those connections were in place, he would begin extending his reach up the spine into the upper limbs.

Gral had not yet attempted to exert his power. He was content for the moment to let his essence act as a filter for impulses coming down from the lowbrain.

But soon he would be in position to assume dominance of the

flesh, overriding Rem's presence and isolating her being in the prison of the leera's skull.

And once he had gained control of the pain centers, her prison would become a living hell.

FIFTY-SEVEN

Scanning the concave bank of viewscreens, Kars Il Jujun stood in the chaos of the command center and listened to the droning litany of the damage report.

Though the center was intact, the air in the chamber was thick with the stench of charred plas and the acrid bite of burned explosives. Many of the screens displayed scenes of devastation or were white with static. His beast's eyes traveled from image to image: shattered atmospheric fighters, burning munitions stores, corridors littered with hetta corpses. So much destruction wrought by a handful of troops—it was incredible.

Despite his heavy losses, Kars could not help feeling a certain sense of admiration for the enemy troopers. They had gone to their deaths valiantly and had left ample evidence of their passage.

Finally—mercifully—the catalog of losses ceased. A long silence stretched over the room. He forced his jujun to turn and face the small assembly of his surviving subcommanders.

"For those of you lacking the intelligence of a raas," Kars began, his beast's voice flat and level, void of emotion, "please allow me a moment to restate the obvious. Last night we were hit by an infiltration team. How they managed to penetrate our defenses is a matter we will discuss in great detail at a later time. For a moment we have a much more serious problem, one that threatens the success of our movement and the safety of the Filitaar."

Kars scanned each of them. Blank hetta faces stared back. Some were scorched with smoke. Others were painted with blood and pocked with oozing wounds. But they knew what he was about to say. The rumors of Gral's abduction were already circulating.

"Most of you should have already guessed that the attack was a diversion, the purpose of which was to distract our attention while the enemy moved against the Filitaar. For the moment—" His voice lowered to a rumbling growl. "—their strategy was successful. The Filitaar has been taken from us."

There was no sign of surprise or shock from the collected officers, their emotions shielded and hidden. Yet he knew a flame of rage burned within them as keen as his own murderous anger.

"But I intend to make certain that their success is only temporary. We believe they are still in the vicinity, probably headed for a concealed landing site. We will search them out. The Filitaar will be returned to his rightful place, and they shall be made to pay for their sins. Am I understood?"

"Yes, Jujun!" A dozen voices shouting in unison.

"Barq and Thul." The jujun pointed to the two officers. "Your sections will be responsible for damage control and defense of the compound. The rest of you, divide your commands into search teams. Your respective search areas will be dispatched via the comm. Though we do not know how many conspirators remain, it is reasonable to assume that the largest percentage stayed behind to create the diversion. So you will be looking for a small group, probably less than five."

At his urging, Kars's beast stepped over toward the control console. One limb reached out to stroke the operating keys. The entire wall of viewscreens went dark, then blossomed into the repeated image of a single creature, an aged leera.

"Among the surviving defilers, you will find this one. Her name is Rem Il Leera." Kars stared up at the displays, his beast's manipulators clenched reflexively. "Our chedo welcomed her into his home and treated her like one of his own. She repaid his kindness with treachery." The jujun turned back to face them. "Once you have secured the Filitaar, you may do what you will with the others. But this one you will return to me alive. Is that understood?"

"Yes, Jujun!" A single thundering chorus.

"Go, then—and find them."

In a heartbeat the chamber was empty. Kars glanced back at the screens, focusing his rage.

After a while, when the thoughts of torture and revenge had faded and he was able to think clearly again, the jujun moved over to the comm and began to divide the compound and the surrounding landscape into search areas.

It was almost dawn when the report of a hetta corpse on the musk road reached the command center.

For a few moments Kars studied the vid-images on the viewscreen: a mangled lump of flesh almost unrecognizable save for the coloring and a vague symmetry that suggested the hetta form. Then he palmed the comm switch and contacted the communication officer.

"Open a channel with the alien shuttle field," he commanded.

Kars had to wade through three underlings before he reached the manager of the shuttle field, a withered Eng by the name of Uhnrutte. They had met before on several occasions, and Kars had found her abrasive and undisciplined, a thoroughly unlikable creature.

And dragging the Eng away from her duties at the present time had done nothing to improve her intolerable attitude.

"This had better be important, Kars," the Eng snapped as she slid into a chair in front of the monitor. " 'Cause it's the middle of the harvest, and every moment I spend sitting here is credit out of both of our pockets."

"I care nothing for your harvest," he said evenly. "Nor would I contact you with matters of little import. I have reason to believe that a band of fugitives is headed toward your location. Their exact number is unknown, five or less, but there will be a leera among them." He touched a switch and transmitted Rem's image. "Should you see them, you are to notify me immediately."

"These . . . fugitives," she said, studying the image on a split screen. "They have anything to do with all the action up at your place last shift?"

"The crimes committed by these defilers are none of your concern." He kept his symb's features neutral. "But until they are caught, you are to close your field. No landings. No departures. Am I understood?"

For a heartbeat the creature was speechless, her wide mouth gaping in surprise. Then she remembered her tongue.

"Shut—shut the field down!" she stammered. "You can't ask me to do that. Not in the middle of harvest! Have you taken leave of your senses?"

"I assure you, my senses are functioning perfectly. And I am not asking you to close the field—it is an order."

"On whose authority? Yours?"

"Gral Il Chedo's."

"I'll need to speak with him."

"That is not possible."

"Then neither is shutting down this field," Uhnrutte said, leaning forward until her face seemed about to protrude from the screen. "We'll keep an eye out for your fugitives. But if you want me to halt all landings and departures, I'll have to hear that from Gral first. Or if you'd like, I'll contact the station and have them get in touch with the Prime back on Verrin. See what they say. But until I'm told otherwise, it's business as usual. Now," she said, her hand moving toward the disconnect switch, "if you don't mind, I've got a post to run."

The screen went dark.

Kars wasted no time brooding about the Eng's refusal. There were, after all, other ways to secure a field. Another touch on the contact switch and he was staring at his communication officer.

"Tell Thul to prepare three armored phalanxes for immediate departure, fully armed and staffed for a Stage One assault . . ."

FIFTY-EIGHT

Dawn. Rosy fingers of light thrusting over the distant horizon.

Fighting fatigue, Rourke navigated the grav-sled up the shallow slope and onto the tarmac. The valley floor was still in darkness, with a few bright stars gleaming in the opaque shell of the sky. Behind them, the distant serrations of the coastal range were painted with brilliance.

As he glanced back, the spine of stone seemed a thousand miles away and a thousand standards in the past. But Rourke knew that was only wishful thinking, an illusion caused by exhaustion. The long night had changed nothing. It had only given the Oolaanian unit squatting by the sea time to generate a few hundred more spear-carriers and brought the opening attacks of the war a few hours closer to reality.

On the landing field the frenzied pace of the musk harvest continued without pause, the flight line alive with chaotic activity. Rourke and Thunder came up along the unloading zone for the musk transports coming in from the interior. Industrial lifts swarmed around the monstrous trucks like carnivorous insects stripping the carcass of some massive beast, electric turbines whining, jaws heavy with pallets of musk bound for the belly of another waiting jumpship. Dust clouds skirled in their wake, a red haze of powdered camaii dung and Jurrume's crimson soil, settling on coveralled crews who were busily rolling drums and barrels into place on another brace of pallets. Still other teams secured stacked loads with banding gear and sprayed them with sealant foam to prevent leakage.

As he maneuvered his sled through traffic, Rourke was overcome by a sudden urge to warn the workers of the approaching danger. The intensity of the impulse startled him, filling his mind with a bizarre visual image: him standing atop a stack of pallets, yelling to be heard over the din like some damned heroic statue on some distant Human battlefield.

The urge passed quickly, smothered by the weight of cold logic. No one would heed his warnings. He had not been in the Mael system very long, but Rourke had already learned that there were no individuals downworld during the harvest. There were only the mindless components of a vast machine, fueled by alien currency, whose prime directive was to gather camaii musk. Inertia alone would keep the operation moving, funneling the loads up through the gravity well, workers driven by the pace of the work and the promise of bonuses.

And the harvest would probably continue right up to the moment the first bombs began to fall.

Uhnrutte was waiting for them in the equipment hanger, stalking toward Rourke and Thunder even before they had cut the turbines on their sleds.

"Thunder," she snarled as the sound of the turbines whined down to silence. "I warned you about involving this post in any of your clandestine insanity!"

"I remember your instructions quite clearly," Thunder said.

"Well, you got a real funny way of proving it!" She whirled on Rourke. "By the slime, if you've gotten me into something that violates contract, I'll have you up on charges! Factor or not."

"Mind telling us what in the hell you're talking about?"

"I'm talking about using my post as a sanctuary for Col fugitives." Her eyes flared again. "I got product to move. I don't have time to be nursing wounded aliens or making up stories for the local authorities. You understand?"

"No." Rourke shook his head. "I don't."

"You don't know anything about a Col leera showing up here about half a shift back demanding that we give her passage up to the station?" Uhnrutte made a wet sound with her huge mouth. "I find that hard to believe, since she keeps asking for you by name."

For an instant Rourke was totally confused. Then the pieces suddenly slid into place, locking into his mind. "Where is she?"

"Thought you didn't know anything about her," Uhnrutte sneered.

"Look, if it's who I think it is, then, yes, I know her. But I sure as hell didn't send her here. Now, where is she?"

"Against my better judgment, I put her up in the crew quarters. Figured I'd let you deal with her when you got back. I'll take you to her." The Eng turned toward her own sled, a five-passenger unit, squat and broad.

"You ought to know that she's in pretty bad shape," Uhnrutte continued as they walked toward the sled. "Wounded. She wouldn't say how it happened, just kept demanding to speak with you. But there was something happening at the Col compound last night. Fireworks, if you know what I mean."

"Fighting?"

"Serious action." Uhnrutte nodded. "For a while it looked like the old volcano was coming back to life. But whatever it was, they got it under control around midshift." She narrowed her huge eyes to gapped slits. "Just before you arrived, a Col jujun contacted us via the comm and ordered us to shut the field down. No flights in, no flights out."

"What'd you do?" Thunder asked.

"Stalled him. Said it'd take more authority than his to shut us down. Offered to contact the station and have you get in touch with the Prime for clarification. And until I heard from them we were going to continue to operate. My bluff seemed to shut him up temporarily. So far we've been lifting without incident. But there's no telling how long it's going to stay peaceful."

Rourke figured the Eng was closer to the truth than she realized, but he kept silent.

"At any rate, before the jujun signed off, he told me to watch out for a leera and possibly a few others. Said if this leera showed, we were to call them immediately.''

"You tell them she was here?''

"No. That's why they pay you the big credit, to deal with slime like this.'' She almost looked as if she believed what she was saying. "I just said that if I saw her, they'd be the first to know.''

"All right.'' Rourke nodded. "You just keep playing dumb until you hear otherwise.''

"I'll play dumb,'' she said carefully. "But I don't want to *be* dumb. I want some answers.''

"You'll get 'em. But first, let's go talk to this leera.''

Uhnrutte climbed into the driver's seat. Rourke stepped up to the platform and hung on. Before Thunder had even managed to get both feet on board, the Eng gunned the turbines and the sled lunged toward the distant exit.

The sleeping modules were parked at the far end of the field, four square pods resting on the tarmac, their solar panels shimmering in the early morning heat. Uhnrutte cut the engines and let the sled skid to a stop, jarring across the ferroconcrete and coming to rest in front of the expansion grate staircase that led up into the last unit.

Inside the module the air was cool, free of dust, purified through a filtration system that pumped it full of oxygen and nitrogen to suit the Eng majority of the work force. Thunder peeled off his mask. Rourke, following his lead, stripped off his own. It felt good to have the bottom half of his face free of the feeder hardware, his nostrils free of the filtering tubes.

A few workers were sprawled in the racks of bunks that they passed, sleeping the slumber of the dead and the overworked, the comalike somnolence caused by sheer exhaustion. Rourke knew from experience, from his days working during the trade conference, that they would continue to snore until tapped for the next shift. Nothing could disturb their rest.

Not even the approach of war.

It was a long walk to the back of the module, crossing through four dividers fashioned of corrugated plastic paneling. The lighting was faint and indirect. Rourke found little illumination even in the infrared band, the radiation blanked out for tired Eng eyes.

The last section was empty of life. A rack of ten bunks that were not in use, flat surfaces stacked with surplus gear and blankets, duffel bags and extra bedding, and cleaning supplies.

An elongated lump disturbed the flat plane of the lower bunk in the corner. Rourke stooped to look closer and was surprised by what he saw. A leera, yes. But the leera who had visited him? What was the name? Rem Il Leera? He found it hard to believe that it was the same creature.

Gone were the neat clothes, the silvered vest and tunic, the black trim. The medallions and trinkets that had adorned the creature's horns were missing. The flesh was dull, the hide dingy, the green breast feathers rumpled and matted. There was a deep cut on one shoulder, dried blood rust-brown on the sleeve of an oversized jacket.

The beast's ragged breathing was unsteady and disturbing.

As Rourke stood watching, the Col's eyes flickered open, staring at him numbly for a moment. Then recognition dawned, the eyes hardening and focusing on his features.

"Rourke," the Col whispered, its horned mouth gaping, the black tongue thick and awkward in its mouth. "At last . . . you have come."

"Yeah, Rem," he said softly, uncertain how to proceed. "I heard you were asking for me."

"I had no choice. The Eng—" she cast a dark glance toward Uhnrutte "—would not grant me passage to the station, so I used your name. I was not certain the message would reach you or that you would heed the call. Humans are not known for their honor." The Col tried to sit up but fell back to the bed and lay panting with exertion. "Dar was wise to choose you, Rourke. He was wise about many things."

She tried to sit again. Rourke grabbed one thin shoulder and helped her raise herself upright.

"You're hurt badly." It was not a question.

"My flesh still draws breath. There are many others who are not so fortunate." She swung to the side of the bunk. "We must hurry. If Kars discovers I am here, the dead will have sacrificed their flesh in vain."

"Kars Il Jujun," Uhnrutte said. "He's the one who contacted me earlier."

"Kars knows I am here?" A note of panic reverberated in the Col's voice.

"Not yet," Rourke said. "But why don't you tell us why the jujun is looking for you."

"That is a Col matter." She scowled at him darkly, pain etched across her imperial features. "It is not your concern."

Her tone touched something deep within Rourke, stabbing into him and releasing a wellspring of frustration and rage. He felt it flood over him, felt his muscles quiver and hot anger burning in his skull like flames behind his eye sockets. He swallowed hard and managed to keep from raising his voice, struggling to keep his tone cold and flat.

"I'm getting damned tired of being told that whatever is happening in this system is none of my business," he said evenly. "You come here with half the Col army in hot pursuit, demanding to be taken to the station. You ask for me, which puts my life at risk. Personal risk always makes the reasons why very important to me. You want my help, I'll need some answers."

For a moment the creature seemed stunned. "I do not seek your help," she stammered, disgust thick in her voice. "You owe a life debt, and I come, in the name of Dar Il Chedo, demanding rightful payment."

"Not until you tell me what's going on."

"You would deny a life debt?" The disgust had become horror.

"As you said, we Humans aren't known for our honor. And if you think you can convince Uhnrutte here to lift you stationward without me, go to it. Otherwise, you know my price."

"But what you ask me to do—it is not permitted." She paused as if searching for words. "To speak of things Col. To speak of sins and abominations. I cannot. My words are for Dar Il Chedo. None other."

"Unless you start talking, you'll never see him alive."

"You would murder me?"

"No." Rourke spread his hands casually. "We'll just turn you over to this jujun who's looking for you. I think he said his name was Kars."

"That would be the same as murder."

"You may be right. But as you said, it's a Col matter. It's not my concern." He stood up and wrung his hands as if wiping them clean. "Let's get this Kars on the horn and tell him we found his fugitive."

Rourke headed for the front; Thunder and Uhnrutte were right behind him. He did not get far.

"All right," the leera called weakly, her voice trembling. "I'll tell you what I know. But if I talk, do you promise to help me?"

"That, my dear Rem," Rourke said as he returned to her bunk, "depends on what you've got to say."

Uhnrutte was the first to speak after the leera had finished telling the tale of Gral's sins and her escape from the compound.

"This is local politics," the Eng said, "and none of our affair."

"Last shift I might have agreed with you," Thunder rumbled. "But not now, not after seeing what is sitting on the coast about two hundred klicks west of here."

The Eng gave Rourke a puzzled glance.

"An Oolaanian corporal unit." he explained. "It couldn't have gotten there without Col help."

"It's true, then," Rem whispered. "As Dar suspected, Gral has conspired with aliens."

"Apparently so."

"I do not understand," Uhnrutte said. "These aliens, they are trying to usurp our contract?"

"More likely the whole blasted system," the boar said.

"Thunder's right," Rourke said to the Eng. "This is beyond business. It's war." He stared hard at Rem. "If we get you and your hitchhiker to Verrin, will your people support us?"

"I cannot speak for the Prime," the battered Col replied. "But I will do what I can."

Rourke looked back at Thunder. "What do you think?"

"She would seem to be our only hope. Besides . . ." The Wormat shrugged. "Even if we gave her back to this Kars, chances are he will kill us all anyway. Gral cannot afford to leave any witnesses alive."

"It's settled, then, we take her to the station." Rourke turned his attention to Uhnrutte. "How soon can you have your people ready for evacuation?"

"You can't be serious." The Eng gawped. "This is the middle of the harvest!"

"Forget the musk. Sooner or later Kars is going to figure out that Rem headed here. And then he's going to guess that we interfered. Anyone who's still on the ground when his troops arrive is going to die very quickly and messily. Understand?"

The Eng swallowed hard and nodded silently.

"Good. Now, how soon can you get everyone off the ground?"

"There are three shuttles on the field at present," Uhnrutte said. "Two others en route. If we do not load them, there should be enough room to transport most of the staff."

"She should probably stick to the normal flight schedule," Thunder said. "Sending up five flights at one time is bound to draw the Col's attention."

"Agreed. Can you do it?"

"You are the factor," the Eng muttered. "What choice do I have except to do as ordered? But I assure you, I will gladly testify as to whose orders I was obeying."

"And I hope you get the chance," Rourke said. "Now, let's get Rem to the shuttle and clear the atmosphere before Kars and his troops show up."

Rourke and Thunder lifted the wounded Col between them and headed for the sled.

Before the gleaming orange orb of Mael had cleared the horizon, they were aboard a shuttle and racing toward the distant imaginary safety of the station.

FIFTY-NINE

Kars Il Jujun was aboard the lead hover as the line of armored vehicles crashed through the flimsy barricade of cyclone fencing and swept onto the shuttle field.

Following their orders, the hovers ignored the shuttle that lifted as they arrived. If Gral was aboard, they could not risk his essence by shooting it down. Six of the armored units headed for the two remaining launch craft, their weapons trained on the squat spacecraft, ready to fire if they showed any sign of an attempted ascent. The rest of the gun platforms spread across the complex, startled workers scattering before them like chaff before a cleansing wind.

Kars's phalanx made for the administration offices; its jamming units were broadcasting a wide band of static to silence the alien comms. The hovers halted, and troops boiled out of the rear hatches even before they had come to a full stop.

As anticipated, there was no resistance, and by the time Kars walked from his craft, the perimeter was secured.

"What in Hoth's name is going on here?" Uhnrutte bellowed as she stormed from the entrance of the administration complex.

As Kars stared at her livid, imperious face, he allowed his jujun a moment of gloating satisfaction. "This field is closed until further notice."

"You have no right to do this." the Eng protested, marching toward him, her features pale with rage.

"I have every right," he said calmly, his symb drawing its weapon with practiced ease. "This is still a Col planet."

"Be assured that I will notify your superiors of this outrage!"

"I doubt that," Kars purred as his symb pulled the trigger.

The pistol was set on maximum power, the muzzle opened to its widest beam. Shot at such close range, the Eng's head simply ceased to exist. Her still spasming body toppled forward, blood gouting from pulsing arteries.

Around him, Kars heard the roar of other weapons, saw the muzzles flash and the bodies spinning in a slow dance of death. The troopers stormed forward, up the stairs and into the building.

Within a quarter span there were no living aliens anywhere in the complex.

The hetta officer who reported to Kars stood stiffly at attention, a bad omen that spoke of failure. The search of the facility had obviously yielded nothing.

"You did not find them," Kars stated flatly before the hetta could speak.

"We have not, my Jujun. There was evidence of a leera presence, but we were unable to locate the flesh. Shall I order the troops to expand the search perimeter? Perhaps she has hidden somewhere near the field. Her spoor is fresh; she could not have gone far."

"Additional searching would be a waste of time," Kars said softly. He stared out toward the two shuttles burning on the landing field. Smoke billowed up in thick black clouds. The battle for Jurrume was over; the next battle would take place at Mael Station.

"The leera is no longer on Jurrume," he continued. "The aliens have taken her to their station—but they will pay dearly for their interference." Kars looked back at the rigid officer.

"Assign a detail to hold this position. Recall the rest of your troops. We are returning to the compound."

Back at the fortress, Kars ordered the two ships on ground-based rotation readied for flight. Then he sent word to the tran to prepare himself for departure with the fleet. Though Kars had little use for the whining priest or his trembling prayers, the tran would be a necessary evil if Gral was returned in need of immediate medical and spiritual attention.

As a final task, Kars spend a moment dictating a transmission to be broadcast to the station on a repeating loop. It was a simple, nonnegotiable demand:

"We are in pursuit of one Rem Il Leera and an unknown number of Col nationals suspected of conspiracy and high treason. Aforementioned fugitives have fled to your station. You will relinquish said beings immediately upon demand. Failure to do so, or any other form of additional interference, will be deemed an act of war and result in the commencement of open hostilities."

That the hostilities had already begun did not trouble Kars. In fact, he felt it only helped to emphasize the conviction inherent in his words.

Less than half a span later he was at the helm of one of the two ancient battlewagons that lifted off from Jurrume. The two Col ships had been on ground-based rotation during the conflict. Roaring up through the thin atmosphere, they pivoted in formation, arcing toward the midpoint coordinates where they would rendezvous with the rest of the fleet before proceeding to their objective—the alien orbital.

Though still deep in the Gulf, the main reasoning center of the Ssoorii Unity was aware of the Col fleet's movement almost as soon as the launch was initiated. The instant the lift was detected, one of the shielded sensors orbiting Jurrume fired a coded tachyon message at the Unity and then expired in a brief scintillating flash. Other sensors intercepted and forwarded the Col ship's communiqués. Still other devices scattered throughout Col Space noted the sudden course changes among the vessels on patrol and broadcast their extrapolated routes back to the Oolaanian mothership.

No longer cluttered with the input of construction information, the data was shunted almost instantaneously through the communication node and into the reasoning center, where it was plugged into the reality interface. The smaller remaining segment of the Designers' future plan was reduced by a third, one of the three paths vanishing.

Only two vectors remained, both pointing directly at Mael Station.

Orders flickered out from the reasoning center. In a microspan the battle group was in motion, shields off and impulse engines rapidly powering up to maximum survivable sublight acceleration.

SIXTY

Rourke returned to a station in chaos.

The turmoil came as no surprise—the shuttle had not yet reached the halfway point of the flight when it lost contact with Jurrume. No one on board believed that the sudden profound silence from the comm was due to a temporary hardware failure, especially since the last transmission received seemed to have been an aborted cry for help.

All attempts to reestablish a link proved futile. It was as if the landing field had ceased to exist.

They were still a long way out when the Col transmission overtook the shuttle on its way to the station. The terse demand confirmed Rourke's worst suspicions. The landing field had ceased to exist. A stunned silence settled over the refugees crowded onto the vessel as they thought of coworkers and friends who had been left behind.

The news of the suspected attack had wrought almost immediate changes on the station itself, a sudden transformation driven by caution and fear. Even before the shuttle had entered the station's flight control zone, the controller began requesting the shuttle's identity code, demanding the regurgitation of an old security sequence that Thunder said had not been officially operational for almost five standards.

In addition to the verbal scrutiny, before being allowed to enter the flight zone they were visually inspected by a vessel from the station's volunteer navy, a battered single-ship commandeered for duty during emergencies. The rusted hull was armed with a modified signal laser that might have been able, given an unlimited power source, to burn a hole through a stationary target in slightly less than a standard. Still, the implication was clear: Mael Station was expecting hostile visitors.

The docks were a disaster waiting to happen. Rourke felt all eyes lock on him as he and Thunder stepped from the air lock, the Col leera slung between them like a crippled ancient. Stevedores stood around in loose groups among larger crowds of migrants and support staff suddenly cut loose by the stoppage in the flow of product. Uncertain whether to quit and go find an open bar or wait for something further to happen, the throng stood idle and traded gossip back and forth, the rumors becoming more ominous and desperate with every telling.

Rourke heard the murmur of questions and speculation pass through the collected beings like a wave. He could feel the growing swell of fear and anger, the muttered protests sprinkled amid the whispers. And from past experience Rourke knew that if someone did not intervene soon, the milling labor force was going to be transformed into a panicked mob looking for any means to escape from what it had decided was a doomed station.

"I'll get some officers down here immediately," Thunder said, reading his mind, "Start organizing some civil defense brigades. Give this bunch something to do besides talk."

"An excellent idea."

There was a tram and driver waiting on the docks with explicit instructions to bring them immediately to Nebuun as soon as they arrived. The driver, a slender Eng male, took his orders seriously, herding them across the quay.

Stepping into the vehicle, the trio settled onto the rear bench. The Eng slid in behind the operating controls and turned back to confirm that they were seated. His huge yellow eyes lingered on Rourke for a moment.

"Is it true?" he asked finally. "Has the shuttle field been attacked?"

"I don't know," Rourke answered.

They both knew he was lying.

The Eng turned back and stomped on the throttle. Turbines protesting loudly, the tram whirred away down the concourse.

The tumult continued within the crowded confines of the factor offices. Beings jammed the ersatz lobby, supervisors and crew bosses, labor representatives and contractors, all trying to get answers and information for their constituents. Ianiammallo and the twins were working the comms, fielding questions and requests and stalling for time.

Due to the turmoil, Rourke was halfway across the work area before he noticed the strange absence of pounding in his skull—no throbbing alarm from the surveillance detector. He stopped for a moment and carefully swept the room. Still no warning pulse. Someone had done a very thorough search and destroy on the listening devices. Another sign of impending war.

Nebuun was in the "conference room," the makeshift chamber at the far end of the storage unit that they were using as a temporary factor office. The Eng was not alone. The rest of the department managers were seated around the table—Yevaan and Vuuni, Kiintaart, Fenlint, and Abbanimeer—all of them talking and shouting at once.

"A misunderstanding . . . an unjustified attack . . . perhaps we are misinterpreting the information . . . we should not . . . until further confirmation . . ."

Their voices fell suddenly silent as Rourke and his two companions entered the room. They stared at him for a moment as though—despite arranging for a driver and tram—they had believed him to be already dead.

A few long heartbeats of oppressive silence ticked past, then the simultaneous yelling continued, only this time they were hollering at Rourke instead of Nebuun.

It took Rourke and Thunder a while to detail everything they had managed to uncover in the past few cycles about the complex machinations of the Oolaan-Col-Human conflict in which the station found itself inexorably entangled. Sorting out the progression of events that had occurred on station during their absence was only a slightly less complicated job.

First the station had received the garbled Mayday and had lost contact with the shuttle field. A short time later a hopper from an interior post had made a rapid flyby of the landing complex and reported that it seemed to be occupied by Col forces. Holo transmissions showed burning shuttles and scattered corpses on the tarmac.

Consequently, when the Col demand had reached the station, no one had doubted the threat of violence contained in the brief communiqué, not after viewing the scenes of carnage beamed back by the hopper pilot. Nebuun had ordered a general alert and initiated a search for the fugitives. Next, he had fired off a statement of protest to the Col—both the Verrin and the Jurrume contingents—and contacted the Quadriate for help that he was certain would be too little and too late.

Then he sat back to wait for the Col's next move and tried to guess the motive for the unprovoked attack on the shuttle field. He did not have to wait long. Flight control reported a multiple launch from Jurrume, Col signatures, battlewagons. Moments later multiple signatures were detected on long-range scan— some Col and a large group of other vessels of unknown origin. All appeared to be converging on the station. ETA approximately one shift.

Interpretation: serious trouble.

Nebuun had then called an emergency session of the station operations team. They had just begun discussing their limited options when Rourke and his companions had made their appearance.

"So," Rourke said, summing up the situation for those gathered around the table. "It appears Gral Il Chedo is making a power grab for control of the Col Empire. The Oolaan are supporting him, evidently hoping to put him in place in return for access to a new nexus somewhere in the Col Restricted Zone. And the Human Alliance is making moves to keep the Oolaan from succeeding. Which puts us right in the middle of a hellacious mess."

"A situation made even more untenable by your foolish decision to interfere," Vuuni muttered. "Bringing the leera here has endangered all of us."

"No," Thunder growled, his voice a rumbling threat from deep in his massive chest. "Being in the wrong place at the wrong time endangered us. The fact is, by getting involved, the Human has given us some leverage we wouldn't otherwise possess. Remember, we have Gral. Certainly that must give us some bargaining power."

"The Wormat speaks the truth," Nebuun said quietly. "Gral is our only bargaining chip. But how best to utilize him?"

"Utilize him?" Vuuni was incredulous. "By Hoth, we should return him to his people! Have you forgotten what happened to those on the shuttle field? They disobeyed this Kars Il Jujun's request. Where are they now? Food for scavengers, as we will be as well if we listen to this fool." She thrust one webbed hand toward Rourke.

"Great idea," Rourke replied. He reached down to his belt, detached his pistol, and slid if across the table toward the wizened Eng. "But before you send Gral back, why don't you pick up that Spencer and shoot her?" He jerked a thumb toward Rem. " 'Cause they're sure as hell gonna kill her—real slowly. So you might as well do it now."

"What the Col do to their prisoners is not my concern. This station is my concern."

"Then you ought to know that giving Gral back is only a temporary solution," Thunder said. "It doesn't solve the basic problem, which is that we are sitting in the middle of what's about to be seriously disputed property."

"What good is property if we are all dead?" Vuuni exclaimed, her voice querulous and shrill.

"Odds are that we're dead anyway." Rourke glanced at each of the faces around the table. "Our lives were forfeited the moment Gral and the Oolaan struck their bargain. We've just been living on borrowed time. And giving Gral back won't change that fact, because I don't think he can afford to leave any witnesses. Mark my words, the moment Gral is safely back with his troops, this station and all of us are going to vanish in a blaze of glory."

"Then what do you suggest?" Nebuun asked. The amphibian leaned forward, his eyes watching Rourke intently.

"I suggest we get some help—and fast."

"I have already contacted the Quadriate." Nebuun shook his head slowly. "But they are at least ten cycles away. I doubt we can hold out long enough for them to arrive."

"Perhaps assist the Prime might us," Abbanimeer ventured hesitantly. "As well they threatened are."

"Impossible," Thunder countered. "Gral is the commander of the bulk of their military forces and ships. I doubt they have the firepower to counter him. And even if they do, they can't handle Gral and the incoming unknown forces as well. We need major muscle."

"Or we need to make them think we've got major muscle," Rourke said softly. "Tell me, the woman—Weiss—is she still alive?"

"Yes." Nebuun nodded. "She awakened from her coma last shift. Why do you ask?"

"Just checking the hole card."

The beings gathered around the table turned to stare at him blankly.

"Any of you ever play poker?"

Continued blank expressions.

"Well, folks . . ." Rourke grinned at them. "You're about to get your first lesson in the ancient and time-honored art of bluffing."

"And what exactly is bluffing?" Nebuun inquired.

"In poker, it's a method of convincing someone that you've got a much better hand than he does. In this case, it's convincing somebody that you've got bigger and badder friends than he does."

"I don't follow you."

"Look at it this way: Would Kars still be willing to hit us if he thought he'd be going up against a superior force?"

"Maybe. We do not have enough information about Kars to guess his reaction to such a scenario."

"Granted. Which means we have to play the percentages. And the prevailing wisdom says that a rational being won't attack if vastly outnumbered."

"This is a moot argument," Vuuni snapped. "We have no numerical superiority."

"When you're bluffing you don't need to hold the high cards, all you have to do is make your opponent think you've got them."

"You are proposing that we attempt to stop Kars with a phantom armada?" The Eng looked ill.

"Exactly."

"How would we do this?"

"Well . . ." Rourke shrugged. "The only organization with enough firepower to stand against the Oolaan is the Human Alliance. If Kars and his friends thought that we had a mutual defense pact with Humanity, they might not want to risk attacking this station."

"Need I remind you that such a pact does not exist?" Nebuun asked evenly.

"Kars doesn't know that. Neither do the Oolaan. What I'm proposing is a small-scale video production, something designed to convince them that we just negotiated this treaty. If we can get our Human prisoner to cooperate, we can probably make it look very authentic. Broadcast it out to Central on an open dispatch, something both the Oolaan and the Col can easily pick up on their communication hardware."

"That would give us a treaty," Thunder agreed, scratching his jaw thoughtfully. "Yet we would still be lacking a fleet."

"True. But if we were to follow up the first transmission with a message to a fictitious Human Battle Group requesting immediate military support, Kars might withdraw to regroup and consider his options."

"Only until he realizes no Human ships will be coming to our aid."

"But we will have bought some time. And if we can rig some type of transmission relay system, it might be possible to make it appear that an armanda is on the way—at least, for a little while longer." Rourke glanced around slowly. "I don't have to remind you that every minute we delay the attack puts us a minute closer to the arrival of a Quadriate battle group. And there is one other possibility. If Weiss really is a Bureau operative, there just might be a Human fleet close enough to reach us in time."

"But why would they come to the aid of a Quadriate station?" Vunni stammered, her voice filled with frustration.

"To fulfill the terms of our mutual defense treaty."

"But there is no such document!"

"When you're bluffing," Rourke said, giving the Eng a grim smile, "you've got to fool everyone who's playing the hand."

The assembly gathered at the table looked at each other expectantly, hoping that someone—anyone—had a better idea.

"It is insane," Vuuni said finally.

"A trick most elaborate parlor." Abbanimeer swallowed hard. "Utilizing words much instead of smoked mirrors."

"You are both quite correct," Nebuun agreed. "But well-chosen words have been used to stop bullets many times in the past."

"And it is better than sitting here waiting for the final blow to fall!" Thunder slammed his fist onto the tabletop. "What can I do to help?"

"You can gather your volunteer navy and set up a defensive perimeter," Rourke began, his voice picking up speed as the details of the plot clicked into place. "Make it look like we intend to stand our ground. And for the time being, place Rem into protective custody, just in case someone tries to grab her and circumvent our negotiations with a private bargain. Nebuun—" He turned toward the Eng. "I'll need some help drawing up the necessary documents. As for the rest of you . . ."

Within a few short minutes the plan had been approved, duties had been assigned, and each had gone scurrying off to attend to his or her respective tasks.

SIXTY-ONE

Without a whimper of protest Rem allowed herself to be led away to the safety of a small cubicle in the security office.

There was a blessed relief in being a "prisoner" of the station. For the first time in what seemed like an eternity, all sense of responsibility had been lifted from her mind. No need to worry about her next move. No need to run. Her fate was no longer under her control. Live or die, her future was an unknown variable to be resolved by the actions of others.

And with the sense of relief came a sudden tidal wave of exhaustion washing over her symb. She let the beast collapse onto the small cot and lie still. It was as if her mind were detached, floating above her numb flesh. No pain. No fear. No thoughts or questions about Gral's presence in her flesh. No thoughts at all.

She spiraled slowly down into unconsciousness.

Sensing Rem's slide into the dark pit of oblivion, Gral had to fight to keep his elation from seeping out of his essence and flooding into the flesh. He concentrated his efforts on maintaining the constant flow of subduction fluids into the circulatory system and fine-tuning the anoxia he was inducing within her unsuspecting intellect, rendering her helpless yet keeping her alive.

It was a fine line he trod—a razor edge between success and failure. Though he had spliced his mind directly into a large section of the beast's central nervous system, he was not yet in position to assume complete domination. Rem still controlled enough of the leera's autonomic responses to terminate the creature if she should realize how close he was to accomplishing his mental coup.

And to survive, Gral needed her flesh intact.

Gral could not see the shape of his essence within the leera, but he could imagine the bulge it created on the middle of the sloping back, a large protrusion where the bulk of his mass had burrowed into the muscle through the gaping stab wound. He visualized the tuberous swellings of his probes along the length of the spine, ending just slightly below the neck and the fan of horns projecting from the base of the skull.

He was less than a claw span from his goal.

Slowly, Gral gathered excess mass at the perimeter of the lowbrain's medulla. He directed a stream of nearly pure subduction poisons at the area, deadening all sensation, heightening the feeling of well-being that pervaded Rem like the warm glow of an excess of sacramental wine.

One hair-thin filament pricked the dura mater.

No response from Rem or the leera. No screams of surprise or rage.

A gentle push, and then Gral was inside the muddled lowbrain.

SIXTY-TWO

There were guards outside the suite, a pair of Wormat security officers looking awkward but deadly, huge riot guns gripped in their massive paws. Rourke scanned them briefly as he approached, wondering if the two of them knew exactly what it was they had caged inside the hotel room. If the woman decided to escape, Rourke was certain they would have been only a minor inconvenience on her way out the door.

He knew firsthand what a top-flight Bureau operative could do in a fight. It wasn't pretty.

Inside, the room was dimly lit, with soft shadows spilling across the furnishings. Alexis was seated in a chair facing the door. If she had suffered any ill effects from the gassing, they were not external. She stared at Rourke as he entered, her eyes following his every move as he slid onto the low Vostian bench opposite her place.

"I thought it would be you," she said after a moment of

silence. "It just seemed to me that interrogating prisoners was probably the duty of a factor. Frontier justice and all that."

"I am here in my official capacity as factor," Rourke affirmed. "But there won't be any interrogation. I don't think there's anyone on station who doesn't believe you're an operative for the Bureau of Human Affairs. In fact, we're counting on it."

"I see," Alexis said, smiling slightly. "And why would that be?"

"Because if you aren't Bureau, we're all going to end up very dead—very soon."

"Sounds ominous—and interesting. Care to explain just how you think I can help?"

"In due time. But first indulge me for a moment, will you? I want to know how close I got to the truth." Rourke took a deep breath. "The way I figure it, this whole mess got started when the Oolaan found an uncharted nexus . . ."

Alexis listened intently to his tale, the faint smile dancing on her lips. She did not interrupt. And somewhere along the way she decided to drop her pretense of innocence.

"How'd I do?" Rourke asked when he had finished rehashing his hypothesis.

"Pretty damn close." She nodded admiringly. "Right down to the fact that the Rath was working with me."

"What happened to her?"

"Don't know. She never made it back from the surface." Alexis was silent for a moment, as if she couldn't speak. Then she cleared her throat. "So what's my part in all this? What do you want me to do?"

"Call in the cavalry."

"Say again?"

"You aren't here alone," Rourke said with a tight smile. "There has to be a fairly sizable chunk of Human Alliance navy somewhere nearby."

"What makes you so sure?"

"Two things. First, you sure as hell can't neutralize an Oolaanian force by yourself. Second, remember that Wormat who attacked us back at the Golden Horn?"

Alexis nodded.

"He was pissed off because a Human warship almost rammed him at the Malacar nexus. Malacar is pretty damn close to Mael. So I figure there must be at least one battle group in a shielded position somewhere in this area, just waiting for an undercover operative to give them the signal to move in. I'm going to give you that chance—with a few minor strings attached, of course.''

"Such as?''

Rourke picked up the small folder he had brought with him to the suite and took out a sheaf of hard copy. The documents were on official United Trading Authority stationery, thick white vellum with gold seals emblazoned with the signet of the Quadriate. He handed them to her without explanation.

"What the hell is this?'' she asked, skimming the Patois.

"A mutual defense agreement between this station, as a representative of the Quadriate, and you, a representative of the Human Alliance. Gives the Human Alliance official Quadriate permission to come into the Mael system and kick some Oolaanian ass.''

"You expect me to believe that this is a valid treaty?''

"Actually,'' Rourke said with a loose shrug, "it's more important that the Oolaan and the Col believe it's valid. I'm hoping that they won't want to attack for fear of uniting the Quadriate and Humanity in a future war.

"But the truth of the matter is that this station is the Quadriate's official representative in this system. And as the factor, I've got the legal right to make binding treaties. Now, maybe we're stretching things a bit with your authority, but somehow I don't think we're bending the rules too far.''

"Okay,'' Alexis said, fingering the pages. "Let's say, for the sake of argument, this paper will hold up in court. Why should I agree to sign it? What's in it for the Human Alliance?''

"Access to the new nexus.''

"Sole access?''

"Don't be ridiculous,'' he chided. "Shared access between the Quadriate and the Human Alliance. But shared access beats the hell out of your alternatives. You certainly don't want it under Oolaanian control. And you can't afford to come storming in here and take the nexus without permission from the Quadriate, 'cause Humanity can't afford to have the Quadriate as an enemy any more than the Oolaan can.''

"You sound pretty sure of yourself.''

"Sure enough that I brought the ident unit.'' He dug in the pocket of his coveralls and produced the small square device.

"I'll need some time to study the contract.''

"Take all the time you want.'' Rourke held out the ident. "As long as it's not more than five minutes. I mean—I don't want to rush you, but I'd feel much better if I knew the good guys were en route.''

Alexis looked at him for a long moment, then her smile returned.

"You scheming bastard," she said, taking the printing unit from his hand. "I sure as hell hope you know what you're doing."

SIXTY-THREE

The defense of Mael Station began with a pair broadcasts from the flight control center.

The first transmission was a halo-vid of the formal treaty-signing ceremony. Alexis Weiss represented the Human Alliance; Casey Rourke, the Quadriate League. It was pure theater, but even Vuuni had to admit the performance possessed a certain impressive mock authenticity.

A second dispatch was beamed from the station a short time later, a concisely worded hailing intended for the as yet unseen Human fleet:

. Hostile units approaching vicinity of Quadriate colony at Mael Station. Per terms of recent mutual defense agreement enacted between the Quadriate and the Human Alliance, we are requesting immediate assistance to repel attacking forces. You are to consider this request as authorization to engage any enemy forces encountered in the Mael system.

> Kenneth Christian Rourke
> Factor, Mael Station
> Alexis Weiss
> Lt. Commander, HAN
> W114-97-111ALPHA

The message was transmitted on a broad-band sweep, all frequencies, and repeated ten times for emphasis.

Shielded within the oort cloud on the fringe of the Mael system, Admiral Etiane Rusch listened silently to the broadcast just received from the Quadriate station.

"Your evaluation?" she asked her second in command as the message looped through for another repeat.

"The halo is quite unorthodox, Admiral," the officer said. "But the verification code on the request for assistance is correct."

"Opinion?"

"I'd say it's what we've been waiting for, Admiral."

"So would I." The gray-haired woman leaned forward and touched the comm panel. "Communications, open channel for transmission to all ships. Stand by for orders."

The fleet swung out of the cloud and powered up to full speed as soon as it was clear of debris, its coordinates set for the distant navigational beacon of Mael Station.

On the bridge of his flagship Kars Il Jujun allowed his symb to pivot the helm chair slightly as he considered his next move.

Kars had anticipated any number of possible responses to his ultimatum and subsequent launch: pleadings or negotiations, capitulation or flight. But the news bulletin and subsequent statement from the station requesting outside intervention had come as a complete surprise.

As had the sudden appearance of another fleet on his ship's forward screens.

The distant vessels far outnumbered his meager collection of lumbering craft. They were sleek and fast, their projected course arrowing them straight toward the alien habitat.

For the first time since he had detected their presence, Kars was glad to know that the bulk of the Oolaanian battle group was coming in on his flank. Together with his allies, he would have numerical superiority if the Humans were engaged.

The jujun glanced toward his flight crew, catching sight of the priest cowering on a bulkhead jump seat. Vaz Il Tran was a stone statue, the plates of his beast's face rigid with fear. Kars felt a twinge of disgust burble up from his symb's lowbrain, nauseated by the nearness of the piteous creature.

"Observation," Kars commanded. "Give me projected time of arrival at the station for the Human ships."

"One zero one five, my Jujun," came the hurried reply.

"And our own ETA?"

"Zero eight zero six, Jujun."

"Excellent."

Two-tenths of a span differential in his favor. Enough time to wreak havoc and be gone . . . if the aliens were foolish enough to turn over Gral without hesitation.

On a collision course from the opposite side of the system, the ships of the Ssoorii Unity were already at maximum acceleration. At their present rate of speed they would have reached the orbital several million deca-spans before the Humans or the Col. More than enough time to destroy the facility should it be deemed necessary.

But then the sequenced transmissions from the station entered the communications node, were passed on to the reasoning center, and impacted the small fragment of the Designers' plan that was still intact.

One of the two surviving options winked out of existence. A solitary track remained, a brief series of actions leading inexorably to a single acceptable outcome.

No doubts arose within the reasoning center as it viewed the final resolution of the Mael Gambit. Nor did the intellect feel any sense of anticipation knowing that its assignment was near completion. It saw nothing beyond the small segment of the future spreading before it and the short list of necessary offensive maneuvers.

A burst of commands was discharged from the reasoning center.

The fleet altered course, a slight lateral deviation. The new end point of its vector was several hundred navigational units distant from the station, directly in the path of the approaching Col battlewagons.

All weapon systems were elevated to battle station status.

Each and every member of the motley crowd of beings gathered in the station's flight control center was fully expecting to die. Rourke was no exception.

"Run the program again," he said, keeping his eyes locked on the screen, where a trio of intersecting lines formed an asterisk on the station's spatial coordinates.

"Being program running times thousand many," the Lling flight controller protested. "Not changing being item one. See?"

On the screen, the lines retracted and advanced at rapid speed, seeming to flicker over the stylized image of Mael Station.

"The Lling's right," Alexis said glumly. "No matter how you figure it, the Col and the Oolaan are going to reach us first."

Which means it's over, Rourke thought silently. Because there was no way the station's ragtag navy was going to stop the incoming warships.

The silence in the room indicated that everyone else was having similar thoughts. The grand gamble had come up short.

There had been one brief moment of wild elation when the blips representing the Human fleet had shown up on the screen, a single shout that had seemed to echo through the station, resounding from other crowds gathered around other screens, public comms, and private monitors.

Then the cold reality of the numbers had been tallied. The Human ships were too far out to reach the station in time. Even at maximum acceleration, there was little doubt that the orbital would be nothing more than a cloud of debris when they arrived.

The shouts and cheers had faded into whispered prayers.

For a time Rourke had clung to the slim hope that the enemy fleets would turn back. But evidently the Oolaan and the Col were quite capable of crunching numbers. The ships swept on toward them, the only change a slight course deviation in the Oolaanian approach.

"Intersecting they will here be," The Lling confirmed, pointing to a spot still some distance away from the station. "Moment now, time any. See?"

"I see," Rourke muttered.

Still, the course change was an unexplained phenomenon. And Rourke chose to interpret the shift as a sign that all was not lost. If that was foolish, so be it.

But then, he had always thought that dying men had a right to dream whatever they wanted in their last few moments of life.

Kars Il Jujun was watching the Oolaanian course change with growing suspicion, an emotion that became increasingly acute as the distance between the two fleets narrowed. Once again he was reminded that he had not contacted the Oolaanians. He had not asked for their help. Yet here they were, an enormous cluster of blips on his screens, closing with his small fleet as if for battle.

"Communications," he snarled, his symb's gaze fixed on the approaching scintillations. "Open a channel with the Oolaan."

"Channel open as commanded, my Jujun."

"Unidentified Oolaanian vessels, this is the Col flagship *Ver-*

rin. Request you state intentions before proceeding on present course.''

A profound silence greeted his words.

''Comm?''

''There is no response, my Jujun.''

''I repeat. Unidentified Oolaanian vessels. State your intentions immediately!''

A longer hush was filled only by the beeps and ticks of the bridge. And then he heard the whisper of the litany of peace. Who would dare to show such fear?

Whirling, his symb's eyes found the tran.

''Shut up,'' he snarled.

The sibilant hiss faded to a keening whine.

''Detecting course change, my Jujun,'' The observation officer announced. ''Formation turning. Heading zero-two-zero. ETA to intersect three point one deca-spans.''

Kars stared at the screens, unaware that his jujun was gaping and trembling.

What in the name of the All Knowing were the Oolaan doing?

In the hot and stale atmosphere of the flight control center Rourke felt a small chill as he saw the Oolaanian battle group come about on the display.

''Frappin' hell,'' he whispered to no one in particular. ''Are they doing what I think they're doing?''

''If I didn't know better,'' Thunder replied, his deep voice starting to rise with hope, ''I'd say those sireless bastards were crossing the tee.''

''About coming,'' the flight controller confirmed. ''For side broad shooting to prepare. Barrage of firing. Understand?''

Of course Rourke understood. He had spent too much time at the front not to know an attack maneuver when he saw one, and the Oolaan were definitely preparing to engage the Col fleet.

The question was, Why?

Rourke had never thought of himself as a religious man, but the prayer he was whispering under his breath was the genuine article, a fragment of New Catholic doctrine dredged up from deep in his past.

''Our Father, who art in heaven . . .''

Kars Il Jujun reached the same conclusion as Rourke had at almost the same instant.

''Approaching ships acquiring targets, my Jujun,'' the observation officer reported, a hint of tremor in the beast's words. "I have sighting lock. Two—no, three!"

The jujun continued to stare at the screens in disbelief, at the cluster of gleaming images converging on his fleet.

"Your orders, Jujun?"

"Shields up," he snapped, his symb's voice breaking. "Bring all weapons systems to bear. Select nearest targets. Prepare to fire on my command."

It was a futile exercise. Kars knew little about the Oolaanian vessels, but he was certain his second-rate shields would not hold long against their weapons.

"Comm," he snarled. "Is the channel still open?"

"Yes, Jujun." Fear laced the hetta's voice, an incredible breach of decorum.

Kars ignored it.

"Oolaanian ships . . . Oolaanian ships . . . disengage. We are friendly. I repeat . . . we are friendly . . ."

"I have launch," the observation officer shrilled. "Multiples . . ."

A rising shriek echoed through the bridge. Kars jerked around. The tran was on his belly, forelimbs raised in supplication, eyes tranfixed by the images on the screen, his prayer an incoherent wail.

Time slowed as Kars turned back toward the helm, as though the expansion of the universe had shuddered to an infinitesimal crawl. He thought he could see the incoming spheres of energy hurtling toward his ship, glowing orbs that smashed through the feeble shields like stones through a paper screen.

He never even had the chance to return fire.

The Col fleet vanished in an almost simultaneous flash of blinding incandescence.

Aboard the mothership of the Ssoorii Unity the main reasoning center studied the input flooding in from the external sensors. Empty space, six rapidly expanding spheres of gas and debris, no signs of life in the immediate area.

That information was funneled into the remaining fragments of the design. A completion glyph emerged, a simple message:

Objective achieved. Disengage. Abandon system and return to base.

The reasoning center did not question its orders, not did it wonder what its efforts had accomplished during this brief interval spent along the edge of the Gulf. Such inquiries were meant for other minds—far-seers and long-thinkers—entities who understood that manipulation was the purest form of control. The Ssoorii Unity was a simple combat unit, and like all soldiers, it was content to have achieved the goal it had been given.

The new orders were dispatched through the node to the rest of the fleet. And as a collective entity, it altered course and headed for home.

For several seconds there was a deathly silence in the flight control center. Then, as the reprieved saw the Oolaanian ships departing and realized they had been spared, pandemonium erupted.

Vostians flatulated happily, the cinnamon stench filling the air. The Lling flight controller was warbling at the top of his lungs, his song throbbing, harmonizing with Nebuun's undignified squeals and grunts. Someone found a couple of jugs of Wormat ale and a tub of lyki. Very little of the beverages actually made it down any throats. Most was sprayed on the cheering crowd.

Rourke suddenly found Alexis in his arms, and a moment later they were both swept up in Thunder's crushing embrace.

"It worked," Thunder bellowed, lifting them both off the floor and squeezing until Rourke thought his lungs would burst. "By my grandsire's testicles, your damned bluff worked! You cunning motherless bastard!"

For an instant Rourke was afraid the Wormat was going to kiss him. But luckily, Weiss beat the boar to his lips. Rourke dimly felt the Wormat set them down and move off to find another celebration.

The Battle of Mael Station was over, and so far, the residents of the orbital had not even fired a shot.

SIXTY-FOUR

The celebration had spread throughout the habitat, the din of a glorious party echoing through the narrow passages.

Rourke was just finishing his fourth, or possibly fifth, mug of Wormat ale when Alexis pointed through the milling throng jamming the corridor outside the flight control center. He followed her gesture and spotted Thunder coming out of the doorway. The big boar glanced around, noted Rourke, and started shoving his way through the joyous celebrants.

Reaching the pair of Humans, the Wormat squatted beside them, leaning over so that he could be heard above the noise.

"Just got word on the comm," Thunder said, his shout barely audible. "The Col Prime is sending a ship for Rem and her hitchhiker."

"How long before they arrive?" Rourke asked, his own yell but a whisper in the tumult.

"Be here by the end of the shift."

"I suppose one of us should go tell her the good news. She probably doesn't even know it's over." Rourke stood slowly, his aching muscles protesting, his tired body a half step away from a coma. "I'll be right back."

He left the woman in the safe company of the Wormat and headed forward the security office.

Gral's final assault on the leera was brief and brutal, the struggle for control over almost before it had begun.

It was as Gral had expected. He had already completed the hardest tasks, working patiently to establish his position, slipping around inside the flesh, staying hidden and quiet, biding his time until all was prepared. Her chance to stop him had long since passed.

His strategy was simple, a rapid manipulation of the leera's pain centers. The first stroke was the touch of flame, a burning concerto of agony crackling across the leera's flesh and up into

Rem's dazed intellect. That was followed by a second wave of torture, the feel of razors slicing through open eyeballs. A third stab, steel biting into every joint, popping sinews and tendons. The fourth movement was the sharpness of glass grinding through her beast's guts and bones, which were smashed to bloody splinters.

He felt/tasted/heard Rem convulse, her probes recoiling like a hand jerked back from a bed of coals. Then Rem was in full retreat, instinctively withdrawing her control filaments from the lowbrain, trying desperately to escape the agony of her tortured flesh.

And Gral swept in to fill the void she had left in the lowbrain.

He could have destroyed her the moment he assumed control, constricting the blood supply to the skull cavity until her essence withered away from anoxia. But thoughts of revenge stayed his mental commands.

She had dared defy him, dared defy the wishes of the All Knowing. Surely Rem should be made to pay.

The globule of essence quivering in the skull pan was helpless, little more than another lowbrain for him to torment as he wished. And Gral had an infinite catalog of torments filed away in his brain.

Rem would live a while longer.

But she would wish she were dead.

He drove a thick filament deep into her essence, brutally raping her intellect, probing and twisting to establish a one-way pain-transmission link. Then he began flooding her mind with a continuously cycling loop of his sadistic fantasies, an almost autonomic response that did not require his attention.

And the waves of terror seeping from her membrane filled Gral with joy as he settled down to relearn the physical limitations of the leera form.

There were a half dozen Wormat security officers gathered in the front of the office, passing a jug and toasting the spirit of the moment. Their riot guns were stacked against the wall, the fronts of their uniforms open for comfort. All froze as Rourke entered the room.

"Carry on," he said quickly, smiling at their sheepish faces. "I don't expect any more trouble this shift."

"Not unless we're making it," one of the guards roared heartily, raising his jug. The rest laughed loudly.

"The Col leera still here?"

"Yes, Ser Rourke. Haven't heard a sound out of her all evening. Last cell on the end."

"I'll be taking her out with me," he informed them. "Her people are sending a ship. I guess that means you can call it quits for tonight."

They did not have to be told twice. The guards were gone before he reached the short hallway leading to the holding cells.

The leera was crouched in the center of the floor in her cubicle, her thin legs crossed, her skeletal arms waving in a ritualistic motion. She stared at Rourke as he opened the door, no recognition in her dark eyes.

"You can come out now, Rem," he said, pushing the barred gate back. "It's all over."

"Over?" The voice seemed strangely slurred.

"Yeah. Didn't anyone tell you?"

No response.

"The jujun—hell, the whole damn Col fleet—they're gone."

"What are you saying?"

"I'm saying you don't have to worry about Kars Il Jujun anymore. The Oolaan took him and his ships out and then fled the system."

The leera's horned mouth gaped, its breath hissing in great gulps. She staggered unsteadily to her feet.

"You . . . lie," the beast spit, a low rumbling deep in her throat.

"It's the truth," Rourke insisted. "I swear it. Come see for yourself if you don't believe me."

"No!" It was an agonized shriek, a wail of despair and hatred. And then the leera was charging him.

Maybe it was his lack of rest. Or maybe is was the five Wormat ales. But whatever the reason, Rourke could not seem to get his feet to move. The leera hit him hard, her head down, one horn goring him in the shoulder.

Spinning, Rourke pulled himself free and stumbled back, flipping over the cot to crash onto the floor. The crazed beast hit him again, its claws ripping at his belt. He got one foot up, planted it in her stomach, and kicked hard. The leera jolted into the wall, but when she came up, she was gripping his Spencer, the muzzle pointed directly at his skull.

He was still trying to rise as her digits pulled back on the trigger.

And then the leera exploded, her midsection from hips to neck vaporizing in a bloody mist of fluids and meat. A full third of the body simply disintegrated, transformed into a marbled red stain on the opposite wall of the cubicle.

In the doorway a single Wormat stood clutching his riot gun, a thin haze of blue smoke drifting up from all four of the fist-sized bores.

The guard had come back to the office to pick up the jug he had left in the cooler, had heard the noise, and had investigated.

For his diligence, Rourke promised him an unlimited supply of imported ale.

When the Col arrived at the end of the shift, Rourke let them have what was left of Rem: the two parts of the severed corpse and the hardening oval of gelatinous fluid that had boiled from the dead leera's skull.

No fragments of Gral's essence were ever found.

BOOK FIVE

THE NEXUS

Heroes are created by popular demand, sometimes out of the scantiest materials.

—Gerald White Johnson

SIXTY-FIVE

The Great Temple of Selkirk was quiet; only the crackle of coals in the glowing braziers interrupted the silence.

On the dais, a chedo was stretched out supine, its back against the cold stone. It was a young beast, its fur still silver-tipped, its claws long and black. The creature drew a deep breath, its limbs stirring experimentally, its movements stiff and slow as if it were a marionette.

At the first movement the tran priests rose from their kneeling positions on the circle surrounding the dais. Each sprinkled the welcoming incense onto the brazier at its side. Blue, fragrant smoke coiled up in a twisting arc.

The chedo sat erect, rising to stare out at the tran priests who stood before it. The beast displayed no fear. No hint of wild chedo rage was visible in its features. It looked at each of them in turn, its primitive eyes filled with knowledge and understanding.

"Welcome, Chedo," the high priest proclaimed. "Your presence enhances our wisdom."

"As yours does mine," the chedo replied, its voice tentative and hesitant, half growl, half whisper.

"We would know how you will be called," the high priest inquired.

There was a moment of silence as the newborn chedo considered the request, searching its newly formed intellect, sifting through the meshed images of three separate lives suddenly forced into one, trying to determine which was ascendant in the new intellect that filled its skull.

"The name I choose," the beast said finally, "Is Rem Il Chedo."

The tran bowed low and turned back to the congregation gathered at the steps of the temple. It spread its spindly arms toward the throng, raising the scepter of knowledge.

"Blessed be the thoughts of the All Knowing. This day we

have been given a new chedo. It is my honor to present Rem II Chedo.''

A cheer rose up from the crowd as the sun broke through the intermeshed leaves of the jungle, light striking the Eye of the All Knowing so that faceted jewels of illumination spilled over the new entity like a celestial benediction.

Seated in the place of honor at the front of the throng, Dar II Chedo thought the gleam from the Eye was a very good omen, promising a bright future both for Rem and for the entire Col race.

SIXTY-SIX

Nursing a cup of synth, Rourke sat in the darkness of the observation deck and stared out at the vista beyond the plasteel barrier.

The once-empty space around Mael Station suddenly resembled a military shipyard more than a frontier trading port. Warships were clustered in stationary orbits: sleek Human craft, slender and deadly and studded with weaponry; boxy Quadriate vessels, armament pods sprouting like angular growths. More ships arrived every shift, consolidating the positions of both forces in the sector. Some held the station; others moved out to secure the new nexus.

Spinward, Rourke could see a portion of an enormous sphere, the temporary habitat erected to house the negotiations between the Alliance and the Quadriate. The nacreous surface eclipsed the light of Mael. Inside, representatives from both governments were hammering out the details of the Southern Arm Mutual Defense Compact, an agreement born of the treaty he had drawn up with Weiss.

As he watched, a shuttle approached the sphere and docked— another load of diplomats or supplies. Two more shuttles waited, holding position with slight flares of their attitude jets. A fourth arced up from somewhere below his line of sight. More activity in a few minutes than he had seen in ten cycles during earlier, less hectic times.

"I thought I'd find you here," a familiar voice drawled. Alexis Weiss slid in next to him on the bench. "A criminal always returns to the scene of his crime."

"You saying all this is my fault?" Rourke gestured out toward the clustered ships.

"Your signature is on the treaty."

"So's yours."

"Don't remind me." She produced a flask and broke the seal. Taking a healthy swig, she handed the bottle to Rourke. "Scotch. From the private reserve of the captain of the *Glasgow*. Drink up. This is one of the immediately tangible benefits of what we did here."

Rourke took the bottle and tipped it. The liquid burned a scalding path down his throat. He savored the warmth in silence.

"I've got to ask you a question," she said after a moment. "Something's been bothering me for a while."

"What's that?"

"Well, I've been thinking about your so-called bluff. It wasn't, you know."

"Wasn't?" He glanced at her.

"A bluff, I mean. You knew I had ships in support. It's not a bluff when you've got a good hand."

"Is that what you think?" Rourke laughed quietly. "Hell, Alexis. Fooling the Oolaan—sure, that was part of it. But that wasn't the real bluff. The real trick was getting you to believe the treaty was valid."

"But it is."

"Granted. But I sure didn't know that at the time we drew it up."

"You thought it was fake?"

"Didn't think it was worth the paper it was printed on."

It was her turn to chuckle. She nodded toward the scene beyond the window. "All this, and the original treaty was a scam."

"You really think we accomplished anything?" Rourke asked.

"Yeah." Alexis gestured toward the habitat. "It's happening out there right now. I don't know the details, but significant progress is being made. You know, the Quadriate and the Alliance were never really that far apart. What we did here—it made everyone see the benefits of mutual defense. There's even some talk of a formal coalition. God knows where that might lead. But it should give the Oolaan reason to worry."

"I think we all have reason to worry." He took a deep breath and let it drain slowly through his teeth.

"Why's that?"

"The way the Oolaan pulled out of here . . ." Rourke shook his head. "It just doesn't make sense."

"If you start making sense of the Oolaan, you let me know. The Alliance high command will be real interested in talking to you."

"Yeah." He nodded knowingly. "I guess you're right. But they had a whole damned battle group. They could have held the nexus, at least for a time. Maybe long enough to bring in reinforcements." Rourke stared down at the table top, brutal memories washing up into his skull. "When I was on the front, there were many times that the Oolaan fought us to their last biological unit. No surrender—even when the odds against them were incredible. Why not here?"

"I don't know." Alexis shrugged. "Prevailing wisdom says that they weren't prepared for the size of our force. Personally, I'm not so sure. The Oolaan have withdrawn from strong positions before, many without a shot having been fired. No rhyme or reason to it. And trying to figure out why has put a great many Human strategists into padded cells. But sometimes I get the feeling that we're playing chess with an opponent that doesn't just think a few moves ahead, they're thinking games ahead. And I'm not sure whether we're opponents or just pawns.

"But for now," she said, picking up the bottle and giving him a mock salute, "we'll just have to be content with winning this one. That's all that matters."

Outside the window another shuttle entered the docking pattern. Scotch gurgled in the sudden silence.

"Hear anything from the Col?" she asked, wiping her mouth with her sleeve.

"As a matter of fact, I did. Rem made it, survived her elevation."

"I'm not surprised. Hell, they should have given it to her without the trials. She'd been through more than enough to qualify." Alexis grinned at him. "And rumor has it she's not the only one up for a promotion. Thunder is going to get his own station. And I understand your name is being tossed around as a candidate for a job with the new Compact organization. Special adviser to the general secretary or some such crap."

"I've heard that, too."

"If it's offered, will you take it?"

"Maybe. It's tempting." Rourke shrugged. "Besides, I don't think the United Trading Authority is planning on having me on the payroll much longer. They're very grateful to me for keeping their station intact, but my methods evidently leave a lot to be desired. Violated company policy and all that rot."

"You should take it. The Compact position, I mean. We'd probably run into each other occasionally. Allies have a tendency to do that, you know."

For a long time Rourke said nothing. Then he cleared his throat with a cough. "So what are you saying?"

"I've been reassigned." Alexis looked down at her hands. When she looked back up, her eyes were gleaming with sudden moisture. "I'm shipping out in the morning."

"Figured as much." Rourke took another pull on the bottle. The burning liquid failed to wash away the constriction in his throat.

"But—" The woman reached out to take his hand. "—I've got a full shift before I have to report."

"That's funny," Rourke said, laughing softly. "My schedule is wide open until tomorrow, too. And I believe I still owe you a dinner."

"You owe me more than that, Ser Rourke. Much more. And I intend to collect." Standing, she looped her arm through his and snagged the flask of scotch. "There's another one of these waiting back in my room. And I bribed the hotel clerk to give us an extra ration of water for the hygiene unit, enough for a hot bath."

"Madam, you are incredible."

"You ain't seen nothing yet."

Arm in arm, they walked from the deck. Behind them the glowing orb of the temporary habitat filled the vista, rising like a new sun above the vast darkness of the Gulf.

About the Author

A native Californian, Joel Henry Sherman was born in Pomona, a suburb of Los Angeles. At the age of twelve, he moved with his family to the mountain metropolis of Wofford Heights (pop. 426), trading the white shirts and navy slacks of St. Dorothy's Parish School for the bootcut denims of Kern Valley High. Reading was the preferred alternative to the marginal programming on the three local television stations. He learned the basics of writing from a ten-year-old correspondence course discovered in a box in the attic.

Joel has a BA in English from California State College, Bakersfield, and is presently employed by the state of California, operating under the dubious title of Worker's Compensation Insurance Specialist II. He and his wife, Carolyn, make their home in Bakersfield. His major hobbies include snow skiing and backpacking.

His short fiction has appeared in *Amazing SF* and *Aboriginal SF* as well as numerous small-press magazines. *Random Factor* is his second novel.